Another Woman's Husband

Also by Sarah Duncan

Adultery For Beginners
Nice Girls Do

Another Woman's Husband

Sarah Duncan

headline
review

First published in 2007
by HEADLINE REVIEW
An imprint of HEADLINE PUBLISHING GROUP

1

Cataloguing in Publication Data is available from the British Library

ISBN 978 0 7553 3097 3

Typeset in Garamond by Avon DataSet Ltd,
Bidford on Avon, Warwickshire

Printed and bound in Great Britain by
Mackays of Chatham plc, Chatham, Kent

Headline's policy is to use papers that are natural, renewable and
recyclable products and made from wood grown in sustainable
forests. The logging and manufacturing processes are expected to conform
to the environmental regulations of the country of origin.

HEADLINE PUBLISHING GROUP
An Hachette Livre UK Company
338 Euston Road
London NW1 3BH

www.reviewbooks.co.uk
www.hodderheadline.com

To Steve, without whom this book would have been written faster,
but life would have been in black and white.

Acknowledgements

There's an element of team work in any book, and I'm eternally grateful to my 'team': my friends Rachel Bentham, Linnet Van Tinteren, Sue Swingler and Nancy Kinnison, who read and gave feedback on the manuscript; my agent Lavinia Trevor; and, above all, my editor Marion Donaldson, who has the patience of a saint and more tact and wisdom than I'll ever possess. I'm also grateful to Jonathan and Rebecca Wright, who gave me an insight into the subtle differences between Goth, Emo and other teenage tribes, David Moore, who ran the Bath Marathan and endured a complete stranger asking impertinent questions, Jane Riekemann, who provided inside info on teaching, Isabel de Larrinaga, who took over the research when I was on overload, and Craig Davey, who helped with the research for *Nice Girls Do* – in a senior moment I forgot to thank him in the acknowledgements for that book. Thanks also to my fabulous family for their support over the last couple of years: Menna, Eric, Annie, Isabel and Nicholas, and Steve, whose eyes hardly ever glaze over when I'm banging on about writing.

Chapter 1

Why does it always have to be 'cheese'? Becca thought as she grinned at the photographer, her hand resting lightly on Lily's shoulder. She realised that Lily was nearly as tall as herself. This last summer she must have shot up a couple of inches without Becca noticing.

'Can you all come a little closer?' Crystal said, taking her photographer duties seriously. 'There are rather a lot of you to squeeze in.'

Becca hardly knew many of the extended family that had gathered to honour her parents' golden wedding anniversary. Frank and June had both been part of large families so had acquired nephews and nieces, first cousins and second cousins, and then all those that were removed, as if Pickfords could deliver cousins by the truckload. Her own family of Martin, Lily and herself seemed small and contained compared with the fecundity of everyone else, including her only sibling, Joanna, co-organiser of the golden wedding party and proud possessor of five children.

'I still can't get everyone in – can you move up?' Crystal had backed as far as she could. If she went much further back she'd be in the hybrid teas.

Obediently, they all shuffled a little towards the centre where June and Frank were seated, patriarch and matriarch. Martin trod on Becca's foot, vulnerable in summer sandals. 'Bloody hell, Martin!' Becca squeaked as the camera clicked.

'Lovely. Thank you so much, Crystal,' Joanna said, breaking out of the family group.

'Oh, no, couldn't we go again? I wasn't saying cheese,' Becca called out, literally caught on the hop.

'Stay where you are, everyone. We're going for another photo,' Joanna called out as her twins peeled off from the group with the speed and grace of miniature Red Arrows, hurtling towards the far recesses of Frank and June's garden. 'Becca wasn't quite ready. Twins – come back!'

'Martin trod on my foot,' Becca said, then immediately wanted to kick herself with her good foot for being defensive.

'Yup, it's all my fault,' Martin said cheerfully, and put his arm around Becca. 'Never mind, darling, you always look lovely.'

'We can always retouch the pictures in Photoshop,' Joanna said.

But . . . but . . . but, she wanted to say. But I don't want to be stuck on the family Christmas card and sent round to every ancient aunt or distant cousin who couldn't make the party, caught next to Joanna looking like something from *Vogue*, and me captured mid-squawk, like before and after photos.

'I'll get the twins,' Norman, Joanna's husband said, sprinting after them. He was notoriously keen on sport, and kept trying to inveigle Martin into a game of squash, which Martin avoided with a display of agility that would have done him credit on court, had it been transposed into physical action.

'Are we doing another photograph or not?' Crystal said.

'I don't think we'll see the twins again,' Joanna said, looking towards the garden shed with a worried expression. 'I could get Norman back.'

'It doesn't matter,' Becca said, thinking there were worse things in life than a wonky photograph. It would have been nice to look stunning in the photo, but after a morning preparing party food it wasn't likely. The larger family group had begun to disperse anyway. 'Can you do one of my lot and Mum and Dad?' Becca held out her arm to Martin. They stood side by side behind June and Frank, and Lily sat on the ground in front of them. This time Becca managed to say cheese at the right moment.

'How about that?' Crystal said, as she and Becca looked at the digital screen.

'Perfect,' Becca said bending over the image. Everyone was looking happy in the late July sunshine; June was laughing, Frank looked relaxed, even Lily looked cheerful despite having said, earlier that day when Becca needed help with the cooking, that she'd die if she had to get up before twelve. Her family. 'That's perfect.'

June had originally said she wanted fifty guests, fifty guests for fifty years of marriage, but this had long since gone out of the window, what with the golf-club crowd, and the art-club set and the accumulation of friends and acquaintances garnered over the years, as well as some of Joanna and Becca's long-time friends, like Crystal who taught English at the same tutorial college as Becca. There must have been over a hundred people crammed into the garden.

'Do you think we'll get as many people to our golden wedding party?' Becca said to Martin when they bumped into each other having been circulating with drinks for the guests. 'I hope there's enough food.'

'You're assuming I don't have a mid-life crisis and run off with one of Lily's friends,' Martin said, lifting up his bottles of champagne to the light to see how much was left in each. 'And speaking of food, where is it?'

'Ugh, she'd be a bit young – only fourteen.' Becca checked her watch. 'You're right, I should have got the food underway ages ago.'

'I'll have to wait a few years then,' Martin said, giving Becca a quick kiss. 'In the meantime, both these bottles are nearly empty. Give me yours, and you go and do the food.' Becca nodded, handed over the bottles and went into the kitchen.

'There you are,' Joanna said. She'd put on one of June's aprons, the Mondrian pattern working well with her white shirtwaister dress. She looked crisp and modern. Trust Jo not to choose the frilly apron, Becca thought. 'I wasn't sure what to do,' Joanna said.

Becca took charge. She'd more or less done all the food during the preceding week and brought it up to June and Frank's house earlier that morning. Joanna, who'd flown in from New Zealand only a few days earlier, was asked to organise the decorations. The house was swathed with gold fabric looped with gold ribbons. Gold candles burned, creating warm air currents so the gold balloons bobbed against the ceilings. Tiny gold hearts were sprinkled across the dining-room table and little gold baubles hung from a pair of standard roses in tubs, Joanna and Norman's present to June and Frank.

Into this setting, Becca and Joanna now distributed dishes of food. Salads of various kinds, bowls of cherry tomatoes glistening like rubies, cold sausages, egg mayonnaise and coronation chicken for the conventional, spiced beef, peppered honey-roast ham and a tagine for the more adventurous.

The sisters surveyed the scene. 'It seems a shame to spoil it,' Becca said.

'After all that work?' Joanna raised her eyebrows. 'Let's get everyone eating.'

'I've heard so much about you,' Crystal said, settling down next to Joanna on one of the kitchen stools at the breakfast bar. Becca turned away from the oven, a tray of mini pizzas in her hand. She couldn't remember ever discussing Joanna with Crystal. School issues; Crystal's succession of boyfriends and ex-boyfriends and would she ever get married; Martin's late nights at work, yes. Siblings, no.

Joanna took off one of the heavy earrings that Martin had said looked like half-sucked gobstoppers. 'All good, I hope.'

'Becca wouldn't say anything bad.' Crystal caught Becca's eye and grinned at her. 'She's a very loyal sister.'

Becca shoved the tray into the oven, and slammed the door shut with her foot. 'They'll be ready in ten minutes.'

'So, what have you heard?' Joanna said, massaging her ear lobe where the earring had been. Becca felt a mean pulse of satisfaction that the earrings, though decidedly glamorous, pinched.

'Oooh, that you're an interior designer, and you live in New Zealand, and you have loads of children – how many is it actually?'

'Five,' Joanna said smugly. Becca wondered if she was conscious of the smugness, or the way she smoothed the front of her dress down, drawing attention to an impossibly flat stomach. It would take more than a pair of magic knickers to get Becca's stomach to that shape, and she'd only had Lily.

'Wow,' Crystal said, wide-eyed. 'How do you manage with five, and work?'

'Oh, we just muddle through, everyone's pretty laid back in New Zealand. I've got a nanny, which helps of course. She's about some-where,' Joanna said, looking around her vaguely. Becca assumed once you'd got to five children you probably became pretty relaxed over their whereabouts. 'S'funny, I never intended to have so many kids. I always thought Becca was the one who'd have loads.'

The ties of Becca's apron had come undone and she did them up again – she'd ended up with one of June's flowery frilly ones, so she hoped she didn't look too much like Mrs Tiggywinkle. 'Lily's plenty for me,' she said looking around the kitchen. Everything seemed pretty much done.

'When we were little,' Joanna said, 'you were always the one who was going to have hundreds of children, and dogs and cats and ponies and live in the country, which is what I've more or less ended up with.'

'Times change,' Becca said. 'You were going to be a ballerina.'

'Despite not being able to balance. I'd have been the wobbliest ballerina ever,' Joanna said, shaking her head so her hair swung in a bell around her. Becca had always envied her fine, straight hair that never strayed out of place, unlike Becca's which had a fondness for taking off in its own direction especially when there was the merest hint of dampness in the air. 'Do you remember when I broke my arm falling off my bicycle?' Joanna added.

Becca shook her head. 'It must have been when I'd gone off to university.'

Joanna looked vague. 'Oh, yes, it must have been.'

'So is there a big age difference between you?' Crystal looked between the two sisters. They spoke at the same time.

'Six years.'

'Five years.'

Becca frowned trying to do the maths in her head. The trouble was, there came a point in life when you genuinely forgot how old you were, so keeping track of other people was impossible. 'I'm sure it's five.'

'Six.' Joanna smiled.

'Well, I'm forty-three, and you're—'

'Thirty-seven. Six years, see?'

'But it's your birthday next month, and I've just had mine so . . .'

Joanna clicked her tongue as if Becca was being needlessly pedantic. 'Whatever. You're older than me, anyhow.'

I know that, Becca thought. Older, frumpier, boring-er – not that that was a word in the dictionary, but it was how she felt. She didn't see Joanna that often, given that Joanna lived on the other side of the world, but whenever Joanna did come home, she was irritatingly exactly the same as before, while Becca felt herself sliding further into middle age. 'Those mini pizzas must be ready.' She opened the oven and a delicious scent of baked tomato and fresh dough filled the kitchen. 'Let's pass them round.'

Becca and Martin had brought up their own garden table and chairs, and with June and Frank's assorted furniture, they'd got enough to seat most of the guests, with picnic blankets ready for the young.

'People can sit on the walls,' June said. The house was on the northern slopes of Bath, looking out across the golf course and park towards the centre of the city. June had designed it using a book of oriental art as her inspiration. Close to the house was a pergola with vaguely Japanese crossbars, as carved by Frank, and a rectangular lily pond where he kept koi carp. Some of them were quite big now. Over the years Frank had built a number of retaining walls to contain the slope and make a series of terraces and flowerbeds. He was quite happy to let June be the designer, while he built. The biggest wall was nicknamed the Great Wall of China, and June had intended to plant azaleas and acers along it, but Frank had diluted the effect by planting hybrid tea roses of all colours. 'Let's hope the walls are up to the strain.'

Becca started with a group of elderly women sitting under the shade of an umbrella. Golfers rather than artists, Becca guessed, judging by the flowery frocks and smart shoes that looked painfully stretched across bunions. They had appeared deep in conversation, but when Becca approached they turned to her with wide smiles, as if she were a welcome diversion. 'Weren't they lucky with the weather?' Becca nodded, trying to remember the woman's name. She knew June complained she had a habit of turning up on their doorstep, unannounced and expecting tea. The woman nodded too, her eyes bright under a fluff of white hair. Becca could see the scalp underneath, pink, like a white mouse. 'I said to your mother, what on earth will you do if it rains? It doesn't bear thinking about, does it? It would have been a disaster. You'd never have got everyone in the house now, would you?'

Becca smiled at her. 'As you say, we've been lucky. Mini pizza? And there's lots of food laid out in the house.'

'I went to a wedding last week, and it poured,' another woman chipped in. 'A complete washout. They'd hired a chimney sweep to bring good luck, and all the soot ran down his face.'

'How dreadful,' the white-haired woman said with tones of great satisfaction. 'The whole day must have been ruined for them. And the bad luck – they won't be making fifty years.'

Becca glanced across to where Martin was circulating, champagne bottle in one hand, orange juice now in the other. He was bending solicitously over one of her great aunt's glass, filling it up to the brim. As he straightened up he caught Becca's eye and smiled. She smiled back at him. Fifty years did seem a long time but they were nearly halfway there, and it didn't seem longer than a few minutes.

Becca handed round the pizzas, picking up snippets of conversation as she went. 'And it comes out, sweet as a nut. Lovely action, really well engineered,' one of Frank's cronies was saying, miming pulling a cork from a bottle before scooping up a mini pizza. 'Thank you, my dear. Now, as I was saying, you've got to check for the ratchets – the cheap ones are made from plastic, and you've got to have metal.' The other men nodded, mouths full.

'It's amazing what they can do, nowadays.'

'Japanese, I expect.'

'Or Taiwanese.'

'There's lots of food in the house, please, help yourselves,' Becca said before moving on. She looked round the garden, wondering where Lily had got to. Fourteen was an awkward age, leaving Lily marooned between being one of the children scampering through the guests, and one of the cousins who had miraculously turned into young adults while Becca wasn't looking. Now she knew why aunts and uncles went around saying 'My! And haven't you grown' to their nieces and nephews. Ah, there Lily was, sitting with her grand-mother, and June's old friend from way back, the very arty one with chopsticks securing her bun, and beads that looked like toffees around her neck. Good, they'd all got food. She turned back to see who else she could offer a mini pizza to. There was a general drift of guests both towards the house, and back out into the garden with plates laden with food. It was time to put out the puddings.

Before she went in she spotted Martin talking to Norman, or

more accurately, Norman was talking at Martin. Norman's pink shirt emphasised his high skin tone, his fair skin was tanned to a shade just darker than the shirt and topped by hair bleached to nearly white. Pink had been Joanna's favourite colour when she was little, Becca remembered. Norman had been involved in property in Hong Kong, which was where he'd met Joanna. Now they ran a development company together in New Zealand.

'You have to speculate to accumulate,' Norman was telling Martin with gusto. Everything Norman did was energetic, he radiated determination. Martin swigged beer from a can. He'd obviously given up trying to get a word in edgeways and looked bored. 'Waterfront developments – that's where to put your money.'

'Mini pizza?' Becca asked.

'Ah, Becca, I was just telling Martin here that he should be looking at waterfront developments for his investment portfolio.' Norman put a bear-like arm around Becca and gave her a hug.

'Really?' As far as Becca knew their investment portfolio consisted of a handful of underperforming shares and an old Post Office savings account Martin had started when he was nine, and had forgotten to close. With compound interest, it had nearly reached the giddy sum of ten pounds. Becca avoided looking in Martin's direction in case she giggled. 'Well, lunch is ready, so help yourselves. You'd better go quickly, or there won't be any left.'

'What about you, have you had anything to eat?' Martin said. 'Let someone else do some of the work for a change.'

'I like doing it,' Becca said. 'I want Mum and Dad to have the best party ever.' She looked around; everywhere people were sitting, eating, talking, laughing. The sun was shining, children shrieked and played tag in the bushes. Becca had a feeling of pure satisfaction that everything was just as it should have been.

The afternoon continued, guests talked, glasses were refilled, someone got pavlova down their skirt and needed sponging, one of the great nieces, or maybe it was a cousin three times removed, fell off the Great Wall of China and needed a bandage for a grazed knee, and three people stepped back without thinking and ended up in the lily pond. The noise of people talking and laughing mixed with knives and forks chinking as plates were scraped, and glasses were drained and refilled yet again. The sun was hot and many of the older guests took refuge inside. Others, including Frank and June, sat under the shade of the trees. Joanna was sitting with them, and Frank was gently snoring when Becca approached.

'Typical,' June said, shaking her head. 'He can't stay awake the whole day.'

'I was saying to Mum she and Dad ought to come out to New Zealand and visit,' Joanna said, looking up at Becca with her hand shading her eyes against the sun.

'I'd love to. I thought it looked wonderful in the films.' June had been to see all of the *Lord of the Rings* films with Lily, Becca and Martin, although Frank couldn't be bothered after the first one.

'We could go to some of the places where they filmed, if you like. Perhaps do some hiking. Dad could go fishing.'

'What?' Frank sat up, blinking furiously. 'What's that?'

'You could go fishing, Dad.'

'Where?'

'New Zealand. If you and Mum came out. We could go fishing, maybe a bit of a tour round the wine-producing areas, bit of hiking.'

'It's too far,' Frank said, yawning.

Joanna and June exchanged glances. 'You could do the journey in stages, if you wanted. People often stop off in the Far East, or California. Maybe you could do it as part of a round the world trip.'

'We're far too old for that sort of thing,' Frank said. 'We need peace and quiet at our age.'

'Speak for yourself,' June said. 'I'm only just seventy. I'd love to go.'

'No, you wouldn't,' Frank said. 'You don't like foreign food.'

'I do, so long as it's not too spicy,' June said. 'And it wouldn't be that different in New Zealand from here, would it?'

Joanna shook her head in confirmation. 'You'd have a great time,' she said. 'I'd love to show it to you.'

Becca saw Crystal on the top terrace by the pergola looking round and she waved at her. Crystal waved back, and started to weave her way down through the guests towards them.

'It'd be too expensive,' Frank said. 'Think of the flights.'

'But we'd stay at Joanna's house when we were there. It wouldn't have to be expensive,' June said.

'I'd help you out with the tickets, as your golden anniversary present,' Joanna said.

Becca wanted to step in and say she and Martin would chip in too, but knew she couldn't, a hangover from when Martin had been made redundant several years before. He'd got a job, at last, but money was still tight.

'I don't know why you want to go anywhere else other than this country,' Frank said, shifting in his deckchair like an old owl fluffing up his feathers. 'It's got everything a person could want.'

Crystal came over. 'Sorry to interrupt, but I just wanted to say thank you so much for having me. It's been a wonderful party. Happy Anniversary.' She bent down and kissed Frank and June.

'Thank you so much for coming and being our photographer, dear,' June said. 'Are you going somewhere nice on holiday?'

'Yes, my boyfriend's taking me to Barcelona later in the month.' Crystal grinned. 'It'll be boiling, but fabulous.'

'All those wonderful Gaudi buildings. I'd love to see the Sagrada Familia,' June said.

'Er, yes,' Crystal said, looking blank. Becca knew architecture wasn't her strong point. 'We're only going for a week. I'll see you at the start of term, Becca.'

'She's such a nice girl,' June said when Crystal had gone. 'I don't know why she doesn't get married. She must be getting on a bit.'

'Mid-thirties,' Becca said, leaning back in her chair and feeling she could sleep for a week. 'She never meets the right man.'

'Is there ever such a thing as a right man?' June said. 'Don't you just take the best that's around at the time?'

'Mum!' Becca and Joanna said in unison. They all looked over to Frank, who was fast asleep again and the three of them burst out laughing.

Becca sent Lily straight up to bed when they got home, while she and Martin unloaded the car. 'What am I going to do with all these profiteroles?' She shook her head at the sight of the bowl.

'Eat them!' Martin responded, picking one up and taking a mouthful.

'Aren't you stuffed?' Becca said. The thought of food disgusted her right now, although she knew that would pass. She emptied the plate into a smaller bowl, a mix of chocolate, cream and beige pastry, and pushed it into the fridge.

Martin put his hand on her shoulder. 'You look all in,' he said. 'Why don't you go up to bed, and I'll bring you a cup of tea.'

Becca looked around at the kitchen. 'But I've got all this to do.'

'We'll do it together in the morning, it'll keep until then.' Martin gave her a gentle push towards the door. 'Go on. Upstairs.'

Becca swung round. 'I love it when you're all masterful.'

'Do you?' He gave her a kiss, then patted her bum. 'Go on, hop it.'

Becca gave a last look around the kitchen. Martin was right, she could do it in the morning. 'Are you sure?' Martin pointed at the door. 'OK, I'm going.' She yawned as she went upstairs. Her legs felt heavy and her whole body lethargic. Post-party blues, she supposed. God, but it was hard work organising someone else's bash. She sat on the edge of the bed, knowing she should be getting undressed, taking off her make-up, but feeling unable to move.

'I couldn't do it for a living,' she said as Martin came into the bedroom. He settled a milky cup of tea on her bedside cabinet.

'What? Catering?'

'Mmm. But I think everyone had a good time, don't you?'

Martin sat next to her, his arm around her shoulder. 'I think everyone had a great time. It was a wonderful day.'

Becca rested her head on Martin's shoulder and closed her eyes. 'I think Mum and Dad enjoyed it.'

Martin squeezed her shoulder. 'Course they did. All their family around them, all their friends . . . you're tired, love. Get ready for bed.'

Becca yawned and stood. 'There was something a bit sad about it though.'

'What do you mean?' Martin got up and went over to his side of the room, pulling his sweater over his head as he went.

'As if their lives were over.' Becca undid the zip of her dress. 'As if that was the end, and it was all downhill from there.'

'You're just tired. We all are.' Martin stretched. 'God, remind me not to get stuck with Norman again. I must have aged about a hundred years.'

'I thought you liked him.'

'In small doses. But he's getting worse. All he can talk about is how much money he makes, and how many deals he's won, and how many impressive people he knows. His dick is probably this big.' Martin indicated a minute gap between his thumb and forefinger.

'He's got five kids,' Becca said without thinking.

The air between them froze for a second. She could see everything clearly, although the room was filled with diffused light, then, as if it were a television picture, normal service resumed and Martin carried on getting ready for bed. 'I couldn't care less about price-earning ratios and square footage. We're not meeting up with them tomorrow, are we?'

'No, they're off to visit friends near Guildford.' Becca went through to the bathroom. She stared at her face in the mirror, knowing she ought to take her make-up off, but feeling too tired to lift her hand. 'Would you like it if I wore the same sort of stuff Joanna does?'

'What do you mean? You looked great.'

'I feel . . . old. Frumpy.'

'Better than mutton dressed as lamb.'

'Perhaps I should cut my hair.' Becca tried holding it up to see what it looked like short. Now her face seemed to have sagged downwards. She dropped her hair and put her forefingers on either side of her jawline and pushed upwards to make the skin taut. She lost five years immediately. She let her fingers drop, and her face drooped with it. Up – thirty-eight. Down – forty-three. Up! Down. Up! She kept her fingers there. No wonder people had facelifts. 'She looks a lot younger than me though.'

'She *is* a lot younger than you. Isn't she?'

'Six years.'

'There you are then.'

Becca let her fingers fall one last time. 'Perhaps I should buy more expensive clothes and stuff.'

'But you wouldn't want to have a whole load of designer stuff, would you?' Martin sounded as if he genuinely wanted to know.

Becca buzzed the electric toothbrush around her upper gums. 'Noooo,' she said. She guessed Joanna's handbag had cost at least £500, maybe more. She'd seen the Prada label. 'I don't know. Perhaps.'

'You look great in what you have.'

'There speaks a man whose idea of dress sense is ironed or not ironed.'

Martin came and stood at the entrance to the bathroom. 'Are you implying I'm not at the forefront in fashion?'

'In that T-shirt?' Becca gave it a fond tug. 'How could anyone suggest that a man caught in possession of a "Frankie says Relax" T-shirt is anything other than up to date?'

Martin smoothed the front of the T-shirt he wore in bed over his chest. It had been washed so many times that the word 'Relax' had nearly faded away. 'It's vintage, I'll have you know.'

'Oh is it?'

'Oh yes. All the stars wear vintage nowadays. Julia Roberts, people like that.'

Becca turned her toothbrush off. 'Now, how on earth did you know that?'

'There are lots of things I know,' Martin said, looking coy.

Becca prodded her face one more time. 'I can't be bothered to take off my make-up tonight.'

'Tsk. Slut,' Martin said cheerfully, squirting toothpaste on his brush as Becca left the bathroom.

She paused, hanging in the doorway. 'Come to bed and find out . . .' She didn't wait for his reply, but carried on into the bedroom. Sliding under the sheets she felt overwhelmed with relief that the day was over. No hitches, no disasters. A successful family party. Everyone had enjoyed themselves. Everyone had said how amazing Joanna was.

'Do you think I'm boring?' Becca said as Martin got into bed next to her and turned the light off. He snuggled up to her.

'Not at all. Why on earth would you think that?'

Becca hugged his arms around her. 'I mean, compared to Joanna – she's got her business, and they obviously entertain a lot and do lots of socialising, and go to the theatre and the opera. And art exhibitions.'

Martin yawned in her ear. 'Thank God you don't do all that stuff.'

Becca thought about it. 'I don't know why I don't. I'd like to, but somehow the opportunities go by. We ought to go to the theatre more at least.'

'Do we have to?' Martin grumbled into her shoulder.

Becca twisted round to face him. 'Perhaps me and Lily can go. Being with Joanna makes me feel . . . inadequate I suppose. She's a bit of a superwoman.'

'You're a superwoman.' Martin's hand traced the curve of her back. 'You're *my* superwoman.'

'Am I? Am I really?' She cosied up even closer to him.

'Very much so,' Martin said, his hand going lower. 'Is that nice?'

'Mmm,' Becca sighed. 'Very much so.'

Chapter 2

The thing is, Becca thought to herself as she lay in bed emerging slowly out of sleep. The thing is, nothing changes. It was more than a month since the party, and her life was just the same, running on predictable rails, stopping at the usual stations: birth, childhood, work, marriage, motherhood.

Becca yawned and stretched. Only retirement and senility to come. She thought about shutting her eyes and trying for a bit more sleep, then shook herself. Martin had got up early to go off on a work team-bonding day, and she thought she could remember him bringing her a cup of tea. She found it, and sipped. Yuck, luke warm, with a scummy surface. She yawned again. Right, let's get going. Let's be dynamic, let's be effective. Let's get up and do a hundred sit-ups! But bed was so warm . . . Fifty sit-ups? If only I could invent an exercise system that could be done in bed and didn't involve sweat, I'd be a millionaire, she thought, snuggling down under the duvet. But now she was awake properly and there was no denying the truth. Nothing was going to change, unless she actually did something about it.

She swung her legs out of bed and stared at the carpet trying to visualise herself down there doing sit-ups. After three seconds she gave up – sit-ups simply weren't going to be part of her new dynamic life. But she had a more or less free Saturday: she could investigate a new career, find an exciting hobby, join a gym, go swimming. She could get cultural: there was a whole world of art exhibitions and performances, concerts and museums out there, just waiting for her to walk through their doors. Go, Becca, go! She scurried into the shower and ran it cool, all the better to energise her ready for her new life.

Downstairs she made herself breakfast (no point in waiting for Lily) and started on the day's chores. Unload dishwasher, fill it with Martin's and her breakfast things, wipe down surfaces. Newspapers into recycling bin, sift through post, throw most of it away, read postcard from Crystal in Barcelona – the post must have taken ages, she'd have been back for a week – peek at gas bill, thank heavens it was from the summer months. Load washing machine, go into hall to yell at Lily to get up and clean out hamster, realise yelling is futile, go back to the utility room.

Becca held the hamster in her hand, Lily's Christmas present from the year before. The hamster stared at her, black eyes shining, nose twitching. Then, obviously unimpressed with Becca, it turned its back on her, tiny feet scuffling Becca's palm, and got on with the serious business of washing.

'You could be a bit more grateful,' Becca told it, as it cutely cuffed behind its ears as if auditioning for a Beatrix Potter watercolour. 'You're not in the desert now you know. If I didn't look after you, you couldn't rely on Lily.' The hamster yawned showing small but sharp teeth. 'You're not listening to me, are you?' she said. 'Never mind, no one else in this house does so you're not alone.'

Becca popped the hamster on the worktop, put on rubber gloves, then began cleaning the bottom of the cage. That done, she replaced the bedding in the hamster's little house and spread a clean newspaper over the bottom of the cage. A headline caught her eye: 'Daring canal boat rescue!' She began to read the article, and then the next, caught up in the irresistible lure of out of date and discarded newspapers, so much more interesting than when the news was fresh. Then her attention was caught and she read more intently. An amateur dramatics group were auditioning for a production of *The Country Wife*. Oh, but that took her back. She'd been in a production at university in her first year. Becca sat on her haunches as she tried to remember the plot. Lots of bed-hopping, Restoration style, with *Fie*! and *Foh*! and *La*! and heaving bosoms and tapping the fops on the shoulder with your fan. The cast had got into the spirit of things, the quantity of romping increasing offstage as well as on as the term wore on, and a party each night after the performance complete with at least one person being sick in the garden, one girl weeping in the upstairs loo, and three couples glued to each other while slow dancing to 'Lady in Red'. She'd done her share of that with – now, what was his name? She scoured her mind for the answer. Strange how she could remember details like his curly hair and that he came from Rotherham, but not his name.

'Happy days,' Becca told the hamster as she went back to the article. Then all thoughts of her romance with Rotherham man skipped out of her brain. There were going to be open auditions all week, finishing on Saturday 2 September. Today. This morning. Becca checked her watch. Now.

Becca pushed open the door, her heart beating as if she was entering the dragon's lair instead of a converted church on the outskirts of Bath. She'd driven past it often enough, as it wasn't far from her house, nor the school where she taught. The walls of the entrance lobby had the slightly lumpy effect of having been painted fast with thick paint to hide the poor quality surface underneath. It gave the place a subtle makeshift feel, like nightclubs in daylight.

There was nothing subtle or makeshift about the young woman lounging against a desk, however. She was wearing a purple feathery bolero and black velvet shorts, long legs encased in thick, horizontally striped, black and white tights ending in red leather Doc Martens. At the other end, half her black hair snaked over her shoulders while the other half was in two high bunches at the top of her head like a manga cartoon.

Becca nearly turned tail and ran. 'Is this the right place for the auditions?' she asked instead. She'd chucked on her usual Saturday uniform of jeans and sweatshirt, but compared to the glories of purple feathers she felt horribly mumsy and conventional, mutton dressed in Boden. This was a bad idea.

The woman picked up a clipboard. 'Name?' she asked with a smile, Biro poised.

'I won't be on your list – I only saw the notice this morning,' Becca said, stumbling over the words. 'I don't expect there are any spaces. It was just an idea. It doesn't matter.'

'It's fine, if you don't mind waiting,' the woman said, smiling with a friendliness that was at odds with her startling appearance. 'I can pop you in at the end – we're running a bit late but I'm sure he won't mind,' and she indicated with a tilt of her head someone behind the double doors that presumably led to the main body of the church.

Becca gave the woman her details and sat down carefully so as not to disturb an elderly man slumped on the chair who Becca guessed was thinking himself into his role. That, or he was in a coma. There were six other people waiting, all women, apart from the coma man. Even at ten minutes per audition, it was going to mean waiting over an hour.

'Have you auditioned for us before?' the woman asked, hair bobbing. She was not as young as Becca had originally thought, judging by the fine tracing of lines around her eyes. Becca shook her head. 'It's quite a commitment, you know.'

'I hadn't thought . . .' Becca wondered if she should go now. She couldn't give up too many evenings a week, not during term time.

'Mind you, you should be all right with this play – there's a big enough cast. With some of the smaller plays, the actors have to turn up three nights a week, but I wouldn't have thought it'd be more than once a week. Assuming you got cast. And assuming you won't get the lead role. Which you won't.'

Becca immediately longed to get the lead role, just to prove her wrong, although three nights a week would be practically impossible. Perhaps the biggest roles went to the actors who'd been there longest. 'How do you know I won't get the lead role?'

'It's a bloke.' Becca mentally kicked herself; she should have remembered that. The woman carried on. 'And the lead female role is – and I don't mean to be rude – going to go to someone younger than you. There's a hardcore of about thirty of us, but lots more dip in and out, and we've built up a loyal audience. We do three plays a year, usually modern, occasionally a musical. Are you interested in musical theatre?'

'Not really,' Becca said. 'I can't sing.'

'Pity. We're always on the look out for sopranos. Do you want to go in now?' she said to one of the waiting women as another came out, then hardly without breath went back to Becca. 'We did *Guys and Dolls* last year, I did all the costumes, it looked great though I say it myself. Are you interested in wardrobe?'

'Acting mainly, though I'd be happy to help.'

'I couldn't bear to act, all those people looking at me.' She gave a theatrical shudder as Becca wondered why you'd dress in purple feathers if you couldn't bear people looking at you. 'Is that your phone?'

'Sorry, yes.' Becca rummaged in her bag, expecting it to be Lily demanding to know where she was. But it wasn't Lily, it was her mother.

'You're not at home,' June said, without preamble.

'No, I'm in town.' Becca bit back the impulse to tell her mother what she was doing, not wanting anyone to know she'd had a go at auditioning – unless she was cast. Then she'd tell everybody.

'When will you be back?' June's tone was abrupt, but then June always was when calling a mobile phone, worried that she'd end up with a ten-pound charge for a ten-second conversation. How she thought Lily managed without bankrupting Martin and Becca was anyone's guess.

'I don't know.' Becca looked round, calculating. There were now four people waiting to audition. 'Perhaps in an hour and a half?'

'I'd like to come round.' June lowered her voice. 'I've got something to tell you I don't want to say on the phone.'

'What is it?' Becca said immediately. But June wouldn't say. How strange, Becca thought as she dropped her phone back in her bag.

'Hello, sorry to have kept you waiting.' The man behind the desk at the far end of the hall stood up, his tone warm but brisk. 'I'm Paul Fitzwilliam, the director. And you are . . . ?'

'Becca Woods,' Becca said, crossing the length of the hall to take his outstretched hand. She'd waited long enough to have second, third and fourth thoughts about auditioning and had been on the point of leaving when Purple Feathers had called her in.

'Please sit down.' He indicated a chair in front of the desk, picked up a pen and looked expectantly at Becca as she sat. He was good looking, with strong dramatic features and she could imagine him being used as a model to sell suits to businessmen, although he was dressed in jeans and a T-shirt with 'I don't smoke' written on the front in hazy, smoky writing. The thick dark hair swept back over his ears was streaked with grey, so she guessed he was in his late forties or early fifties. 'Tell me a bit about yourself.'

'My name's Becca Woods and . . .' Becca's mind went blank. She couldn't think of anything to say about herself, beyond her sudden, absolute, desperate need to go to the loo.

'What made you come to the audition?' he said, his tone gentle. His blue eyes were understanding and Becca locked on to them.

'I saw a piece in the paper. When I was cleaning out the hamster. It was just spur of the moment, really.' Her face felt as if it were scarlet. What a stupid thing to say. But his expression didn't falter.

'So you decided to come in.' He nodded, as if hamster-cleaning was the usual route to auditioning. 'Have you done any acting before?'

Becca nodded. 'At university. I've been in *The Country Wife* – I played Alithea.'

'So you know the play?'

She shook her head. 'I can't really remember much.'

'And after university?'

'I thought about it but . . .' She shrugged, not wanting go into the details of the mess that had been her final year. It had been quite dramatic enough without any additional acting. 'I suppose there's always a bit of you that says – what would have happened if I'd pursued it.'

Paul laughed. 'That's the actor's curse. Never mind, you're here now. As I expect you know, after the restoration of the monarchy in 1660, there was a backlash against puritanism and people indulged in all the vices that had been banned – theatre, alcohol, dancing, generally having fun, and of course, sex. The plays of the time reflect the change of mood in the country as a whole. *The Country Wife* is one of the most famous from this period. The plot centres around Horner, who's notorious for having affairs with people's wives. He comes up with the idea of spreading a rumour that he's impotent so that the men think he's safe – but all the wives know the truth.'

Becca nodded. She could remember this bit of the plot about Horner – oh, it had been Rob! Rob from Rotherham. He'd been lovely.

'One of the men, Pinchwife, has had the bright idea of marrying an innocent girl from the country with the idea that she won't know the ways of the town wives, and therefore won't have affairs.' He smiled at her, and Becca smiled back, wondering how many times today he'd given this précis of the story. 'That's the main plot, but there's another plot involving a husband and wife – the Fidgets –

who are bored with each other and are looking for fun and games elsewhere. Do you feel like doing a little bit of reading for me?' He made it sound as if it was optional, rather than an expected part of any audition. He handed her a script. 'Perhaps you'd like to read for Lady Fidget.'

Becca looked at the page he'd marked and quickly scanned it. 'Oh! Is this the china scene?'

He grinned, his eyes lit up with amusement. 'I'll read Horner.'

Becca tried to remember the scene. As Alithea she'd had little to do with the Lady Fidget–Horner relationship, but she knew that this was the scene guaranteed to get the audience laughing. The characters discussed buying, having and enjoying china, but some were doing it innocently and others were using china as a euphemism for sex. Lady Fidget was an experienced, knowing woman of the world.

Becca sat up straight on her chair, imagining herself in a corset, trying to forget she was Becca Woods in jeans and a sweatshirt. As far as she could remember Lady Fidget was bold, confident, sexual. A hungry woman. Becca started to read. ' "Well, Horner, am not I a woman of honour? You see, I'm as good as my word." ' She looked across the desk at Paul with what she hoped was a bold, confident, sexual look. A look of surprise flashed across his face for a second, then was replaced by a more intense expression. Becca felt a surge of confidence.

' "And you shall see, madam, I'll not be behindhand with you in honour. And I'll be as good as my word too, if you please but to withdraw into the next room." ' He made a gesture, his eyes fixed on Becca's.

Becca trailed her hand along the top of the desk inches away from his. ' "But first, my dear sir, you must promise to have a care of my dear honour," ' she drawled. Would it be too much to lick her lips? What the hell.

Paul took her hand. ' "If you talk a word more of your honour, you'll make me incapable to wrong it." ' He kissed her fingertips, his eyes on hers. Underneath her sensible sweatshirt, Becca's bosom gave a little heave. ' "To talk of honour in the mysteries of love is like—" ' There was a sudden loud noise behind her. Paul stood up abruptly. 'What is it? I'm auditioning here, I'm not to be disturbed, I—' He caught his breath.

Becca turned round. A slim woman with sunglasses perched on the top of her blond-streaked head was standing in the doorway, hands on hips, and effortlessly glamorous in a way Becca tried, but knew she failed to achieve. If that was the competition, there was no way Becca would get a part.

But when the woman opened her mouth, it was obvious she wasn't intending to audition for any part, except possibly Fishwife. 'Where the hell have you been? You promised you'd collect the boys. I've had the school on to me saying where are you, I've had to drop everything to go and pick them up.'

'God, Suzy, I'm sorry, I've lost track of the time.' Paul ran a flustered hand through his hair.

'Is that what you're going to tell the boys? "I'm sorry, I lost track of the time"?' She mimicked Paul's voice with bitterness. Becca shifted in her chair, feeling acutely uncomfortable at being a witness to a domestic scenario she knew only too well. His children must be at a private school, to have school on a Saturday.

Paul turned to her. 'I'm terribly sorry,' he said, and she could tell that he was mortified with embarrassment. 'If you'll just wait there for a second.'

'Of course,' Becca said, trying to give an understanding and sympathetic smile. He nodded, then walked to Suzy, and they left the hall.

Becca flicked through the playscript, trying very hard not to listen to the angry cadences of Suzy's upraised voice through the swing doors. Oh dear, she was giving him a hard time. If she hadn't turned up at the last minute, he'd have been able to get away earlier.

Becca glanced at her watch. She was going to be late for June too at this rate.

The door opened and Paul came back in, and walked stiffly towards her.

'I'm sorry about that,' he said. 'You were doing very well.'

'It doesn't matter,' Becca murmured.

He settled himself back down at his desk, then gave a little shake as if discarding himself of his family man persona, becoming entirely professional. He picked up the playscript. 'Let's start again, from the top.'

Becca rushed back to find her mother standing on the doorstep.

'Sorry, sorry, sorry,' she said, fumbling in her bag for her house keys. 'I was held up.'

'Where have you been?' June wore her pale blond hair in a short bob, the waves carefully arranged each week at the hairdresser's. Today she had clipped the front section to one side away from her face with a childish slide, but there was nothing childish about her tone.

'Auditioning,' Becca said, letting herself into the house, a classic late-Victorian end of terrace, identical to thousands throughout the country although theirs was faced in honey-coloured Bath stone. 'Lily? Are you there?'

No answer. Becca slung her bag over the newel post and went through to the kitchen, June following. 'Cup of tea?' Without waiting for an answer she filled the kettle, water splashing all over the place. The house had cost more than they'd budgeted for, and in the renovations items like taps had to be the cheapest. Over the last ten years Becca told herself at least once a day she must redo the kitchen, usually when the water splashed all down her front, just as it had done now. As she dabbed at her wet tummy with a tea towel she saw that Lily had left a note, now damp, on the side: 'Gone to town. Can you pick me up at 3? Luv U. Lily.'

Becca's mouth twitched. Oh Lily. Get a bus! Or walk! But nothing, not even Lily's assumption that her mother had nothing else to do with her life except run a taxi service could dent the uplifted feeling she'd got from the audition.

'Did you say auditioning?' June's tone was of disbelief.

'Yes, I thought I'd have a go. Am dram, of course, but it'd be fun to do something different. Not that I expect I'll be cast.' She felt charged with energy, like being enveloped in a glowing balloon of light.

'Won't that take up a lot of your time? What about Lily? And Martin?' June tidied the stack of catalogues and brochures Becca had left on the kitchen side having forgotten to put them out for recycling.

Becca took them from her. 'I doubt very much if I'll get a part, but both Lily and Martin are old enough to look after themselves for an evening or two a week.' The glowing balloon dimmed. I don't care if she thinks auditioning is ridiculous, Becca thought, dumping the catalogues in the bin with a frisson of guilt about the environment. 'What did you want to see me about? You said there was something you wanted to tell me.'

June gave a little gasp, as if caught out, then pressed her lips together, her gaze fixed downwards. Her face looked every one of its seventy years, the lines pronounced. Becca felt a cold chill of panic.

'You're not ill, are you?' She took her mother's hand. 'Are you OK?'

June squeezed her hand. 'No, I'm not ill. And your father's fine, just fine. Don't worry, it's not serious.' The lines around her eyes tightened as if she was going to have to force out what she wanted to say. 'Well, it is serious, but not terminal. Not illness.'

'What then? What's the matter?'

June put her other hand on Becca's, her eyes fixed on her daughter's. 'I've decided to leave your father.'

Chapter 3

Becca couldn't take it in. It was impossible. Her parents' marriage was a fact of life, like dogs walking on four legs and credit-card bills being larger than expected. Yes, you knew there was the possibility of variation – she'd seen a photograph of a dog who'd lost his back legs and had been kitted out with a two-wheeled carriage for his rear end – but you didn't expect it to happen. And not to her parents. Perhaps she'd misheard her mother.

'Did you just say . . . ?'

June nodded. 'I'm leaving Frank.'

Becca gawped at her. Everything seemed to have gone into slow motion, but still her brain couldn't keep up. 'But why?' was all she could manage.

'Because . . . Oh, I don't know. It's difficult to explain.' June gave an apologetic smile and sat down at the kitchen table, as if hiding behind a chunk of scrubbed pine would protect her from awkward questions.

'Try to – I want to understand. I thought you were so happy at the party. Both of you.' Becca clasped June's hands, feeling her finger joints, hard and bony. She looked up at her kitchen pinboard; among the clutter of discount offers from loyalty cards, Crystal's postcard, the programme for the Theatre Royal, was a photograph taken at the party. There they all were, Becca, Martin and Lily,

Joanna, Norman, all their children, and at the centre, Frank and June. Everyone was smiling in the summer sunshine. Genuine, unforced smiles – of course, they'd already had a couple of glasses of champagne at that point so it was hardly surprising they were happy, but it really had been a golden day for a golden couple. Frank and June, and their descendants. The family unit.

'Funnily enough, it was the golden wedding party that made up my mind,' June said. 'I looked around at everyone and thought: is this it? Everyone's being lovely, but no one expects anything more out of me and Frank except to go on living and not making too much fuss out of it. My generation put up with what we got and didn't expect too much from our marriages. And a good thing too – Frank and I have nothing in common. At the party, all the talk was of what you young people were doing, and I realised I hadn't done anything with my life. I don't regret having been nothing more than a wife and mother, but the fact is you've got your own lives. You don't need me to be there any more. It's OK for Frank, he's had his career, and now he wants to vegetate, but I don't want to be a cabbage. I've got at least ten years of good health left to me, if I'm lucky, and I want to do things.'

'What sort of things?'

'I'd like to travel.'

'You could do that with Dad.'

June snorted. 'Hardly! He's determined not to move more than a hundred yards from home – he says he's seen everywhere that's worth seeing.'

That rang true. 'You could travel on your own.'

'But then, what's the point in being married? Everything I want to do, he doesn't. And I don't want to do the things he does. Why do we have to stay together, just because we're old?'

Becca wanted to say, Cos you're my mum, like a little child would. She shook her head to try and clear the confusion. 'Have you talked about this with Dad?'

'I don't have to ask his permission to go,' June said tartly.

'No, I didn't mean . . . I'm sorry, I'm being really stupid, but it's such a shock. I'm completely thrown. I never expected this.' This feels like a dream, Becca thought. This isn't happening to me. In a minute, I shall wake up, and everything will be back to normal. She looked across at June. 'Is there anything I can do?'

'What do you mean?'

'I don't know.' I want to wave a magic wand and make the clock go back, I want you to go back to just being my mother. 'Is this a trial separation or are you just moving out for a bit? Perhaps you need a holiday . . . leaving sounds so permanent – are you certain?'

'Oh, Becca, what do you think? I'm not leaving your father for fun. It's taken me years to get to this point, and now I'm going, I want . . .' She stopped, her face suddenly less defiant, more pleading. 'I want your support.'

Becca gripped the edge of the table, trying to shut out the wail of no, no, no that rocked her body. I don't want to support you, I don't want you to leave my dad, I want life to carry on, safe and secure. 'You're my mother,' she said quietly.

'That's not an answer,' June said, sharp as lemons.

'I know.' Becca fiddled with her necklace. The catch was always getting tangled in her hair. Think. 'You are my mother, and I love you, so of course I'll support you. I'll do whatever you want,' she said, looking directly across at June. 'But I also love my dad.'

'So you're on his side?'

Becca squeezed her eyes shut then opened them. 'I'm not on anyone's side. Or I'm on both of your sides. I don't know, Mum, I can't think straight.'

June leaned forwards. 'You don't have to think straight, Becca. It's not your decision.'

She needed to stall for time. 'Have you spoken to Joanna?'

June shook her head. 'Not yet – I will later.'

Becca glanced at the clock. Two in the afternoon here, two in the morning on the other side of the world. What would Joanna say? But it didn't matter, time was short. Becca would have to do this on her own. She looked across to June, and couldn't think of a single thing to say.

They both jumped as the back door burst open and Lily arrived, lugging her bag over her shoulder as if she was hauling a sack of coal. Coal was appropriate as she was dressed in black and her eyes were rimmed with soot, although her hair was the same light brown as Becca's. Somewhere underneath was Becca's pretty, fresh-faced, fourteen-year-old daughter but at times it was hard to see where.

'I had to wait for ever for the bus,' Lily said, dumping her bag in the middle of the kitchen table. 'Hi, Gran.'

Becca darted a warning glance at June. She mustn't say anything to Lily, not now, not yet. Lily would be shocked, upset, and Becca wasn't sure she could cope with her own emotions, let alone Lily's. 'Gran just popped round for a cup of tea,' she said brightly.

June raised her face to be kissed, just as normal, just as if she hadn't made her extraordinary announcement. 'Hello, love. Have you been into town?'

Lily slumped in a chair next to her grandmother. 'Me 'n' Grace went shopping. This woman, you wouldn't believe, it was really sly, she was like trailing us round the shop, like we were going to steal something, it was like, so random.'

It was all as normal and yet things had changed. Becca realised she was shaking. She cleared her throat. 'I thought you wanted me to pick you up at three.'

Lily looked as if her life force was dwindling to nothing. 'No one was around, so I came back.'

Becca glanced at the clock. 'Have you had lunch?'

'Kevin gave me some of his pizza,' Lily said. Despite most of her mind being on June and Frank, Becca clocked Lily's cheeks getting pinker. Obviously 'Kevin' was someone significant.

'Is that enough? Do you want something more to eat?'

'What is there?'

Becca opened the fridge door. It was full to bursting as she'd squeezed in a megashop on Friday afternoon, and yet her brain seemed to have stopped making connections as if the synapses had fused. All this food, and she couldn't think of a single thing to make. She tried to concentrate. Lunch, lunch for Lily. 'Cheese on toast?'

'No thanks. What else is there?'

'I don't know.' Becca stared at a pack of yoghurts as if they might hold the answer as well as a healthy dose of friendly bacteria. Perhaps they did. 'Yoghurt?'

Lily pulled a face. 'Yeah well, like I said, I had some pizza.'

June pressed her lips together. 'It doesn't sound like much for lunch.'

'I don't think she's going to starve just yet,' Becca said shortly, shutting the fridge door.

Lily looked between the two, picking up the undercurrents, but disinterested in them, being covered in a layer of self-absorption as soft as puppy fat. With a surge of sudden energy she bounded from her seat, and shot off into the sitting room. 'See ya.' The door slammed behind her.

'I must be going too,' June said, getting up. 'I only dropped in to tell you the news face to face.'

'Mum, don't go. Stay and we can talk some more. I'll make a fresh pot of tea and . . .' She waved her hand, realising she hadn't got round to making the first pot, trying to think of something more enticing than tea. Something that would make June stay. 'I feel like you sometimes,' Becca said quietly. She swallowed to try and rid herself of the great lump that had suddenly turned up in her throat. 'I think every married woman with children knows the feeling of suddenly turning round and thinking – where have I gone? And sometimes, sometimes, you feel the only way of finding out is by leaving the situation.' She glanced up at the photo. Martin had his arm around her shoulder and she was smiling up at him. Lily stood in front of them, shyly smiling at the camera. Her family. 'But leaving isn't the answer. It really isn't.'

June sighed and stared out of the window. 'Let's have that tea.'

Becca realised she had been holding her breath. She busied herself with making the tea, finding release in the noise of clattering the cups, and the water whooshing out of the tap and into the kettle.

'Tell me about this audition,' June said.

'It's nothing,' Becca said, as she poured boiling water into the pot. 'Silliness, really. It was just an impulse to do something a bit different.'

'You always liked acting at school. Thanks,' she added, as Becca handed her a mug of tea.

Becca sat down with her own mug. The tea was pale – she hadn't left it to brew long enough – but it was hot and refreshing which was all she needed. She looked across to June and realised that in her agitation she had given her the mug that had been Martin's Christmas present to her a few years ago. 'A Mother's Place is in the Wrong' was emblazoned in red across it. 'Don't go,' she whispered. 'Don't leave us.'

'Oh, Becca.' June reached out for Becca's hand, her face creased with anxiety.

'Sorry,' Becca sniffed. 'I don't know why I'm so upset. I'm behaving worse than Lily.'

'I'm sorry, it's such a shock. Didn't you have any idea?'

Becca shook her head. 'None. It never occurred to me . . .' But now, thinking back she could remember little things – the expression on June's face when Frank had said going to New Zealand would be ridiculous for example. She took a deep breath. 'You have to do what's right for you. And whatever that is, I will try – I really will – I will try to be supportive about it. But please, don't do anything in a hurry. Give Dad a chance. He does love you.' Becca said the words, but then she thought – how do I know that? I just assume he does.

'I didn't expect you'd be so upset,' June said slowly. 'I thought you'd realised years ago that me and Frank weren't happy.'

'Never,' Becca said. 'Never.'

June lifted A Mother's Place is in the Wrong and sipped. 'This is a foul cup of tea,' she said, putting the mug down and standing up. 'I must go. I've got things to do.' She snapped on her gloves, shooting her fingers to the ends. Supple brown leather, good quality, bought to last a lifetime. She arranged a scarf around her neck, one Becca hadn't seen before, rainbow colours in a fuzzy chenille-type wool. She turned to Becca. 'I'll think about it. I don't think I'm going to change my mind, but I will think about it. And I promise you that I won't do anything in a rush.' She prodded the mug. 'I expect that's Martin's idea of a joke.'

Becca nodded. 'I didn't realise I'd given it to you.'

'Don't worry.' June kissed Becca's cheek. 'Don't worry about anything. It'll all be fine.'

By the time Martin came home she felt as explosive as a shaken bottle of lemonade, though distinctly less sweet. The fact that June had said she was going to think again about leaving Frank inhibited Becca from discussing the situation with anyone else, such as Crystal or Lily in particular. Lily would be devastated by the news. The only person she felt she could freely talk to, apart from Martin, was Joanna, but June hadn't yet told her. Perhaps the whole thing would blow over, she thought, brightening. Perhaps it was a momentary lapse.

The choice seemed grim: June was serious about leaving Frank, or she'd got senile dementia. She rang Martin, but his phone was switched off. She left a message: 'Ring me. It's urgent.' All her plans for making the most of her more or less commitment-free Saturday went out of the window. Stuff culture, all she wanted to do was talk to someone, anyone. And eat chocolate. At the local mini-supermarket she had a compulsion to pour out her woes to the checkout girl. It took all her willpower not to babble about her mother, and keep the exchange at the till to a three-second conversation about the weather. Where was Martin? Busy bonding with his team. Typical bloody man, she thought, knowing she was being unreasonable, feeling close to tears again. Why can't he be here when I need him? She checked her watch, although she knew he wouldn't be back until eight at the earliest.

But he didn't come back. At ten, Becca started getting ready for bed, still hoping that any minute she'd hear his key in the lock. She turned to the comfort of Jane Austen and *Sense and Sensibility* but gave up when she realised she'd read the same paragraph three times. Reluctantly she turned the light off. She thought she'd never sleep, but had just dropped off when she was woken by Martin stumbling over the corner of the bed.

'Martin?' she mumbled, groping for reality from a complicated dream state.

'Sorry, love,' he whispered, switching on his bedside light. 'Didn't mean to wake you.'

'Did you have a good day?' Becca said, snuggling back into a foetal position, arms folded across her chest.

'Yeah, it was brilliant, but God, I'm knackered. They're all about half my age, you know,' he said with a yawn, sitting heavily on his side of the bed. 'I'm going to be covered in bruises tomorrow.' He pulled his sweater off and examined his right side. 'Look, you can see where Helena got me, the cow. God, that woman's tough. I got her back though.'

'I thought paintballing was a guy thing,' Becca said.

'Don't be so sexist.' Martin pulled on his T-shirt. 'The girls were worse than the guys, totally ruthless.'

'My mother's leaving my father,' she said suddenly.

Martin swivelled round to her. 'What?' He looked blurred, his hair unruly. 'Relax', his T-shirt said. Becca felt she would never relax again. 'What about their golden wedding party?'

'She said that was the trigger. She said Dad wanted to vegetate, and she didn't want to be a cabbage.'

'Blimey. She's got a point, of course – your dad's hardly a New Man, and your mum's all into her art but . . . you don't think about people splitting, not at their age.' Martin ruffled his hair so it stuck up on his head like a parrot's. 'So she's going to leave him, just like that?'

'We talked a bit, and she said she wouldn't do anything in a hurry.' Becca thought back to her mother, her determined face. 'I'm frightened she means it.'

He turned his light off, then swung into bed. 'Poor you, having to deal with it. You should have rung.' His body was cold against hers.

She tucked her warm feet away from his. 'I did, but your phone was off.'

'I'm sorry – we were in some forest, miles from a signal.' He stroked her hair. 'Poor Becca.'

She twisted round to face him. 'I'm confused, Martin, I don't know what to do.' She snuggled into him, feeling like a child searching for comfort in his physical presence. With Martin holding her, cuddling her, she would be safe.

'Do you have to do anything?' He kissed her head, and she could smell the beer on his breath. 'Your mum's an adult, she can do what she pleases.'

'I know.' It was so hard to articulate the confusion she felt, the mix of worries, anxieties, to distinguish what was childish fear, what was irrational, what was anger. It would be worse if she were Lily's age, of course it would, but that didn't mean she could be rational about it. Martin's hand moved to her breast. She shifted so his hand missed its target. 'Not tonight. I'm all wound up.'

'It'll relax you.' His hand resumed.

Becca felt like a kit that he'd once assembled and had now memorised the instruction manual. A minute here, a minute there, then, with the foreplay boxes ticked, a heave-ho and he would be on top. She gave a more decisive push. 'No it won't. I need to be relaxed first.'

He tensed, then twisted away from her, rejection in the outline of his shoulders. 'Fine.' She could hear the hurt in his voice.

She put her arms around him, feeling his back against her chest. Everything felt jangled and wrong, she needed him to smooth out the sharp edges, to console her. She nestled into his back, needing the comfort of his body, stroking his chest as if she was soothing his injured feelings. 'Can't we just cuddle?' she whispered.

Martin sighed deeply and half turned to her. 'I'm too tired for all this – do you want to, or not?'

Perhaps he was right. Perhaps it would relax her. 'Yes.'

He rolled right round to her at that, lurching at her body. They had been married a long time; she knew the routine. She wanted to get there, she needed the release, but the more he pushed at her, the less engaged she felt. Relax, relax, she told herself, but her muscles tightened into hard dense knots, determined not to be unravelled. Her body felt dry, not just inside, but outside, as if she were made of brittle bark as Martin's body sawed against hers. And when it was over, she held him in her arms, like a mother with a child at her breast. His breathing, relaxed and untroubled, changed into the deeper rhythms of sleep. He meant well, she thought, stranded in no-man's-land.

What had June said at the party? Something about there not being a right man, just settling for what was about at the time. And they'd all laughed. Becca didn't feel like laughing now. Poor Frank, being the man June had settled for. She frowned, not wanting to believe that's what June had felt fifty years ago. Besides, in a way, it was logical that you 'settled' for whoever was about – you couldn't go out with a man who wasn't there, whom you hadn't yet met. A bit like house-buying, you had the choice of what was on the market at the time of looking. You couldn't just decide you liked a particular house and demand to buy it.

Martin twitched and rolled over. Becca looked at his back, wondering if she had settled for him. At the time, he had been her saviour, her rock, her steady shining light. Her best friend. He'd been there for her when everyone else had let her down. Becca rolled over on to her side, her back against Martin's, remembering.

It had been her second year at university and she'd fallen desperately in love with one of her lecturers. In tutorials she'd lose track and watch his hands, his mouth as he talked, and drift off into daydreams of love. Then the miracle happened. He noticed her, and their affair started. They had to keep it quiet, of course, because of his career. They met in pubs outside the city, or more frequently, at his house. He wasn't married, and his previous partner was living in America. What she didn't realise was that his previous partner wasn't quite so previous. She was taking a sabbatical, and halfway through Becca's third year turned up at the house where Becca and the lecturer had spent so many lazy Sundays lolling in bed amid the Sunday papers. Her bed, it turned out. The lecturer was apologetic, but clear: he thought Becca had understood, had realised that he was committed elsewhere in the long term. Becca hadn't.

She had finally understood why people said their hearts were breaking. Hers had been slowly torn apart. She'd pictured it like tearing a crusty baguette, the spongy inside separating, the chambers like air holes, all dripping. The pain was incredible. It was hard to believe that it was entirely in her head and not some physical amputation without anaesthetic. She could hardly stand, kept sliding down walls into a foetal position, hugging her knees to her chest and weeping burning tears. She'd missed half her final exams, wrote nothing on at least one paper that she did turn up for. Her flatmates had kept her supplied with tea and sympathy, and shoulders to cry on. Becca had closed the curtains and left them closed. She lay on her bed, face turned towards the wall, hearing her flatmates come back from a night out, full of giggles and chat. She didn't blame them for wanting to be with their boyfriends. Life was carrying on, but hers was over.

Except that Martin was there. Reliable, gentle Martin, who listened to her maundering on about the lecturer with tolerance. Who held her head on the night she got drunk and was sick. Who finally and decisively told her it was time to let the sunshine into the room, wash her hair, have a shower and come out to the pub. She'd wept at his cruelty, but allowed herself to be steered towards the bathroom, to be taken down the road, her knees as wobbly as a newborn calf, and for a pint of Guinness to be plonked in front of her while Martin told her she was a wonderful person who didn't want to waste a minute more of her precious life weeping over a complete toerag. It had taken time to wean herself off the idea of herself as dramatic, wronged heroine, but gradually she realised that she wasn't Marianne from *Sense and Sensbility*, but Elinor. Or if she was Marianne, then Martin was her Colonel Brandon, and they married two years after graduation. It hadn't occurred to her then that she was settling for Martin, and if it was a rebound relationship, it had been a successful one lasting for nearly twenty years. And yet . . . and yet . . . now in the darkness she lay and wondered if in her own marriage there should have been something more.

The next day, after Sunday lunch (which they always had together, as a family), Becca dragged Lily out of her festering bedroom – it was appropriate that her favourite band was Cradle of Filth, given the state of her bedroom, the land the Hoover had forgot – and to the local museum where an archaeologist was demonstrating flint-knapping. Lily put up a token protest, saying it was the last day of the holidays and she'd rather die than go to a museum, but Becca insisted, knowing that history was one of Lily's favourite subjects at school and, until the last few months, a trip to see an archaeologist demonstrate flint-knapping would have been a treat, not an appalling example of abuse worthy of a call to Childline.

The archaeologist selected his flint and examined it closely, looking for the best place to strike. The flint was a dull and chalky white on the outside, knobbled and ugly. Yet he turned it gently in his hands to find the hidden axehead beneath. Then, using another flint, he struck a sharp tap on the side and a chunk flaked off. Then another and another, each time turning the flint in his hands to see the best place to strike, judging the fault lines. The blows started hard and the chunks big. Then they diminished in scale until the last blows were like feathers and the pieces minuscule and in his hands he had a thing of great beauty, an axehead, the dull brown translucent at the edges, edges formed by scallops like overlapping scales. The whole thing was so perfect, so lovely Becca found it hard to believe it had been created there in front of their eyes. And this thing of beauty would have been used to chop trees or whatever, and as it blunted more would be chipped off until it diminished in size and finally was no longer of use. 'At which point it would be discarded and chucked away for an archaeologist like me to discover four thousand years later,' the man said.

'Wasn't that interesting?' Becca said to Lily when it was over.

'No,' Lily said with a yawn. Once she'd have wanted to find her own flints and experiment herself but those days had gone.

Mind you, Becca thought as they walked to the car, I'm not sure I'd have been that interested in flint-knapping at her age. Or, if I had been, I wouldn't have been able to admit to it. She drove them back home, thinking about life's phases. Perhaps we start out as interested, outward-going children, get derailed by sex and relationships, and then gradually revert to being interested, outward-going adults. Maybe that's what's happening to June, she thought. She's done with the relationships bit, and now wants to explore the world with a child's curiosity. And I'm somewhere adrift in the middle.

• • • 40 • • •

The phone started ringing as she turned the key in the back door, and carried on ringing. Where was Martin? She pushed the door open, and grabbed the phone. 'Yes?' she said crossly, not bothering with any niceties of phone etiquette. It was bound to be someone selling double glazing anyway.

'Is that Becca Woods? It's Paul Fitzwilliam. Is this a bad time?'

It took her a few seconds to realise who he was, and then her heart started thumping so hard she could hardly hear what he was saying. 'No, it's fine. Goodness. How are you?' Don't get excited, this is the 'thanks, but no thanks' call, she told herself.

'I'm fine. I was phoning about the auditions. As I'm sure you were aware, lots of people auditioned for this production . . .' Becca braced herself for the rejection. 'I was phoning to see if you'd like the part of Lady Fidget.'

Chapter 4

What would Martin say? She had the feeling he was going to laugh and think it daft. Perhaps she'd made a humungous mistake in accept the part. The thought of actually being onstage in front of an audience was terrifying. What if she forgot her lines? What if she missed a cue, or tripped up? Everyone would see. Luckily December was a long time away, so she didn't have to think about that now, but she did have to think about Martin's reaction.

I suppose I could lie and say I was doing some other evening class, she thought. Life drawing perhaps, or Spanish or the Russian Revolution. But that would mean lying to Martin, and I can't do that. Besides, he might get suspicious that I never progressed beyond *Ola*! or the storming of the gates of the Winter Palace. Perhaps he'll think I have a lover! He'll follow me to the arts centre and sit in the car and wait, drinking coffee from cardboard cups and eating doughnuts like in American detective stories.

The house shook as a door slammed upstairs, and then settled into a steady shake-shake in time with the bass of Lily's music. Becca went into the hall and called up the stairs. 'Lily, Lily. Guess what?' She waited. No response. She yelled again.

A few seconds later the house stopped shaking. 'What is it?'

'I've got a part in a play. I'm going to be Lady Fidget in *The*

Country Wife.' Becca swung round the newel post at the foot of the stairs, waiting expectantly for Lily's response.

Silence. Then, 'What?'

'Oh, never mind,' Becca said, going back into the utility room and hanging up her coat. 'I've got a part in a play. How about that?' she said to the hamster. The hamster's response was as inert as Lily's. 'You could be a bit excited for me, I did clean your cage yesterday,' she said, giving the cage a little prod, but the hamster carried on sleeping. 'I suppose you think I ought to think about supper.' She paused. I've got a part in a play. I'm going to be Lady Fidget. That was all she really wanted to think about, not supper.

She waltzed into the kitchen humming tunelessly. It would have to be a pasta bake. What did people eat before pasta became a staple? She put a pan of water on to boil. The meals she gave her family were so different from the meals she could remember June producing. Pasta had been something exotic and new when she was a child, along with eating in restaurants which only rich people did. Rich people like Lady Fidget. I'm going to be in a play! She gave a little skip. Yesterday morning she'd been lying in bed thinking about how dull her life was, and now here she was, an actress with a part in a play. Not that she and Martin ate out much now. She paused, pasta packet in hand, trying to remember the last time she and Martin had gone out to a restaurant, just the two of them. Light years away.

She poured the pasta into the boiling water. All the women's magazines recommended making special time for your partner, booking a weekly date so you could have 'couple' time together. Ask him questions, like you would on a first date, what are his hopes, his fears. We ought to do that one evening, Becca thought, pushing the pasta with a spoon to check it hadn't stuck together. There are loads of places to eat in Bath. We could try that new gastro pub round the corner – pick a Friday night when Lily wants to be out. Becca heard Martin coming down the stairs.

'Hello, love. How was the flint-knapping?'

'I thought you were out – didn't you hear the phone ring?' She wondered if he'd heard what she called up to Lily.

'I was working in the study with my headphones on.' So he hadn't heard. What would he say?

'The flint-knapping was really interesting. I think Lily enjoyed it – though she'd die rather than say so.' She prodded the pasta, thinking of the best way to tell him her news. Perhaps she ought to wait until supper, and then she could tell Martin and Lily at the same time, see both their amazed and delighted faces together.

He gave her a peck on the cheek. 'I'm going to pop out for a run.'

'A run?' It seemed so unlike Martin, whose idea of exercise was more usually traversing an eternal triangle between fridge, sofa and biscuit tin.

'Yeah. Could do with shifting some of this.' He slapped himself on the stomach, which quivered slightly. 'The paintballing was good fun, but I was sweating like a pig. Most of the team are practically half my age. You talk about something that happened in the eighties, and they look at you and say something about only being a toddler then.'

'Perhaps I should come with you.' She had a picture of them together, jogging along, her hair tied up in a ponytail, a sweatband around her forehead.

'If you want to . . .' He dragged on an old sweatshirt that he'd last used when painting the sitting room, tousling his hair even more than usual.

Becca's imagination couldn't make the leap into seeing herself running. Who was she kidding? It was difficult enough running a bath let alone running to the end of the street. And as for Martin . . . She looked at him, seeing him for what he was, a middle-aged, completely unfit man. But what was the alternative? Vegetating, like Frank? 'Don't overdo it. You don't want to have a heart attack first time out.'

He grinned and blew her a kiss. 'I'll try not to.'

'It's better to do it little and often.' Cripes, I sound just like June, she thought. Don't overdo it, little and often. When did I become so limited? But I'm not limited. I'm an actress. She took a deep breath. 'Martin, I've got something to tell you.'

Martin stared at her. 'Christ, you're not pregnant, are you?'

Becca gave a start. 'No, nothing like that. What a weird thing to say.'

'Sorry. It's just the way you said it.' He shrugged, not meeting her eyes.

Becca felt cold as all those years of trying flashed before them, the ups and downs, the feeling of failure as yet another period turned up, the joy. When Lily finally appeared, the mourning when she realised that Lily would be an only child. 'Would you have liked me to be?'

'God no, it would be unbelievably inconvenient, starting over again with a baby after all these years.' Martin fiddled the laces of his trainers.

'Yes, it would.' There was a silence between them. Martin was right, Becca thought, that was all in the past. They had Lily, and their future before them. Becca smiled brightly. 'Anyway, I'm not. Pregnant, that is.'

'Phew!' He wiped imaginary sweat from his brow.

'I'm probably too old now, anyway.'

'Probably,' he agreed. 'So, if you're not pregnant, what did you want to tell me?'

'Oh. I've . . .' Now the moment had come, Becca hesitated. Would he laugh when she told him? 'I've been offered a part in a play.'

'What?' Martin looked puzzled.

'In a play – it's a Restoration comedy. *The Country Wife*. I auditioned.' She shrugged, trying to appear nonchalant. 'I got a part.'

'You're kidding me,' Martin said, a smile starting to spread on his face. Becca shook her head. Don't laugh, she pleaded inwardly. Don't laugh. 'You're going to be in a play, on a stage? Where? Who with?' Martin scratched his head. He didn't have the amazed and delighted look on his face she'd imagined 'What on earth for?'

'It's an amateur theatre group, they're quite big and well established.' She drained the pasta, feeling her excitement draining along with it. 'They put on three productions a year. Including musicals. They did *Guys and Dolls* last year.'

'You can't sing,' Martin said. 'You have many talents, but that's not one of them.'

'No, but I can act,' Becca said. She dug out an ovenproof dish from the cupboard and poured the pasta into it, followed by a jar of sauce. She had been going to make her own, but her brain was full of acting, not pasta sauces. Except according to Martin obviously it should have been. She glanced over to him.

Martin began to laugh. Not a jolly Green Giant 'ho ho ho' sort of laugh, but a sniggering spluttering laugh as if the idea of Becca acting was utterly ridiculous and preposterous. He shook his head. 'Sorry, darling, I shouldn't laugh. Just that – well, it seems so unlike you. You've never done it since I've known you. You've never shown any signs of wanting to.'

'I do want to. I've been offered Lady Fidget – it's quite a good part actually.' She put the pasta in the oven, then remembered that she'd forgotten the cheese, so took it out again.

'Ah, don't be upset.' He took her in his arms. 'I'm sure you'll be brilliant.'

Becca wasn't mollified by the indulgent tone in his voice. She wriggled out of his arms and went to the fridge to get the cheese. 'I thought you were going running.'

'I am, I am.' He sighed. 'Becca, I'm sorry I laughed.'

'It means a lot to me,' she said, vigorously grating cheese all over the dish and the kitchen side. She hadn't realised quite how much before. It had been just a momentary whim to audition and if she hadn't been cast she'd have accepted that, but now she'd got the part, it did matter. 'It's not just about the acting, it's about getting something more into my life.' She stopped, caught by the echoes. Hadn't June said something similar yesterday?

'I'm sorry if I've offended you.'

'That's OK,' Becca said, feeling confused by her emotional swings – up with acting, then down at the thought of June. She wanted to reach out for Martin and steady herself, but he was edging towards the door. 'Go on, off you go. And don't be long; I want to have supper early, it's the first day of term tomorrow.'

'I'll be quick.' He grinned. 'Actually, I'll be very slow, but I won't go far.'

Becca looked up as Crystal breezed into the staffroom, as usual the last of the teachers to gather. 'Any biscuits? I need about a thousand calories before I can face another Monday staff meeting – oh God, it's so depressing, just thinking we've got a whole term to go before it's Christmas.'

Crystal obviously hadn't changed over the summer holidays. Her capacity for chocolate had, in the eight years Becca had known her, been surpassed only by her unerring ability to whiz through men. They all started off as Mr Right, but were soon revealed to be either wet and pathetic or utter bastards. Becca grabbed the biscuit tin from where it had been left on the side by the other members of staff, who had already settled down for the meeting, and peered inside. 'On the bright side, start of term equals chocolate biscuits.'

'HobNobs?' Crystal had the sort of metabolism that could devour biscuits and chocolate without any apparent side effects. Perhaps it was her height, or her restlessness that twitched away the calories.

Becca shook her head as she helped herself to two biscuits before handing the packet to Crystal. 'Digestives. Plain chocolate though.'

'It's funny, isn't it, how some things are better plain chocolate, while others are better milk. You couldn't have a milk chocolate jaffa cake, now could you?' Crystal folded herself on to a chair, long legs wrapping round each other.

'How was Barcelona? I got your postcard – thanks.'

'Oh, it was brilliant, you and Martin must go. And David was fabulous – he spoke Spanish, and knew all these wonderful places to eat.' She chattered on about a meal she'd had, rice cooked in fish stock and squid until it turned black, absolutely heavenly, just like David.

Becca listened, waiting for an opportunity to tell Crystal her news, although she wasn't sure which she'd start with: June's announcement or the part in the play, or even Martin's decision to start running. She was saved from having to choose by the door crashing open and Bill Malcolm, head teacher and owner, entering.

'All he needs is a cape, and he could double for Dracula,' Becca whispered to Crystal.

'Greetings, greetings, one and all. I'm surprised you haven't already started the meeting. No need to wait for me.' He shot a quick glance round the room, bushy eyebrows working. Becca knew he could switch from twinkling charmer to frog-eyed bully in seconds if it suited him. 'Let's gather in a circle, my friends, and get this show on the road.' The edge to his voice galvanised the staff, who quickly rearranged themselves into a circle of chairs. Bill waved his hand at the deputy head. 'Proceed, my boy, proceed.'

'Thank you, Bill.' Richard shuffled his papers together, looking more like one of the pupils than a teacher. 'There are just a couple of health and safety issues I'd like to run through with you . . .'

The Hamilton House Tutorial College had been founded by Bill presumably more than sixty-five million years ago, given that Bill was the last remaining dinosaur in the educational business. He'd started with a large Victorian semi-detached house, bought cheap because the garden had been sliced off to build a main road, and later had expanded into the other half of the building so that Hamilton House had two staircases, two front doors, and one combined driveway with In and Out signs that looked impressive in the brochures. Bill's motto for Hamilton House was *Esse Quam Videri*: 'To be rather than to seem', ironic given that Hamilton House was a good example of seeming. It didn't look nearly as impressive from the back, the main road being busy all day, and beyond it the trains hurtled past along Isambard Kingdom Brunel's viaduct, making the sash windows rattle and dust collect so the light in the classrooms was perpetually filtered through a grimy layer.

The college crammed and coaxed the students through their exams, with a surprising success rate given that almost everybody in the building was a failure of some sort: the pupils because these were usually resits, the staff because no one with the opportunity of working elsewhere could possibly fail to do so. Becca, with her miserable degree and no teaching qualifications (which meant she could only teach in the private sector), fitted right in. The job had originally been a temporary stop-gap when Lily was a baby, but she'd stayed for over ten years teaching English to an assortment of students, who varied from the bright but lazy to the dim and dismal.

She looked around the staffroom at the weird and wonderful collection of teachers Bill had amassed, sitting in varying degrees of catatonia, apart from those rhythmically munching biscuits like cows chewing the cud. By tradition no one ever listened to Richard, knowing that power lay with Bill, but in general the staff were well disposed towards him. For most, dropping off quietly while Richard droned on was preferable to teaching. Becca actually enjoyed what she did, although Hamilton House etiquette demanded that she kept that information to herself. According to the staffroom, it was the worst-run, worst-managed, most anachronistic private tutorial college in the world, and it was a wonder that any of the students passed their exams. But they did, and often enough to keep

Hamilton House lurching through the educational undergrowth for another year.

'Coffee, must have some coffee.' Bill sprang up from his chair. 'Carry on, carry on. Don't mind me, I'll just potter.'

'As I was saying . . . Richard continued with his talk and Becca tried to listen, but it was hard to follow the thread while Bill pottered. It seemed to involve a lot of clattering: teacup, saucer, spoon, whooshing water, kettle clicking on and off. She looked around the staffroom and could see that while Richard was holding their attention, most people looked slightly baffled. She put an intent listening expression on her face and leaned forward, chin cupped on one hand.

Bill waited until it looked like Richard had run out of steam then clapped his hands. 'Excellent, excellent. And what a lot of splendid jargon you know, many thanks for sharing it. But now I think it's time for something far less interesting, and perhaps a little more,' he paused for effect, 'a little more immediate.' He beamed around the room as Richard's face froze except for one nerve twitching in the side of his jaw. If he'd been a cat it would have been his tail twitching.

'I've decided that this year we shall extend the cultural horizons of our students,' Bill continued, apparently oblivious to Richard's surprise.

Crystal rolled her eyes at Becca. 'That probably means he got a bum inspector's report,' she whispered.

'We shall inculcate our wayward charges into the wonders of the Bard, disseminating the glories of the English language at its most muscular and poetic.' Bill's gaze fell on Becca, who felt anything but poetic, let alone muscular. His eyes swept on to seek other victims. 'We shall have workshops, and productions, and visits and speakers. We shall organise trips to art exhibitions, to theatres, to museums. We shall—'

'What about the curriculum?' Crystal piped up.

'Crystal – always so quick with a positive suggestion.' He gave a sharkish smile in Crystal's direction, who wilted. 'We shall over-come the limitations of our political masters with careful planning and nifty footwork. Now, who would like to help organise this great endeavour?' Bill scanned the room with the expression of a magician who's just asked for a willing volunteer to be sawn in half.

Becca looked round at the staff, who appeared to be auditioning for a production of *Night of the Living Dead*. Very wise. Like the trenches and World War I, never volunteer for anything. Besides, the spirit of Hamilton House was to do the bare minimum accept-able, it should have been the college motto. On the other hand, if you didn't volunteer you often got dumped with the worst things. Becca put her hand up. 'I couldn't take on organising the whole thing, but I'd help out, perhaps do a theatre workshop.' It flashed across her brain to tell Bill and the rest of the staff she was acting in a play, but she decided to keep it to herself.

'I'd help Becca with that,' Crystal added.

'Splendid, splendid! And who else?' Bill scanned the room gathering more unwilling suggestions until he'd got enough offers to be satisfied, including Richard being co-opted as the organiser as everyone knew he would be. 'Right, I think that just about rounds off our meeting. If that's agreeable with our estimable deputy head and organiser supreme?' He turned to Richard who nodded, lips tight together. Becca knew he was thinking the stress of dealing with Bill wasn't worth the extra pay. 'Then onwards and upwards, my fellow educators. Onwards and upwards.'

There was a general movement to gather books, bags and belongings. Becca checked she'd got all the files she needed for her morning sessions, then set off for her classroom. Just before entering the room she paused. The best tip she'd ever been given when she'd started teaching had come from Bill.

'Remember,' he'd said, eyebrows bristling. 'People are like sheep. They want to be led. And you, as teacher, are the sheep dog. You need to take charge of the space, show them who's boss, and they'll love you for it. Nip their heels if needs be, but above all, never let them see you're scared. If you act like the boss, they'll treat you like the boss. Enter that classroom as if you own it.'

It had been good advice. Now, taking charge of the classroom was like second nature. She took a deep breath, and opened the door. 'Hello, everyone,' she said in a clear voice and purposefully made her way to the teacher's desk at the head of the class. Out of the corner of her eye she checked out the students. A mixed group, perhaps a few more girls than boys. Most were sitting up, as if ready to start the lesson, but a few boys were still lounging around the window.

'If you'd like to take a seat . . .' Becca said pleasantly, but firmly. Two of the boys at the window were about a foot taller than her, grown men with bum fluff on their chins. *Never let them see you're scared.* She pointed at a couple of empty seats and they shambled into place. Strange to think that if she'd had a son, he might have been one of these clumsy giants in boys clothing.

Take charge of the space. It was now a habit, although when she'd started the effort of making her body language appear relaxed, open and confident had made her sweat all over so her clothes were damp within two hours. Ten years of teaching later it took no effort at all to appear confident. She waited until they'd settled and were silent, then smiled at the class. 'My name is Mrs Woods, and I'll be taking you for the AS and A-level English Literature resit . . .'

A week later, Becca sat on the edge of her chair trying to look relaxed and happy to be at her first rehearsal. Paul Fitzwilliam had greeted her with a friendly smile and handed her a copy of the play, which had made her feel welcome, but he was now busy discussing something with the woman with the clipboard at the top of the table as the other actors drifted in. They all appeared to know each other, kissing cheeks with much smacking of lips and cries of

'Darling!' Becca was the only one sitting at the long trestle table. She smiled at everyone, trying to send out friendly 'I'm not feeling horribly self-conscious' vibes.

She glanced at Paul Fitzwilliam. He was wearing a pinstriped jacket and blue jeans, but the jacket was made of smoky-blue velvet and had a deep purple satin lining that flashed as he reached across the table for a piece of paper. Conventional with a twist, Becca supposed you'd call it. She couldn't imagine Martin ever wearing such a thing.

Today Purple Feathers was wearing red and black stripes and a wide buccaneer's belt, dangling necklaces and glittering ruby earrings, not dissimilar to a pirate after a week stuck in Ali Baba's cave. Paul said something to her and she clapped her hands. 'Can we get underway, please?' It was the cue for everyone to come to the long trestle table.

'Hello, I'm Brian, and this is Victoria,' a man said, sitting down next to Becca and holding out his hand. He was wearing short sleeves, but the ghosts of leather patches circled his elbows like wreaths of pipe smoke. 'Sir Jasper, and Old Lady Squeamish.'

'Oh, you're my husband,' Becca said, shaking his hand. His palms were sweaty, despite the short sleeves. 'I'm Lady Fidget. Becca.'

'We thought you were,' Victoria said, settling down on her other side. She too had a nautical air, wearing a Breton striped top that emphasised a bust suitable for the figurehead on a warship. 'Have you done much theatre before?'

'At school and university,' Becca said. 'But this is my first play for ages. I'm a bit nervous, to be honest.'

'Never mind, we don't bite,' Brian said, despite having the teeth for it.

'I'm so excited to be working with Paul Fitzwilliam – you know he used to be with the Royal Shakespeare Company,' Victoria said.

'Goodness,' Becca said, looking up to where Paul sat at the head of the table. 'I'd no idea.' He suddenly looked up and smiled at her, making fine creases at the corners of his eyes as the skin stretched over high cheekbones. She smiled back, feeling reassured.

Paul knocked on the table to get the cast's attention. 'Thank you everyone for coming. We're rehearsing mainly Tuesday, Wednesday and Thursday evenings from now until December – Angela has the schedule, but this may vary depending on how the production goes, illness and so on, so please make sure she has your contact details in case we need to change your call.' He looked around the table. 'And now, before we do our read-through, perhaps we can do a name check.' He put his hand to his chest. 'Paul Fitzwilliam, Director.' He turned to Purple Feathers.

'I'm Angela Sinclair, Stage Manager.' How funny, Becca thought. She didn't look like an Angela at all, more like an Esmeralda or an Anastasia. Even an Angie. Angela turned to the young blonde girl to her left.

'Rosie Justin, Margery Pinchwife.' The leading lady, Becca thought.

'Michael Hendon, Horner.' And the leading man. Becca could only assume he was an excellent actor because she couldn't imagine him as a serial seducer, not with that greasy hair.

It took quite a long time to go round the table, as there were nearly twenty people gathered round, roughly half male and half female. Most were either students or in their fifties onwards, although the man playing Horner looked as if he was in his thirties.

And then came the read-through. Becca felt nervous to begin with, but soon relaxed into her role. Brian, as her husband, was a bit creaky and pompous – no wonder Lady Fidget cuckolded him. There was quite a lot of teasing among the cast as they went through the script; she realised that most of them had known each other for some time.

At the end of the read-through there was mention of going to the pub, but Becca thought she ought to get home. 'Next time,' she called to them as she left the church hall.

Angela went down the steps at the same time as Becca. 'Which way are you going?'

'Manvers Street car park.' Becca smiled, hopeful of her company on the walk through Bath.

'Me too. What did you think of it?' Angela said as they turned right towards the abbey. 'Most of us have been doing it for ages, we're old hands, but did you enjoy it?'

'Oh yes,' Becca said. 'I wasn't sure I was going to – it's years since I've done any acting, and I was a bit worried to be honest – but it was fun this evening.'

'Paul's very good, isn't he?' Angela said.

'He seems to know what he's doing. Is he your usual director?'

'I wish!' Angela gave a rueful laugh. 'No, one of us usually directs, we can't afford a professional director, but he got in touch with us, and hell's bells we weren't going to turn Paul Fitzwilliam down, even if he'd said he wanted to do an avant garde version of *Noddy* meets *Godzilla*. Victoria says his wife's some sort of legal hotshot who's moved job to Bristol, so that's why they've moved here. How he's ended up with us instead of somewhere like the Tobacco Factory, or the Old Vic, I don't know. We got lucky, I guess.'

'Is he well known, then?'

'Victoria says he used to run a repertory theatre up in the north, then went freelance. He's directed all over the world, the US, Japan, Australia. Shakespeare mainly – he uses this incredible theory about how Shakespeare should be acted, it sounds absolutely brilliant. Cue scripts, they're called. Victoria's trying to lean on him to do a production here.'

'Directing in Japan sounds impressive,' Becca said, thinking that anyone leaned on by Victoria would be flattened fairly quickly. 'I think I'm out of my league.'

'Don't worry about that – he cast you, didn't he? So he must think you're up to it. He's the expert!' She giggled. 'It is a bit like being given a Ferrari to drive instead of an old banger. He's quite demanding, knows exactly what he wants. But then, I suppose he's used to working with the best.'

They'd reached the car park. It had been practically full when Becca had parked, but now her car was one of a handful left marooned in the sea of concrete. 'This is mine.'

'I'm just over there.' Angela indicated with a nod of her head a small hatchback painted with stripes all over. 'See you next week.'

Becca got into the car and put her seat belt on, and as she did, her attention was caught by something white. It was a couple entwined in an embrace over the far side of the car park. Eating face, as Lily called it. She started the car and slipped the handbrake off. She and Martin hadn't snogged like that since . . . when? Had they ever? Perhaps snogging wasn't something married people did, it was a teenage thing. She glanced sideways at the couple as she drove past, vaguely thinking how sweet, then her mind abruptly switched into focus.

It was Lily.

Chapter 5

Becca marched Lily into the house via the back door. 'Right. You've got some explaining to do.' Lily looked balefully at her with sooty eyes. Becca could see the start of a love bite forming on her neck. The hamster started to run on its wheel, rattle rattle rattle. 'You're not allowed out on a school night, you know that. Who was that boy?'

'None of your business.' Lily's face was white and set. 'Why were you spying on me?'

'I wasn't spying, I just saw – I'd have thought half of Bath saw too.'

Martin came into the utility room. 'What's all this noise about?'

Becca turned on him. 'Ask her where she's been.'

Martin frowned. 'She's been upstairs . . .'

'God – I don't know who to be more angry with, you or her.' She spun round to Lily. 'You're grounded.'

'Don't care,' Lily said, sticking her chin out. Rattle rattle rattle continued the hamster. 'I'm old enough to look after myself.'

'Lily, you can't even look after that hamster let alone yourself.' Lily's lower lip stuck out like a Borneo tribesman's, but there were dark shadows under her eyes. Becca felt the fight seep out of her. She could control a classroom of adolescents but not her own daughter. 'Go on, just get to bed now. We'll talk about this tomorrow.'

'What's happened?' Martin said as Lily escaped past him. 'Has she been out?'

Becca took a deep breath. 'Your daughter went out without you noticing,' she said, enunciating the words carefully. 'What kind of father are you?'

'I went running, and then I did some work, OK? As far as I knew, Lily was upstairs.'

'Did you think to check? Did you think to make sure she was in bed, or reading, or . . .' Becca ran her hand through her hair, trying to keep some control over her temper and the huge sense of injustice that threatened to overwhelm her. 'All I expect you to do for one night – one night! – is the stuff I do on every other evening of every week. I really don't think it's too much to ask, do you?' Martin opened his mouth to answer then shut it again. 'Can I ask if you've supervised her homework? Checked on her maths? Looked at what she needs for her coursework? Made sure her school clothes are ready for tomorrow?'

'I was going to do that later,' he said, checking his watch. 'I didn't realise it was that late.'

'Do you know where she was? Do you? She was snogging some boy in the middle of town, in a car park of all places. What were you doing?' She meant it as a rhetorical question, but Martin took it at face value.

'You don't know the pressure I'm under at work right now,' Martin said. 'There's another round of redundancies coming, and I don't intend the axe to fall on me. I won't get another job so easily – not at my age, not in this business.'

Becca felt deflated. She leaned against the wall. 'You didn't say.'

'I didn't want to worry you.'

The silence between them grew. Becca was caught between feeling guilty at being angry with Martin, and justification at her anger. He should have kept an eye on Lily. It was only one night, for heaven's sake.

'Perhaps I should give up the play,' she said, dull with disappointment. One evening that was hers, and she was offering to give it up. She hadn't realised before how much the play meant to her. 'Better to give up now, than let everyone down later.'

Martin moved to the kitchen sink. 'You don't have to do that. I can manage.' He turned to her. 'Hey, I'm a pretty useless father if I can't.'

Becca bit her lip. 'Make me a cup of tea?'

He nodded, and filled the kettle. 'I'm sorry about tonight,' he said. 'I should have been paying more attention.'

Yes you should, she wanted to say, but Martin's face worried her. She noticed he had threads of silver running through his tawny hair. 'Are things really that bad at work?'

Martin shrugged. When he'd been made redundant before, it had taken him two years to find another job. 'I should be safe, I've worked my guts out for them but who knows? But this running thing . . . the company puts forward two teams for the Bath half marathon, one male, one female. It'd be good to be chosen.'

'You? Run a marathon? You must be kidding.'

Martin shook his head. 'The beginners pre-training programme starts in three weeks time and lasts for eight weeks. Then it's a question of getting my speed and distance up for December when the training programme proper starts. I can run with Una and Ian, from my department.'

Becca's head bulged with the information. Pre-training, training? It was so unlike Martin. 'When is the marathon?'

'Half marathon,' Martin said. 'March twenty-fifth.'

'That's six months away. Are you going to be running every day?'

Martin poured out a mug of tea. 'There's a proper schedule of which days, how long for, et cetera. Four times a week, mostly twenty minutes or half an hour.'

Becca took the mug from him. Four times a week. Probably the equivalent of her one night for rehearsal. And it was getting him fit, which was more than could be said of acting. 'Do you think you'll do it?'

'I can but try.' He grinned at her, his expression mischievous.

She couldn't imagine Martin running a marathon, but he was a tortoise, not a hare so maybe marathon-running would suit him. But not at Lily's expense. 'We need to work as a team.'

He nodded. 'We are a team, aren't we?'

'Of course.' Becca yawned. 'I'm going up to bed.' She took her tea and climbed the stairs, quite exhausted from the rehearsal followed by the emotional turmoil.

Lily was waiting at the top of the stairs. 'I'm sorry, Mum.'

'You mustn't do stuff like that,' Becca said. 'What if something had happened to you? We wouldn't have known where you were.'

'I'm not a child.'

Becca looked at her face, plump and unlined. 'I know that. But you're not very old either. And quite apart from the safety angle, what really upsets me is you sneaking off without saying anything. It's just so dishonest.'

Lily stared at the landing carpet. 'You're not going to get divorced, are you?'

Becca blinked with surprise. 'Why on earth would we?'

'Because of me. Because you and Dad are always arguing over me. I make you have rows, and then I think you're going to get divorced.' She began to cry. 'I don't mean to cause trouble, but I do. I wish I was dead.'

'Oh, Lily darling. Don't cry.' Becca put down her tea, and hugged Lily. 'Of course Dad and I aren't going to get divorced, you're working yourself up about nothing, sweetheart.'

'But you were shouting,' wailed Lily into Becca's shoulder.

'I was cross. Your father should have known where you were. But just because I was cross with him, doesn't mean that we're going to get divorced. Just because I was cross with you, doesn't mean I don't love you, does it? Mmm?' She held Lily's face. 'Because I do love you, very much. Now. No more sneaking out without telling anyone. Promise?'

'OK.' Lily scampered off.

June and Frank never argued, because Frank said he didn't like rows. He liked life on an even keel, with no highs or lows. She'd thought June liked life like that too – 'A place for everything, and everything in its place' was one of June's favourite sayings. Becca picked up her tea mug. She hadn't heard anything more about her mother leaving her father, and Joanna hadn't rung so presumably she'd changed her mind and decided that her place was at home, with Frank. Becca smiled. How stupid of her to get worked up just on the possibility her parents might get divorced. She'd been letting her inner drama queen get the better of her common sense. Divorce! She smiled into her mug. Ridiculous.

'I want a divorce,' June said, wiping down the kitchen worktop. The kitchen at June and Frank's house looked much as it always had done, what an estate agent would probably have called ripe for modernisation. Given that nothing had been done to it for at least thirty years, that was probably accurate. It was a showcase of what had been fashionable (but also reasonably priced) back in the seventies: Moroccan-patterned orange wall tiles that Becca could remember her father picking up as seconds as the pattern didn't quite match, and rustic oak cabinets with fiddly balustrades that June dusted regularly. Becca felt overwhelmed by the thought that June might not dust the tiny spindles again.

June tidied away the cloth under the sink. 'I don't see much reason in hanging around for any longer – I'm no spring chicken, you know.'

'Divorce, though. It's – well, it's awfully final.'

'And your point is?'

Becca wasn't sure what her point was. 'It shouldn't be something you do without really thinking through all the options.'

'Do you think I haven't?' June sighed. 'I know you don't like the idea, but I don't want to live with him any more. I want some space of my own. I'm going to devote the rest of my life to art.'

For a second Becca wondered who Art was. 'Who's Art?'

'Art,' June emphasised, as if Becca was especially dim. 'You know, painting.'

'Painting,' Becca echoed with relief. So not some dreadful old man who was seducing her mother from her father. 'Are you serious?'

'I've always been serious about my painting,' June said with dignity. 'Although I know no one else has been. Huh! Your father can't even discuss art without going blue in the face.'

'But . . . to leave Dad for it?'

'It's not just about art.' She lowered her voice. 'He stifles me. I can't breathe when he's in the room. I have to go.'

Becca could hardly breathe herself. It was all happening too fast. She couldn't cope. 'What about Dad? How's he going to manage?'

'He's an intelligent adult, with functioning arms and legs. I expect he'll do just fine.' June narrowed her eyes. 'Don't you expect Martin to help round the house?'

'That's different. Dad's not used to cooking and cleaning.'

June felt the soil of an African violet on the windowsill. The purple blue was electric against the orange tiles. 'Perhaps he ought to be.'

'How could he? You always did everything.'

'So now's his chance. I think you underestimate your father,' she said quietly, carefully pouring water into the saucer under the plant pot.

Becca glared at her. 'Where is he anyway?'

'In the sitting room, I think, watching telly.'

Frank was indeed in the sitting room watching television. She felt a pang at the two chairs arranged so comfortably centre stage in front of the television, each with a small side table beside them, just the right size for a cup of tea and a slice of Battenberg. How was her father going to manage with suddenly becoming a singleton after being one half of a couple for so long?

'Mum says she wants a divorce,' she said.

Frank briefly looked up from the snooker. 'It's all talk,' he said, not meeting her eyes, and she thought she could sense his fear of what was happening around him, unsettling his life. She felt a sudden stab of sympathy with the old man's denial, however frustrating. 'She won't go.'

'But what if she does?' He didn't move, but his gnarled hands gripped the chair arms. Becca could see the tension in the knotted blue veins snaking past the liver spots and blotches. He was an old man, unaccustomed to change, trying to pretend none of this was happening. But it was, and he needed to act. 'Dad. You've got to take it seriously.'

Frank shook his head, hardly moving his eyes from the screen. 'It's not going to happen, Becca, so there's no point getting het up about it.'

'But I am, and so should you,' Becca said, practically jumping up and down in agitation. She grabbed the remote and turned the television off. 'There's no point in pretending nothing is happening, because it is.'

Frank sighed, a sigh that whizzed Becca back to her own teenage years. 'Rebecca,' he said slowly, the awful voice that had initiated a lecture about the size of the phone bill. 'Please return the remote to me and stop being so melodramatic.'

The word brought her up short. *Don't be so melodramatic. Don't be so emotional.* But I am emotional, she thought. My mother is going to leave my father, of course I'm emotional. But he didn't see it like that. Frank's emotions had always been kept strictly under control. Feeling the sour taste of defeat in her mouth, Becca slapped the remote into his hands.

'Thank you.' He switched the television back on.

Becca stared at him. She hated to admit it, but June had a point. He really did look as if he was melding into the easy chair. But they'd been married fifty years. If he was like that, then part of it was June's fault. She knelt down beside the chair. 'I know you think it's all ridiculous, but couldn't you make a bit of effort? You've been married fifty years and—'

'So if she doesn't like me now, she's had plenty of time to find out.'

It was a good thing that Becca had been kneeling; if she had been standing she thought she might have fallen over with the shock. 'I don't understand,' she said. 'Aren't you even going to try?'

Frank expertly flicked the paper. 'She's a grown woman, she can make her own decisions. Not that she will,' he added smugly. 'Once a faffer, always a faffer.'

'Don't talk about Mum like that,' Becca said standing up. Frank widened his eyes in surprise. Without realising it, she had switched into the mode she used with the worst of the students. Sheep dog mode. Lead, and they will follow. *Nip their heels if you have to.*

'I'm going to get Mum, and you're jolly well going to be nice to her,' Becca told him. 'Because if you're not, and she does go, don't expect me to take over the cooking and cleaning. You'll be on your own. So be nice. Yes?' Frank nodded, and Becca realised he had never before seen her take control. It felt . . . good, but also scary.

Fired up with her new-found parental powers, she marched down the hall to chivvy June back into the fold. 'Come and talk to Dad,' she commanded with a slight menace.

June paused from the washing-up. 'Please don't try to push me around,' she said in a cool voice, and Becca's sheep dog powers vanished.

'Please, Mum,' she said, feeling like a little girl begging for a treat. 'Please come and talk.'

June pulled off her yellow kitchen gloves with a snap. 'What's the point? Your father's not going to change, and nor am I. How's Lily?'

'She's fine.' Becca thought of her snogging Kevin in the car park. 'She's discovered boys.'

June chuckled. 'Ah, I remember that stage. It's a tricky one.' And how, Becca thought. 'You and Joanna were both dreadful. You were the worst, though.'

'Was I?'

'Oh yes. It was one long hormonal rollercoaster. Up down, up down, true love one minute, bitter hatred the next. I don't envy you the next couple of years,' she said, shaking her head with apparent satisfaction as she stowed the gloves under the sink. 'Come and have a look at what I've been doing.'

Strange how your parents could turn you back into a child so easily. Becca struggled to regain her adult self as she followed June upstairs and into what had once been Joanna's bedroom, a temple to pink and purple and all things girlie, but which June had converted into a studio about ten years ago. There were canvasses leaning against the plain white walls, a chest with an array of jam jars holding brushes and pencils on top, and biscuit tins full of half-squeezed tubes of paint: acrylics, watercolours and oils. One wall was covered with images torn from magazines, interspersed with postcards from art galleries and photographs June had taken. In the centre of the room stood a large easel with June's latest painting on it – an abstract that made Becca think of fried eggs in the night sky, or maybe lemons at sea.

'Look,' June said, her cheeks pink as she picked up an art magazine and pointed at the cover. 'That's what I'd like to do.'

Becca stared at the cover. A woman with a startling resemblance to Samuel Beckett challenged the viewer. She was seated in front of what appeared to be a disembowelled nude, tubes spewing forth from her stomach.

'Most of the class want to do nice little landscapes, but I'm for expressionism.'

'Are you serious about getting a divorce?' Becca said. 'Have you spoken to a solicitor?'

June picked at a tube of paint. 'Not yet,' she conceded. 'But that doesn't mean I'm not serious.'

'If I booked a session, would you try Relate?'

'What good would it do? There's nothing your father has to say to me any more, and to be honest, there's nothing I want to say to him. Except goodbye.'

'Please. You've been married for fifty years.'

'And don't I know it!'

'It's got to be worth a try. Just one little session, to see how it goes.'

'Becca, if people don't want to change, they won't. Relate, or any other marriage guidance won't make a difference.'

'But will you try? Please?'

June shook her head. 'No. How's Martin?'

'Oh, fine. He's taken up running,' Becca said, annoyed that her mother was changing the subject again.

'Really? At his age? He'll have a heart attack if he's not careful.'

'Martin's not old,' Becca said, mentally scrabbling to get the conversational train back on the tracks. 'But that's not what I'm here for. Look . . .'

June looked, a sceptical expression on her face. Becca took a deep breath. 'Please don't do this. Don't go for a . . . divorce.' She didn't even like saying the word. 'Have a trial separation, if you must but give it time. Give Dad a chance. He wants you to stay, I know he does. Come downstairs and talk to him. Please.'

June pursed her lips. 'Very well. But it's not going to change my mind.'

Slipping into sheep dog mode again, Becca trotted down the stairs and back into the sitting room. Frank was still watching television. Becca shook her father's shoulder. 'Do something,' she hissed at him. 'Be nice.'

Reluctantly Frank stood up. 'Now, June,' he said as Stephen Hendry potted yet another black behind him. 'Don't you think this has gone a little far?'

'Not far enough,' June said cheerfully. She trotted out of the room.

'Dad!' Becca turned to her father. 'Was that being nice? Do something. Swear undying love. Anything!'

Frank sniffed. 'I'm too old for all this. I can't change just like that, even if I wanted to – which I don't. This is who I am. I don't want to go gallivanting around, and I like things to look like what they are, I don't like them looking as if they're made out of jigsaw pieces gone wrong. And I think that conceptual art is nothing more than a big con. You can tell her that from me.' That was obviously the clincher. He settled himself in his armchair, pulling his dilapidated cardigan round his thin chest. At some point June must have mended a small hole by the pocket, Becca could see the darn slightly lighter than the wool around it. Her eyes pricked at this evidence of wifely duty fulfilled.

'Couldn't you at least try a bit . . .' Her voice trailed off. It all seemed to be hopeless. Frank wasn't going to change, June seemed determined to go off in new directions. In a way it was funny, the idea of them arguing over conceptual art. Except that it wasn't funny at all. Tears welled up. She searched in her pockets for a tissue, but couldn't find one. 'I'll be back in a sec,' she said, her voice all croaky.

'Don't you worry about me.' Frank coughed pathetically as Becca went to find some loo paper. 'I'll manage.'

June was in the hall, unruffled, undisturbed as if nothing momentous was happening at all. She looked up at Becca and smiled. 'Do you know, I never really liked that wall paper.'

Becca shook her head unable to speak.

Frank stuck his head round the living-room door. 'Did someone say something about a cup of tea?'

* * *

'The thing that gets to me is that they're both so matter of fact about it all,' Becca said, loitering in the doorway to Martin's study. It was the smallest room in the house, above the front door and next to their bedroom.

Martin's eyes were fixed on the computer. 'Perhaps that means that it's the right decision.'

'How can you say that? They've been married for all that time, and then suddenly June gets it into her head to go off. I wish I'd never organised that party for them.' She picked up a paperclip off his desk and fiddled with it. 'How could I have known it would lead to this?'

'I don't think it's entirely your fault,' he said, flicking a glance in her direction before going back to the computer. 'Ah . . . that's interesting . . .'

'And all that stuff about conceptual art – I mean, what was that all about? They've been together fifty years, they don't have to agree on everything, it's not compulsory for couples to agree, but you don't have to get divorced over it.'

'Mmmm,' Martin said.

'I can't bear it,' Becca said trying to keep her mouth from wobbling. 'Everything's going wrong. How are they going to manage? What will happen to them? Mum's saying she's going to go and live in a flat, but what about Dad? He won't be able to cope on his own, he'll go to pieces.'

'He'll be all right.'

'That's easy to say, but he won't, he's always lived with Mum, and she's done everything for him. And she'll end up in a bedsit alone being eaten by cats.'

Martin swivelled round on his chair. 'Don't you think you're being a bit, well, overemotional about this?'

'It's my parents! Of course I'm emotional! It's a normal human reaction to get emotional,' she said, as the tears ran down her cheeks. 'My parents are splitting up!' She wanted Martin to hold her, comfort her, say it would be all right, say everything would be all right.

Instead he rubbed his nose. 'Yeah, but . . . you're not a child, are you? You're a grown woman, with a child of your own.'

'But I am a child, I'm their child,' Becca shouted at him. 'Can't you see that? It's natural I'm upset. How would you feel if your parents split up?'

'I wouldn't be prancing around like a drama queen, that's for sure.'

Becca stopped. 'Is that what you think of me? Is that what you—'

'I'm sorry, I take it back, I didn't mean to—' Martin put his hand up in surrender.

'No, no, that's what you think, isn't it?'

Matin sighed. 'I think you're being a bit . . . excessive.'

'Excessive.' Becca wiped her face. 'Excessive.'

'Listen, love, give me a chance to finish this bit of work, and then we'll talk about it, OK?'

Becca stared at the wall. It was covered with bits of paper, graphs and charts, business cards, lists and memos. Down one side was a diary Martin had sellotaped together to make one long list headed 'Weekly Programme' and divided into four neat columns – Distance: Target/Actual, Time: Target/Actual. He'd filled in the first couple of weeks. There was a huge star at the bottom marking 25 March. The Day! Becca felt exhausted just looking at it. It was so very organised. So very Martin. 'I need to talk about my parents now,' she said, feeling the moment slipping past them.

'Yes, in a minute.'

She swallowed. 'I need your support.'

'I'll come through in a sec.' He smiled at her and she nodded, hugging herself. She was cold, and the room felt empty and barren.

'In a minute,' she repeated, knowing they wouldn't talk about it.

He grinned at her. 'By the way, I think conceptual art's a bit of a con too.'

She knew he meant it as a joke, something to lighten the mood. She smiled the best she could. 'Don't stay up late.'

'I won't,' he said, turning back to the computer screen. She watched him for a while, then turned and went into their bedroom. She undressed, and got into bed where she lay staring at the ceiling, feeling lost and alone. She could hear the clatter of Martin typing on the computer keys.

After a while she turned out the light, and tried to find sleep.

Chapter 6

She found it hard to concentrate the next day at work. Her first class was on *Pride and Prejudice*. She always enjoyed the students' discussions, the girls keen on the book (although Becca knew that the familiarity usually came from television or film adaptations), the boys having to be coaxed into an appreciation of the finer points of Austen wit and subtlety. The theme she had centred this class on was choice, particularly the life choices men and women faced in Regency England. Was the men's choice between the navy, church or army less restricting than the women's of marriage, governess or spinsterhood? Discuss. They did, hesitantly at first but then getting into it as Becca gently steered them. Were modern-day choices less or more restrictive? Was it the same for their parents or grandparents? Was more choice always a good thing? Some talked confidently, others needed encouragement and proffered their opinions with diffidence, although she knew that all believed they were the centre of the universe. Their faces were so young, so unformed, Becca thought. They hadn't encountered any real life choices yet; life for them was still black and white and not shades of grey, and the universe was fundamentally benevolent rather than arbitrary.

She smiled, remembering how she'd resented her father telling her she'd understand when she was grown up, and that feeling of thinking she was grown up aged seventeen and perfectly able to go hitchhiking round Europe or go to an all-night party in the middle of the school week. It struck her that she had felt more confident and grown up then, more certain of maturity than she was now. If anything she was regressing into childhood.

Suddenly the whole June/Frank situation flooded her brain. Her parents were splitting up. Choices could be made, but ultimately life could be derailed by the arbitrary decisions of others. Last night June said she wanted a divorce. She was making choices and leaving Becca to cope with the results. There was a buzzing in her ears. I mustn't cry, she thought, not here, not in class.

She shuffled her lesson plans, the typed sheets blurred. Her hands were shaking. She made herself listen to what one of the boys was saying. He was one of the more hesitant ones, with mild blue eyes behind gold-rimmed glasses and he was saying something about money and marriage, and she nodded, although she had no idea what he was referring to. 'Thanks, Eddie.'

As she spoke she regained her equilibrium. The lesson plan swung into focus. 'Now, let's look at the options Lizzie Bennett is offered and what she chooses, and compare them to those of some of the other characters, particularly Charlotte.'

Crystal was in the staffroom making coffee. She looked up as Becca came in, then looked again. 'Are they that bad? My lot are quite sweet.'

'It's not them.' Becca shook her head. 'It's just one of those days.'

'Christ, and it's only ten thirty-five. What's up?'

Becca washed out a mug. She hadn't said anything to Crystal so far about June and Frank, hoping that it was a passing whim of June's. She wouldn't have said anything to a colleague, but Crystal was her friend, she knew June and Frank. 'It's June . . .'

'It's not cancer is it? God, that would be so typical, she has that wonderful party, dead by the end of the year.'

'No, it's nothing like that,' Becca said, disconcerted. 'It's . . . well, she says she wants to leave my dad.' She gave a rueful smile, trying to put a brave face on it.

'No! You poor sausage! How dreadful!' Crystal gave Becca a hug, and Becca felt some easing of the tension. 'How come?'

'I don't really know. She just wants to do her own thing.'

'I can't bear it, I really can't. All those years together.' Crystal's mouth quivered, and to Becca's horror her eyes had gone all watery. 'How's Frank? How's he going to manage? You'll have to look after him.'

'He's not that old,' Becca said, taken aback.

'But it's all awful. There's just no point, is there, for any of us.' She gave a huge sigh, her breath catching as if she might burst into tears. 'Let's go and eat all the chocolate we can find.'

'What's the matter?' Richard said coming over to them. 'You OK?'

Becca felt her news was being hijacked. Perversely it made her want to play it down. Besides, she didn't want it to be staffroom gossip. 'It's nothing,' she said, tension making a hard knot of her voice.

'How can you say that?' Crystal turned on her. 'It's the most terrible thing I've heard all week.' Her voice squeaked as she choked back a sob. 'It's so sad.'

Richard gave Becca a baleful glance as if she was the problem, and put his arm around Crystal. 'Would it help to talk things over?' he said to her, his voice dripping with sympathy and pastoral care.

'It's actually my problem,' Becca said sharply. 'And actually I don't want to discuss it.'

But she did. If only Martin had been more understanding, more sympathetic she thought as she drove home. Once he'd been the most brilliant shoulder to cry on, tolerant and gentle, endlessly patient with her interminable moanings. Had he thought she was overemotional then? Melodramatic, even? What was the word he'd used last night? Excessive, that was it. Excessive. Becca snorted. He wouldn't have called her excessive if he'd seen Crystal's reaction.

Lily was at home when Becca got back, frantically tapping on the computer keyboard with a noise reminiscent of jungle drums. The gossip travelled on MSN like jungle drums, Becca thought, who did this, who said that.

'Have you got much homework tonight?' No response. Becca tried again. 'If you've got homework, can you make a start now before *Hollyoaks*.' She tried to make her voice authoritative, but tiredness kept the edge off.

'Yessssss,' Lily hissed, as if Becca was insisting on an intolerable and completely unnecessary procedure to be carried out. 'In a minute.' The frantic typing continued, clattering into the sore places in Becca's brain.

Becca knew 'in a minute' meant some time in the far far distant future. 'Lily. Homework. Now, please.'

Clatter clatter clatter.

'Now.'

Lily flung her hands off the keyboard. 'I've said I'm going to do it, can't I just relax for one minute, I've been at school all day, I've just got home, I just want to relax for one minute. One minute, that's all. Surely I'm allowed one minute. But no, I've got to do it all now, now, now. It's so unfair, no one else's mum makes them work the second they come home, you're so mean and uptight, you don't let me do anything except work, work, work, you think I'm a slave . . .'

Becca thought she would snap in two, the pain in her head was intolerable. She turned and walked out of the room, and kept walking. She walked to the front door, and then out into the street, and just kept walking.

She had walked to the end of the street before she realised that she'd gone without her bag or coat, the need to get away had been so powerful. She checked her step, then carried on. Lily probably wouldn't notice she'd even gone. Martin wouldn't. She strode down the main road. Why shouldn't she go out for a walk? Martin went running most evenings.

Cars whizzed past. People rushing home from work, people with happy lives, happy families, happy children. She walked on, not sure where she was going, or what she was going to do when she got there. Perhaps she would just walk for ever and never come back. The idea had a certain appeal.

She reached the point where Royal Victoria Park ran alongside the main road and for want of anywhere better to go, she turned into the park. There were boarders at the skatepark and she watched them for a few minutes, marvelling at their agility and flexibility. On the other side was the children's playground. On a sunny weekend it was heaving with children and parents but this evening it was quiet. Everyone was at home having their tea, she assumed.

She walked further into the park, past the boating lake. The ducks quacked and waddled towards her, hopeful of bread. She walked more slowly towards the botanic gardens. Walking out like that was childish. What would Lily be thinking? Becca sighed, knowing that if Lily had noticed her absence she'd probably assume that Becca had popped out on some domestic errand.

It was a pleasant evening, the sun still strong although getting lower in the sky. People walked along the central path that bisected the park. Some were dressed for the office, obviously making their way home after working in the centre of the city. Two were in tennis kit, heading for the courts near the playground. Others just strolled: tourists, dog-walkers, people taking the late afternoon air. Mothers pushing babies and toddlers, perhaps after an afternoon at the playground, now heading home for tea and bed.

Becca sat on a bench under a tree. She closed her eyes, feeling the sunlight playing intermittently on her face as light filtered through leaves gently swaying in the breeze. She opened her eyes to recognise the splayed pattern of horse chestnuts. Green conker cases hung, acid green, tightly closed, but soon they would ripen and discharge their cargoes. Becca wasn't sure if small boys were interested in conkers still; Lily hadn't been. There was something satisfying about their brown glossiness, a sense of potential waiting to be fulfilled.

. Unlike her own. She felt old and used, a husk of a woman. Uptight, Lily had called her. That had stung. She had hated Lily at that moment with a fierce passion. Becca shifted in her seat. She couldn't blame June for wanting to get away. It was the same impulse she'd experienced after the party, that sense of: is this it? June was off to find herself, and never mind those left behind. She leaned forwards on to her elbows, her mind in turmoil. Martin had said she was excessively emotional; her father had said melo-dramatic. Perhaps she was, but she couldn't help feeling that your mother leaving home after fifty years was a reasonable excuse for emotional excess.

It hurt that Martin hadn't taken her in his arms – that was all she had wanted from him, just something that said her anguish, however excessive, mattered more than some stupid spreadsheet. It hurt that Crystal hadn't reacted in the way she'd hoped either. It hurt that she was supposed to be adult and controlled when inside she felt like a mass of molten lava waiting to explode. She banged her fists against her forehead three times, frustration and anger bubbling under the surface. But it didn't help. I don't want my mum to go, she sobbed inside. Hot tears ran down her face, and she pressed her fists into her eyes. I don't want things to change, I don't want to be alone. People walked past, feet clicking purposefully on the asphalt path, or silently in trainers, and she hunched into her hands, not caring if they looked at this strange weeping woman on the bench, rocking in misery.

Feet walked past. Then came back, closer. 'Are you all right?' A man's voice.

'Fine, thanks,' Becca managed to say in a tiny, tight voice, hoping the voice would go away. The feet moved away. Suddenly a wet black nose pushed between her knees. She couldn't stop herself from jumping.

'Sorry – come here, bad dog.'

The dog stayed where it was, panting heavily so a healthy pink tongue lolloped out from a black, hairy face.

'I'm sorry,' the man said, grabbing the dog's collar and clicking a lead on. 'I hope he didn't frighten you, he's only being friendly.'

'It's all right,' Becca said, looking up for the first time. 'I like dogs. Oh!' She looked back down again as she recognised the man as Paul Fitzwilliam, and quickly wiped her face with her hands.

'Here.' He held out a large handkerchief. 'It's clean.'

'Thanks,' Becca said, taking the handkerchief and still not looking at him. Bad enough being caught sobbing by a stranger, but at least you'd never have to see the stranger again. But Paul Fitzwilliam she'd have to meet on Thursday. She wiped her face again.

'You've made it worse,' he said. 'Here . . .' He sat down next to her and took the handkerchief from her, then dabbed at her face. His expression was neutral, as if mopping up weeping women was all part of his day's work. 'I think that's most of it.'

He hesitated, then handed her back the handkerchief. Becca clutched it in her fist as if it were a lifeline against further flooding. It was quite damp. 'I'll return this when I see you,' she said, not looking at him.

'Whenever. No problem.'

Go away, Becca thought. She blew her nose on his handkerchief. Paul stayed where he was. The dog had lain down on the path, its chin resting heavily on her foot.

'I'd be happy to listen, if you wanted to talk,' he said.

'I don't want to bore you . . .' Becca shook her head. 'I expect you've got lots you ought to be doing.'

'I'm supposed to be walking the dog, something I find excruciatingly dull.' The dog presumably had recognised the word 'walk', as it stood up, tail wagging. Paul stood too. 'We could walk and talk. Or not. Up to you. But I'd be pleased with the company. Do you have a dog?' Becca shook her head, but she got up and fell in step with Paul. 'It's a weird situation. Somehow a dog gives you the right to talk to people you'd never talk to normally.' He bent down and released the dog from the lead and it rushed off, nose to the ground in search of some elusive scent. 'Sometimes you think you're the first person they've talked to all day. Sometimes they're the first person *you've* talked to all day. Apart from the dog of course.'

'You work from home?' Becca said tentatively.

'At the moment. I used to run a theatre company and have minions doing things for me, but that's no more. I have to be my own minion now.' The dog had found a stick and was prancing in front of them. Paul took it, and threw it. The stick arced impressively high as the dog raced over the grass for it. 'Why were you crying?'

Becca blinked at the direct question. She watched the dog retrieve the stick and trot back in their direction, tail high.

'You don't have to answer that,' Paul added. 'It's a bad habit; I'm notoriously nosy about people.'

'It's all right,' Becca said. 'It was silly of me to cry. My parents are separating and it's been a bit of a shock.'

'That sounds like a perfectly legitimate reason to cry.' The dog dropped the stick in front of him and he picked it up. 'I cry over everything – give me a hint of violin on the telly and I'm off. And I've no excuse to cry.' He threw it again, and the dog raced off. 'Have they been married long?'

'Fifty years. I organised a party for them in the summer. I don't know – my mum just says, that was it. She thought, fifty years, and she'd had enough.'

'It is a long time,' Paul said. 'Half a century. No hint beforehand?'

'None,' Becca said with a sigh. 'Or at least, none that I picked up.

I suppose there were hints she wasn't one hundred per cent happy, and hadn't been for ages. But if people are going to break up, you sort of think they're going to do it sooner. And everyone seems to think I'm being pathetic by being so upset. I mean, *I* think I'm being pathetic most of the time. It's not as if I'm a child, I've got my own family. This shouldn't affect me.'

They stopped at the road, having come to the end of the path. 'Should is an interesting word to use about emotions,' Paul said. 'It implies we can control how we feel, and I don't think we can. We can pretend we can control it, of course, sometimes even to ourselves. But I think what we feel is what we feel, and no one should be ashamed of that.'

'Let it all hang out, you mean? That's not very British of you.'

'Must be my theatrical background coming out.' He turned and started to walk back along the path. 'For what it's worth, in my opinion it'd be downright odd if you didn't find your parents separating upsetting, regardless of your own age.' He smiled at her, and Becca felt as if a weight had lifted from her shoulders. Stupid, because what did Paul's opinion matter to her, but she felt validated.

'I like your dog,' she said.

'Do you want him? Drives me mad.'

'Why do you have a dog then?'

'My wife's idea. She thought it would be good for the children to have an animal to look after. I wanted to get a mutt, but she insisted on this breed.'

'What is he?'

'A flat-coated retriever. He's a very posh dog actually. Got a pedigree as long as your arm.'

'Are you going to breed from him?'

'Suzy wanted to, but he kept wandering away and shagging all the local dogs, so she whipped his bollocks off. Not personally, you understand,' he added. 'At the vet's.'

Becca wasn't sure what to say. 'I always wanted a dog when I was little,' she said. 'But my father doesn't like them, so we never did. Sometimes I used to walk the dog from across the road, and I'd pretend we were winning Crufts, or saving people from drowning, or winning obedience classes.' She pulled the dog's silky ears. 'What's his name?'

'Oberon,' Paul said straight-faced. 'King of the Fairies. You haven't got yourself a dog since?'

'We've got a hamster. At least, it's my daughter's but I've ended up looking after it most of the time. As you do.' It was strange how she felt she could talk to Paul. Perhaps it was because he was a near stranger, but she could imagine telling him anything about herself, and know that he would listen intently as if really interested. Perhaps being a director made him good at listening. 'I'm sorry I dumped all that stuff about my parents on you. Please ignore it.'

'It was a privilege.' He called the dog to him. 'Besides, I need to keep my actors happy. I don't want you dropping out halfway.'

'I did wonder if I ought to, what with my parents and everything,' Becca said, thinking of Martin and his running schedule. 'I'd hate to let you down later on.'

'I'd understand if you did, but it'd be a disappointment. You're a good actress,' he said. 'I need you.'

Chapter 7

Becca's fears that she might have to give up the play proved unfounded. Over the next few weeks home life reached some sort of equilibrium. Martin went running, Lily mooched around presumably dreaming of Kevin, Becca got to know the students and dreamed of the days when she went to rehearsal. Being Lady Fidget was fun. She wasn't called each evening – the Fidgets were a subplot, not the main story, and she only went to about one in three rehearsals – but the sessions had become characterised by her turning up at seven, and then suddenly looking up at the clock and realising it had miraculously become nine thirty and the intervening two or so hours had evaporated. Freed from the responsibilities of carrying the main plot, Becca was able to relax and enjoy herself. Paul was a wonderful director.

Not that she had many others to compare him with, but she gathered from her fellow cast members that they were impressed. And he was funny. Brian had a tendency to quibble interminably over some teeny element of Paul's direction, which could make Becca feel she was losing the will to live, but Paul was good at deflecting him. Once he'd told Brian that acting wasn't a democracy. 'It's a dictatorship,' Paul said with a carefree grin. 'My personal fiefdom.' It was a bit like Bill, and his comment that people wanted to be led, except that Bill was serious and Paul had made them all laugh. Well, everyone except Brian of course.

The only flaw in Becca's life was June, who said she was determined to leave Frank, and Frank, who refused to take June seriously. Frank had a point, as June hadn't instructed a solicitor, although she had moved out of their bedroom and into what had once been Becca's room. Becca trotted between the two of them trying her best to keep them together. She deliberately didn't tell Lily, hoping that the situation would blow over, but on her last visit June had said she was going to live elsewhere and Becca knew she had to let Lily know at least some of what was going on between her grandparents. But it was hard to find a good time.

'Just tell her the truth,' Martin said, filling his water bottle up at the kitchen sink.

'Whose truth?' Becca said, thinking she ought to start cooking supper. 'June's or Frank's?'

'The truth as you know it – that June's not happy and is going to move out for a while, maybe for ever, maybe not. You don't have to give her details. Where is she, anyway?'

'Upstairs, making herself beautiful in the bathroom.' Becca looked up, as if she could see Lily through the floor. 'When do you want supper?'

'Half an hour? I'm starving.'

'I was going to do a casserole this evening, but it won't be ready in time . . . you could always eat something now and then supper could be later.' Becca looked at the clock.

'I've already had a banana – the book says to eat carbohydrate an hour before running so you don't get hypoglycaemia. Couldn't we have the casserole tomorrow?' Martin turned towards the kitchen door as it opened and Lily came in. 'My God,' Martin croaked.

'Oh no,' Becca murmured, eyes wide, hand over mouth in horror.

It looked like Lily, but instead of the pretty light-brown hair was a shock of jet black. 'I dyed it,' she said, unnecessarily.

'Go and wash it out this minute,' Martin said, his finger pointing towards the door. 'It looks dreadful.'

'Can't,' Lily said, looking horribly pleased with herself. 'It's permanent.'

'It'll have to be chopped off.' Martin turned to Becca. 'You'll have to sort something out.'

'Me? Why me? Why not you?'

'It's a girl thing.' He shrugged. 'I'm off for my run.'

'You can't say it's up to me and then run off,' Becca said. 'She's your daughter too.'

'Stop arguing,' Lily butted in, cheeks flushed. 'It's my hair and you've got no right to tell me what to do.'

'We're your parents, we've got every right,' Becca snapped back.

'I can't be doing with this,' Martin said. 'See you later.' The back door slammed behind him.

'Martin!' Trust him to go just when he'd got everyone upset. There was a inexorable feeling about the situation, as all the arguments she'd had with her own parents whooshed back. Platform shoes and dog collar chokers and: 'You're not leaving the house dressed like that, young lady.' It was like the nightmare where you suddenly find yourself on stage performing a role that you haven't rehearsed, except in her case she felt she was taking part in a play she had rehearsed years ago, but now she was playing a different role.

Lily's chin was high in the air, but her eyes were miserable and her mouth downturned. We mustn't argue in front of Lily, Becca thought. What did I want when I was her age? I wanted them to see *me*, not a child. She shook her head, letting the heat dissipate and fade. 'Why?'

'Why not?' Lily shrugged, less defiant now her father had gone.

Becca touched the jet-black spikes, close to tears. 'Your hair was such a lovely colour.'

'I'm a goth,' Lily said as if that explained everything.

She stroked Lily's hair again, remembering the baby fine softness of fourteen years ago now transformed into damp black strands. There was a sense of overwhelming sadness and – yes – a strange tingling fear. Her child, her only child, was growing up and away from her.

'I don't see why it's such a problem. It's not his hair.' Lily's lower lip stuck out. 'Anyway, you dye your hair.'

'Yes, but . . .' Becca's hair was an artful selection of honey, caramel and toffee. Sweetie shades, to hide the grey that was starting to emerge. A few years ago she'd been to a school reunion and everybody had looked exactly the same, but blonder. 'It's different.'

'Why?'

'I'm an adult. Look,' Becca said, swiftly moving on as she knew it wasn't a particularly good answer but unable on the spur of the moment to come up with anything better. 'I'd rather you hadn't, but I suppose in the greater scheme of things it could be worse. Can you lay the table for supper please?' Becca deliberately kept her voice flat and non-confrontational, so she didn't give Lily anything to react to, and went to the cupboard to pull out carrots and onions, not looking at her. They'd have pasta – again – tonight, but she'd get a casserole ready for tomorrow when she'd got back from her rehearsal. She began to scrape the carrots, keeping her back towards Lily as if there was no question about her laying the table as asked. After a short silence she heard the cutlery drawer open, and the clatter of forks and knives.

Becca began to chop up the carrots, enough to make two casseroles, one for tomorrow night, and the other for the freezer. At least that would be two home-made meals. Carrots done, she moved on to the onions. Lily came back into the kitchen and rested her head against her mother's arm.

Becca smiled, knowing it was a peace gesture. 'Put your hand out.' Lily obediently put her hand next to Becca's, and Becca stopped chopping onions and laid her hand over Lily's. 'Look,' Becca said. 'They're the same.'

'No they're not,' Lily replied, wriggling her fingers. 'Your fingers are longer than mine.'

'My hand is bigger overall, but it's the same shape.' She compared the two hands. Lily's nails were bitten down to the quick, the rough cuticles red in places as if sore. 'See?'

Lily inspected their hands. Becca wondered what she was thinking. Did she want to have hands that were like her mother's, or did she long to be different? Hard to think that you were predetermined by your genetic material, that however much you rebelled against your parents you were stuck with being a product of them. Fifty per cent from each. But which fifty per cent?

Becca tried to picture June's hands, wondering if they too were similar, but could only conjure up an image of wrinkled skin, the wedding ring embedded deep in the flesh, so deep you wouldn't have thought it could be removed. But that was what June was intending to do. She was going to have to tell Lily sooner or later about June and Frank.

She squeezed her hand, remembering the baby Lily had once been, the simplicity of dealing with childish problems: grazed knees, a melting ice-cream cone. So unlike the prickly teenager she had become. 'I've got something to tell you,' she said. 'It's about Gran and Grandpa. The thing is, Gran feels that she wants to live on her own for a bit.'

Lily frowned. 'What do you mean, live on her own? Where? And what about Grandpa?'

Becca shook her head. 'I don't know where Gran's going. I'm not sure she knows herself. And I don't know what's going to happen to Grandpa. We just have to see how things develop.' God, that sounded lame. Becca bit her lip. It was hard to articulate things you didn't really understand yourself. She supposed it was like being a politician, having to defend a position you didn't agree with because your party had voted for it. That, or resign. But you can't resign from being a mother.

Lily looked at her with the blue eyes she'd inherited from June. 'Are Gran and Grandpa getting divorced?'

Becca started chopping onions again. 'I don't know,' she said. 'Aren't they too old?'

'I don't think there's an age limit.' She peeled the papery skin off another onion. 'Be a love and grab me a bit of kitchen paper. These onions are stinging my eyes.' Lily handed her the paper and Becca wiped her eyes. She began to brown the ready-cubed meat.

'By the way,' Lily announced. 'I've become a vegetarian.'

'So you're now the child of a broken home.' Crystal stuffed a pile of exercise books into her pigeonhole in the staffroom. 'Join the club.'

'Do you think Bill would let me off lunch duty because of it?' Becca said. They were now five weeks into the term, with half term coming up. She wondered why she always seemed to have twice as much to take home as Crystal.

'Fat chance. You'd have to be suddenly orphaned at the bare minimum. One parent buggering off wouldn't get a look in,' Crystal said, collecting her coat from the hat stand. She flicked her hair out over her collar. 'I put it down to too much reading of *Saga* magazine. It gives unreal expectations of life past retirement, all trips to Cuba, and Petra by moonlight. I wish.'

'Speaking of expectations, what are you up to tonight? A date with David?' Becca gathered a stack of exercise books together, thinking about unrealistic expectations.

'You're so behind – didn't I tell you? He was all right at first, but whenever we went on dates he'd start to tell me something and then kept saying "You're going to love this" and "This is so funny", and then tell some long-winded story that wasn't at all funny. I couldn't stand it. In the end I said: "I can decide for myself if it's funny or not, I don't need you to tell me." Then he went off in a huff and I just went off.'

'So you're back on the hunt.'

'I'm not sure I ever left it to be honest. Are there any nice blokes at your drama group?'

'Only if you're looking for either a toy boy or an old boy.'

'What about the director? He sounds quite nice.'

'Paul? He's all right.' It was now mid-October and Becca had had six rehearsals to date. At the heart of each rehearsal had been Paul, encouraging, coaxing, teasing. And then afterwards in the pub, he was the centre around which they all revolved. Not that he put himself forward, but it was natural that they as amateurs should defer to him, the professional. Becca had been surprised that he came to the pub afterwards, given that he attended every rehearsal, but Angela said he didn't always. She remembered the last time, when he'd worn that velvet striped jacket again, the one that brought out the colour of his eyes. Becca giggled. 'Actually, a bit more than all right, to be honest.'

'Mmmm,' Crystal said smacking her lips as if eating a particularly delicious chocolate with a cream centre. 'Tell me more.'

'Nothing to tell – and if there was, you'd be one of a long, long line. I think all the women have a bit of a crush on him. 'Spect some of the men do too.'

'Sounds promising. Introduce me.'

Becca shook her head. 'Married. And I've seen his wife. I don't think I'd be wandering if I was him.'

'Gorgeous?'

'Yes.' Becca remembered the woman who'd burst in on the audition, her glossy hair, her stylish clothes, her perfect make-up. 'But also scary. Apparently she's a terribly high-powered lawyer, one of those women who make me feel completely inadequate. An alpha female.'

'I hate her already. Us beta girls have to stick together.' Crystal linked her arm in Becca's. 'And how's Martin? Still running?'

'Does lots of fartlek, apparently. That's a mix of running and walking,' she said in mock seriousness to the sniggering Crystal. 'You wouldn't believe how much there is to know about running, you could write a book about how to choose a pair of shoes, and that's not including everything else.'

'I went out with a runner once,' Crystal said. 'Nice bum.'

Becca thought about Martin's bum. It did seem to be shaping up a bit. 'I must get a move on, I've a rehearsal tonight and I need to grab a shower after wrestling with *Othello* all afternoon.'

The traffic home was kind to her so she got back, hoicked something out of the freezer then nipped upstairs for a shower. Lathering her body all over, she thought she might as well wash her hair. She poured shampoo into the palm of her hand and massaged it into her hair, feeling like a girl in an advert. At the pit of her stomach was a feverish throb of anticipation. I love acting, she thought. Rehearsal evenings had become the highlight of her existence.

Washing, and then blow-drying her hair had nearly made her late for the rehearsal. Downstairs she grabbed her bag, then put it down again. She'd go to the loo before setting off. Quickly she ran back up the stairs.

Why was it that she never noticed the loo paper had run out until the critical moment when it was too late? Knickers round her ankles, she hobbled over to the airing cupboard and reached for the stack of loo rolls. She snapped the roll of paper on to the holder. It was a simple but necessary job, so why was it always her who got landed with it? Something stirred in Becca's memory. She could just remember her mother muttering in the same way: 'Why is it only me who changes the loo rolls?' This was the definition of domestic drudgery, the changing of the loo roll, a necessary function that everyone else was oblivious to. I bet if I asked Martin or Lily, they'd say they didn't know where the loo paper was kept. She took a couple of rolls from the packet in the airing cupboard and placed them prominently in the bathroom cabinet. One of the loo rolls kept falling off the shelf despite her pushing it back. She reached inside the cabinet. Yes, there was something at the back of the shelf, like a pencil. It took a few seconds for her to register what it was.

A pregnancy-testing stick.

Chapter 8

The pub was crowded, but the theatre crowd found a mostly free table and squashed themselves around it. In honour of impending Halloween, the landlord had decorated the bar with strings of black plastic bats and orange pumpkins. Lily should get a job here, Becca thought despondently. She'd fit right into the vampire theme. Becca sipped her drink, listening with half an ear to the other actors round the table and trying to hide the fact that she was sick with anxiety. Lily was only fourteen. It was far too young. And who was the boy? Kevin, presumably. When she'd seen the stick, for a second she could have committed murder, but now she was trying to be rational about it. Teenagers experimented. She had, Martin had, heavens, half her *Othello* class definitely had. It was just that most fourteen year olds didn't go as far.

She'd wanted to talk to Martin about it before she tackled Lily, but Martin, red-faced from his running, had been edgy. Girl's stuff, he kept saying. Women's department. And then she'd had to leave or she'd have been late for rehearsal. She was going to have to tackle Lily about the pregnancy-testing stick when she got back. At least it was negative.

Victoria leaned forward. 'How long have you been married, Becca?'

Becca started and brought herself away from Lily and back into the discussion. 'Oh. Twenty years?' She did the maths in her head. They'd been married for five years before Lily came along, and Lily was fourteen. 'No, it must be nineteen.'

'What about you, Brian?'

Brian looked smug. 'Thirty-five.'

'Thirty-five!' Victoria beamed at him. 'That's incredible – what's your secret?'

'I always do what I'm told.' He looked around the table for approval. Becca smiled politely, although she was pretty certain that Brian was an old-school misogynist. She could just see him complaining that things went downhill when they gave women the vote. He'd do it with a little smile as if to say, I don't really believe this, I'm just being a playful tease, what's the matter, can't you take a joke?

'I don't know why we make such a fuss of people who've been married for ages as if it's some kind of great personal achievement,' Becca said. 'Surely they've just been lucky.'

'I don't think so,' Victoria said, frowning. 'You have to work at marriage.'

'Hard labour, in my case,' Brian chipped in, looking as sleek and smug as if he'd never done a day's work in his life, hard or otherwise.

'What about you, Paul?' Victoria said, turning the full wattage of her smile on to Paul as he approached their table, moving up to create a space beside her. Instead Paul sat down next to Becca.

'What about me?'

'Do you think people with long marriages have just got lucky?'

'That, or they're scared.'

'Ooh, you cynic,' Victoria squealed.

'A lot of people stay married because the devil you know is better than risking being on your own.' There was something in his tone that made Becca look closely at him. 'At least during the Restoration there wasn't any pretence about marrying for love. That was a late eighteenth-century concept. You took friendship where you could find it, and lovers – once you'd done your duty and provided the heir.'

'And what about poor people, who didn't have land or money?' Becca said. 'Did they marry for love?'

'The average age of marriage was twenty-six for women, twenty-eight for men. Which isn't much different from now. People saved up to get married, acquired property. Sure there were shotgun weddings – Shakespeare being a prime example – but generally everyone was hard headed about marriage. They simply didn't expect to find love in their marriage.'

'I didn't know Shakespeare had a shotgun wedding,' Victoria said. 'How romantic.'

'To be fair, we don't know that it was a shotgun wedding,' Paul said. 'She had a baby six months later so that's the assumption.'

'Didn't he leave her his second-best bed in his will?' Becca said.

'That doesn't sound like love,' Brian said, sniffing.

Paul sipped his beer, then leaned forward. 'Attitudes were different.' As he talked about Tudor and Jacobean attitudes to possessions she realised that he'd sidestepped the question about people being too scared of loneliness to leave a marriage. Was he unhappy in his own marriage? His wife had seemed frighteningly bossy that day at the auditions. And there was something restless about him, a sense of power being controlled, you could see it sometimes in the set of his shoulders when Victoria kept on getting her lines wrong, or Brian couldn't remember whether to turn upstage or down. It must be hard for him to be working with a bunch of amateurs when he'd directed professionally all over the world, Becca thought.

She traced round the edge of one of the beer mats. What would she have done if Lily had been pregnant? Not a shotgun marriage à la Shakespeare, despite Lily being the same age as Juliet had been. She was going to have to have a talk with Lily. She drained her glass. It frightened her to think of Lily – her baby – having sex, needing a pregnancy test. And she was going to have to deal with it, especially as Martin looked as if he was going to opt out of any responsibility. Perhaps if they'd had a boy, Martin would have seen him as 'his' department and gone off for man to man bonding sessions over football and fishing.

'That was a big sigh,' Paul said, his voice low.

'Sorry.' She looked around, but no one was looking at her. Victoria, Angela and Brian were deep in some other discussion, Michael was chatting up Rosie. 'I was somewhere else.'

'I'm the one who should be sorry, I was obviously boring for England.'

'Not at all,' Becca said. She looked around the pub, the rest of the cast chatting and drinking, their eyes bright. 'It was fascinating.'

'So much so you drifted off.'

'Sorry, I'm a bit distracted.' She took a sip of wine, then realised the glass was empty. 'I hope it didn't wreck the rehearsal.'

He shook his head. 'Of course not. I don't suppose anyone noticed.'

'You did,' Becca said.

'It's my job to notice.' Paul smiled at her, his eyes sympathetic. 'How are things?' he said.

She opened her mouth to say fine, but found herself talking. 'I found a pregnancy-testing kit at home just before I came out.' If he'd looked surprised, she'd probably have stopped. As it was he nodded, and sipped his beer. 'My daughter's only fourteen. I mean, she's too young to be having sex, let alone risking pregnancy.'

'You can't be sure she's having sex. She might have bought the test out of curiosity.'

'It was used. She'd done the test.'

'That still applies – assuming it was negative?'

'Thank heavens.' She leaned back against the high wooden seat. 'Have you asked her about it?'

She knew she didn't want to ask Lily about it, because of the reply she might get. Becca shook her head. 'I found it literally the second I had to leave to come to rehearsal, so I haven't had a chance.' She wished she could pass the responsibility to Martin but she had to face it, it would come right back.

'Perhaps you could have a more general discussion, but not say anything about the test. She might volunteer the information anyway.' He sipped his beer. 'My kids are too young, but I'm not looking forward to talking about sex. I'm sure they already know far more than I did at their age. Probably far more than I do now.'

'Oh yes, Lily always says "But I've already done it at school". God, I hope that's not literally true.'

Paul laughed, and she felt a stab of pleasure that he had picked up the double meaning. 'You're a teacher, I think Victoria said. Surely you have to deal with this sort of issue in the normal course of your job.'

'It's very different when it's your own child.' She shook her head and got up. 'I must go home and talk to her.'

'I ought to go as well.' Paul stood. 'Where did you park? I'll walk you to your car.'

'Oh, Becca, are you off?' Angela perked up. 'The calls are a bit different next week because someone had already booked the hall. I think you're on Tuesday. Or maybe Wednesday. I'll ring you.'

'Great. Bye, everyone.' Becca smiled at them, there was a chorus of goodbyes from the others, then Paul's hand was in the small of her back, steering her through the pub and out on to the street.

'Which car park do you use?'

'Manvers Street.'

'That's the one towards the railway station?' Becca nodded. 'See? I'm getting my bearings.'

'What about you?'

'Oh, we live up on Lansdown.'

'But that's the other direction.' The posh bit, she thought.

'I can't have my leading lady being mugged.'

Becca shook her head. 'I'm hardly your leading lady, and Bath's perfectly safe. You don't need to walk me to my car.' He smiled. Becca looked at him. 'You're going to insist, aren't you?' He nodded. 'Then I shall accept your company gracefully. Thank you.'

They walked past the abbey which was lit up and silhouetted against the ink-black sky. 'Are you enjoying rehearsals?' Paul said.

'They're the highlight of my week. I'm really grateful to you for giving me the chance,' Becca said, sticking her hands into her pockets and thinking she'd have to get her winter coat out soon. 'It's a major achievement I haven't yet fallen off the stage or bashed into the furniture.'

'It's a pity you didn't take it further – I think you said you thought about applying to drama school after university?'

Becca nodded. 'But I didn't want it enough to follow through, and I think acting's the sort of profession where you have to really, really want it. Perhaps I should have tried. Maybe I'd have become a film star and gone to Hollywood.' She laughed. As if that was likely! 'Or maybe I'd have struggled for work and worked in an antique shop to make ends meet. Or maybe I'd have ended up teaching English after all. Who knows.'

'It's never too late to find out. You could always apply again.'

'What – at my age?'

'Why not? There are lots of courses for postgraduates and mature students. You could do it if you tried.'

'What, audition again, and go to drama school? No, I couldn't.'

He turned away as if disappointed by her immediate dismissal of his preposterous suggestion. Because it was preposterous. Fancy going to drama school at her age. It was ridiculous. You sound just like your mother, she told herself. Or rather, the old version of June. The new version would probably be leaping at the thought of going to drama school.

'This is me.' She smiled at him. 'Thanks for walking me to the car.'

'My pleasure. I hope things work out with your daughter.'

'I'm sure they will.' She jiggled her car keys. 'Till Thursday.'

'Till then.' He hesitated, then leaned forward and kissed her cheek, the lightest of touches but somehow strangely disturbing.

'I'm so fat,' Lily moaned, clutching her tummy as she stretched the seat belt over it. There did seem to be more of it than usual, bulging over her school trousers in a muffin top. Pregnant, Becca thought feeling cold all over, despite knowing the test had been negative.

'Perhaps if you ate more sensibly,' Becca said, slipping the car into gear and setting off from Lily's best friend Grace's house, where Lily had gone after school. 'Fewer biscuits and chips, more salads.'

'I don't like salad.' Lily's lower lip stuck out.

'Fruit, then. It might help your skin too,' Becca said, looking straight ahead as if she was just saying it casually. Lily's skin had always been beautifully smooth, with delicate colouring, but recently it had flared up into a band of teenage acne. She was undoubtedly a pretty girl, but the last few months had not been kind. The contrasting jet-black hair didn't help either.

'What's wrong with my skin?'

'Nothing. It's just having a bit of a reaction to the hormonal changes you're going through.'

'Great. My mother thinks I'm spotty and fat.'

'I never said that.'

'You're supposed to be supportive.'

'I am being supportive.' Becca struggled to keep her temper under control. You're the adult, she's the child, she muttered to herself. You're the one in charge. She needs to let off steam in a safe place, and who safer than her mother. But it was hard not to mutter 'not fair', like a more mature version of Lily herself. Not fair, not fair.

'It's not fair,' Lily said. 'Why did I have to inherit Dad's legs, why couldn't I have inherited yours? Everybody else is really skinny except me. It's not fair.'

'Life's not fair,' Becca snapped back. 'Do you think I want to be stuck in a car in a traffic jam with a moaning teenager? Because I don't. I'm fed up too, but I don't go on and on about it.'

Lily started to sob. 'It's all wrong, everything is useless, I'm useless, there's no point in doing anything, it's all hopeless.'

Becca felt swamped with remorse at losing her temper even momentarily. 'Lily darling, of course it isn't hopeless. Of course you're not useless.'

'You're just saying that,' Lily sniffed. 'You're angry with me because I'm a disappointment.'

'Of course you're not, darling.' It was terrifying how fast they could go from the most anodyne of conversations to nihilism. Lily's hormones may have been on a rollercoaster, but did they have to drag Becca along too? She felt giddy from the ride. Best to try distraction. 'How was Grace? I haven't seen her for ages.'

'Why are you trying to distract me? I'm not a child,' Lily said. Becca winced. Lily was sharp at spotting ruses and tricks. On the other hand, saying you weren't a child was practically positive proof that you were immature.

'Oh, look there's Kevin!' Lily sat up.

'Where?' Becca swivelled her head round, eager to catch a glimpse of Lily's object of affection.

'Don't look,' Lily said, subsiding in the passenger seat. 'He might see you.'

'Isn't that a good thing?' Becca saw a youth shuffling along the pavement who she guessed was Kevin. He was stocky, as far as she could tell from his baggy clothes. And older than Lily by quite a few years, she guessed. Old enough to get a girl pregnant. This was her opportunity to find out some more about him. 'Do you want to hop out and say hello, or give him a lift somewhere?'

'Shut up, don't look,' Lily hissed. 'Drive on.'

'Really? I thought he was your friend,' Becca said. The lights changed and she moved forwards, past Kevin on the pavement. As they did, Lily turned round to look at him, then settled back in her seat, texting furiously.

'Sort of.' Lily's fingers rattled over her mobile phone.

The mysteries of teenagers, Becca thought. Still, at Lily's age she'd gone out with different boys all the time, in what seemed like, in retrospect, a complicated rotation around her class at school. The pregnancy-testing kit floated in front of her imagination. She had to ask about it.

'I know you're not a child,' she started, hoping that this might be a way of approaching the subject. 'You're becoming a lovely young woman. But that means you have to think about some other things, like taking responsibility for yourself.'

'I am responsible.'

'I know you are.' Becca couldn't think how to open up the subject. Perhaps it was better to just say it straight out. 'When I was cleaning the house I discovered a pregnancy-testing kit in the bathroom cupboard.'

'It's none of your business.' Lily's tone was of shocked outrage.

'I'm your mother, and it is my business.' Becca took a deep breath. 'You're too young to be having sex, but if you are, you must take precautions.'

'I know all this.'

'Well, you obviously don't know, as you've had to take a pregnancy test.'

'I'm not pregnant.'

'So I saw, thank heavens. Darling, I don't want to pry or discuss your private life, but—'

Lily cut in. 'It was Grace's idea. We wanted to see what happened.'

Becca's heart lifted. 'So you haven't . . . ?'

Lily made a face. 'No,' she said, managing to squeeze about five vowel sounds indicating disgust and horror into the single syllable. But while the thought may have seemed disgusting and horrible to

Lily, it made Becca feel light-headed with relief. It was all right. Paul had been right. She felt a wave of gratitude towards him as Lily carried on. 'All the boys round here are creeps. Except Kevin. Anyway, Mum, I know all about it. We've done all this at school, ages ago, in PHSE. They're always going on about it: don't get pregnant, use a condom, AIDS can kill you.'

Becca felt quite taken aback, thwarted in her motherly role of information provider. 'Promise me you'll always use a condom.'

'Yes, yes, I promise. Oh, this is so embarrassing. Can we stop now pleeeease?'

Becca nodded, relieved that it was over and that they had arrived back at the house with her mission accomplished and a happy outcome.

'Mum?' Lily's voice had that two-note wheedling tone that indicated that whatever Lily was about to ask, she didn't expect her mother to agree easily. 'There's Battle of the Bands on Saturday at Moles, and I want to go.'

'What is it?' Becca reversed into a small space trying to avoid touching next door's car.

'Lots of bands play, and then they decide who's best. I'll stay over-night with Hannah,' Lily said brightly as she undid her seat belt.

They got out of the car and went through the back gate. Drat, I should have done the planters this weekend, Becca thought. Never mind, they said tulips were better planted in November, didn't they, so she had a few more weeks. Becca had her hand in her pocket for the back-door keys when Martin opened it.

'Hello.' He gave her a quick peck on the cheek. 'I was just popping out for a run.'

'Hang on a sec. Lily wants to go to some thing late on Saturday night.' She thought back to what Lily had said. 'Isn't Moles a club? You're only fourteen. And who's Hannah?'

'She's my best friend.' Lily's lower lip was sticking out again, ready for a fight.

Becca blinked. As far as she knew, Lily's best friend was Grace, and had been for years. 'What about Grace?'

'She's a friend too.'

Becca looked at Martin who shrugged. 'You girls sort it out between yourselves. You don't need me.'

'I do, I want your opinion.'

'I've got to go – I said I'd meet Una at the corner five minutes ago.' He gave a huge sigh as if it was all too much. 'OK, my opinion is: she's too young, she can't go. Right, I'm off,' and he loped away leaving Becca to cope with the fallout.

'That is so unfair. You never let me do anything,' Lily shouted, slamming through the back door. 'You just want to keep me here locked up.'

Becca followed Lily into the house. 'Lily, be reasonable.' Was that a reasonable thing to say to a teenager? Silence. Becca waited, then climbed the stairs. She could hear sobbing from behind the bathroom door. 'Lily?' More sobs. 'Darling?'

'Go away.'

What to do? Go away, as Lily suggested or talk through the gap. Or break it down and drag her off by her hair to some teenage bootcamp. Becca could see the appeal of boarding schools, pack them off and don't worry about them until they were eighteen, let the teachers deal with teenage tantrums. She was saved from having to decide which course of action to take by the phone ringing.

'I'm just going to get the phone,' she said to Lily. 'But I'll be right back.' By which time she hoped she would have come up with some magic formula, some crafty line, some ingenious solution to Lily's teenage years beyond disowning her.

'Hello?' Becca said, her mind on Lily.

'Ah, Becca . . .' Her father's voice quavered down the line. 'I wonder if you could come over.'

Becca's heart sank. 'It's not a great time, you've caught me in the middle of something.'

'It's about your mother. If you could just come round and talk to her . . .'

'What is it?' she said. 'Is Mum OK?'

'Yes,' he said, drawing the word out. 'But on the other hand, no. I suppose it depends on who you're talking to.' His voice went into humble mode. 'No, it's too much trouble. I shouldn't have rung.'

She had to go. If Martin was there he'd say it was emotional blackmail, but Martin wasn't there, he was off running. Becca put the phone down and went back to the bathroom door. The sobbing had stopped. 'Look, I've got to go up to Gran and Grandpa's. Work out what it is you want, put Hannah's address and phone number on a piece of paper for us, and we'll see.' Audible sniffs. 'I'm sure we can work something out.'

'Like going to Moles?'

'Oh, Lily, you're only fourteen. It's too young to be going to pubs and clubs and things.'

'You just don't want me to have any fun,' Lily flung back.

'Yes, well.' Becca could feel a headache developing at a point just above her left eyebrow, as if a small and evil elf were drilling for oil. 'We'll talk about this later. I have to go.'

'Later, it's always later. You never have any time for me,' Lily wailed through the bathroom door. Emotional blackmailing skills were obviously inherited. Becca's sense of duty was neatly torn in half. Who came first, her parents, or her daughter? And what about me?

Lily was working herself up. 'I'm just inconvenient,' she sobbed. 'It would have been better if I'd never been born. That's what you'd like. You wish you'd never had me.'

'Oh Lily,' Becca said, not able to keep the smile out of her voice. You had to laugh really, all things considered. Lily hadn't yet learned that less was sometimes more in the blackmail stakes. 'You silly pickle, you're the most important thing in my life, as you well know, but I'm just going up to see your grandparents. You could come too, if you like. I'm sure they'd love to see you,' she added.

'I might die of neglect, and you wouldn't care,' came tragically through the door.

'We've all got to die sometime,' Becca said cheerfully. 'Never mind, I'll be back soon to sort out your funeral.'

Chapter 9

'Rebecca! How nice to see you,' Frank said, sounding surprised even though he'd known she was coming.

'I said I'd come. What's the problem?'

'It's your mother.' He rubbed his hands together, fingers twisting. 'She says she's leaving.'

Well, yes, Becca wanted to say. Have you only just realised? 'I know it's difficult for you to accept,' she started to say in her gentlest voice, but Frank cut through it.

'Yes, yes, I know all about that,' he said, dismissing his wife's desire for a divorce with an irritated wave of his hand. 'But she says she's going now, for months! And when she comes back, she's selling the house. What will I do? What will happen to me?'

'I've decided to visit Joanna,' June said cheerfully when Becca was on her own with her mother. 'I fancy seeing the scenery. They say it's spectacular.'

'But what about Christmas?'

'They have it in New Zealand too. Frank's got to get used to me not being around. Besides, I'll get the chance to see my other grandchildren at Christmas.'

'We always have Christmas at my house,' Becca said forlornly. Everything around her seemed to be crumbling. 'I was going to order one of those bronze turkeys. When are you coming back?'

'In February. That'll give me time to get the house ready for selling.' June took Becca's hand. 'Becca, you've got to accept this. Frank's not the only one in denial.'

'So, what are you going to do about Mum?' Joanna said, crystal clear all the way down the phone from New Zealand.

Becca tapped the phone in annoyance. Why did she have to do something about Mum? Wasn't she already doing everything she could? And it was Thursday morning, she'd have to get up in a minute and go to work, whereas Joanna, on the other side of the world, was winding down. Martin started to stir, making snuffling noises like a piglet dreaming of truffles, his face blurred with sleep. He looked younger when asleep, the lines and wrinkles smoothed over. Probably gravity performing the same function as a facelift, stretching the loose skin over the skull underneath. Not that it mattered for men, Becca thought with a niggle of resentment. Men were allowed to get craggy and wrinkled, it added to the character. 'What did you have in mind?' she said to Joanna.

'Talk to her. Tell her she can't just walk out on fifty years.'

If only it were that easy. 'I have talked to her. I have told her. What do you think I've been doing?' Not that Martin was going the craggy direction. Over the years of their marriage he had thickened around the middle to the point that in certain lights he looked five months pregnant. Not that she could complain, having said good-bye to size ten many years ago herself. On the other hand, the running was definitely having an effect on his physique. As if he could read her mind, Martin on the other side of the bed stirred and raised an eyebrow in a questioning way. Joanna, she mouthed back. Martin nodded and rolled out of bed, rubbing the sleep from his eyes.

'I don't know. It just seems a bit odd that she should suddenly up sticks and leave. You don't think she's gone doolally?' Her accent was noticeably antipodean, which was new.

'Ask her if Norman's got hairy feet yet,' Martin said, and yawned. Becca frowned at him, not getting what he meant. 'You know, hobbits. Middle Earth. *Lord of the Rings.*' Martin gollumed off to the bathroom, a big grin on his face at his early morning wit.

Becca shook her head at him with irritation, then went back to Joanna. 'What sort of doolally did you have in mind?'

'Senile dementia? Alzheimer's? She's got to have been through the menopause years ago. I mean, you must be getting round to it yourself.'

'Thanks.' Becca felt stonier than an Easter Island statue. 'No, I don't think Mum's gone doolally. She's just got fed up with living with Dad, that's all.'

'She was fine when we were there.' Joanna emphasised the 'we', as if implying it was Becca's fault that June had now gone off the rails. 'She can't just get fed up. That's completely irrational.'

'Is it?' And was it equally irrational for Becca to be quite so annoyed by Joanna's tone? 'Would you want to live with Dad? I don't notice you offering to have him come and live with you.'

'A, I didn't marry him and B, I live on the other side of the world.' Joanna paused, and Becca imagined her taking a sip of chilled New Zealand Sauvignon. 'You've got to talk to her, Becca, make her see sense.'

'She's coming to stay with you, so you can talk to her. You can make her see sense. I've tried quite enough.' Martin's electric razor buzzed merrily in the bathroom, accompanied by snatches of singing. Becca cradled the phone under her chin. 'Martin says that we ought to bow out of their relationship. If they don't want to stay together, then perhaps it would be best to let it go. It's not compulsory to stay married for ever.'

'It's none of Martin's business.' Joanna's voice was crisp.

'But he may have a point.' There. She'd said it.

Joanna heaved a sigh. 'I'll sort it out when Mum comes over. I expect everyone's getting worked up about nothing.'

'Nothing?' Becca couldn't believe what she was hearing. 'Nothing?'

'Sounds to me like you're the one being a bit menopausal. It hits any time in your forties.'

Becca tried and failed to control her temper. 'I am not menopausal and Mum isn't doolally,' and with that slammed the phone down.

Martin came back in with wet hair and a towel round his middle. 'Isss everything OK, my preciousss?' he hissed like Gollum as he sat on the bed next to Becca, dripping cold water on her.

Another time, Becca would have played along with him, but now was the wrong time, the wrong mood. She had more important things to be worrying about. She gave him a shove. 'Get off, Martin, do.'

'Good morning,' Martin murmured, rubbing his hair with the towel. 'And did you sleep well?'

Becca looked at him. 'I was abducted by aliens who took me up to their spaceship, ripped all my clothes off, used and abused me, then dumped me back in the middle of Milsom Street outside Waterstone's and I've only just managed to crawl home.'

'So you're not in a filthy mood because of your sister?'

'I'm not in a filthy mood.' Martin raised an eyebrow at her. 'She asked if I was menopausal.'

'Bit young for that, aren't you?'

'Yes – I am!'

That evening, with Martin out running and Lily tapping furiously on MSN, Becca decided the time had come to clean the oven. Life was stressful enough at the moment, oven-cleaning couldn't make it any worse. Except . . . Running over the conversation with Joanna in her mind as she gave the oven a therapeutic scrub, she stopped. Was she getting menopausal? She was forty-three. Perhaps she was. She felt anxious a lot of the time, and had tremendous mood swings from the elation of rehearsals to the troughs of domestic life. Perhaps the menopause was the answer.

She sat back on her haunches and took off her rubber gloves. Her hands looked wrinkled. And was that a hot flush she was feeling, or just a toxic combination of irritation with Joanna and scrubbing? She patted her face, suddenly feeling wizened like a little homunculus. Soya, wasn't that what you were supposed to have?

She stood, feeling her joints creak in an imminent hip replacement sort of way, and wrote the word 'soya' in big letters on her shopping list. Was it almonds? Or something else? Apricot kernels maybe? She'd have to get a book. She turned to go back to the cleaning, then went back to the shopping list, and added 'menopause book'. The menopause meant the loss of fertility. Ageing. No more babies. She crossed the book off the list. She wasn't menopausal. She was far too young. She was just tired – roll on half term.

Half term came and went, and Becca was beginning to panic about the performances. Paul had said they'd be just before Christmas, and in September that had seemed light years away. Now the Christmas decorations were up in the shops and the performances were only a month away. The rehearsal schedule had become more onerous, with Becca being called several times a week and sometimes, like today, on a Monday.

She'd managed to clear the backlog of homework marking over the weekend so when she was climbing the stairs up to her classroom, trying to keep a pile of exercise books from slipping out of her grasp, she didn't feel too guilty when she heard a voice calling her name.

Bill was standing at the foot of the stairs. 'Becca, a word, if you'd be so kind. It'll only take a few seconds.' Bill showed no signs of moving up towards her so Becca swivelled round and made her way back down the stairs inwardly cursing him. If she dropped these exercise books it would all be his fault. Why couldn't he have come up to her? It was just an assertion of power. But she should be used to Bill by now.

She stood on the bottom step. Here she was directly face to face with his shaggy, craggy head. His hairline was receding and something about the way it receded made it seem as if it was pulling the whole of his face with it. His pale watery eyes blinked behind his glasses. His was the sort of celtic skin that never tanned, although there was a smattering of freckles over the bridge of his bulbous nose and high domed forehead. She'd always found him attractive, in an avuncular way, but looking at him from this level there seemed something unsettling about him. She took the final step down and waited.

'I understand you know Paul Fitzwilliam,' he said, peering down at her with pale watery eyes magnified by the glasses.

Becca nodded. 'I wouldn't say I know him, but, yes, he's the director of this play I'm in.'

'Extraordinary – I'm sure you appreciate who he is?'

'I know he's supposed to be quite well known.'

'Quite well known.' Bill shook his head. 'One of the leading exponents of Shakespearean theatre direction, articles in papers and journals, internationally in demand – ah, dear me. Quite well known.'

'It's a Restoration play I'm doing, not Shakespeare—' Becca started to say before Bill interrupted.

'I want you,' and he pointed his finger at Becca's chest like the Lord Kitchener poster, 'to ask him to take part in our cultural endeavours this coming year. What, exactly, would be up to him.'

'I wouldn't have thought he did schools – he's directed Shakespeare around the world.' She wanted to add, especially if he's as well known as you're implying.

Bill put up his hand to silence her. 'Let's not be defeatist, Rebecca,' he said, his dark voice rumbling. 'It's time for you to take a more active part in the department. At Hamilton House, all the staff have something extra to offer.'

It must have been a line he used with prospective parents, Becca thought. 'I don't think Paul Fitzwilliam is an extra I can offer.'

Bill pressed the tips of his forefingers together and tapped them. 'There's something else I wanted to ask. There's a conference in Oxford next Spring on theatre and teaching. It'll involve a weekend at a lovely hotel, all expenses paid by Hamilton House of course. I immediately thought of you.' He patted her shoulder, and one of the exercise books slipped to the ground. 'Would you like to go?'

'Yes, of course,' Becca said. 'It sounds really interesting.'

'Splendid. I'll make sure our esteemed school secretary organises the place for you. And in the meantime,' he said in his most comfortable voice, patting her shoulder again, sending a few more books cascading down to the ground. 'You can ask Paul Fitzwilliam about giving us a mere morsel of his time. Surely it's possible for you to ask.'

Meet Bill Malcolm, Becca thought as she knelt to pick the books up, the most manipulative man in the world. The stick and the carrot. At least the carrot sounded interesting, and a weekend away might be fun. She supposed it wouldn't be too embarrassing to sound Paul out. For all she knew he might love teaching in schools – there had to be someone who had to. 'I'll ask him this evening.'

'Good, good.' Bill beamed at her. 'So pleased to hear it. Now, you'd better get a move on, you're a little late for your class.'

Becca had been waiting for about five minutes outside the very dark and very locked church hall before Paul strode around the corner. 'Gosh, I'm pleased to see you, I thought I'd made a mistake.'

Paul frowned. 'Isn't Angela around?'

'There's no one. I've been here for about five minutes.' She stamped her feet. It was a cold evening, and the stars were shining brightly.

Paul made a hmm noise, then picked up his mobile and went down the steps. Becca waited, arms folded across her chest. It wasn't so much that it was cold, just that she'd been standing still. If she'd known, she'd have worn a hat. Angela had obviously forgotten about the rehearsal, judging by the squeaks emitting from Paul's phone, and his exasperated expression. 'We're pushed for time, I can't afford to lose a session through incompetence,' she heard him say. Becca felt sorry for Angela who did more work and gave more time than any of the actors, and she didn't get paid for it. It was a bit mean of Paul – but on the other hand, as the company had employed a professional director, they shouldn't be surprised if he demanded professional standards. Finally he clicked the phone shut.

'I'm sorry,' Paul said. 'You've been dragged out for nothing. Angela got confused about the schedule changes. She's a nice girl, but a bit scatty. Let's go for a drink, and we can at least discuss the play.'

Becca wasn't sure she liked the idea of discussing the play with a cross Paul. 'Don't you want to get home to your family?'

'They've all trooped off somewhere. No, come for a drink.' He grinned, and his face lifted. 'I've got an evening off, you can't let me spend it on my own weeping into a takeaway watching trash TV because nobody loves me.'

Becca thought for two seconds about the washing, Lily's coursework that had to be done, the hamster which needed cleaning out yet again. The thought of dealing with soggy newspaper did it. 'A drink sounds good.'

They began to walk up the high street towards the pub. 'I had a friend who inherited a cottage in a village outside Bath,' Paul said. 'We used to pile down there from London at the weekends when we were all students. I can't remember the name of the village.'

'You're not in touch?'

'God no. That was years ago. Before my wife came on the scene.' He sighed, but didn't elaborate.

'I've lost touch with most of my old student friends too,' Becca said. 'There are a couple I meet up with about once a year, and a few others I exchange Christmas cards with, but – I don't know – it's easy to lose touch. We're all so busy nowadays.

'I'm not,' Paul said to her surprise. 'I'm at a bit of a loose end, you could say.'

'But I thought . . . Angela said you did a lot of directing abroad and gave talks about Shakespeare.'

'Oh that. Yes, I do that, but my wife wanted to move here for her career, and I offered to play house husband for a bit.'

'That's very good of you.'

'Not really, just being fair. She hadn't wanted to move away from London and go north for my career when we first married, so it's my turn to take second place.' He stopped walking and gave a snort of amusement, then turned to her. 'I've had a mad idea. Would you like to – no, I can't ask you. I'll do it some other time.'

'What? Ask me,' Becca said, intrigued.

'No it was stupid. And presumptuous.'

'That's for me to decide, surely. Go on. What was it?'

'I've remembered where that village was. I was going to suggest having a drink at the pub there, but I know it's mad so forget it.'

'No, I'm not expected back home for the evening so there's no reason why I shouldn't go,' Becca said. 'It'll be an adventure.'

Chapter 10

Becca and Paul drove off from Bath in Paul's sleek silver sports car. Becca had a moment of anxiety about getting into a stranger's car but dismissed it as ridiculous. Paul wasn't a stranger, he was her director. When they got to the village, Paul parked by the green. He got out and peered at the houses then pointed at one. 'That's where my friend lived,' he said triumphantly.

'It looks very dark,' Becca said doubtfully. It looked shut up to be honest. 'I don't think your friend can be there.'

'Oh, I expect he's moved on long ago. Probably sold up and in the Bahamas,' Paul said cheerfully. 'The pub's further up the street.'

They walked up and found the pub. Becca had imagined roaring log fires, and horse brasses and curious agricultural implements on the walls, perhaps a snoozing springer spaniel or two in front of the fire, but it wasn't that sort of pub. It did have a log fire, which was welcoming, but next to it was a flashing fruit machine.

'How's the line learning coming along?' Paul said, putting down his beer with a satisfied sigh.

'Pretty much OK.' Becca sipped her own glass of wine. 'I'm a bit dodgy in some places.'

'That's nearly always a sign that you're not a hundred per cent certain of the emotions behind what you're saying. Tell me which bits you're finding difficult,' Paul said.

'Well . . .' They talked about the play. Paul knew so much, there was always something to be discussed or elaborated on. And then they moved to other subjects: films, books, art exhibitions, the conversation never stopping but easily flowing, like handling a skein of silken threads, each different and shining, but linked and connected. The pub filled while they were talking and suddenly she became aware that the noise level was high.

'Another drink?' Paul said, but Becca shook her head. She didn't particularly want to go back, but nor did she want to stay in the pub.

'What a wonderful night,' Becca said, looking up at the deep black sky as they walked to the car. The stars were bright and the moon hung large and silver in the sky. 'My mother calls that a hunter's moon.'

'It seems a shame to go back to the city. When I was a student we used to spend evenings out at the circle.'

'The what?'

'Surely you've been to the circle.' He looked at her, as she shook her head in bewilderment then grinned. 'A treat's in store for you.' He led the way past the car and up a side road. It looked surprisingly suburban, given the rural setting, with modern houses and cars parked in every driveway. Becca couldn't think what or where 'the circle' might be, but it was magical to be out in the moonlight, with the world turned silver and black and the crisp air chilling her cheeks. Then they turned right, to a large five-barred gate. There was a smaller wicket gate next to it with a notice saying '£1 admittance'. An honesty box was attached to the gate.

Paul rattled the gate. 'It's locked.' Becca pointed to the notice on the gate stating that the circle was open between 9 a.m. and sundown. 'Take no notice of that,' Paul said, as he began to climb over. Becca looked around expecting alarm bells, raised voices, shrieks of protest at the trespassers as Paul neatly dropped over to the other side. He held out his hand. 'Come on,' he said. 'Have an adventure.'

She took his hand, clambered over, feeling as ungainly as a camel, and jumped down onto the other side. Paul walked on, but Becca surreptitiously popped a couple of pound coins in the honesty box and heard them rattle down inside. She might be a trespasser, but she was determined to be an honest one. They walked a little way between two high walls, along what seemed to be a farm lane, smooth tarmac with the occasional tuft of grass or dried clod of mud. At the top of the track was a high stone wall with a kissing gate, then they were funnelled right along a grass pathway, which led to another kissing gate and out into a field. On the far side the grass was dewy with autumnal mist. Becca looked around, but even though the moonlight was strong she couldn't make out much beyond field and the white shapes of scattered sheep.

'It's further into the field. Do you need a hand?'

'I'm OK,' Becca said, practically tripping up and spraining her ankle on a tussock of grass. Her feet were feeling damp in the light trainers she wore for rehearsals. At least she wasn't wearing smart leather shoes, or they'd be ruined by now. As it was, she was conscious of her handbag swinging over her elbow, far too citified for a walk in the country by daylight, let alone moonlight. Suddenly she gasped as something white loomed out of the darkness. She stopped, hand to beating heart. It was a stone, a granite monolith ten feet high pointing towards the sky like an accusing finger. Beyond the stone she could make out the ground dipping and there were other stones, roughly arranged in a circle about sixty feet in diameter. Some of the stones were toppling sideways, others had already fallen. The whole circle looked like a mouthful of broken teeth.

'This ring isn't the best one,' Paul said, striding across the middle. 'There's another, better one further down.' Becca trotted after him, not wanting to lose him in the middle of a dark field. The ground gently sloped down and she saw more stones, closer together. Paul walked to the centre and spread his arms out, his coat swirling around him. 'May I present the Dancing Maidens,' he said, giving a flourish with his hands and then bowing.

Becca looked around at the stones, grey shapes in the darkness. 'How many are there?'

'In this ring, nine or ten, I think but I've no idea about the bigger ring – it's bigger than Stonehenge, but hardly any stones are still standing.' He led the way to a couple of stones that had fallen against each other at the outer edge of the ring. 'I think this was supposed to be the start of a ceremonial way off to another ring, but it's where we used to hang out. Come and sit here, it's more sheltered from the wind.'

Becca found a ledge on one of the fallen stones and sat, making sure her coat was tucked under her. Sheltered from the wind it may be, but it was November and not high summer. Paul sat on the edge of the other stone.

'I had no idea the stones were here,' Becca said, thinking she'd have to bring Lily out to see – in daylight, of course. She could imagine the stone she was sitting against being used for sacrifices. It wasn't a comforting thought. She felt as if she were being watched, as if the surrounding stones had eyes. 'What exactly is it?'

'A wedding party who were turned to stone for dancing on the Sabbath, of course,' Paul said, turning the collar of his coat up against the wind that ruffled his hair. 'Seriously? No one knows, beyond it being a stone circle probably as important in its day as Avebury or Stonehenge. I don't know if it's still true, but when we used to come here there hadn't been any previous archaeological excavations. So whatever theory you like is as valid as any other.' He rummaged inside his coat and brought out a flat tobacco tin and flicked it open with his thumbnail.

It was one of the things she liked about being with Paul: he knew a lot about a wide range of subjects. He wasn't just a narrow special- ist, knowing only about theatre and Shakespeare. The unwelcome image of Bill popped into her head. 'I've got an embarrassing question to ask you,' Becca said, watching him pick out a hand-rolled cigarette from the tin.

'Don't tell me – you're secretly the next Grand Wizard? You want to have my babies? You've got a birthmark that shows where the Holy Grail is buried in Rosslyn Chapel?'

'Nothing as exciting, sadly,' Becca said, laughing. 'My head teacher . . . well, he's decided that this academic year we're going large on culture, and he asked me to ask you if you'd come and do something.'

Paul struck a match, then cupped it in his hands as he bent his head to light the cigarette. The light shone golden on his face, illuminating the strong line of his nose, the high cheekbones. His hair whipped across his face as he sat up. He took a long drag. 'I don't want to sound ungenerous but . . .'

'The answer's no.' Becca smelled a familiar sweet smell on the wind, one she hadn't come across for years, not since her student days. 'I didn't expect you to say yes. That's why it was embarrassing to ask.'

'The thing is, I'm not a teacher. I've only worked with pro-fessional actors in the past. I can't see myself working with children. Besides, it's been hard enough for me to gain credibility within the profession and academically. If I start doing schools . . . I can't. Sorry.' He held the joint out to her, his wrist white in the moonlight.

Becca shook her head. 'No thanks.'

'I expect you think it's childish and immature.' Becca started to protest, but he carried on. 'It's what my wife thinks. Which is of course in part why I carry on. Now, I do agree that that's childish and immature.' He took a long drag, the end of the joint crackling red against the darkness.

'What did you do up here when you used to come as a student?'

'Sit around drinking and smoking dope mostly.' He hunched forward. 'We were always going to have an orgy, but the girls chickened out in the end.'

Becca laughed. 'When I was at uni, the boys were always trying to get us to play strip poker.'

'And did you?'

'Once. As far as I remember, several people got down to their underwear, but no one actually stripped off.' She looked up. It was years since she'd seen such a big sky. Living, as she did, in a city – albeit a small one – it was easy to forget what the countryside looked like away from artificial light.

'The energy that comes up through the stones is incredible.' Paul lay back and closed his eyes, his face bathed with moonlight. 'You ought to try it,' he murmured without opening his eyes. Becca hesitated, then moved up to lie back on the stone next to Paul. She thought they must look like effigies of a medieval knight and his lady, except that Paul was very much alive lying next to her. 'It may seem very New Age and all that,' Paul continued, 'but I believe that there's an energy we can all tap into, that comes up from the earth. It makes us grounded, centred. But it's all too easy to lose touch with it. Get swept up into material things. Lose our way.'

Becca watched Paul's mouth as he talked. It was a beautiful mouth, well shaped and almost feminine in the curve of the upper lip, balanced by the masculine sweep of his full lower lip. A mouth you could imagine seeing on a Roman statue, except instead of cold marble, Paul's was warm. She could have drawn it from memory. He'd only have to roll over a little and their heads would be together, his mouth on hers.

Bad thoughts. They were both people with responsibilities. She sat up. 'What are your children called?' she asked, hugging her coat around her.

'Jack and Willow.' He breathed out a cloud of smoke creating a temporary haze across the night sky.

What I want, she realised, what I really want is to kiss him. She stared down at the stones, which seemed the safest option given the startling thoughts hurtling round her head. We're talking about his children. Concentrate. 'Willow's a pretty name.'

'I met Suzy when I was playing Willoughby on tour in a production of *Sense and Sensibility*.'

Yes, she could see him as the romantic hero sweeping Marianne Dashwood off her feet and kissing her thoroughly. No. Don't go there. 'And Jack?'

'After Jack Absolute in *The Rivals*. That's set in Bath, as I expect you know.'

'I hadn't realised you were an actor as well,' Becca said, trying not to think of Paul in breeches and top boots.

'It's how I started.' He rolled over towards her, and leaned on his elbows, his eyes intense in the moonlight.

'Amateur theatre's all very well, but you could be doing something better.' He touched one of the buttons on her coat. 'You *should* be doing something better.'

'Like what?' she said as he traced a finger around the button. Becca's heart was beating so fast it was a surprise her coat didn't pulsate. 'Besides, professional actresses are always complaining that there aren't enough roles for women my age, so I can't imagine I'd stand a chance.'

To her surprise Paul leapt up. 'Why so defeatist?' he cried. He spread his arms wide and swung around in a circle. 'Look at this wonderful place. It's amazing to be here. Can't you feel the magic in the air, the starlight pouring down on us. The people who built this place didn't say, oh well, I don't suppose anyone will remember who we are in a few hundred years so what's the point? They got on with their dreams and made them happen. You could do that too.'

'I don't see how,' Becca said. 'I'm too old, too married, with a job—'

'Irrelevant!' He jumped down into the stone. 'Start applying for work – Bristol's on your doorstep, they're always looking for people to be in *Casualty*, and there are loads of other productions being made in the area. If that seems too much, then go to drama school for a year.' She could feel the energy sparking out of him. It fired her up, made everything seem possible. Perhaps she could become an actress. He held out his hand to her. 'All you have to do is take the first step.'

She took his hand, and he pulled her to her feet. She looked up at him, the distance between their heads only a few inches. The moonlight poured over them and the stone, his eyes dark and intense upon hers, drawing her in.

'The question is, do you want it? Because if you do, then what's stopping you?'

'I don't know.' She turned her head away from his searching gaze.

'Do you want to follow your dream? It could all be there, waiting for you. You have the talent, the ability. Do you have the will? Do you want it?'

Becca could feel the cold power of the stones surge up from the earth running through her to the stars. Paul's hands were on her shoulders, steadying her. Her body was trembling from the cold, from the power, she didn't know.

'Do you want it?' Paul murmured again, his eyes dark, his face white in the starlight, his mouth only inches from hers. She felt stripped naked, taken back to the Becca she once had been, a Becca who had hopes and ambitions and dreams. 'Do you want it?'

This is madness, utter madness, Becca thought, her breathing shallow. She could feel herself being drawn to him, leaning forwards, her eyes closing, lips yearning and— 'Oi! What's your game? Get over here!' Torchlight swung round.

'Quick!' Paul grabbed her hand, and they were off, running as fast as they could through the stones, the man shouting behind them, the torch bright like a prison searchlight, their scampering shadows large ahead of them, coats flapping, hearts racing, the man still shouting behind. She stumbled but was saved by Paul's hand in hers, running, laughing, stumbling, through the first kissing gate, then the second, Paul's hand was warm, all thoughts of shoes and mud gone in the exhilaration of running away. The man's voice – 'bloody vandals' – became fainter, the only sound now her panting, clouds of breath condensing in the sharp air. Then up and over the gate, a tearing sound as her jeans caught on the lock, Paul catching her on the other side, his arms around her, and then more running, past the farm buildings, past the houses, along the green and back to the car.

'Quick, quick!' She grabbed the door handle and collapsed into the passenger seat, hand to chest, desperate to get some air in her aching lungs. Madness. Madness. Paul revved the engine and they accelerated away into the darkness, way over the speed limit for a residential area.

She turned to Paul, who was doubled up catching his breath. His eyes met hers and then they were laughing, laughing amidst the panting, and it was uncontrollably funny, tears streamed down her face, hysterical giggles: Becca's sides ached she was laughing so much, she hadn't laughed like this for years.

Her breathing came back to something approaching normal as she looked at Paul, his face vital, dark hair shining in the moonlight. Becca thought, I've just broken the law. I'm a vandal. I could have been caught. What would Martin have said? Madness, utter madness – but oh, it was good to be alive.

Chapter 11

After Paul dropped Becca off back at her car, she drove home on a wave of adrenaline, let herself into the house and slipped off her muddy trainers. Tsk! Running over muddy fields at her age! She caught sight of her face in the mirror as she hung her coat up. It was glowing and alive. She caught her lower lip in her teeth, thinking she hadn't looked this young for years.

'Hi there. Did you have a good rehearsal?' Martin came into the kitchen, the glasses he used for reading perched on the end of his nose, and the newspaper folded to the crossword under one arm. 'I was just going to make myself some cocoa – do you want one?'

'No, thanks. You'll never guess what I did this evening.' She hung her bag up over her coat and turned to him. 'There was a mix-up over the rehearsal times so Paul and I went for a drink and then we went to this stone circle. It's incredible, Martin, like Avebury or Stonehenge.'

'At night? Surely it wasn't open?'

'Course not – we climbed over the gate. I'm going to have to go back and take Lily, I had no idea it was there. Anyway, we sat on the stones for a bit just talking, and then this man came and we just ran away, and he chased us a bit, but we got to the car and drove off.' She gave a yelp of laughter. 'I can't believe I've just done that.'

'I don't understand – why did you run off?' Martin looked puzzled.

'We weren't supposed to be there, of course. We'd climbed over the gate.' Becca grinned at him, feeling irrepressibly wicked.

'So, you broke into this stone circle that's probably a protected ancient monument and sat on it, then ran away when you were challenged.' He looked at her over the top of his glasses, like some ancient Oxford professor with an unruly student. 'What if you were caught?'

'But we weren't,' Becca said, feeling as sulky and rebellious as Lily. The atmosphere of joie de vivre that had encircled her evaporated like cheap perfume. 'I wish I hadn't told you now.'

'I don't understand what you were doing there in the first place,' Martin said, getting milk from the fridge. 'I thought you were going to rehearsal.'

'I was,' she said tersely. 'But no one else turned up.'

'So why didn't you come home?'

'Because I wanted to have a bit of fun, and not be some old fuddy-duddy,' she snapped at him. 'Because it seemed a good idea at the time.'

'I see.' His voice was cool. Martin looked at his crossword, pen flicking on the paper. Becca could see that he'd nearly finished it. Her sparkling mood had vanished to be replaced by a dull nagging ache in her heart. Martin put a spoonful of cocoa in a cup, mixed it with milk and put it in the microwave. The clock ticked into the silence between them. Becca stared at the ceiling, arms folded. She knew that Martin was expecting her to make the first move towards reconciliation; she knew that she had no intention of doing so.

'Your mother rang while you were out. She didn't leave a message.'

'Thank you. I'll ring her tomorrow.'

'Suit yourself.' Ping! The microwave had finished. Martin collected his cocoa. 'Well, I'm sure you will. I'm going to bed now. Good night.'

'Good night.' Becca said. She stood frozen in the same position for ten minutes after Martin had left the kitchen, thinking. Recently any knock or rub against the surface of their marriage and something flared up, raw as eczema. They didn't seem to be able to talk any more. I've lost my way, she thought.

An echo chimed in her head, something Paul had said, about the stones. They grounded you, centred you, focused you on the things that mattered. Her focus switched to Paul and the moment when they had been close, so close, their mouths just inches apart. It would have been so easy for them to kiss. She touched her mouth. So easy.

She gave herself a shake. That was what running about in the moonlight gave you – ridiculous ideas. Now. Be sensible. Paul had been talking about drama schools, and how she could apply. He'd made it seem within her reach. She grabbed her tea, went into the dining room and switched on the computer. As she was waiting for it to boot up, she ran her finger across her upper lip. It would have been quite romantic, though, a kiss in the moonlight circled by ancient stones. She smiled. Definitely something not to tell Martin about. She went to Google. Into the search box she typed 'drama schools'.

At the end of November Becca drove June to the airport. 'You don't have to,' June had said, but Becca had insisted. On the journey Becca ran through a checklist: have you got your passport, tickets, anti-embolism stockings? June replied patiently that she'd got all those things and more.

'Don't worry about Dad, I'm going to have him over every Sunday, and for supper a couple of times during the week.'

June looked out of the window. 'I'm sorry I'm going to miss your play. I'd have liked to see it. I'm sure you'll be fantastic. I've asked Lily to tell me all about it. By the way, I've left her Christmas present all wrapped up in my studio, along with things for you and Martin.'

Becca felt her mother had mentally already left England and was in transit to the other side of the world, a place about as far away as it was possible to go. 'You will phone, and send emails, won't you?' Becca said.

'Don't worry. You concentrate on having a lovely Christmas, and I'll be back in no time at all. Just drop me off at departures,' June added. 'Don't bother with parking and all that.'

'You're coming back in February,' Becca said. 'It's more than two months, and of course I must park. I've got to see you off properly.'

June sighed and they drove the rest of the way in silence. At Heathrow, Becca parked in the short stay car park. She unloaded June's baggage onto a trolley, not that there was much, just a suitcase and a brand new rucksack. The queue to check-in seemed interminable.

'Don't waste your precious day off on queueing,' June said. 'I'll be fine.'

'I want to wait with you,' Becca said. June shrugged. 'Do you want a paper, or some magazines? I could keep your place in the queue while you went and got something to read.'

'I'll get something when I'm through customs.'

'Or I could go for you now. They might not have a copy of *The Times* on the other side.' Becca trotted off, ignoring June's rolling eyes which she must have picked up from Lily. She found the newsagents, and picked up a copy of the paper. As she was going to the checkout she saw plastic bottles of water. They were on special offer, three for the price of two. Becca hesitated. June probably only wanted one bottle; on the other hand, the price for one was extortionate. She balanced three bottles in her arms. By the water cabinet was a stand of travel accessories. Perhaps there was something here that would be useful for June. Becca added a blow-up pillow to the bottles, then a mini torch and special wristbands that promised to reduce motion sickness.

While she'd been looking at the travel accessories, the queue to pay had bloated. Becca stood jigging up and down. Perhaps June had reached the check-in already. Perhaps she should dump everything and make sure June was all right. But that would mean going back empty handed. She dithered as to what was the right thing to do, trying to look through the people on the concourse as if she were able to see June standing in the check-in queue around the corner. The boy at the cash desk was incredibly slow, totting everything up without any apparent concern that these were people with planes to catch. Becca had to stop herself from asking him to hurry.

She shoved the things in a carrier bag and rushed back to where June should be. But wasn't. A moment of blind panic. She'd lost her mother. Perhaps she'd already gone through, perhaps Becca had missed her. Becca swung round, trying to identify June's pale hair from all the different-coloured heads in the queue. There she was! Near the front.

'I thought you'd gone through,' she panted as she rushed up to June's side. 'Look, I've bought you some things.' Becca fished out the water, the pillow, the mini torch and showed them to June. 'You must drink lots of water – the flight takes for ever. You needn't take all the bottles if it's too heavy to carry.'

'Darling, it's sweet of you but you can only take water which you've bought on the other side, beyond customs. Something to do with security.' Becca stared at the plastic bottles, feeling like a complete idiot. She'd known that, so why hadn't she remembered? 'Never mind,' June continued. 'The pillow I'm sure will be very useful.'

'And the torch,' Becca said, holding it out to her.

'Very useful too,' June said. At what point did children realise that their parents were humouring them? It wasn't a conscious awareness on either side – Becca knew she'd pandered to Lily's sense of well-being, letting her win at games, taking an interest in her cartoon drawings and so on, without ever consciously trying to.

'There are exercises you're supposed to do on flights, aren't there? Drat, I should have downloaded some, I meant to, but—'

'I've got an exercise sheet. Becca dear, you don't have to mother me. I'll do just fine by myself.'

Becca fidgeted with the bag strap. 'This queue's going on for ever. Are you OK standing for so long? You could perch on the edge of the trolley. Oh look, there's someone in a wheelchair, they're getting fast-tracked. I should have ordered you one, it would have been brilliant, I could have wheeled you round, we wouldn't have had to worry about the luggage or anything, we'd have skipped all the queueing.'

'Becca . . .' June put a hand on her arm. 'Stop fretting. Why don't you go home, mmm?'

'But I want to wait with you . . .' Logically Becca could see there was no point in waiting, that there was nothing practical she could do for her mother, but she wanted to stay around in case there was something. Anything. She bit the side of her thumbnail.

When it was finally her turn, June was brisk and efficient. She had all the relevant papers in her bag, produced her passport and ticket, loaded her own bag and rucksack, answered the questions. Becca loitered, ready to help, but wasn't needed.

'Do you need to go through immediately?' Becca asked. 'Your flight's not for a while. We could have a coffee.'

'No, I think I'll go through customs straight away,' June said, tucking her papers back into her bag. 'I fancy doing a bit of duty-free shopping. You go home now.'

'I want to wait.'

June sighed. 'Becca, it won't make any difference. Please. Go home.'

They embraced, Becca pressing her face against June's cheek, her eyes squeezed shut. And then June was off through customs and passport control with a jaunty little wave of her hand.

Becca waited in the cavernous hall of Terminal Four watching the departures board click round. She was surrounded by people kissing, chattering, worrying, surging about her in a non-stop ebb and flow of humanity, all going to exotic destinations, to have wonderful holidays, meet long-lost relatives, have business meetings. The noise of excited voices bounced off the high ceilings and buffeted her ears, the swirl of people passing, some jostling into her as she stood still, watching and waiting. And in the midst of all that seething flow, she had never felt so alone.

When Lily had been younger Becca had loved Christmas. It had been a magical time, the three of them doing things like visiting Father Christmas at Longleat, or going to see the lights. Christmas shopping had been fun, both for Lily and with Lily. In the last few years Bath had put on a Christmas market, in imitation of the continental ones. Small huts decorated with lights and greenery were arranged around the abbey square, mulled wine and hot chocolate were on offer, and a silver band played Christmas carols. Becca wandered round the various stalls, wishing Lily had come with her to the fair, but Lily had gone back to bed, rolled up tightly into her duvet like a hibernating black-haired dormouse. She'd already told Becca that the Christmas market was, variously, sad, gross and for losers.

Last year they'd gone round the stalls together. Lily had taken her job as present-buyer seriously, writing down a list of who were to receive presents and working out what she could afford for each one. Some of the choices were eccentric, like the comb she gave Martin's older, balder brother, but generally she was a good chooser and if in doubt her standby was a slab of chocolate, the bigger the better. But that had been last year, when Lily was still a child. This year she hadn't even bothered to open a single door in her advent calendar.

Many of the traders had stalls in the regular market or were local shop owners but the band playing and the air scented with mulled wine made the atmosphere special. Dangling earrings hung from black velveteen boards, jewelled necklaces draped over red satin spread out over trestle tables. Furry hats from fantasy animals like the long-coated zebra were stacked up in dazzling patterns. A charity was selling tickets to Name the Teddy on behalf of the local hospital. Becca picked the name Evangeline as the least likely teddy bear name on offer; the last thing she wanted was to win a teddy.

There were several stalls selling baby clothes ranging from delicate sweet almond colours to bold and bright stripy jumpers. Becca fingered a pair of filigree booties, rimmed with a lacy frill. I suppose buying things like these will be one of the joys of being a grandmother, she thought. She could remember a tiny pale-blue cap June had given Lily with satin ribbons that had disappeared beneath the bulging curve of the newborn Lily's chin. It had always seemed a miracle to her that the weight of a baby's head could be supported by the delicate stem of its neck.

And what would I have done if Lily had been pregnant? Becca thought. Insisted on an abortion, put it up for adoption, or looked after it myself? She didn't know the answer. An abortion would be agonising, adoption heartbreaking, especially after all those years when she herself had longed for a child. A baby to look after again . . . She felt a pang as she remembered nuzzling into baby Lily's soft, warm neck, that special baby's scent . . . Becca put the booties down. She wasn't at the grandmother stage yet, and thank heavens for that. Her life was full of opportunities. What opportunities she didn't quite know, but she could feel them out there, waiting for her. She felt like a hawk ready to fly, letting the wind run through its wings, testing the air.

'Hello there.'

'Paul!' They kissed like old friends completely relaxed in each other's company, except that Becca felt dizzy with delight. Thank heavens she'd bothered to put on her make-up before coming out.

'Christmas shopping I presume?' Paul said, smiling down at her. 'Is your daughter with you?'

Becca shook her head. 'Far too grown up for this. She's still in bed. My mother always said that I was a horrible teenager, so I expect I'm getting my comeuppance.'

'Surely not. I can't imagine you as a horrible teenager.'

'I can remember slamming lots of doors and being in tears and perpetually saying it wasn't fair.' Not much different to now, she thought. Just now it's internal, rather than external.

'And I expect your mother answered, life's not fair.' Becca nodded, thinking of June, all those thousands of miles away. She missed her, even though she'd only been gone a week. 'Mine too,' Paul said. 'Although I was quite a well-behaved teenager. I often think I should have been more – oh, I don't know, more rebellious, less conformist. Do you fancy a mulled wine?'

Suddenly, drinking at four in the afternoon seemed an excellent idea. They made their way to the drinks stall, and Paul bought their wine. Becca watched him. He was taller than anyone else waiting, his presence seemed in sharper focus, as if the other shoppers were blurred and unformed. She smiled as he returned to her, two plastic cups of mulled wine in his hands.

'You looked very pensive over there at the baby clothes.'

'I was thinking . . .' She couldn't say she'd been thinking about babies and being a grandmother. That would sound too old and sad. 'I was thinking about opportunities, and what I want to do with my life.'

'And have you made any decisions?'

'I've sent off for some drama school brochures.' She looked up at him feeling suddenly quite shy. 'It's just to see them. I haven't decided that's what I'm going to do.'

'Well done you.' He touched her arm. 'But I thought you'd decided. At the stones . . .'

'I know. I'm not sure acting's the answer though. We'll see.'

'If you need a reference, just ask.'

'Thanks.' They exchanged smiles and Becca's heart sang. They started to weave their way through the stalls, stopping every now and then as if this was how they'd always planned to spend the afternoon. They were like a regular couple out on a shopping trip, a pair of tourists perhaps, come to sample the delights of Bath on a romantic weekend away. She had to stop herself from tucking her hand into Paul's arm.

They stopped at a joke stall. Becca bought some small presents for stockings, and Paul bought a magician's outfit for his son. 'He's hoping to wake up on Christmas morning and discover he's Harry Potter.'

'A normal boy then.'

'How's your husband's training getting along? He's running the half marathon next year, someone said.'

'He hopes so – he doesn't know. He doesn't know if he's fast enough to get asked to join the proper programme, which starts the week after next. It's been bad enough on the pre-training programme, heaven knows what he'll be like when the real thing starts.'

'I'm impressed he goes running at this time of year. Will he be out running over Christmas?'

'I hope not,' Becca fervently wished. 'I really hope not.' She fingered one of the hats, a velvet cloche in a delicate pink with a poppy-like flower made from feathers. Just a few months ago and she'd have got it for Lily, but now there was no point. Even the black one would be no good, because it was pretty. Becca tried on a furry hat, hoping she looked cute rather than stupid under the brim. 'Should I get it?'

'You look like a Russian countess. You ought to be whisked along in a horse-drawn sleigh, covered with furs.'

'With a balalaika playing in the background?' Becca glowed. Russian countess said exotic and romantic to her, much more appealing than cute.

'They're all original designs,' the stallholder said. 'You won't see another person wearing that hat.'

'Should I buy it for you?' Paul said, and touched her cheek.

'Oh, no, no,' Becca said quickly, scarlet with embarrassment and pleasure. She turned to the hovering stallholder. 'I'll take it,' she said.

'I have an announcement,' Martin said at supper on Tuesday. Becca paused from doling out sausages to everyone. 'I've made the marathon team!'

'Brilliant,' Becca said, amazed he'd managed the times, but genuinely delighted for him. 'Well done.'

Lily jumped up from her place and hugged him. 'Dad, that's great.'

'What team's that?' Frank said. Since June had gone, Frank had been to supper twice a week, and to lunch on Sunday, and she'd made sure his fridge and freezer were well stocked with meals.

'Martin's company is putting in a team to run the bath Marathon next year.'

'I'll be looking for sponsorship, Frank...' Martin said, a mischievous look in his eyes. Frank looked vague.

'I'll sponsor you, Dad,' Lily said. 'I'll give you five pounds.'

'Thanks, love. I'll need all the help I can get – we're supposed to raise at least £250 each. Could you put up a sponsorship form at the college?'

Becca nodded. 'But I'll do it at the beginning of next term.'

'Wouldn't now be a good time? Season of goodwill, and all that.'

'It'll get lost in all the Christmas stuff. But I'll ask at the theatre. I expect you might pick up a lot of sponsorship there.'

'Thanks – how are the rehearsals going?'

Becca groaned. 'I can't believe we're nearly finished – only ten days to go and I'm not nearly ready. I don't know that I want anyone to watch now, it's going to be so embarrassing.'

'You'll be great.' Lily took her plate from Becca. 'I can't wait.'

'I can come on the first night, or the last night,' Martin said. 'I've got the team Christmas meal on the Friday. Which night do you want me there? Or I could come to both.'

'We've got to come to the first night,' Lily said. 'You'll come, won't you, Grandpa?'

'What's that?' Frank paused mid-sausage.

'Mum's play. You'll come, won't you?'

'It doesn't sound like my sort of thing,' Frank said, looking cagey. 'When is it?'

'End of next week,' Becca said. 'And then it'll be Christmas and another year will be over.'

'I don't know where the time goes to,' Frank said mournfully. 'One minute I was a young man, with a wife, and a baby on the way, and my whole life before me, the next—'

'Have another sausage,' Becca said, ladling one onto his plate.

'Thinking of plays,' Martin said. 'What about us all going to the new Harry Potter film as a Christmas family treat? We could go this weekend. It was only a suggestion,' he added, as there was a resoundingly unenthusiastic reaction to the idea.

'It's a great idea,' Becca said, rallying even though she didn't want to see the film. 'You'd like to see it, wouldn't you, Lily?'

'I was going to go with my mates . . .'

'You could see it twice. It'd be something we could all do together. D'you fancy it, Dad?'

'What is it?'

Lily rolled her eyes at his ignorance as Becca answered. 'A film, about a boy wizard.'

'Doesn't sound like my sort of thing,' Frank said. Nor mine, Becca thought, but it's about going as a family.

'I tell you what I do fancy going to see,' she said to Martin. 'And that's the French film on at the Little.'

'Subtitles?' Martin said. Becca nodded, knowing Martin didn't like subtitled films because of his mild dyslexia. 'I'd rather go to Harry Potter.'

'It's not an either/or situation, we could do both,' Becca said. Martin didn't look convinced.

'What do you want for Christmas, Grandpa?' Lily dipped her sausage in ketchup and ate it, vegetarianism long forgotten.

'Oh, don't you mind about me. I don't want anything,' he said in a pathetic little voice that sounded as if he had been starved for most of his life. Certainly that chimed with the way he was helping himself to seconds of potato.

'But you've got to want something.'

'Well. There was something . . . but it's too much bother.'

Becca caught Martin's eye, and had to stare at her plate to prevent laughing.

'Go on, Grandpa, spit it out,' Lily said, a rather unfortunate expression as Frank's mouth was full of Becca's roast potatoes. 'What was it you wanted?'

Frank chewed as they all watched, if not exactly with bated breath, then at least polite attention. 'Since you ask . . . it's a circular saw with a laser guide.'

'That must make cutting very accurate,' Martin said leaning forwards. 'Mains or cordless?'

'Mains,' Frank said. 'You lose too much power with cordless.'

'Depends how much cutting you were going to do,' Martin said. 'Most things you can get a lot of power out of a full battery, and if you have a second battery pack on rapid charge, it's as good as mains.'

'But what would you use it for?' Becca asked, baffled as to why Frank would want a circular saw.

Frank sucked his teeth. 'Lots of things. The one I saw in the catalogue had a tungsten carbide blade.'

'What d'you cut with that? Thirty mill? Forty?' Martin chipped in.

'Don't tell me, you want one too,' Becca said. She often got Martin a gadget for Christmas. Last year it had been a special device for uncorking bottles. He'd been so pleased with it, she'd gone back and bought another one for Frank for his birthday present. This year was easy – she'd bought him a watch-cum-heart-rate monitor with split time functions, a countdown timer, and big, easy to press buttons for people on the move.

'Speaking of Christmas presents, was that a new hat I saw you with this morning?' Martin said. 'It looked nice.'

'I got it from the market on Saturday,' Becca said, remembering Paul being with her, how the mulled wine had gone to her head, making her feel hazy with goodwill to all mankind.

'Tell you what,' Martin said brightly. 'Tell me how much it was, and I'll give you a cheque.'

Becca was puzzled. 'I've already bought it.'

'I know, but it can be your Christmas present from me.' Martin looked delighted with the idea. 'You know I can never think what to get you.'

A hard tight knot formed in the centre of Becca's chest. 'But I don't want it to be my Christmas present. I want you to choose something you think I'll like.'

'But you like the hat, don't you?' Martin looked baffled.

'Yes, but—'

'Don't argue,' Lily said, her face creased in anxiety.

'We're not arguing.' Becca put a bright smile on her face. 'More sausages? More potatoes?' Frank nodded. 'I'll just get them from the kitchen.'

In the kitchen she took the food from the oven. To her horror she felt a fat tear slide down her cheek. This is ridiculous, she thought, hands over her face. It's stress, you're tired, what with the end of term and the play rehearsals. It's only a stupid hat.

Chapter 12

Becca sat in the dressing room, not able to remember a single one of her lines. It's first night nerves, she told herself. That's all. Relax and the words will be there. She made a conscious effort to ease her shoulders down. Eyes shut. Breathe deeply. And the first line was . . . She sat up in a state of abject panic. What was it? What was her first line? She picked the playscript up and flicked through. Could she hide the script behind her fan? Pointless – the words made no sense. Everything had gone from her brain amid the clamour of the other actors around her.

Becca scanned the busy dressing room, a simple white room more commonly used to store chairs, now transformed into a riot of colour by the first night good luck cards pinned up on mirrors and arranged on windowsills, and clothes scattered over the backs of chairs. Stiff brocade dresses battled with gravity and cheap wire coat hangers on a clothes rail while the other actresses adjusted corsets and petticoats, fishing around in bodices to arrange breasts so that they were authentically bulging but not actually indecent. Some were tying white stuffed sausages that Becca had learned were called bum rolls around their hips, to make the dresses stand away from the body.

Everybody else was cheerful, chattering and giggling, squeaking when their corset strings were pulled too tight, but wanting to go just that little bit tighter to reclaim waists that hadn't been so small since they were ten years old. Victoria was gargling in the corner, her face covered in white make-up, while Rosie judiciously applied a beauty spot at the corner of her mouth. Becca stared at her own face, white enough without the addition of make-up. Oh, this was such a mistake.

There was a tap on the door, and Lily peered round. 'Hiya, Mum.' She handed Becca a bunch of red roses. 'Good luck.'

'Oh, darling.' Becca hugged Lily, overcome by her thoughtfulness. 'You shouldn't have.'

'Yeah, well.' Lily disentangled herself. 'Are you looking forward to it?'

Becca pulled a face. She found a mug and filled it up with water from the tap in the corner for Lily's flowers.

There was a knock on the door. 'Five minutes. Beginners please.'

Becca closed her eyes. Oh god, it was going to happen. 'I feel sick,' Becca whispered.

'Mum, you're really nervous, aren't you?' Lily's voice was a mixture of amusement and incredulity. Becca nodded, wishing she was anywhere else in the world but here in this room. Why had she had such a stupid idea? Why in the world had she ever thought she could act? How could she have been so stupid? Lily hugged her. 'I love you,' Lily whispered in her ear. 'You're going to be great.'

For a moment Becca relaxed, as if she were the child being reassured by her mother. 'I'm worried I'm going to let everyone down.'

'You won't,' Lily said. She wagged her finger. 'Come on, Mum, don't let the side down now. You've done the work, now show them what you can do.'

Becca smiled, recognising her own pep talks. 'I'll try. Darling, thank you so much for the flowers. You shouldn't have spent your money on me.'

Lily looked pleased. 'I'd better go and grab my seat.'

She turned for the door as Becca remembered. 'Is Dad with you?'

Lily looked a bit sheepish. 'He wasn't back from work so I came in by bus. He's probably here by now.'

'Oh,' Becca said. She twiddled one of her ringlets round her fingers. 'You did leave the ticket somewhere where he'd see it?'

Lily nodded. 'Don't worry, he'll be along.' She paused at the door, thumbs up. 'Go, Mum. Go!'

The only place Becca felt like going was through the exit door with Lily. She inhaled deeply, feeling as sick as it's possible to feel when you're laced into a corseted bodice. She regretted getting Victoria to lace the dress so tightly. She looked across at her. Victoria, resplendent in brocade and a lace headdress that added a foot to her already imposing height, was doing what Becca assumed were vocal exercises. Either that, or multiple repetitions of 'Babbity Bee, Babbity Boo' were a sign of insanity caused by performance nerves.

A knock at the door. 'Enterrrrr!' trilled Victoria.

'Evening, ladies.' It was Paul. 'Just came to wish you good luck. We've got a good house tonight, so remember, enjoy yourselves, and they'll enjoy you.' He came into the dressing room and went first to Rosie with a word of encouragement, then Victoria.

Becca wondered if the good house contained her husband. She splodged powder over her face, thinking she'd never ever forgive Martin if he didn't turn up.

'How are you feeling?' Paul was beside her now.

'Terrified,' Becca said. She'd meant to speak lightly, but all lightness had gone from her.

He laughed. 'You'll be fine. Just enjoy it.'

'I think I'm going to muck it up.' She stared at herself in the mirror and her eyes stared back, black as obsidian. Paul sat on the chair next to hers and took both her hands in his. 'You are hugely talented. Don't forget that. You are going to go on stage and knock them dead in the aisles. Do you trust me?'

She nodded, her eyes mutely on his. They were a clear blue,

the sky on a spring day, untroubled and serene. His hands were warm, she could feel his energy pulsing into her bones. 'I wouldn't have cast you if I didn't believe you could do it. They'll be starting soon, I have to go out front.' He stood up, touching her shoulder in farewell.' At the door he turned. 'Don't worry. I believe in you.'

Becca stood in the wings waiting for her cue. She could see the others on stage. She felt sick. Her head swam. Her heart beat against the cage of her corset. I can't do this, she thought. It's impossible. I want to run. I must run. And there was her cue. Oh god oh god oh god. She took a deep breath and . . .

They bundled offstage after the curtain call, giggling and laughing.

'You missed out the whole of that last speech!' Brian said to Victoria. His wig had half slipped off, giving him the look of a lopsided spaniel.

Victoria took a swipe at him with her fan. 'Don't be so silly, Brian, of course I didn't!'

'You did, you did,' Rosie chipped in.

'I thought something had happened,' Victoria conceded. 'It went very fast at the end.'

'No wonder, with you missing out bits!'

They surged into the dressing room, high on adrenaline, talking in excited voices, no sentences finished, conversations lost as everyone chattered, headdresses bobbing, faces animated. Becca chattered with the rest of them, feeling young, feeling alive, feeling relieved. She had done it!

'Mum, Mum!' Lily tumbled through the door and into her arms. 'You were great, I told you you would be.'

Becca hugged her tight. 'I made so many mistakes, you wouldn't believe it, it must have looked so awful.'

'No, I didn't notice anything. But the play – it's really rude. And it's old!'

Lily sounded so outraged that Becca had to laugh. 'They had sex in those days too – despite it being ancient times.'

'When you went behind the door with that bloke, were you . . . you know?' Lily's eyes were round. Becca nodded, her eyes brimming with amusement. 'That's disgusting.' Lily sounded as appalled as any puritan.

Becca laughed and squeezed her shoulders. 'Never mind. Did you enjoy it?'

Lily nodded. 'It was fun,' she said in surprise. 'Though it's well out of order seeing your mum doing stuff like that. Honestly, Mum, you should have said. It's not right.'

'I see.' Becca gave her a hug, because she was Lily, and she loved her for being there and being so appalled at a 350-year-old play. 'Well, it's only for two more nights, and then like Cinderella, it's back to the kitchen.'

Lily obviously thought that was a reasonable proposition. 'That dress . . . it's a bit, well, don't you think you're a bit old for that sort of thing?'

'It's what they wore. And no, I don't think I'm too old for that sort of thing,' Becca said. She thought she looked rather good as a Restoration wench. 'Did Dad come?'

Lily looked shifty. 'I didn't see him. But that doesn't mean he wasn't there, there were loads of people. Really, loads, I mean I thought there'd only be about six people in the audience and there were masses,' she added, her face earnest, as if that was compensation for there not being a particular forty-four year old man.

Had he forgotten? Or could he simply not be bothered? Becca bit her lip on all the things she wanted to say about Lily's father. She tried to keep the bitterness out of her voice. 'Never mind. You came, and that's all that matters.' She gave Lily a hug. 'Now, I must get changed and take my make-up off.'

A knock at the door. 'Everybody decent?' Paul stuck his head round the door. 'Thank you, ladies, that was wonderful. Mr Wycherley will be happy in paradise tonight. I've just a few notes, so if you could all come tomorrow by six thirty so I can run through them, I'd be grateful. And there are drinks waiting for us at the pub, so I hope everyone can come along and raise a glass to the success of *The Country Wife*. See you there.'

His words galvanised the dressing room, and there was a flurry of unlacing and removal of dresses and petticoats.

'Wait for me, Lily, I'll only be a few minutes,' Becca said, taking her headdress off and throwing it onto the dressing table where it bumped into her only good luck cards, one from Lily, one from Paul. Martin hadn't even remembered that. The elation curdled in the pit of her stomach.

'But aren't you going with the others for a drink?' Lily said.

Becca shook her head. 'I'm not in the mood, and how will you get home otherwise? I'm not going to send you back alone on the last bus. I can have a drink with the cast another night. Go and wait for me in the foyer, and I'll be along in a sec.'

Lily left the dressing room, and Becca quickly changed, glamorous Becca peeling off with the white make-up, leaving ordinary Becca behind deflated like an overblown balloon. Martin hadn't even bothered to show up. Her mouth in the mirror had settled into an upside-down crescent of disappointment. No wonder Lady Fidget wanted to run off with Mr Horner, she thought, when stuck with boring, stupid, careless Sir Jasper. She hung the dress on the hanger, and the sleeves hung down, the cheap fabric limp and tawdry. Hey ho, back to real life.

She made her way upstairs to the foyer, which was full of people in winter coats talking with animation and laughter. Everybody had had a good night out. She spotted Lily's black tufty hair, and next to her was Martin. He came across as soon as he saw her and gave her a hug. 'Becca, I'm so sorry, I got held up at work, I couldn't avoid it.'

She gave a taut smile, wanting to hang on to some of the remnants of her happiness at the performance. It was a reasonable explanation, except he always managed to get home on time if it was a running evening. 'It doesn't matter, Martin. Really. It's just a play.'

'Becca, I am really sorry. By the time I got home, I knew I'd missed the beginning, and there didn't seem any point in coming in for the second half.'

She couldn't keep the anger and bitterness under control, they had to burst out. 'You knew how much it mattered to me.' She stopped, trying to control the sour cauldron of feelings swirling inside her.

'Of course I did, but I was held up – it was a work problem, I had to talk it over.'

'Mum, Dad. Don't quarrel,' Lily said, putting one hand on Becca's arm, her forehead puckered. 'He's said he's sorry.'

'We're not quarrelling,' Becca said, shoving her hands into her coat pockets. She wasn't going to squabble in front of Lily.

Martin put his arm around her shoulder. 'Look, why don't we all go out for a meal and celebrate.'

She twisted away so his arm fell, not quarrelling in front of Lily forgotten in the fatuousness of what he said. 'Celebrate what? My performance, which you couldn't be bothered to come and see? Besides, we've all eaten. At least, Lily and I did earlier, and I left your dinner out for you.'

'Yes, I ate it, it was very nice. Delicious, in fact.'

'So what's the point of suggesting we go out for a meal?' Becca put her hand over her mouth to stop more harsh words coming out. Lily's face was pinched.

Martin's face crumpled like a Labrador puppy's that's widdled on the carpet and is waiting for a smack from a rolled-up newspaper. 'I'll make it up to you, I promise. I can't come tomorrow, but I'll be at the next night, I promise.'

Becca felt exhausted, hating herself for upsetting both Lily and

Martin, but also feeling it was all Martin's fault and somehow he'd twisted it so she got the blame. 'Whatever. I just want to go home now.'

She searched for her gloves in her coat pocket when she felt a tap on her shoulder. 'Are you coming, Becca?' Victoria joined them and tucked her arm in Becca's.

Becca shook her head, politely smiling. 'No, I'm off home.'

'But you can't! First night drinks is an absolute tradition. You can't not come with us.' Victoria boomed. She turned to Martin and wagged a finger at him, obviously carrying the performance of Old Lady Squeamish into real life, like a bona fide Method actor. 'Tell her she's got to come with us, it's compulsory.'

'Why don't you go and have a drink with the others?' Martin said gently. 'I'll take Lily home.'

All Becca wanted was to get home and have a shower, where no one would notice if she was crying, not even herself. She shook her head. 'I'm not in the mood.'

'Go on.' He gave Lily's shoulders a hug. 'We'll be OK, won't we, Lily?'

'Yeah, you go, Mum. You deserve it.'

'I really don't want to,' Becca said, feeling trapped by Victoria's beaming presence, trapped by Martin being so apologetic, trapped by Lily's anxiety.

'Oh don't be so silly,' Victoria said, thumping her on the back. 'You've got first night blues, that's all. What you need is a decent drink or three inside you. See you in the bar!' And Victoria sailed off, roughly the same shape as a Russian doll in her winter coat and scarf.

Martin kissed Becca's cheek. 'I'll take Lily home, and you go with your friends and have a nice time.' He paused, and she knew she should say something to stop him looking so worried, but she couldn't. It was his fault, and saying sorry didn't make it better. He squeezed her upper arm. 'I am really sorry.'

She couldn't bear the look in his eyes and nodded. 'I know you are.' She kissed Lily. 'Thank you for coming, darling, and thank you for those lovely flowers. I'll see you back at home.'

Martin and Lily went through the doors, leaving Becca stranded in the foyer. There were still people milling around, and several times she was asked if she was going for a drink. She gave a non-committal shrug and shake of the head that could mean anything. She didn't want to be with the rest of the cast, with their bouncing good humour, taking part in a noisy post mortem of the performance. She didn't want to go home, to Martin's apologies which good manners said she had to accept and forgive. She decided to take the car and drive somewhere, anywhere.

She rummaged in her bag for her car keys, and then remembered Lily's flowers. So sweet of Lily to think of them, and she'd left them in the dressing room. It would be nicer to have them at home, where she'd enjoy them more. She headed downstairs to the dressing rooms again. It was strange, seeing them empty after all the earlier activity. Victoria's dress had slid off its wire hanger, so Becca put it back, smoothing out the creases. She felt in limbo land; the argument with Martin had unsettled her, bursting into her elation and destroying her sense of achievement. She made an effort for his things, why couldn't he make an effort for hers? Because he doesn't care, the answer came winging back. He doesn't care. The door opened and she turned away to hide her tears from whoever it was.

'Becca? Victoria said you weren't coming on for a drink so I hoped I'd find you before you went.' It was Paul. 'Hey, what's the matter? It's not about the play is it? You were really good, there's no need for you to be upset.'

'It's not that.' Becca sniffed, wiping her mouth with the back of her hand. Her mouth quivered, she gulped back a sob. 'Something else.'

Then Paul's arms were around her, and his voice was murmuring in her ear as though he were soothing a child: 'Shh, don't cry. It'll be all right. Don't cry. Shh.'

She hung on to him, feeling his arms strong around her, comforting. He was taller than Martin so she nestled into his arms, his smell strange and unknown but exciting. It was tempting to stay like that for ever, but her sensible self emerged. 'I'm sorry,' she said, pulling away from him and wiping her face with her hands. 'I think I'm just a bit overtired.'

'It's not about the play?' His face was concerned.

She shook her head. 'No, the play's the one good thing in my life at the moment. It's all the other stuff.' Like Martin. Like June. She tried a smile. 'I hope I haven't got mascara all over your chest.'

He glanced down. 'Looks OK. Anyway, I'm sure it'll come out in the wash.' He grinned at her, but his eyes were sympathetic.

'Send me the dry-cleaning bill, if you want.'

'I wanted to give you something. A first night present. Here.' He handed her a small package wrapped in black paper with a black and white ribbon tied around it. She took it, looking quizzically up at him, then carefully undid the package, smoothing the paper out with her fingers. Inside was a book, hardback with gold along the edge of the paper. 'Shakespeare's Sonnets' was written on the front in gold lettering.

'It's lovely, thank you.' Becca smiled up at him, then dropped her eyes, suddenly shy. She turned the book over in her hands. There was a purple satin book marker and she opened it between Sonnets 22 and 23. 'As an imperfect actor on the stage . . .' she read aloud. She finished the sonnet, her whole body glowing with the richness of the language, then looked inside the front cover. Paul had written in it, his writing looping extravagantly around the Bs and the P: 'To Becca, with best wishes, Paul Fitzwilliam.'

Becca clasped the book tightly. 'Thank you,' she whispered, nodding, feeling she might be overwhelmed by emotions.

'Don't be sad.' He touched her cheek with one finger. One finger, that's all it took for all thoughts of the outside world to vanish, one stroke of a cheek, for Lily and Martin and June and Frank and everything else to evaporate, one slide of skin against skin for her whole being to focus in on what was happening between them, between Paul and her, right there, right now, no past, no future, just present. Then Paul tilted her chin with his hand, and kissed her.

Chapter 13

Did she think about protesting when Paul kissed her? Not for one second. It seemed right. Their mouths came together as if they were old-time lovers, no clash of teeth or awkward dodging around noses. His mouth was soft on hers, sweet and forbidden. She felt as if she had been lit from inside by a ray of pure light, intense and sharp. It was something beyond her knowledge, she was hooked on the present moment, and the sensations that spread out from her obliterated any thought of the world beyond the dressing room.

Her hands slid up round his neck, touching the soft short hair like velour about his collar, his hand clasped the back of her skull holding her firmly to him, securing her compliance. Not that there was any need for that; she was lost in wanting him. They could have been there for a minute or an hour before they separated. He was smiling at her, a smile she hadn't seen before, a smile of warmth and intimacy and she was smiling back the same smile.

And then reality asserted itself. Her arms fell down by her side and she stepped away from him. 'I shouldn't be doing this.' She was shocked at what had just happened. 'I'm so sorry, I shouldn't have, I've never—'

'I know. I shouldn't have either,' Paul said, looking equally aghast now.

'It wasn't your fault, I wanted—' She stopped, uncertain of what she wanted. I wanted to kiss you, and now I have. 'Just ignore it, pretend it didn't happen. I'm so sorry. Oh, this is so embarrassing.' The words were tumbling out of her, she couldn't look him in the face. She retreated to the far side of the room, needing to put distance between them.

The words were tumbling out of Paul too. 'Look, it's OK. Spur of the moment thing, that's all. I'd hate you to think I was taking advantage of you being upset, I wasn't, I really wasn't, I shouldn't have—'

'It wasn't your fault, it was me, I was all over the place, I was upset by something, my husband actually, he upset me a bit – well quite a lot in fact – but it's no excuse, I shouldn't have kissed you, oh dear, I'm so sorry—'

'It was my fault, I couldn't help myself, you looked so unhappy it seemed the obvious thing to do, I don't want you to think I make a habit of kissing married women. Obviously, it'll never happen again, I assure you . . .'

'No, obviously, it would be dreadful, goodness it's embarrassing enough as it is . . .'

'Not that it wasn't very nice, I mean, because it was, but . . .'

'I know. You're married, I'm married. It was just one of those things.'

'Yes, one of those things.'

'Not to be—'

'No, never.'

They stopped. Becca stared at the floor. She could see that a lipstick had rolled under Rosie's table and lodged next to a discarded bit of tissue. She touched her mouth, thinking about Paul kissing her. Had it really happened? She glanced up at him. He was examining the grain of one of the tables, his forefinger tracing the pattern. As if he could feel her gaze, he looked across and met her eyes. The silence grew between them. His eyes were piercing, she felt he could read her soul. She wanted him to kiss her again.

The door opened, making them both jump as if they'd been caught out doing something, and the caretaker peered in. 'You're still here then.' He had an accusing tone.

'Just leaving,' Paul said. 'We'll be a couple of minutes.'

'Right,' the caretaker said. 'A couple of minutes. Everyone else has gone.'

'We're just finishing off here.' Paul smiled at the man, who sighed heavily, then left. Paul looked across to Becca, his expression serious as if he were working something out in his mind. Probably how to get out of the room with the least embarrassment and hassle.

Becca gave herself a shake. It will only be embarrassing if you let it be, she told herself. 'Well, I must be going,' she said briskly. 'Thank you so much for the book. I'll treasure it for ever.'

'My pleasure.' He followed her out of the dressing room, turning the lights off as they went. They walked in silence up the steps to the foyer, Paul's step matching hers, their arms touching from time to time, the brush of his sleeve as electric to Becca as forked lightning. Outside the hall they turned to each other. 'Sure you're not coming for a drink with everyone?' Paul said.

Becca nodded. 'I'd best go back. Tomorrow, perhaps.'

Inconsequential talk, meaning nothing. For a fleeting second he bent his head and kissed her cheek. 'I'll see you tomorrow,' he said, his voice suddenly husky.

'Tomorrow.' Becca walked away from him, desperate to look back, determined not to. Just before she turned the corner at the end of the street she did look back, and he was standing, watching her. He raised his hand in a farewell gesture. She paused, then gave a little wave before rushing on. She couldn't stop smiling all the way to the car.

Once in the car it seemed like a fantasy. Had the kiss really happened? She looked at herself in the mirror. I've just kissed Paul

Fitzwilliam, a man who isn't my husband. She put her hands to her face, and her eyes stared back at her over her fingers, eyes wide and glowing. It had been years since anyone other than Martin had kissed her. Years. Paul was a wonderful kisser.

And that's all very well, she told herself as she started the car up, but it didn't mean anything. It didn't mean anything to Paul, and it doesn't mean anything to me. No, it doesn't. It really doesn't. Everybody knows a kiss doesn't mean anything nowadays. She could remember seeing Dawn French on a chat show, boasting that she was a brilliant kisser, and then snogging one of the other guests, just like that, and she was married. Paul had probably forgotten all about it already.

The noise of a car door slamming further down the street made her turn her head. A couple were arguing by their car. The woman was wagging her finger at the man, who waved his hands ineffect- ually. She wore spiky black heels that mirrored the sharpness of her pointing finger, and had plenty to say. Equally obvious was that the man had no intention of listening to her. He rolled his eyes and shrugged, and heaved his shoulders, but there were no signs of change.

That's what Martin makes me feel like, Becca realised. Her lips tightened. If he'd listened to her, he'd have made the effort to come, even halfway through, because he knew how much the play mattered to her. Turning up at the end didn't count. What had he said? It was some work problem. Typical. Everything with Martin was now work, or running, or both. If Martin had been there, she wouldn't have kissed Paul. So it was all Martin's fault.

She drove back home thinking dark thoughts about Martin. What kind of man was it who forgot something so important to his wife? She saw herself on the witness stand addressing the jury, telling them about the play and how much it had mattered to her and how Martin had forgotten about it until it was too late for the beginning, then calmly eaten his dinner that his wife had lovingly prepared for him, and had pitched up at the end. All eyes turned to Martin standing in the dock, looking appropriately sheepish.

'I'm sorry. I was held up at work,' he bleated.

'That's no excuse,' the judge in Becca's head said. 'You should have made a point of getting home in time. As it is, I have no option but to direct the jury to find you guilty as charged.'

Becca in the witness stand tried not to look smug. The judge turned to her. 'But it's no excuse for you either. Your husband may have been careless, may have been inconsiderate, but that's not grounds for kissing—'

'Yes, well, tough,' Becca said out loud as she pulled into a space outside her house. 'It was only a kiss. It's not as if I did anything else.' People were always kissing, especially actors, and it didn't mean a thing. First night, and all that. She tried to conjure up a picture of Paul laughing and chatting in the bar, but her imagination preferred a wistful Paul staring into his pint while the rest of the cast chattered animatedly around him, dreaming of kissing her again. And again and again and again.

Stop it.

She squeezed her eyes together as tight as possible for a brief second to wake herself up. Stop it now. Think about Martin, think about reality, think about marriage and fidelity and all those other things.

Martin must have been waiting for her, because he opened the door as she turned her key in the lock. 'You didn't stay long. Did you have a nice time?'

'Yes, thanks,' she said tersely, fiddling to get her key out of the lock. It was one thing to think a kiss was nothing, it was quite another to believe it when meeting your husband. She couldn't bear to meet his eyes in case her guilt was written across them.

But he must have assumed her reticence was due to anger. 'Becca, I'm so sorry. I feel like a complete toad for missing your first night.'

'It's OK,' she said, coming into the kitchen and dumping her stuff on the table. She searched the cupboard for a vase for Lily's flowers.

'Why don't I make you a cup of tea? Or would you rather have a drink? I put some white wine in the fridge, or I've got some red open? Tell me what you want.' His puppyish eagerness stung her.

'Nothing. Thanks.' She mustered a smile. 'Really. I'm very tired, I think I'll go straight to bed.'

'Whatever you want.' He put out a hand to touch her arm, but let it drop before he reached her. 'I know I deserve one hundred per cent to be in the dog house, but really, I am genuinely sorry that I missed the performance.'

'You're not in the dog house,' she said, quickly, still unable to look at him in case 'I kissed another man tonight' was lit in neon across her forehead.

'I deserve to be.'

'Yes – and no. Has Lily gone to bed?' she asked, moving swiftly on before she gave the game away. She'd never had secrets from Martin before, she'd always told him everything, and now this great secret lurked like the pile of elephant dung in the corner. Any minute Martin would turn round and see the elephant.

He nodded. 'She went up as soon as we got back. She said you were excellent. The best thing in the play.'

'Hardly that.' Becca smiled. 'She's a good girl, really.'

'Becca . . .' He took her hands and held them. Her arms felt stiff and awkward, unable to relax. 'How can I make it up to you? Shall I grovel? Oh, Becca,' he wailed in mock apology, 'I'm so, so sorry, forgive meeee.'

She had this horrible feeling that if she opened her mouth she might blurt that she'd kissed Paul Fitzwilliam. And worse, had liked it. And even worse, wanted to do it again. But she wasn't going to. No. No more kissing. 'It's OK, you're forgiven.' She disengaged her hands from his, then patted his shoulder awkwardly. 'Really.'

Martin raised his eyebrows. 'Obviously not forgiven. Will try harder.'

'It's my fault, I'm in a funny mood tonight.'

'You're probably coming down from your evening of triumph.' He moved towards her as if he was going to hug her. 'I really am—'

'Just don't say it again,' Becca snapped, instinctively putting out her hands to ward him off. Then she realised what she was doing and dropped them. 'I'm sorry.'

Martin gave a sharp bark of humourless laughter. 'That makes two of us.'

Becca knew she ought to hug him, console him, make up with him, but her arms remained by her side. 'I'm tired. I'm going to bed.'

He didn't meet her eyes and she knew he was hurt. 'I'll be up in a minute.'

As she went upstairs to bed she tried to tell herself that it was his fault, that he should be sorry, that missing her first night was unforgivable. Which it was, but there was no getting round that what she had done was worse by far. *If I feel guilty like this after just a kiss, it doesn't bear thinking about what it would be like if I'd gone any further,* she thought as she undressed and got ready for bed. *I couldn't cope with the guilt. A kiss might not matter to some people, but it mattered to her. This is reality,* she told herself as she brushed her teeth. *This is real. Paul Fitzwilliam is fantasy. Martin is real. And I do love him, even if he can be thoughtless.* She got into bed and turned her light out, but when Martin got in she turned to him. 'Darling? Sorry for being such a bitch,' she whispered.

He kissed her. 'My fault, I deserved it.'

'No you didn't.' She kissed him back, willing the kiss to be as wonderful as with Paul. She pushed herself at him, suddenly hungry, feeling a desperate need to reclaim herself as Martin's wife, not the Becca who kissed Paul with such glowing urgency. Without ceremony or, more to the point, foreplay, he swivelled himself on top of her, as if his need for her was also urgent. She gasped, and in the darkness suddenly it was Paul on top of her, Paul who kissed her neck, her face, her shoulders, she put her head back and arched to receive him, hands gripping, fingers deep into shoulders, legs locked around his back, and her body bucked and writhed and then, and then, and then she almost said his name aloud and bit her lip to stop crying out for him, because she wanted him so badly.

When they had finished, and she had unwrapped her legs, she was surprised to find Martin staring at her, a smile on his face, and it was as if he were a stranger.

Chapter 14

Becca went up the stairs to the church hall, and pushed the door open as conflicting emotions jostled in her brain. Pleasure at seeing Paul. Dread at seeing Paul. Embarrassment that he would remember and be embarrassed himself, worried that he might have forgotten. Given half a chance she'd have left the theatre, but that would have left everyone in the lurch and she couldn't do that. No, she had to brave it out. A moment of madness, that's all it was, for both of them.

Most of the cast were already there, sitting on the front rows of the auditorium. The atmosphere was different. The first night had been and gone, now it was up to them to do it all again. Becca imagined that they now had the air of seasoned professionals, relaxed and willing. She edged into a seat behind Victoria, who turned and smiled. 'How are you feeling?'

Becca nodded. 'Last night seems a bit of a dream.' And how, she thought.

'But fun. We'll have to see what our lord and master thought.' She indicated Paul, who had detached one of the chairs and placed it in front of them. Becca's eyes fixed on him, but he gave no sign of having noticed her.

'Right, everyone. Can we get started? I'm sure you're all raring to go and get ready.' He smiled around at the cast, that combination of steely and friendly that he'd used in rehearsals. Everyone settled down. Paul gave comments – move a little closer at that point, don't forget the business here, you can go further on the comedy there. 'And Victoria, only the director is allowed to make cuts.'

Everybody laughed, and Victoria wailed, 'Oh, I do feel awful, Paul. I'm so sorry, everyone. I'll try not to do it again.'

Becca didn't get many directorial comments, but what he said was delivered in an impersonal way, just the same as everyone else. Perversely she was disappointed. She wanted to be treated differently, to hear his voice take on a warmer tone when he said her name. But no, she got the same friendly but clipped intonation as everyone else.

'And can we pay attention in the curtain call? Remember, it's the last thing the audience sees of the cast, so let's keep it together, keep it quick, keep it tight – on stage, line up, bow or curtsy, then off. No hanging around. Take your cue from Michael and Rosie in the centre. And smile please! Any questions?'

Do you want to kiss me again? Becca thought.

'No? Then, many thanks for your attention, and see you on stage in twenty minutes.'

Twenty minutes? Becca checked her watch as adrenaline rushed through her body. It couldn't be due to start in twenty minutes. She looked up at Paul, feeling stricken. He made a move as if to join her.

'We'd better be quick,' Victoria said, linking arms with Becca, and when she looked at Paul again, he had turned to Angela, and was deep in discussion with her.

'I feel sick,' Becca said, hand to her stomach. Nerves might be called butterflies, but she felt as if the annual migration to the Serengeti was going on inside her. 'I don't think I could do this for a living.'

'Didn't Laurence Olivier keep a bucket backstage so he could be sick into it before going on?' Victoria said as they walked down the stairs to the dressing room. 'It's supposed to be the nerves that keep you on your toes.'

'Sounds horrible.'

Victoria glanced round with a conspiratorial air. 'We're doing a collection for Paul and Angela for a card and a present each,' she whispered as she pushed open the door to the dressing room. 'Do you want to join in?'

'Of course,' Becca said, fumbling for her purse as she followed Victoria in.

'I thought you might have some idea of what he might like.'

'Me?' Becca stared at her, feeling the colour rise in her cheeks as she handed a ten-pound note across. 'Why would I know?'

Victoria took the note. 'You always seem friendly, always chatting to him.'

'No, I'm not,' Becca said, feeling the tension in her voice. 'I never chat to him. Never.'

Victoria looked surprised. 'I thought you seemed quite close.'

'I don't know why you thought that,' Becca said, busying herself with organising her make-up. 'I hardly know him. Certainly not more than anyone else.'

'OK,' Victoria said, backing off. 'I just wondered.'

Every time there was a knock on the door, Becca couldn't help but look up to see if it was Paul, but was disappointed every time. Perhaps because time is short before we go on, that's why he hasn't come round, Becca thought. Oh dear. Perhaps it's because he's mortified.

The play started. Becca was in the first scene, and she was grateful for that, as it took her mind off Paul. No sign of him backstage, either then or at the interval. Feeling restless, instead of waiting in the dressing room she went upstairs and waited in the wings, watching the actors on stage. Rosie, as Margery, was writing her letter to Mr Horner at the dictation of her husband, Pinchwife. It was a funny scene, and they were getting plenty of laughs. '"Though

I suffered last night your kisses and embraces . . ."' Becca turned away and wandered off towards the dressing room, not sure if waiting in the wings was making her more, or less, nervous. She sat halfway down the concrete steps. The china scene was next. As far as she could see, Lady Fidget was happy to make love to anybody, including Horner, the most notorious of lovers, so long as no one knew. But she hates her husband, and I don't hate Martin, she thought.

A hand touched the nape of her neck and without looking she knew who it was. Paul sat next to her, and leaned forward with his elbows on his knees. 'Are you OK?'

She stared at the floor. 'As much as I'll ever be.'

'Not as nervous this time, I expect.'

'Worse,' she said. 'Paul, about last night . . .'

He sat up, and swivelled round to her. 'Say no more. It was a mistake.'

'Yes,' she said, relieved he felt the same way. 'I don't know what got into me, I think it was nerves. I am sorry.'

'Don't be. These things happen I suppose.' He raised her hand to his lips and kissed her fingers, a casual gesture that suddenly became charged as their eyes met. She nodded, unable to speak for the tension between them. He turned her hand over and kissed her palm, the inside of her wrist. Her arm felt heavy as his tongue traced a pattern over her veins. He slid his arm around her waist and pulled her towards him. Their mouths met, deeper and harder this time, urgent and demanding. I shouldn't be doing this, Becca thought, pressing herself against him.

Suddenly Paul pulled away from her, and listened. 'You're on!' He pulled her to her feet and rushed her up the stairs, before she could recover herself.

Victoria and Brian were waiting in the wings. 'Where have you been? We thought you were going to miss your cue,' Victoria hissed.

Becca shook her head, unable to speak, her chest heaving. No wonder they called them bodice rippers, she felt her heart might burst out of the constraining corset. And then she was on. ' "Well, Horner, am not I a woman of honour . . . ?" '

Ten minutes later she was offstage, as the character of Lady Fidget went into Mr Horner's bedchamber, while Sir Jasper waited for her in Mr Horner's living room on stage, assuming she was looking at china. But of course Lady Fidget and Mr Horner had other things on their mind than porcelain.

As she went off, she found Paul waiting for her in the wings. 'Don't do that again,' she muttered. 'My heart won't stand for it.'

'Took your mind off your nerves, though, didn't it?' He grinned at her.

'Practically gave me heart failure,' Becca grumbled, her heart racing with excitement at his presence.

He leaned forwards and kissed her. 'You know you like it really.'

The kiss deepened until Becca was brought back to reality by Brian as Sir Jasper calling: ' "Wife! My Lady Fidget! Wife! He is coming in to you the back way." '

Becca broke off kissing Paul to call from the wings. ' "Let him come and welcome, which way he will." ' There was an authentic breathless quality to her voice, as if she had indeed been making love. The line got a huge laugh.

' "He'll catch you, and use you roughly, and be too strong for you," ' Brian replied from on stage.

Oh, if only Brian knew what Becca was doing, she thought as she answered him. ' "Don't you trouble yourself, let him if he can." ' Paul nipped her ear lobe, and she gave an authentic squeak. More laughter from the audience. If only they knew, she thought again, as Paul kissed her more. If only they knew.

Becca loitered in the dressing room after the show, having arranged with Paul that they'd slip off to have a drink together, away from the others. Lucky for her that Martin couldn't make that night's performance. She took her time to change and take the white make-up off – Paul had been careful not to smudge it earlier – then carefully reapplied a newer, modern layer. It took twice as long to create a natural look as the old-fashioned version.

'I'll definitely come for a drink tomorrow night, I'm not being unfriendly, honestly, but tonight I want to get home early,' Becca told Victoria who was bustling around and organising everyone as usual. She thought it was lucky Victoria didn't register that for someone who wanted to get home early, she was taking a long time getting changed. 'Tomorrow night, I promise.'

Paul must have been lurking outside the dressing room because he slipped in as soon as the others had gone.

'We must be careful,' Becca said as he kissed her. 'What if someone comes back?'

'Then I'll just say: excuse me, can you come back in fifteen minutes as I'm kissing the most beautiful woman in the world.'

Becca smiled. 'You'd be lying.'

'You're right – fifteen minutes isn't long enough. I need hours and hours and hours . . .' He leaned forward, but Becca pulled back.

'Paul . . .' She hesitated, not sure of what she wanted to say. 'Is this right?' It sounded lame and pathetic. Moralistic, even.

'Right?' He touched her hair. 'I've wanted to kiss you for ages. Ever since I met you, in fact.'

Becca felt her heart give a leap of excitement. 'Really?'

He nodded. 'Of course.' He stroked her face, his hand gentle.

Becca leaned into his hand, feeling the dear warmth of it on her chin. She tried to keep a grip on some perspective. 'We're married,' she murmured. 'We shouldn't be doing this.'

'I know,' Paul said, turning away from her. 'I know. But there's what we should be doing, and what I want to do. I can't believe you don't feel the same.'

'No.' Becca kissed the palm of his hand. 'But it's not just about us. There's Martin, and Suzy. Our children.'

'They don't have to know.'

Becca kissed his palm again, playing for time. She wanted him so much, but she also knew that this was dangerous. Stop before you go too far. 'I think we ought to forget it.'

'Forget what?'

'What's happened.' Her voice was very small.

Paul held her face in both hands to keep her locked to him and in her head the violins swelled and the fireworks exploded. There was something about the gesture that seemed to belong in a black and white movie. It was old fashioned and intensely romantic. 'If that's what you really, truly want,' he said. She closed her eyes, in case he could read the naked longing in them. 'Look at me.' Obediently she looked up. 'Kiss me.' So she did.

Suddenly the door opened and they sprang away from each other. 'There you are,' Victoria said, as if Becca had been playing hide and seek as part of a children's game. 'Didn't you know you've got friends upstairs? They've been waiting for you for ages. I said I'd come down and find you.'

'Me?' Becca was sure she was red in the face. She didn't dare look at Paul, who was flicking through a copy of the play. Becca supposed he thought it made it look as if they had been discussing something play related. Like china. She dropped her eyes from Victoria's curious gaze. 'Who was it?'

'Crystal, she said her name was. She watched the play tonight and wants to take you out for a drink at Bar Ha Ha.' Her eyes travelled from Becca to Paul and back again. 'Shall I let her know if you're coming?'

'No, tell her I'll meet her there,' Becca said, grabbing her handbag. 'Paul was just giving me a few notes.'

'I see.' Victoria gave them one last lingering look, then left. Paul checked the door was closed behind her.

'That was close,' Becca said. 'What if she'd caught us?'

Paul shrugged. 'Would it matter? Why would she say anything? She probably knows anyway.'

'Why would she know?'

'It must have been pretty obvious I had a . . . fondness for you.'

'Really? Did you? I didn't notice.'

He kissed her. 'So long as you've noticed now.'

'Oh yes,' Becca said, snuggling into him. 'Very much so.'

'We've ordered champagne!' Crystal said, standing up and waving at Becca, who had just entered the bar. Becca made her way through the press of people towards their table. Crystal hugged her. 'You were wonderful, darling! Isn't that what actors say?'

'I don't know,' Becca said, kissing her. 'I don't know any.' The last thing she felt like was champagne. All she wanted to do was snuggle up in a corner with Paul. Just the thought of him being there in a few minutes' time made her catch her breath. Crystal introduced her to Harry, her latest man. He looked pleasant enough, although Crystal usually favoured men with more dramatic, Mediterranean dark looks and Harry had mousy hair and pale-blue eyes. Perhaps she could quickly drink the champagne and then Crystal and Harry would go. She knew she shouldn't be so curmudgeonly, that she should be grateful Crystal had come to support her, but she longed to be alone with Paul.

Harry poured the champagne out and handed Becca a glass. 'Are you expecting some more people?' Becca asked, noting five glasses on the table.

'Didn't you see Martin?' Crystal said brightly. 'He said he was going to wait for you at the theatre.'

Chapter 15

Becca practically choked on her champagne, and had to be thumped on the back by Harry. 'Martin? He said he couldn't come tonight.' She spoke sharply, cold to her core at the thought that Martin had been in the audience. 'Why didn't he come to the dressing room after the show?'

'Oh, were we allowed to? I didn't know. Drat, I'd have loved to come through.' Crystal sipped her champagne. 'Cheers anyway. You were fab.'

'Where's Martin now?' Becca said. The condensation on the glass was making her fingers cold and damp.

'Oh, he'll be along any second. He's with that girl – what's her name, Harry?'

'Search me,' Harry said. 'Pretty thing though.'

Crystal gave him a not entirely friendly shove. 'Not that pretty. And far too young for you, anyway, so mitts off.'

Becca automatically smiled while trying to work out who on earth could they mean? Why was Martin with a girl, pretty or otherwise? Crystal knew Lily so it couldn't be her.

Her question was answered by Martin pushing through the crowd towards them. 'Sorry to be late,' he said giving Becca a hug. 'You were good, darling, really good. I'm so proud of you.'

'You said you couldn't make tonight.' Becca felt sick. What if

Martin had seen her and Paul in the dressing room? And where was Paul? She had to warn him somehow. She didn't want him to meet Martin, but how could she stop it?

'Four of the team called in sick, so we're going to have our dinner next week,' Martin said. 'I've brought Una along too.' Una was the one who ran with Martin and Ian. She wasn't a pretty little thing, as far as Becca could remember. She was plump, with glasses and frizzy hair. 'She'll be here in a sec – she went to get something out of her car,' Martin said.

'You didn't run to the theatre then,' Becca said sharply. Martin looked at her and she felt herself flush. 'Have some champagne,' she said, making free with Crystal's champagne and handing him a glass.

'Thanks. Ah, there's Una.' He waved. 'Over here.'

A slim girl with sleek hair squeezed through the crush of people to their table. Not the Una Becca remembered. No frizz, no glasses, no plump.

Martin made the introductions. 'A toast,' he said. 'To Becca, and her success.'

They all raised their glasses in her direction. Becca looked around at their cheerful faces. 'Thanks,' she said, wishing they'd all evaporate. Paul would be here soon, and then what? Getting rid of Crystal was one thing, Martin quite another.

They started to talk about the play, asking questions about the characters which Becca did her best to answer with one eye on the door. Then she saw him. Her whole body shot on to alert. 'So Una, how are you finding the running?' she said, fixing her eyes on Una while her body quivered inwardly for Paul.

'It's been much better now Martin's training with us – to be honest, Ian's pretty fit and it's been hard to keep up with him. But Martin's more at my pace.'

Too long a pause. Becca snapped to attention. 'How long have you been running?' Was that the right question? It appeared it was as Una answered.

'Since the new year – I realised I'd put on so much weight over Christmas that I had to do something to lose it, and running seemed the only answer. It was hell at the beginning, but now I just love it.' She nodded vigorously. Becca nodded back, not really listening.

A hand on her shoulder. The lightest of touches. 'Sorry I'm late.'

Every sinew sang as if she were a Stradivarius responding to Toscanini as she turned to face him. 'Paul.'

His face was guarded. 'I'd like you to meet my wife Suzy.'

Becca gave a short gasp, she couldn't help it, then gave her broadest smile and put her hand out. 'Hello, it's a pleasure to meet you.' Suzy's hand slipped into hers for the briefest of moments. Her hand was cold from outside, but her eyes were even colder. Becca forced herself into hostess mode. 'This is my husband, Martin, and Crystal and Harry. And Una. And this is Paul, the director, and his wife Suzy.'

Crystal waved at Paul and Suzy from the other side of the table. 'We loved the play, we thought it was brilliant. Are you an actress too?'

Suzy shook her head, a tight smile on her lips. 'No.' There was a note of complete finality.

'Let me get you a drink,' Martin said, moving towards the bar. 'I'll grab some more glasses.'

'We don't want to disturb you,' Suzy said, smiling sweetly. Normally when people demurred like that it was for show, but there was something about the way she said it that made Martin pause. 'I only came because I thought Paul needed a lift back. He was very late home last night.'

'First night drinks,' Paul said, the edge in his voice as sharp as Suzy's haircut. 'You knew that. And we can stay for a drink tonight too,' he added, looking at her, his jaw tense.

Suzy tightened her lips, then inclined her head slightly. 'Just one then.'

'I'll get the glasses.' Martin flickered a look across to Becca, and winked, obviously noting the little power struggle between Paul and Suzy, but Becca was too thrown to wink back. This wasn't what she had imagined at all. Now there was a whole Greek chorus round the table, including her husband and Paul's wife.

'I hear you're an expert on Shakespeare,' Crystal said, leaning forward and flashing a bit of cleavage, which Becca guessed was for Harry's benefit.

Paul smiled. 'I wouldn't call myself an expert. I leave that to the academics.'

'Were you in the play?' Suzy asked Crystal.

'Oh no. Just the audience,' Crystal said, appearing slightly taken aback. 'Mind you, I can understand why you might make that mistake, I mean, the make-up was extraordinary, I hardly recognised Becca under all that white stuff.'

'I didn't watch the play.'

'You missed a treat,' Crystal said, looking across to Becca with a big smile. 'Tonight was brilliant.'

'I've seen so much theatre all over the world. Nowadays I only go when I know it's going to be exceptional.' Suzy smiled charmingly at Crystal, who looked baffled as if she wasn't sure whether Suzy had been quite as rude as she appeared to have been.

Paul looked across to Becca. Dimly she heard Harry saying something about the play having been jolly funny. She stared down at the table, half expecting it to spontaneously combust from the heat she felt in her eyes.

'Here we are.' Martin had two more glasses, and another bottle of champagne. Becca dreaded to think how much it had cost. He poured it out. Suzy held the stem between manicured fingers, and sipped with caution. Crystal asked questions about Restoration theatre in a bright 'see how interesting, sociable and cultured I am' way, which Paul answered rather distractedly. Suzy watched Paul, and Becca watched Suzy.

Older than Becca had thought when she'd seen her that first day at the audition, but surely some of those blond streaks were to hide the grey. Her face was immaculately made up. Too well done, it looked like a mask. Blow-dried hair, not Becca's own casual leave-it-to-dry effect. Her clothes were in the smart–casual category but she wore them as if the dry cleaner's plastic bag still surrounded them, keeping her separate from the others. She looked stylish and immaculate and untouchable.

Suddenly she turned and caught Becca's eye. Her own eyes had a peculiar flat quality that made it hard to define what colour they were precisely – blue, brown, green, they could have been all, or none. However, there was no problem in defining her body language. She gave Becca a hard stare as if warning her off her property. Trespassers will be prosecuted, those eyes said.

Becca's brain froze. She couldn't think of a single coherent thing to say, when there was a heavy hand on her shoulder and a familiar rumble of a voice. 'Will you introduce me?'

'Bill!' Normally her heart would have sunk but instead she clung to him like a life raft. 'What are you doing here?'

'I've been attending a very fine production of *The Country Wife*,' Bill said loudly, his eyes fixed in Paul's direction. Paul glanced round briefly and Becca thought he would have turned away again if Bill hadn't leaned forward and stuck out his hand. 'Paul Fitzwilliam, I presume.'

'Er, yes, that's right.' Paul shook his hand.

'Your work is fascinating. Fascinating.'

'Thank you,' Paul said looking cornered, as well he might, since Bill hadn't let go of his hand.

'That article you wrote for the *Sunday Times* – marvellous stuff.'

'Thanks,' Paul said, extracting his hand. 'You must have been the only person who read it.'

'What's he doing here?' Becca muttered to Crystal.

'Sorry,' Crystal muttered back. 'He insisted on knowing all about the performance. I had no idea he was planning an ambush.'

Bill was now talking about his cultural plans for Hamilton House and Paul was leaning back with a look of alarm on his face.

'I've already asked,' Becca said, cutting in.

A flash of annoyance crossed Bill's face. 'Now, now, Rebecca. Let's not jump the gun here.'

'If you mean to ask me about getting involved, I'm afraid Mrs Woods has asked me, and I've respectfully declined.' Paul spoke with an air of finality.

'It could be as little as a talk for our students,' Bill said. 'It wouldn't have to be for an entire day.'

'How much?' Suzy's voice cut across Bill's bluster.

'I beg your pardon?'

'How much, for a day?'

'Ah, well. We're a charitable foundation, you know, we're not a commercial organisation . . .'

'He's not a charity. His day rate's a thousand. Non negotiable.' It wasn't just the gates closing, it wasn't even the portcullis coming down. Suzy's refusal was like stainless-steel doors, smooth and shiny. You couldn't see how the mechanism worked, you only knew that you hadn't a hope in hell of getting through unless you knew the security code. Which Bill obviously didn't.

'Well, I'd better be saying goodnight.' Becca had never seen Bill back down so completely before. 'Good to see you all. Great performance, Rebecca. Great production. And Paul, if you change your mind, you, er . . . well.' Bill scribbled something on a piece of paper and handed it to Paul. 'If you change your mind, here's my name and number. Or ask Rebecca.' He gave an uncertain smile as Paul took the piece of paper and put it in his jacket pocket. He lifted his hand in a sketchy wave, and left. There was an uncertain pause.

'You didn't need to do that,' Paul said quietly.

'It really irritates me, people on salaries assuming you can work for peanuts, when you're a freelance.' Suzy shook her hair as if to clear Bill away.

'You still didn't need to.'

'I do, because you don't. And I don't expect you to; you're an artist, you shouldn't have to haggle, that's my job. You shouldn't be bothered with that sort of thing. People have no idea what it takes to be a creative person, to do the things you do, they just assume that because you make it look easy, it *is* easy. People like that – who does he think he is?'

'This isn't the time.' Paul's face was closed and Becca guessed he was hugely embarrassed by Suzy's fierce defence.

'It shouldn't happen, but it does, time and time again. It's an insult really. He knows who you are, so why does he think you work for free? Artists have to eat too.' Suzy looked at them, as if daring someone to suggest otherwise.

'Speaking of food, does anyone fancy going out for a meal?' Martin said after a short pause. 'Grab a curry maybe?'

'That sounds good – we'd be up for that, wouldn't we, Harry?' Crystal said with relief, turning to Harry who nodded obediently. 'How's the marathon running coming along by the way?'

'Pretty well,' Martin said, and the atmosphere turned from awkward and uncomfortable to something more relaxed and friendly.

'I don't know what you want to run a marathon for,' Harry said as he swigged back another glass of champagne.

'Mixture of reasons. Keeps me fit and out from under Becca's feet.' Martin grinned at the rest of the table. He certainly looked fit, young and energetic with an attractive twinkle in his eyes. Becca felt decidedly ancient. 'Our company decided to get a team together this year. Both Una and I are running.'

'That's brilliant,' Crystal said, smiling at Una. 'A double celebration.'

'I'll drink to that,' Harry said, topping up the glasses.

Martin leaned back in his chair with a faraway look on his face as if imagining himself crossing the finishing line and receiving his medal and silver space blanket.

'Congratulations,' Paul said, shaking his head to more champagne.

'It'll be congratulations if I finish.' Martin grimaced at Una. 'I feel like a fat old dog being dragged round.'

'Hardly fat, Martin. You're looking distinctly svelte,' Crystal said.

Martin looked pleased. 'I don't know about that,' he said, even though Becca knew he spent at least several minutes each morning stepping on and off the scales in the hopes that another pound might have vanished.

'Darling, I'm worried about the au pair,' Suzy said to Paul. 'We really ought to be going.'

'It seems a bit early . . .' Paul looked to Becca.

'I expect you ought to be getting early nights too, if you're in training,' Suzy said to Martin before turning to Crystal and Becca. 'Our au pair is Chinese. We thought it vital that Jack and Willow are exposed to Mandarin at an early age, but she's new and not used to staying up late. I'm sure you understand.'

Crystal and Becca nodded, Becca feeling like a nodding plastic dog at the back of a car lacking control over her own neck muscles, drawn along by the power of Suzy.

'Bye everyone,' Paul said, standing up. 'I'll see you tomorrow, Becca.'

She smiled up at him. 'Until tomorrow.'

On Saturday morning Becca got up as usual, got dressed as usual, ate breakfast as usual, did her domestic chores as usual – or so it must have seemed on the outside. Certainly Martin didn't appear to notice anything different about Becca. In a way, that was the most unnerving thing. It seemed impossible, certainly improbable that Outward Becca should not have changed when Inward Becca was churned up. If someone a few weeks ago – Crystal, for example, it was the sort of question she liked to ask in boring moments at Hamilton House – had asked who knew Becca best, she would have answered without hesitation that it was Martin. Of course it was Martin, he was the one who had been with her in her happiest and most desperate hours. You couldn't be with someone for nearly twenty years without knowing them.

And yet, it appeared you could. It wasn't just the fact that she had kissed another man, it was that she wanted to kiss him again. She wanted to be with Paul. She was counting the hours until the third and final night of the play, when she would be in his presence once again without any of the encumbrances of wives and husbands. Thoughts of Paul and his kisses surged in a tidal wave of energy to occupy most of the space in her conscious brain. Only a few specks of Becca were left to devote to the mundane tasks of everyday living. Suddenly her life had slipped from meandering along B roads and on to the motorway, zooming along at ever increasing speed.

Everything she did had an energy around it like a force field. It was as if Paul had found a hidden switch marked 'Overdrive' and had casually flicked it. Surely Martin had to notice that? But apparently not. Which had to mean that either he didn't know her as well as she'd always assumed, or he'd stopped noticing her. Either way, it was an unsettling thought.

The day washed over her, her focus completely on the moment when she could legitimately leave for the theatre. Frank rang to ask about the production, and announced he was going to come after all, as it was the last night. 'I'm not sure you'll like it,' she said, any chance of meeting up with Paul for a drink after the production flying out of the window.

Frank made a noise of irritation. 'You women all act as if I've no culture whatsoever.'

Becca thought of the argument over conceptual art. Poor Dad, perhaps going to a play was his way of making an effort. 'Of course, you must come if you'd like to. I'll make sure you get a ticket.' She could always say there was a last night cast party that she simply had to attend, and then sneak away to be with Paul.

'That's very kind of you,' Frank said. 'And perhaps I could stay the night.'

'What?'

'As I'm coming for lunch on Sunday. It would make more sense that way. Save too much jiggling around.'

Sunday lunch. Becca inwardly groaned. She'd forgotten all about inviting him the week before, anxious that he was alone. But that had been before Paul had kissed her. For a second she toyed with the idea of putting him off, but only for a second. 'You're right, it does make more sense. I'll make sure the bed in the spare room is all ready for you.'

She arrived at the theatre early, hoping to meet Paul before the cast notes, but there was no sign of him lurking about the foyer, so instead she arranged Frank's ticket for that night. By the time she'd done that, more of the cast had arrived and any chance of having a private chat with Paul seeped away. But at least she got to feast her eyes on him as he gave them notes. Again Becca hoped to detect a softer timbre in his voice when he spoke to her, but couldn't hear it. Her energy faltered. Perhaps the debacle of the previous evening had made him change his mind. He maintained a very professional distance throughout, but as he wished them good luck for the last performance he flashed her a look of pure connection, and she was reassured.

'Are you going to audition for the next show?' Victoria said as the cast drifted down to the dressing room. 'It's a nice Alan Ayckbourn – *The Norman Conquests*.'

'I hadn't thought about it,' Becca said. She didn't think she fancied being conquered, nicely or otherwise. 'Is Paul directing?'

'Heavens, no, we can't afford a professional director twice in a row. No, the Ayckbourn will be Michael's baby. The auditions are next week, if you're interested,' Victoria pushed open the door to the dressing room. If she was suspicious about Paul and her, she was doing well at hiding it. 'But what you must do now is sign these.'

'These' were two cards. Becca took them, amused at Victoria's choice – a cartoon dalmation for Paul and a cancan girl for Angela. It was easy to think of what to write for Angela: 'Thanks for everything, love Becca.' But what to write to Paul? She was all too conscious of Victoria waiting. Victoria had written, 'Fabulous, darling, it's been a real pleasure having the opportunity of working with you, love Victoria xxxxxxxxxx.'

Becca bit her finger, looking for inspiration. It had been a pleasure, it was the single most exciting thing in her life for years, but she could hardly put that. And she couldn't say 'love Becca'. Finally she wrote: 'It's been great, best wishes, Becca.' She hesitated, then added a 'x'. She never usually put kisses, hadn't since she was in her teens. Now she wanted to cross her solitary x out, but that would draw even more attention to it. 'What did you get him? Them, I mean,' Becca added, remembering Angela.

'A magnum of champagne each. Well, you can't go wrong with booze, can you, and everyone likes champagne.'

Perhaps Paul and Suzy would drink the champagne together. Suzy, for all the apparent tension between her and Paul, was an attractive woman and probably ten years younger than Becca. Becca handed the cards back to Victoria. 'Thanks for organising the cards and presents.' Becca suddenly felt depressed. Paul hadn't said anything about meeting up again, and she could have misinterpreted that look they had exchanged earlier. In a few hours the play would be over, and Paul Fitzwilliam would be out of her life.

'When can we meet?' Paul murmured, covering her throat with kisses as Becca waited for her next cue. How wonderfully convenient it was that Lady Fidget was offstage for large segments of the play while the main plot line unfolded.

••• 171 •••

'Are we going to meet again?' Becca breathed.

'I hope so.' Paul's hand traced the line of the bodice and her skin goosepimpled at his touch. 'Tonight?'

'I can't – my father's come to see the production and he's staying over at my house tonight.'

'Tomorrow then.'

Visions of Sunday lunch with Frank and Martin and Lily rose in Becca's head, inescapable. But she wanted to see Paul. 'It'll be difficult to get out.'

'You sound like you're locked up in a tower and need rescuing.' His hand was on her breast. Oh, it felt incredible, wonderful, delicious.

'Rescue me.' She tilted her head back, relaxed as butter in sunshine. 'Were dresses really this low cut?'

'Lower, sometimes, so the nipples showed.' Becca felt as if her own were going to burst, hotwired to his touch. 'They called it the Roman fashion. Meet me tomorrow.'

Her brain tried to make sensible connections through the fog of desire. Think, she urged herself. 'I sometimes go to the cinema on Sunday afternoons – art-house films, Martin hates them. Especially with subtitles. I had said I wanted to see something that's on tomorrow.'

Paul laughed softly. 'Suzy hates art-house films too. Meet you tomorrow afternoon at the cinema?'

It would be impossible, especially with Frank there. But she had to go. 'Yes,' she breathed. 'Yes.'

Chapter 16

Becca rushed through Sunday lunch, whisking the plates away as soon as they had finished. 'What's the hurry?' Martin asked, looking wistfully after his plate. 'I was thinking of having a bit of cheese.'

'Cheese would be good,' Frank chimed in. 'I like a bit of cheese.'

'You'll have to get it yourselves then. I'm going out to the cinema.' Becca cleared the plates into the kitchen, dumping them above the dishwasher. How could either of them want cheese after roast chicken and all the trimmings and helpings of treacle tart – double helpings in Frank's case?

'You didn't tell me you were going to the cinema.' Martin came in with their used glasses stacked up.

'I did.' Becca shrugged, feeling guilty because while strictly speaking she had told him, it had been when he was in the shower. 'I told you I was going this morning.'

'Mmm. I quite fancy the cinema this afternoon.'

Becca swallowed, and took the glasses from him. 'If you want. It's that French film I was telling you about. The one with sub-titles.'

'Who's in it?' Martin ambled over to the fridge.

'Juliette Binoche, and that chap who was in *Jean de Florette*. Put the milk in, and the veg, while you're there.'

Martin paused, milk container in hand. 'She's pretty, the girl in *Jean de Florette*.' He rootled around in the fridge, looking for cheese, Becca assumed, like an overgrown rodent.

'Emanuelle Beart. Yes, she's very pretty.'

'But she's not in this one?' Martin had extracted a lump of cheddar which he held in his fingers.

'No,' Becca said, preventing herself from screaming by the narrowest of margins. 'Juliette Binoche is.'

'I quite liked *Jean de Florette*,' Martin said, through a mouthful of cheese.

'Well, this isn't anything like it,' Becca said. 'It's supposed to be a sort of thriller. Heavens, Martin, if you're going to eat cheese, at least get a plate.'

Martin rummaged around and found a couple of plates, and some cheese biscuits. 'That sounds good. I like thrillers.'

'Come if you want to,' she said holding her breath. 'But it's not that sort of thriller, it's French.'

'Was there any cheese?' Frank came into the room.

'Here.' Becca handed him a plate and the cheese biscuits, inwardly panicking in case Martin decided to come.

Martin riffled the Sunday papers so the television guide was on top, and flicked it open to Sunday. 'No, I don't think I'll go. The Grand Prix is on the box this afternoon, I'd rather watch that. You up for the Grand Prix, Frank?' Frank nodded, and Martin turned his attention back to Becca. 'You go, if you want to.'

Becca thought of saying, I wasn't asking you for permission. Actually, I'm going to meet my lover. Not that Paul was her lover. 'If you're sure you don't want to.'

Martin shook his head. 'You have a good time. Oh, look, *Time Team*'s on later. You'll be back in time for that.'

Becca nodded, feeling guilty that Martin was so easy to deceive. 'I expect so.'

* * *

She had forgotten how crowded Bath could get on a Sunday afternoon even without people doing their Christmas shopping. There didn't seem to be anywhere to park. She circled round the one-way system, willing shoppers to return and pick up their cars. Finally she squeezed into a space so small she wouldn't have begun to try unless she was desperate. Wrenching the wheel round and breathing in as if that would make a difference, she did it in two moves. She quickly checked her make-up in the rear-view mirror, noting that her eyeshadow had already creased. She dabbed furiously at it to smooth out the line that had formed. Oh well, it would be dark in the cinema anyway. No one would see. She hopped out, slamming the door shut, and half walked, half ran to the cinema. As she rounded the corner she could see Paul loitering outside, an anxious expression on his face.

'Sorry I'm late,' she panted. 'The parking . . .'

'Never mind, you're here.' He opened the cinema door for her. 'I've got the tickets.' They hurried past the doorman and up the black painted stairs, climbing to the top of the building where the second, smaller screen was. The ads and trailers had already started and Becca blinked into the sudden darkness unable to make out much beyond the screen.

'What about here?' Paul whispered.

'Fine,' she whispered back, unable to see a thing. She followed the outline of his back down a few shallow steps then squeezed past the legs of other viewers, whispering apologies. She realised Paul was sitting, and sat herself, but forgot to put the seat down first so her bottom caught the edge then collapsed it down with a bump. Hardly the coolest thing to do.

'OK?' Paul whispered.

She nodded, then remembered he wouldn't be able to see her. 'Yes, fine.'

The screen flickered, the curtains withdrew a little further, and a notice came up on the screen saying that *Caché* ('Hidden') was passed for viewing at certificate 18. I am sitting in the cinema with Paul, Becca thought to herself. Paul, who is not my husband. Paul who has kissed me. She looked sideways at him. In the darkness she could make out his profile. I don't really know him, she thought. Just through the theatre, and yet I feel he knows me better than anyone else on the planet. We are in tune. She could remember his hands touching hers, and as if he could read her mind, he glanced at her and smiled, his face lighting up. His hand reached for hers, and their fingers entwined. Becca had never been happier, her arm running against his from shoulder to elbow, her fingers linked with his. She felt enveloped in a warm golden haze, like a summer's day. She wanted to lean her head on his shoulder, to rub against his jacket, like a cat. She could feel her body inwardly purring with contentment.

Paul sat attentively, his chin resting on one hand, eyes intent on the screen. He probably knows all the technical jargon, Becca thought happily. I'll have to pay attention so I can say something intelligent afterwards. But hard to feel intelligent when your brain was a happy mush.

Years ago she'd been to a production by an experimental theatre company. One of the characters had worn a tall hat and spooned porridge out of it, as if able to eat his own brains. As he'd eaten more, he lost control of his physical abilities and lurched alarmingly across the stage. But he'd been happy, and got happier as his brain capacity diminished. Just like me, she thought happily, and gave Paul's hand a squeeze. He squeezed back, with a smile that flashed like sunshine in the darkened room.

The film carried on, washing over Becca, who was far too occupied with thoughts of Paul. I must remember every minute of this, she thought. Every minute he is with me, I must remember. We've always been in darkness, or underground, tucked away in corners, snatched kisses backstage or in subterranean dressing rooms.

She stared at the screen having completely lost track of the plot, in more senses than one. At one point a man cut his throat, right there on screen, and she gave a little yelp of horror, so unexpected was it. Paul had also jumped – as had most of the cinema audience – but he immediately turned to her. 'All right?'

'I didn't expect that to happen.'

'Do you want to go?'

'I'm fine.' She tucked her arm into his, and leaned into him, feeling protected. Sweet that he should be concerned. Of course, Martin would have been too, she had to admit. He was always protective of her. Thinking of Martin made her draw back a little. She shouldn't really be here, sitting in the cinema alongside Paul. It's a public space, she reasoned to herself. If anyone saw us, we could just be friends. I did ask Martin if he wanted to come, and he chose not to. She looked around the cinema, as if she could distinguish between the heads in the darkness. Any one of them might be someone she knew, or worse, someone who knew her but she wouldn't immediately recognise – a parent from Lily's school, or a neighbour.

What if I get found out? What if someone sees us together? They could bluff it out, she supposed. And it wasn't as if she'd had sex with Paul. Desire stabbed her insides like a bolt from the heavens, and she knew that whatever her mind might say, her body wanted him. The point is, she told an imaginary audience, the point is, I haven't. And I won't. This is a harmless flirtation that will blow itself out. I bet Martin has wistful yearnings for other women from time to time, she thought. I bet everyone does. It doesn't mean you're being unfaithful. Still, she moved a little away from Paul, and was relieved, when the lights went up, to see that she didn't recognise anyone else in the audience.

'Have you got time for a drink?' Paul's voice was low, confidential. He dug his hands in his pockets as if, unless they were tethered, he'd sweep Becca into an embrace. On the other hand, he might just have been cold.

They walked to a nearby pub, Becca itching to link arms with him. Paul got drinks while Becca found seats. She checked her watch. *Time Team* would have started by now, and Martin was probably asleep in front of the television.

'You look pensive,' Paul said as he sat down opposite her. 'Thinking of the film?'

'Thinking of my husband,' she said.

Paul took a sip from his pint. 'He seemed very nice.'

'He is. Martin is good, and kind, and funny.' She smiled, thinking of Martin pretending to be Gollum. 'Martin's lots of good things . . .'

'But . . . ?'

'Does there always have to be a but?'

'If there wasn't, you wouldn't be here.'

Becca dropped her gaze down to her glass of wine. 'I know marriage is about compromise, but sometimes it feels as if I'm the one doing all the compromising. Martin's just living his life. It's as if nothing touches the sides. It's like when I found that pregnancy test – I couldn't talk to him about Lily. I don't know why but I couldn't discuss it with him. And my parents – I've tried talking to him about how I feel, but he makes me feel silly for being upset about it.' Paul took her hand and squeezed it. Becca sat up. 'Heavens, I don't know where that came from. I'm sorry, you must think . . . well, I don't know what you think.'

'I think you are . . .' he kissed her index finger, 'beautiful,' then kissed her middle finger, 'charming,' he kissed her ring finger, 'sensitive,' he kissed her little finger, 'and talented.'

'Gosh.' Becca felt she was blushing all over. 'I don't think anyone's ever said anything as nice as that to me before.'

'Then the world is full of fools,' Paul said, kissing her palm. For a second Becca wondered if it was a quote, but then Paul often sounded as if he were quoting from something. It must be his theatrical background. Quote or not, it was delicious to be sitting with an attractive man telling her she was beautiful and charming

ANOTHER WOMAN'S HUSBAND

and sensitive and talented and that the world was foolish for not having noticed before.

'Your wife seemed nice too,' she lied, thinking that Suzy had seemed terrifying.

'Ah yes, Suzy. My wife.' He stared at the ceiling as if searching for inspiration. 'My wife is driven. She's ambitious, intelligent, smart, attractive – you can't fault her in any way, as a mother, as a wife, as a career woman. Whatever.'

Previously Suzy had come across as intimidating, now she sounded formidable. Becca felt a hopeless underachiever just hearing Paul describe her. 'She sounds perfect.'

'Oh she is,' Paul said, his mouth downturned. 'Perfect in every way. Everything she does is perfect. She got our last house in a magazine called *Perfect Homes*, or some such. We only moved to our current house a few months ago, and already everything is perfect, everything in its place down to the last picture on the walls. The photographers will be round any minute.'

Becca sipped her wine, thinking guiltily of the picture that was still propped up against the wall of her sitting room after four years. She'd get Martin to help her hang it this very evening. 'I expect you'd find my house very shabby.'

'I'm sure your house is as delightful as you are.'

'I don't think so,' Becca said, thinking of the chipped paint on the doors, the new handles for the kitchen that she'd never got round to changing, the bedroom ceiling that had a water mark from where the roof had leaked two winters ago. It was her home, and she loved it, but no one in a million years could say it was a perfect home. 'Your wife isn't an interior decorator though. Someone said she was a lawyer.'

'She's a corporate lawyer and earns a fortune. But look, let's not talk about her. I want to talk about you.' He leaned forwards and gently kissed her mouth. 'Have you done anything about acting in the future?'

179

'I got the brochures back from some of the drama schools, but the fees for even a year are huge. There's no way I could afford it, and I'd have to give up teaching too.'

'There are always scholarships. If they want you they'll find the money.'

'You make it sound so easy.'

'It is easy. Just decide what you want, and go for it.' His eyes were shining as if he could already see her name in lights in Shaftesbury Avenue, or leading a distinguished cast at the RSC.

Becca shook her head. Paul was so certain, so convincing, and yes, drama school sounded attractive, but was it really what she wanted? 'I know it's what I wanted when I was eighteen,' she began, 'but I also really really wanted Rob Baker to kiss me, and to have a pair of six-inch platforms and go to an Ian Dury and the Blockheads concert, and I don't want any of those things now. Except possibly the Ian Dury concert, and he's dead now anyway, so I can't have that.'

'All the more reason to seize the day. Take your chances now, when you have the chance.'

'I don't know. I loved doing the play, but . . . I'm not sure it's what I'd really want to do. Even assuming I could get work.'

'Don't be defeatist. Of course you'd get work.' He spread his hands out wide. 'I'd employ you any day.'

Becca giggled. 'Is that so?'

'I'd think myself lucky to have you.' His voice had become more serious, and suddenly the whole tone of the conversation shifted as if they were talking about deeply personal and meaningful things. Becca felt her heart beat faster, and her eyes widen. I could fall in love with you, she thought. I'm on the edge.

'I must go,' she said, getting up, her drink half finished. Her scarf was tangled in her coat sleeves. 'I've stayed too long as it is.'

'The clock hasn't struck midnight yet,' Paul said, but he stood too and helped her disentangle the scarf and settle the coat on her shoulders. 'Whatever you want, darling.'

● ● ●   180   ● ● ●

Darling. He called her darling. She turned to look at him, feeling uncertain, insecure in the world. She kissed him hard on the mouth, not caring about who could see. 'I have to go,' she said, and then ran all the way back to her car and safety.

Chapter 17

All she could think of was Paul. It was unfortunate, because she had far too many things she ought to be thinking about instead of him – Christmas, for one – but he was the centre of her existence. They met when they could over the next three days. Paul's dog was a perfect excuse for him to escape, and Becca used the demands of Christmas shopping. She did wonder how Paul managed to be free quite so often at such a busy time of year, but he explained that as well as the Chinese au pair, they also had a housekeeper a couple of days a week. Suzy was very good, he said with a faint sigh, about giving him the freedom to concentrate on his work. Becca remembered the evening in the bar, when Suzy had been so aggressive with Bill.

'It must be good having her support,' she said, sitting as close as possible to him on the park bench.

'It's relentless,' Paul said, fondling the dog's ear. 'Sometimes I feel she's doing to me what she's done to the dog. You have no idea what it's like, living up to Suzy's expectations. That's why it's such bliss being with you, my darling. You're happy to just be.'

'*Esse quam videri,*' Becca said, feeling the warmth of his body. 'To be rather than seem. It's the Hamilton House motto.'

'You're lovely,' he said softly, and kissed her.

Earlier that day, Paul had been to Jack and Willow's nativity play.

'I cried,' he said as they walked across the park towards James' Square where Becca had left her car. 'They were so sweet and innocent – they're only six and eight. And when Jack said his lines perfectly – he was the Innkeeper – I couldn't help myself. I'm useless, I just couldn't cut it in the business world.'

'I always cried at Lily's nativity plays too. She got to be the Star of Bethlehem in her last year at primary school.' She smiled at the memory of the angel telling the three kings to follow the star, and Lily's intent face as she guided them to the stable – she'd taken her duties as a guiding light very seriously.

Paul touched her cheek. 'Your eyes are shining like stars now.'

'It's the thought of innocence growing up,' Becca said, overcome with emotion at his presence. She fumbled in her bag for a tissue. 'Lily's not my baby any more.'

'You're beautiful,' Paul said, his voice intense like dark chocolate. 'I wish I was spending Christmas with you. Perhaps we should run away to a little cottage in the Welsh hills, and be together, just the two of us. We'd snuggle up beside the fire and you'd tell me everything about yourself.'

'Everything? It might put you off.'

'Nothing could do that.' He stroked her cheek. 'I want to kiss you all over.'

Becca felt breathless with longing. 'Darling . . .'

'Oh Becca . . .'

Their previous snatched meetings had ended in the same way, both reduced to inarticulation by the overwhelming feelings that engulfed them. Paul was in fact going skiing in Courcheval for two weeks on Friday and wouldn't be home until after New Year.

'You must meet me tomorrow before I go,' he said, as they stood under the street lamp by Becca's car.

'But won't you have to be at home to help with the packing and everything?'

'Suzy will have that under control, she won't want me around mucking up her organisational skills.' He'd told her before that Suzy had baked, marzipanned and iced two cakes way back in September, one for home, one for taking with them. She'd also managed to find time to buy and wrap presents for over thirty assorted cousins, nephews, nieces and godchildren, bake and decorate gingerbread for a natural, eco tree complete with cinnamon sticks tied with scarlet ribbon. Becca felt exhausted just thinking about it. She imagined their home as a magazine set of the perfect family Christmas with two smiling children – one of each – settled round the Christmas tree with tasteful lights, fire roaring, parents with champagne glasses in their hands and beatific smiles.

'Promise you'll meet me,' he insisted.

What else could she do but promise? She would have promised him anything at that moment.

On Thursday afternoon she finally did the Christmas shopping she'd claimed she'd been doing while meeting Paul. She spent more than she should on presents for everyone, then panicked and bought some more just in case. Her credit card was practically red hot, steaming up the sides of her wallet. She imagined it panting in her wallet: please, don't take me out again, I'm exhausted.

The burning question was, what to buy Paul? It had to be beautiful, tasteful, unique. Something he wanted. Not clothing – he wouldn't be able to wear it. Not a gadget – too much the last resort of the time-strapped wife. Small, so he could slip it in his pocket away from Suzy. Personal, that it would have meaning for the two of them. But she didn't want to be too personal, she wanted to play safe.

He'd got her the Shakespeare sonnets, so poetry in return would be appropriate. The only Restoration poet she knew of was the Earl of Rochester, but she didn't think that his erotic verse would quite fit their romance. In the end she found a nineteenth-century edition of Lovelace's poetry, nicely bound in leather with marbled endpapers. Lovelace was a royalist who died just before the restoration of the monarchy, but she hoped Paul would appreciate the idea.

She walked towards Milsom Street, heading for M&S. She always bought a selection of clothes for Martin, who normally resisted any form of clothes shopping. M&S was perfect. She bought, he tried on at home, she took back what he didn't like. And there was always something he liked so she was safe. He could have been a poster boy for the shop – middle class, middle aged, middle of the road.

The book in her shopping bag was wrapped up in brown paper as if it were pornographic. She felt vaguely dissatisfied. Yes, the book would do, but she wanted to do something more for Paul. A book was playing too safe. And he wasn't a man who played safe, she thought, as she paid for two crew-necked sweaters in olive green and a tawny brown, and a tan casual jacket in a chenille fabric she wasn't sure Martin would like.

She wandered back via the abbey, trying to think about what else she could get Paul. The Christmas market had been dismantled but she could see the ravaged grass on the green where the little huts had stood. She popped into the sweet shop to get some sweets to drop into Lily's Christmas stocking, fizzy lemon sherbets and the ones called pink and green apples that left the insides of your mouth feeling shrivelled up from prolonged sucking. She came out, dropping the little packages of sweets into the M&S bag. Then she had a brainwave. On impulse she went into the shop opposite.

'Darling, that's sweet of you.' He unwrapped her present to him as she watched his face. Their last night before Paul went away, the last of their snatched meetings in pubs and cafés where they thought no one else they knew would be likely to go. This one was noisy, people pressing in around them, full of Christmas good cheer and excitement, but they'd managed to find a tucked-away corner. She didn't want the evening to end.

Paul turned over the book in his hand. '"Stone walls do not a prison make/Nor iron bars a cage."'

'You know Lovelace?' She should have known he would.

Paul nodded, flicking through the pages. 'Though not as well as I should do. I'll enjoy reading this on the flight.' He leaned across and kissed her cheek, even though they were in a crowded pub where anyone might see them. 'Thank you, that was very thoughtful.'

'I didn't know what to get you.' She suddenly felt shy about giving him the other present. It hadn't been expensive and now she thought he would be embarrassed by it.

'You couldn't have got me anything I'd have liked better. Now, for my turn. I'm afraid it won't be nearly as thoughtful as your present.' He pulled out a small square box.

'Oh, I wasn't expecting anything; you got me the sonnets.'

'I wanted to get you something more.' He handed her the box. 'I can't tell you how much I wish I wasn't going away from you, but here's something to remember me when I'm away.'

She didn't recognise the blue box, but the ribbon was printed with the name of the grandest and most expensive jewellers in Bath. Becca untied the ribbon, half hoping, half dreading what she would find inside. Jewellery was so difficult – Martin always got it wrong. One year the necklace and earrings he'd bought had been so not her, she'd taken it back to the shop and got something else but she'd always felt guilty about it. She opened Paul's box. Inside was a delicate silver bracelet, tiny pearls woven with white stones like moonbeams.

'I thought it might remind you of our starlit evening at the stone circle,' Paul murmured.

She looked up at him, remembering the stone circle and the magic between them, the yearning for excitement. She found herself drawn to him, despite being in the middle of a crowded pub, and their lips met. Somehow, the press of bodies made their corner more private, more hidden. Oh, but she loved kissing him. They separated, and she knew that the big grin on his face was mirrored by her own. She bent to put the bracelet on, trying to fix the catch but not succeeding.

'Here, let me.' Paul took her wrist and fastened the bracelet around it, dropping his head to kiss the inside of her wrist.

'It's beautiful,' Becca said, turning it this way and that so it caught the light. She blushed. 'I got you something else.'

'More presents?' He touched her hair. 'You're too generous.'

'It wasn't expensive.' She handed over a small box. 'To keep you safe on your travels.'

It was a St Christopher medal on a fine silver chain. Paul bowed his head and she fastened it round his neck, enjoying the feel of his skin against hers, the way his hair curled slightly at the nape of his neck. She paused after fastening the medal, hands around his neck. 'Take care, while you're away. Come back safely.' She kissed him again, clinging to him because she knew that their time together was nearly up and she wouldn't see him again for two whole weeks. It seemed intolerable. 'Come back to me,' she whispered in his ear.

He hugged her tightly. 'I will,' he whispered back. 'I will.'

They walked through Bath towards the car park. Becca longed to link her hand with his, but knew it was impossible. But it was romantic to brush hands every now and then, and for him to look down at her, and for her to realise that this was, in a way, a date. Oh, but she shouldn't be thinking about things like that. Dates were for unmarried people.

The car park was emptier now it was later in the evening. There was no sign of people, and when their hands brushed Paul held hers. Strange how something as simple as holding his hand made her heart sing. The car-park lights shimmered on the tarmac, the frost edging each of the remaining cars with sparkling white, and she was completely happy.

It turned out they'd parked practically next door to each other, although Becca hadn't realised it. Tonight he was driving a large navy-blue people carrier quite unlike the silver sports car she'd seen before.

They kissed, a deep smoochy kiss. 'I don't want to leave you,' he said when they came up for air. 'I want to stay here.'

Becca leaned her head into his chest. 'Don't be silly, you'll have a wonderful time. Christmas in the snow. It must be magical.'

'Not as magical as being with you.' He kissed the top of her head. 'Don't go just now, stay a little longer.'

'It's cold. We'll freeze.'

Paul looked around the car park. 'Tell you what, hop in the back and we can talk.' He swung the door of the people carrier open.

Becca hesitated, then ducked her head and clambered in, feeling that her bottom must be sticking out in an ungainly manner. Paul climbed in after her, and slid the door back in place.

'Oh Becca, darling,' he whispered, drawing her to him. It was difficult to be comfortable on the seats which resolutely faced forward. She'd once seen an ad which had demonstrated all the configurations the seats could make including picnic table and seats; it had, however, omitted one for illicit lovers. 'You are the only thing in my life that makes it worth being on the planet.'

'You know that's not true,' she said, stroking his hair. 'There are your children and your work and—'

'I don't care about any of them, I only care about you.' He leaned back against the seat, eyes shut, hand holding hers tightly. 'This move south has been difficult for me. Suzy's been – well, Suzy's always been a bit bossy, but now she's unbearable. Her job is hugely demanding, and I do try to support her, but she makes it so difficult. Every thing I do is wrong, and she resents it when I say I must keep my own work going. The play – she didn't want me to do it, you know. Said it was a waste of my time.'

'I know you've done amazing things, and we can't begin to

compete with professionals, but I think it was worthwhile.' She gave a happy smile. 'I thought it was wonderful, to be honest. It wouldn't have been half as good without you.'

'You are lovely,' he said, rubbing his face with his hands. 'I shouldn't slag her off, it's just . . . well, I'm dreading Christmas to be honest. I don't want to spend time with her. I only want to be with you.' He kissed her, his mouth sweet and loving.

Her whole being was consumed with the need to kiss him, to be with him, to hold him, to feel his arms around her. It felt the only time she was whole, and yet it was bittersweet, infused with a guilty sharpness. Paul's hand was on her breast, sending electric currents of excitement throughout her body. Their breathing changed, becoming heavier, deeper, their mouths passionate.

She broke away with a laugh to hide the fact that she was more aroused than she knew what to do with. 'The last time I did anything like this was when I was sixteen, and it was in a Mini. I was a lot more flexible then.'

'Oh Becca.' Paul was breathing heavily, nuzzling her neck, his hand on her shirt. 'I want you so much.'

'I want you too,' she said, her head floating as if she'd had two bottles of vodka, instead of two small glasses of chardonnay. She had a sudden misgiving that perhaps he was going to give her a love bite and shifted slightly. 'Darling, don't you think we're a bit too, well, old for this?'

'You're never too old,' he said. She could feel him pressing against her, and her heart beat even faster with a heady mix of excitement and panic. Her body was squealing 'Yes! Yes! Yes!' but her head was urging her to take her time, to consider. Once she stepped over the line of physical intimacy there would be no going back. Go slowly her head counselled. But I want him, her body moaned. I want him.

Becca was pressed against the car seat. She could feel the seat belt clasp digging into the small of her back. Paul was leaning heavily across her, his hands rummaging up her shirt. He pushed one of her bra cups up exposing her left breast. 'Oh, Becca,' he groaned, and bent his head. 'You sexy woman.'

Becca stroked the back of his head, feeling the underwiring on her bra digging into her chest, and the other cup twisting against the skin. 'Darling,' she whispered. They kissed and Becca felt weak with wanting him. His hand reached up her skirt, touching her. It was instantaneous, like suddenly turning the gas flame full on.

All reservations forgotten she pressed against him, entirely shameless. She could feel him through his trousers, knew that he wanted her as much as she wanted him. His hand was tugging at her knickers and she lifted her hips to help him slide them off. Something crinkled under her buttock, sharp edges digging into soft skin. Paul's hand was at his belt buckle.

'We can't,' she murmured, wanting him, knowing that it was impossible. 'We mustn't torture ourselves like this.' The crinkly something was a lump under her bottom, so she shifted to try and dislodge it but it wouldn't move. Like the princess and the pea, she couldn't get comfortable. Paul must have taken her writhing as encouragement.

'I want you,' he muttered thickly. She heard a metallic click-whirr, as buckle and zip were undone. Her brain whirled with conflict, between sharp desire and the yearning for love. Yes, she admitted it, she wanted Paul to make love to her, but not like this. Not this desperate groping, with her back starting to ache from the peculiar position on the seat, with a hard lump digging into her behind.

'I want you too, but we can't.' Her tights had wedged themselves into an uncomfortable roll at the crease of her buttocks, forming a latter-day chastity belt that Paul tugged at ineffectually, trousers slipping down. Tentatively she stroked his back, under his shirt and sweater, feeling his skin slightly roughened against her fingertips. 'We mustn't.'

He hushed her with kisses, one hand trying desperately to push the wodge of material further down her thighs. She wanted him to calm down, to take things more slowly, to seduce her properly instead of this frantic flailing.

'Slow down,' she whispered. 'Darling? We don't have to rush.'

'God, but I want you.' He pushed against her, his excitement ever more obvious, and an equal response flared inside her, smothering the desire for romance. Now she tugged her pants too, like an adult variation of *The Giant Turnip* fairy tale. The tights responded by twisting themselves even more firmly into a knot. Becca could feel them tighten like tourniquets around the top of her thighs. She tugged them up, thinking the only solution was to start again, but Paul continued tugging down.

'Up,' she panted. 'Up, up.'

'Please, Becca,' Paul groaned, tugging down, down. There was a ripping sound and the tourniquets eased. 'My darling.'

He pushed at her, and to make it easier she shifted sideways, banging her head on the window. The shock made her open her eyes and . . . Oh God, there was someone coming.

A couple were walking towards them, clearly lit in the car-park lamps. Becca pushed at Paul. 'There's someone coming,' she hissed, trying to sit up and stuff her errant breast back into the bra before anyone could see. Oh, the shame and humiliation of being caught out. Her fingers fumbled with her shirt buttons. She could hear their voices, cultured and considered. They'd probably been to a classical music concert. And they were heading straight for them. Just their luck, they probably owned the only other car parked near them. She leaned forward, hearing an ominous tearing sound, trying to pull her ripped tights and knickers up her legs. Her fingers touched what felt like acres of bare skin, the tights must be in shreds. The couple were nearly at the car, they'd be able to see. Panic. She lurched forward into the footwell, hoping not to be seen.

'Sit up, sit up,' Paul hissed, pulling at her shoulders as he tried to retrieve his trousers from round his thighs. 'Or they'll think you're . . .'

Becca's brain whirrled – the kneeling woman, the man with half-mast trousers. She sat up promptly and caught Paul's face with a smack that reverberated round her skull.

Paul gave a muffled yell, hand to nose. 'You've bloody broken it.'

'Sorry, sorry.' She reached out to him, but he pushed her hand away.

'Don't worry about me.'

She smoothed her skirt down over her knees, trying to make a stab at respectability. Her left breast ached as she hadn't managed to pull her bra far enough down. The couple were near now, about to pass the people carrier. She couldn't pull her bra down properly now or they'd notice. The couple gave them sideways glances as they passed. Becca thanked heaven for being British. At least there wouldn't be any passing comments, or even faces peering into the window. The worst would be surreptitious glances. She stared straight ahead, feeling her breast squelching out either side of the bra band. At least they couldn't see the state of her tights. The couple unlocked their car and got in. It felt as if her left breast was being cut in half. They adjusted their seat belts.

'Come on, come on,' Paul whispered. 'Turn the engine on.'

Becca could see they were in their sixties, white haired, ultra respectable in sensible woollen coats. They were having a discussion. Probably about us, she thought. They're saying it's disgusting, and shouldn't be allowed. They're deciding if they should report us. The man checked the rear-view mirror. Whatever was under her bum was setting up permanent residence for itself. She looked down and saw that her buttons were buttoned up all wrong.

Yes! The man started the engine. They were going very very slowly, as if they were having to negotiate the *QE2* out of dock instead of a Nissan Micra from a virtually deserted car park, the car edged forwards and Becca and Paul were alone again.

Crinkle crinkle. She reached under her bum and hauled out a sweet paper with the remains of a large gobstopper, obviously spat out by one of Paul's children. The remnants of her passion turned to ashes. 'I'm sorry,' Becca said, fishing around inside her shirt to sort out her bra. 'I can't do this. Call me old fashioned, or just plain too old, but I can't have sex in a car. Not even a people carrier.'

'I'm sorry too. I got carried away.' Paul's brow creased in anxiety. 'It's not because you don't want to?'

'Of course not.' She held his hands, trying to will away the sordid memories of the last twenty minutes, to regain the romance of earlier. He stroked her face. They kissed gently, the intense passion gone, but the sweetness remaining.

Becca nestled under Paul's arm, feeling happier. 'I'm sorry about your nose.'

'I'll survive.' He squeezed her shoulders and sighed. 'You are so beautiful and lovely, I can't bear the idea that I'm not going to see you for two whole weeks.'

'I can't bear it either,' Becca said. 'The thought of Christmas fills me with horror.'

'We'll stay in touch with text, though.' He kissed her hands. 'And I'll try and phone whenever I can.' He kissed her hands.

Becca shook her head. 'Darling, that could cause problems. It's best not to.'

He held her face between his hands. 'At this moment, all I want is to be with you, to touch you, to hold you, to kiss you. I can't tell you how you make me feel. You won't forget me, will you, when I'm away?'

'Never,' Becca whispered.

Chapter 18

'At last,' Crystal said, coming into the staffroom. 'I thought this term was never going to end.'

'Look what I got,' Richard said. 'Four bottles of red, two of whisky and a bottle of champagne. They've obviously decided I'm an alcoholic.'

'You've done better than me – mine think I'm a smelly old witch who needs a good shower. I've had more gift sets of bath gel this year than ever. What about you, Becca?'

'Me? Oh. The usual,' Becca said. Normally she'd have been eager to compare their respective hauls of end of term presents, but she'd hardly been listening to Crystal and Richard. Her mind was on Paul, probably in the air by now, winging his way to France. She hoped he was wearing the St Christopher to keep him safe. Becca wanted to think of him as he was when they walked through the park – romantic, caring, gentle – but her mind kept slipping back to the session in the back of the people carrier. She felt grubby, as if the romantic bubble they'd been in had been smeared with something unwholesome.

'What are you up to for Christmas? Something nice?' Crystal asked Richard as he lugged his briefcase off the desk.

'Nothing special, just eating too much and drinking too much.' He waved a plastic shopping bag which clinked. 'This little lot will do for starters. Happy Christmas.'

In the end the three of them left the staffroom together. The cold hit them as they went outside. Richard was in high spirits, chatting about what he was planning to do that night. High spirits were appropriate as it seemed to involve a lot of visits to various clubs and bars.

'I don't know how you have the energy,' Becca said, thinking about Paul grabbing at her tights. Was it just about sex? Was that all it was for him? She couldn't bear the idea that the most romantic man she'd ever met actually only wanted sex. But perhaps she'd got that wrong. It had been so long since she'd had anything to do with romance and dating, that maybe her reactions were all wrong. She needed to talk to someone, someone who knew about things like that.

Becca huddled into her coat feeling that whatever the thermometer might be saying, the atmosphere with Crystal would be considerably frostier than the air temperature if she said she was seeing someone apart from Martin. But perhaps if she phrased it right, made out she was contemplating an affair rather than actually having started one . . .

At the car park Richard waved goodbye and went to his car.

'Happy Christmas,' Crystal said cheerily to Becca, rootling in her bag for her keys.

'Crystal?' Becca called. Crystal stopped by her car, jiggling her keys in hand. 'You wouldn't have a moment for a chat, would you?'

'Oh Becca, I'm really pushed for time – I'm going to a party with Harry tonight, and I've got to wash my hair, it's completely disgusting.'

'OK. Have a lovely time. Say Happy Christmas to Harry for me.'

Crystal looked serious. 'Was it something important?'

Becca shook her head. 'Not really.'

'It was.' Crystal checked her watch. 'Will it keep until after Christmas? Let's meet up and have a nice long chat then. Let's go to the Pump Room – I haven't been for ages, and it's always lovely.'

'OK,' Becca said. That would give her time to think it over

herself, and then perhaps she might have reached her own conclusions. But meeting up with Crystal would be fun anyway. They embraced. 'Have a wonderful Christmas.'

You know you're getting old, Becca thought, when your child stays up later than you on Christmas Eve. Becca had been longing to go to bed, but felt she had to wait until Lily had settled down before creeping in with her Christmas stocking, bulging with a wide selection of goodies. Martin always said she overdid it on the Christmas present front, and she supposed she did. But Lily was her only child, and Christmas was a time of indulgence.

She had to tread carefully across the room trying to avoid discarded clothes, books, make-up, whatever. Lily's body was a mound of duvet topped by a spray of jet-black hair just peeping over the edge of the duvet cover. My darling girl, Becca thought, as she placed the stocking over the edge.

'I know it's you,' came a little voice.

'It's Mother Christmas,' Becca whispered. She put the huge teddy bear she'd won at the Christmas market next to the stocking and hoped Lily would christen it something other than Evangeline. 'Go to sleep.'

'Love you,' Lily murmured.

Becca touched the sleeping mound. 'Love you.'

As she crept back into bed and snuggled against Martin's warm and sleeping back she wondered if Paul was doing the same. His children were younger, so his creeping would have been earlier in the evening, leaving him and Suzy free.

She hadn't really thought about Suzy much, but now, cuddling up to Martin, she wondered about her. She was obviously good at her job, good at everything in fact. Becca wondered what she'd be like on holiday, where all she had to do was be happy and carefree. Were she and Paul making love right now? The thought made Becca feel sick. She didn't want to think about it but she made herself.

This was the reality of her situation. Paul was probably making love to Suzy even as Becca lay in bed with Martin. The best she could hope for was he was thinking about Becca. Martin's back was warm and soft. She nuzzled against him, his smell as familiar as her own, all the while thinking about Suzy. She was Paul's wife, and though he didn't speak of her with much affection, he must have loved her once. Perhaps he still did. Perhaps Becca was nothing more than an amusement, an escape from reality, an excursion into a fantasy world. It was clear that Suzy was the breadwinner. Perhaps he didn't like that, and his relationship with Becca was more about getting his own back on Suzy than any deep affection.

Becca twisted over into a foetal position, wanting sleep. Oblivion was far more attractive than thinking about Suzy and Paul. He's a man married to a highly competent, highly intelligent alpha female. Perhaps his way of dealing with that was flirtation. Perhaps Becca was just another flirtation in a long line of flirtations.

Despite the warmth of Martin's body she felt cold all over, thinking about the escapade in the car. She had come very close to stepping over the line that divides the adulterous from the virtuous, not that she was exactly virtuous, and maybe it was all semantics – how far do you go before you're unfaithful? She was absolutely certain in her own mind that groping was one thing, penetration another. Neither were things a good wife went in for, but to her there was a clear dividing line.

She was shocked with herself that she had come so close to having sex with Paul in the back of a people carrier, with one of his children's spat-out sweets stuck to her bum. It wasn't an attractive thought. And if she had done it? If she had crossed the line? She felt cheap.

Becca squeezed her eyes together so tightly red sparks danced. Sleep, she thought. I have to sleep. But sleep didn't come to order. Instead an image of Suzy came into her head, the fierce stare she had given her at the bar that said 'trespassers will be prosecuted'. Fierce, determined. Vulnerable? Becca couldn't remember ever giving a warning stare like that to another woman. That might mean that Suzy was hyper-jealous, super-vigilant. Or it might mean that she'd had cause to worry.

Martin rolled towards her, the contours of his face catching escaped light from the street lamp outside. He looked young, his face blurred with sleep, and in the planes and angles of his bone structure, Becca caught sight of Lily underneath like a palimpsest of the people who meant the most to her.

In the morning it took repeated bouncing on their bed by Lily to wake Becca up. 'C'mon, Mum, let's do presents!'

Becca felt the only present she wanted was another five hours sleep. 'Go away.'

Lily bounced some more. 'Do wake up.'

It had always been their tradition that Christmas presents were opened in Becca and Martin's bed. When Lily had been little she had snuggled in between them, but as she'd grown up, she'd chosen to sit at the foot of the bed, her feet tucked under the duvet. She was there now, like some imp of Satan, Becca thought.

'She's made us tea,' Martin said. Becca could hear the yawn in his voice.

Becca dragged her body to sitting. 'What time is it?'

'Time for presents!'

Eventually Becca managed to wake up. She drank her lukewarm tea. The bedside lights threw a soft glow over the room as Becca snuggled into the cosy nest of the duvet, Martin to one side, Lily tucked in at the foot of the bed. Everything was suitably oohed and ahhed over. Chocolate coins scattered over the covers like pools of gold, red and green wrapping paper crackled, a tangerine rolled off the side of the bed. Lily squealed as she unwrapped her new iPod. Martin immediately put one of his new sweaters on over his T-shirt. 'And this is for you,' he said, hauling out a big box from under his side of the bed.

Becca was excited at the large box, though less so when it turned out to be a set of saucepans. 'They're Swiss made and guaranteed for twenty years,' Martin said, stroking the box reverently. 'The Rolls-Royce of saucepans.'

'They're lovely,' Becca said. And they were, just not exactly what she'd secretly hoped for, something small and shiny in a little box tied up with satin ribbon, like the moonstone bracelet she'd hidden in the top left drawer of her chest of drawers. 'I hope they weren't too expensive.'

'Nothing's too expensive for you.'

She looked at him, his face open and trusting, then to Lily, absorbed in her iPod. The thought of hurting either of them was intolerable. 'They're just what I wanted,' she said, and kissed him.

'Becca?' Frank shuffled into the kitchen at lunchtime later that day. 'Do you think it's possible for me to have a little something?'

Becca paused from wrestling the turkey out of the oven for another basting. 'I know it's a bit late, but we'll be having lunch pretty soon – couldn't you hang on for just a little a bit?' She got the pan onto the trivet and began spooning juices over the gleaming bird, nicely browning. Her mouth watered in anticipation.

'The doctor said I should have little and often.' He started to poke around in the fridge, pulling out dishes and placing them higgledy piggledy on the side. Since June had gone to New Zealand Frank had acquired a lot of vague, unspecific illnesses, all of which affected his ability to do anything domestic while not interfering with anything he actually wanted to do. Becca bit her lip with exasperation. Had her father always been such a hypochondriac? Or was it stress brought on by June's departure?

'Cor, that smells good.' Martin came in from running. He put one arm round Becca and kissed her, while with the other hand he sneaked a sausage out of the roasting tray and popped it in his mouth.

'Mitts off!' Becca said, tapping his hand with the spoon. 'No food unless you're dressed properly.'

Martin was dressed in his usual running kit, but had chucked on a Father Christmas-style red hat, with a flashing light at the end, in honour of the day. 'What, don't you like my hat?'

'You look ridiculous,' Becca said, laughing. 'Go and have a shower. I want us to eat today not tomorrow.'

'When's lunch going to be?' Lily came into the kitchen, pulling one of the iPod ear phones out.

'Soon,' Becca said, feeling crowded. She pushed a strand of hair out of her eyes, feeling her hot and sticky forehead.

'Have you downloaded the tracks already?' Martin asked. 'That was quick. It's good then?'

Lily grinned. 'It's brilliant. Though I'd rather have had a puppy.'

Becca rolled her eyes. 'You can't look after a hamster, let alone a puppy. Speaking of which, have you sorted Truffle out?'

Lily nodded. 'Yeah, I'll do him after lunch. When's it going to be?'

'As soon as everyone goes off and leaves me alone,' Becca said. Lily put the ear phone back and ambled off. Becca opened the oven door to put the turkey back in.

'Here, I'll do it.' Martin lifted the tray and slid the roasting tin back into the oven. Becca slammed the door shut.

'Oak or mahogany?' Frank said.

Becca wasn't sure what Frank meant. She glanced at Martin, who raised his eyebrows indicating similar incomprehension. Frank sighed as he examined the contents of Becca's fridge. 'Oak or mahogany? For my coffin.'

'Dad! What are you talking about?'

'I know I'm in the way. Useless. Worthless. The only thing to do is die. I thought I'd plan my funeral now. It'll save you a lot of trouble when the time comes.'

'Makes a lot of sense,' Martin said, winking at Becca. 'Pre-planning, thinking ahead. Were you going to make your own? Oak's nice to work with. You could put that circular saw to good use.'

'I hadn't thought of it,' Frank said. His eyes narrowed. 'But now you come to mention it . . . it'd be an interesting project: some nice dovetails, a few chamfered joints.'

'You could borrow my new router, if you wanted,' Martin chipped in.

'Martin, stop it. Of course you're not in the way, Dad,' Becca said, torn between guilt and laughter. 'You mustn't think like that. It's Christmas. We're supposed to be happy, not talk about funerals.'

'I don't mean to be in the way,' Frank said, heart-breakingly humble. 'A little bit of cheese would do.'

She felt a sharp stab of sympathy for her mother, which she stifled as she sliced cheese on to a plate and put a couple of oatcakes to go with it. 'There you are,' she said, handing him the plate. 'And I'd go for mahogany if I were you. Takes a polish better.' She stared at him, willing him to laugh.

Frank took the plate of cheese and biscuits with eyes as mournful as Oliver Twist's. 'What about brass handles?' he said.

After lunch Lily settled at the computer to organise her iPod, and Martin and Frank settled in front of the television, while Becca cleared up. Martin had offered to do the clearing, but Becca had shooed him to the sofa to keep Frank company. She was, to be honest, a little fed up of her father's company. He was so relentlessly determined to be hard done by. He had sat in a little cloud of gloom, and no amount of joking could shift him from it, not even the awful Christmas cracker jokes: What award did the door knocker win? The Nobell prize! Everyone else had laughed, it wouldn't have hurt him to join in.

She wondered what Paul was doing now. Schussing down the slopes, or having Christmas lunch. Perhaps he was telling a joke right now: Why does Sir Lancelot need five hundred pairs of glasses? Because the knight has a thousand eyes! She couldn't picture Suzy going in for cracker jokes somehow. Perhaps Paul was telling jokes and Suzy, the au pair and Willow were sitting in varying degrees of linguistic incomprehension. Only Jack, his little boy, would laugh out loud. Boys liked dreadful jokes, she smiled, even if they grew up and got grumpy like Frank.

Clearing up done, she peered in at the sitting room where Martin and Frank were gently snoring in unison, adding marathon digestion to marathon running. Frank still had his Christmas cracker hat on. Martin's mouth had dropped open. I've married my father, Becca thought, as she turned the television off.

Frank shook awake. 'I was watching that,' he said, before going to sleep again.

Martin opened one eye, saw Becca and stretched out an arm in welcome. Becca went over and he pulled her onto his knees. 'Stop doing stuff,' he said. 'Come and relax.'

Becca leaned into him. Martin stroked her hair, and she felt as cosy and secure as a well-fed cat. 'Any minute I'll start purring,' she whispered and in response he pulled her closer to him.

In the evening, Becca rang Joanna. After the usual Christmas exchanges of goodwill to all her nephews and nieces, she asked to speak to June.

'Hi, Mum, happy Christmas.' Do you miss us? she wanted to say.

'It's a fabulous day here. The sun is shining, and we're going to have a barbie on the beach for lunch.' June didn't sound as if she was missing them at all.

'Sounds amazing. Do you want to speak to Dad?'

There was a pause on the other end. 'Not particularly.'

Becca pressed the phone to her ear. 'Are you sure?' She heard June's exasperated intake of breath and quickly carried on. 'I've got Lily here, I'm sure you'd like to speak to her.' She handed the phone to Lily.

'Hi, Gran, are you having a good Christmas?'

Judging from Lily's expression, June was telling Lily about having a barbie, the wonderful weather and so on. Becca left them to it, and went to the sitting room.

'June's on the phone. Do you want a word?' she said to Frank.

He hesitated. 'Not particularly. Send my love to Joanna.'

Becca rubbed the back of her neck. 'Will do.'

I want us to be a family, Becca thought as she went back into the hall where Lily was still on the phone. I want to keep the threads that hold us together strong. Lily was chattering exitedly about Christmas, her eyes shining, the child in her coming to the fore. This is what I risk if I carry on seeing Paul, Becca thought. But I want to see him. I want to be with him.

Lily held out the phone to Becca again. 'She wants to speak to you.'

Becca took it from her. June's voice was hesitant. 'Becca darling . . . are you all right?'

Not really, Becca wanted to say. And it's all your fault. The ties that had bound them together as a family seemed to be dissolving in June's absence, as if what they'd all thought had been the weaker thread had actually been the tie that held them all together. 'I'm fine,' Becca said. 'A bit tired from Christmas. But otherwise, I'm fine.'

'This is nice,' Crystal said looking around her. 'I haven't been to the Pump Room for – oooh, ages. We ought to come more often.' She sipped her cappuccino. 'Anyway, what did you want to talk to me about?'

Becca looked around too. The Pump Room had been the heart of Bath society more than two hundred years ago – and a string trio had played since 1706. Jane Austen had been in the same room Becca and Crystal were in now, and had drunk the waters for her health. You could still drink the lukewarm water, packed with minerals, although it was the boiled egg taste of sulphur that was most in evidence. The double-height windows on one side looked out onto the Roman baths, on the other the abbey courtyard. In Jane Austen's day the main space would have been open so visitors could perambulate and socialise. Now it was filled with linen-covered tables, just right for two ladies enjoying a coffee and a cake, with the refined sounds of the trio playing in the background. Less refined were the thoughts tumbling through Becca's head.

'This mustn't go any further,' she started.

Crystal leaned forward, her eyes bright, ready to receive Becca's confidence. 'I promise.'

'Not anyone. Not Harry.'

Crystal stared at the table. 'Actually, Harry's dumped me.'

'I'm sorry,' Becca said, relieved that she'd been pulled back from the brink of telling Crystal about Paul. 'I thought you two were . . . did something happen over Christmas?'

'I thought we were doing just fine, but not according to him. He'd apparently been unhappy with our relationship, but didn't want to dump me just before Christmas. Bastard,' she added, with enough vehemence that the ladies on the next table glanced in their direction.

'You poor thing,' Becca said, feeling quite inadequate. It was always tricky to know what to say – Crystal was quite likely to get back together with Harry, so words needed to be chosen carefully. 'Didn't you have any idea?'

Crystal sighed heavily. 'Yes. And no. I mean, I knew we were going through a bit of a rough patch – we'd had a couple of rows about stuff – but I didn't think they were important. Obviously I was wrong.' She picked at the pink carnation in the centre of the table, her face despondent.

'Let's have some chocolate cake,' Becca said, turning to catch the waiter's eye.

'Why do all my relationships end in disaster? There's obviously something wrong with me,' Crystal said after Becca had ordered.

'Rubbish, you just haven't met the right person yet.'

'I meet loads of right people,' Crystal said. 'And it always seems great at the beginning. It just never seems to go anywhere – either I get bored, or they do, or we fight, or they've got problems. All the good men are married, so I'm dealing with the leftovers as it is. The men I meet are either congenitally incapable of settling down, or they've been there, done that, and got three kids to prove it. You're so lucky to have Martin.'

Becca fidgeted with her teaspoon. 'There are lots of lovely men out there.'

'Yes – and they're all married, as I said. Take you and Martin. You've been together since university, right?' Becca nodded. 'I missed that moment. And now it's too late. I'll never get the sort of relationship you and Martin have.'

The waiter came and gave them their cake, to Crystal's squeaks of delight. The cake certainly looked delicious, all glossy chocolate icing and light sponge. Becca picked up her fork, not feeling like eating cake at all. 'I think you've got a romantic idea about marriage,' she said, choosing her words carefully. 'Marriage has to be worked at. It can be hard work sometimes.'

'Yeah, but people like you and Martin have got it sussed.'

'Have we?' Becca spoke lightly as she pushed a bit of cake around her plate, not able to face eating it.

'You and Martin – hey, the world's going to crumble before you two . . .' Crystal's voice trailed away as she caught the expression on Becca's face. 'Shit. Oh no.' She clapped her hands to her face. 'Martin's leaving you.'

'No!' Becca said in astonishment. 'Why would you think that?'

'I'm sorry, it was just the look on your face. I thought – never mind what I thought, it was stupid of me.'

Becca shook her head. 'Why would you think Martin would leave me?'

'You know, mid-life crisis, all this running. He's looking great at the moment, really fit. I can't believe I said that, I'm so stupid. I'm sorry.' She slapped the side of her face. 'What a twit.'

'Martin isn't having a mid-life crisis,' Becca said, putting her fork down and giving up any pretence of eating her cake. 'It's me.'

Chapter 19

Crystal stared at Becca, mouth open. 'You?' She managed to get about fifteen vowel sounds in the single word.

'I've met someone . . .'

'No! I don't believe it. You?' Crystal shook her head. Becca wasn't sure if she should be flattered or offended by Crystal's astonishment. 'You're having an affair?'

'No,' Becca said quickly. 'It hasn't gone that far.'

'Have you . . . you know?'

'Of course not,' Becca said, starting to regret telling Crystal about it. 'We've just talked and . . . kissed.'

Crystal gave a sharp intake of breath. 'Who is it?'

Becca shook her head. 'I don't want to say. You mustn't tell anyone about this, promise me?'

Crystal nodded, her eyes concerned. 'Of course I won't. I'm just a bit stunned, that's all. Whoever he is, he must be pretty special.'

'Oh, Crystal, you've no idea. It's so romantic.' Becca smiled, thinking of the text messages Paul had been sending at least three times a day. She couldn't stop herself from sharing. 'I feel he understands me, really deep down. He knows so much more about me than Martin ever did.'

'Come off it.'

'No really. Sometimes I don't even need to say anything, and it's as if he knows what I'm feeling, what to say to make me feel better.'

'Becca.' Crystal took her hands in hers. 'Everyone feels like that at first. Take it from me. I'm the queen of new relationships. I know what it's like, it's wonderful when you first meet someone, you can't eat, you can't sleep, all you can do is think about him. All good sense goes right out of the window. You're no different from anyone else – except you have Martin and Lily. You're playing with fire.'

'I know,' Becca said. 'I know you're right. I know I ought to stop seeing him. But there's knowing what you ought to do, doing it is quite a different thing.'

'Is he married?' Becca nodded. 'Kids?' Becca nodded again. Crystal sat back in her seat. 'If you leave Martin for this man, you wreck so many people's lives. You know how upset you've been over your parents. Now think of what it'd be like for Lily.'

'I didn't say anything about leaving Martin.'

'But that's where it ends up, isn't it? You can't just go on meeting, having heart to hearts and passionate kisses and that's that. Sooner or later one of you at least is going to want more.' Becca turned away from her but Crystal persisted. 'It's all very well saying this is romantic, but no red-blooded male is going in for just kissing. It's bound to go further. Give it up now before it does.'

Becca felt like sticking her fingers in her ears and going la-la-la so she couldn't hear what Crystal was saying. There were altogether too many resonances with the scene in the people carrier. But Paul wasn't like that. She knew he wasn't.

Crystal caught hold of her hand and stared into Becca's face, her expression creased with anxiety. 'Please, Becca. For Lily's sake, if not for Martin's.'

For Lily's sake. I don't want to give him up, Becca thought. I don't want to be found out either. Martin would be devastated if he knew. What should I do? Paul seemed more real at that moment than either Lily or Martin. She could see him in her mind's eye, his face as he concentrated on fastening the bracelet round her wrist. She was wearing it now, and twisted it round and round. Aren't I entitled to a bit of romance? she wanted to wail.

'Give him up,' Crystal said. 'What you and Martin have is really precious. You're so lucky to have someone like him. Stop before you go too far.'

What to do what to do what to do? rattled round in Becca's brain as persistently as the hamster ran on its wheel. Becca frowned. She hadn't heard the hamster for ages. She made her way to the utility room to check, what to do being replaced by could she do it could she do it could she do it? She knew what she should do, it was the doing that was going to be difficult. She thought of Paul, his energy, his dear face. Impossible to let him go.

Becca peered in the cage. It looked OK, hardly any droppings anywhere, and most of the bedding neatly inside the little plastic house the hamster liked to make a nest in. She could see the curve of hamster fur tucked up in its nest. It was suspiciously still. She opened the cage and gave the little plastic house a nudge. Nothing happened. She pushed it again, harder this time. The hamster carried on sleeping. If it were asleep.

Her heart beating fast she reached a trembling finger and prodded the body. She took a sharp intake of breath. Quite stiff. Oh God, the poor little thing. The hamster was dead. How? Why? Her eyes swooped to the food bowl – empty. The water bottle – not a single drop.

She stormed to the bottom of the stairs. 'Lily,' she yelled upwards. Lily had been in her room all afternoon. 'Come here right now.'

'What?' Lily's voice drifted downwards.

'Come here now,' Becca shouted. The memory of the starved little body, curled around itself fuelled her anger as surely as Lily hadn't fuelled the hamster. 'I mean it. Right now. I've got something to show you.' Becca waited while Lily dragged her body downstairs, more zombie than teenager. She took Lily's arm and dragged her to the utility room. 'Look.'

'OK, I'll do it later,' Lily said, pulling away and rubbing her eyes. 'Just not now, Mum, I'm a bit—'

'No. Look.' Becca undid the clips that held the top of the cage onto the base and pulled out the little house. 'Truffle's dead. I told you you needed to look after him. The poor little thing has starved to death.'

'I did feed him,' Lily said, tears welling up. 'I did. I did.'

Becca felt torn between wanting Lily to realise the dreadful thing she had done and compassion for her wounded white face. 'OK. When did you last feed him?'

'I . . . I . . . I . . . I can't remember. Just recently. I know I did.'

'He needed you to look after him, he couldn't go out and find food on his own.' Becca felt her own guilt rise. She should have reminded Lily, but she'd nagged her so often, at what point did it stop? Her own eyes filled with tears. I should have checked, she thought, I should have nagged Lily more. She imagined the hamster frantically licking at the water bottle, tiny incisors scratching the ball bearing in the hope of finding some moisture. Its needs had been so small, so minimal and yet they hadn't managed to fulfil even those. It had lived its lonely life, going round and round on its wheel frantically running to nowhere.

Tears were now rolling down Lily's face, and Becca hugged her. 'I'm sorry, Lily, but you've got to learn. Otherwise there was no point to Truffle's life at all.'

'I didn't mean it.' Lily sniffed, her mouth making a perfect downwards semicircle. 'I didn't mean it. I loved him.'

'But not enough to feed him, and give him water,' Becca said gently to soften the truth that had to be said.

Lily was crying properly now, great sobs that shook her shoulders. 'Everything's gone wrong,' she wailed. 'Everything's awful. I wish I were dead.'

'Oh, sweetheart, it's not that bad.' Becca hugged her, feeling the sobs shaking Lily's body. 'We'll give Truffle a proper burial in the garden.'

'It's Kevin,' Lily wailed. 'He's going out with Hannah. Grace texted me. They've been going out with each other for ages. Kevin says Hannah's really fit and I'm too fat.'

'You're not, darling, you're perfect, just as you are,' Becca said, stroking Lily's hair.

'Everything's so dreadful,' Lily wailed. 'Kevin gone off with Hannah, and Truffle's dead. Gran and Grandpa are getting divorced and he's all on his own, and going to die just like Truffle cos no one will look after him, and it's awful, I can't bear it.'

'Darling, don't worry, it'll be OK,' Becca said, patting her back. 'I'm sure Grandpa is going to be fine, I think it's going to be years before he needs a coffin, brass handles or not.' She hoped that was true.. 'Let's have supper in front of the television and watch something nice, just us girls.'

'There isn't anything to watch.'

Becca settled her in front of the television. 'Look, *Casablanca*'s on in a couple of minutes, we could watch that together.' She managed to persuade Lily that it wouldn't be boring, and quickly made turkey and salad sandwiches for them both. Lily was looking small and fragile, as if she had diminished over Christmas. Lily leaned against her, and as the film progressed, Lily's head became heavier and heavier. Becca stroked her hair, thinking that sleep was the best thing for her. Poor Lily, it had been a bit of an emotional time.

Ingrid Bergman as Ilsa glowed in black and white, Humphrey Bogart as Rick was rugged and manly. Paul Henreid as Ilsa's husband Victor Laszlo reminded her of Paul in a way, both being tall and thin with defined cheekbones and a slightly receding forehead. Paul was probably gliding down the piste at this very moment, or drinking Glühwein. They'd drunk Glühwein together at the Christmas market. Becca could feel the spiciness on her tongue, the scent of cinnamon and cloves.

Crystal had said she was playing with fire. I can't give him up, she thought. Not like this. Not without . . . Without what? Without sex?

Stop it now, Crystal had said. Stop it before you go too far.

Lily shifted against her shoulder with a grunt. When she'd been a baby she'd made little grunting noises when she slept, like a piglet rootling for acorns. She'd been a beautiful baby with thistledown hair, nestling into the crook of Becca's arms as if she'd been made especially for them. My baby, she thought, kissing the top of Lily's tousled black head. My love.

Lily stirred and sat up, mouth opening in a pink yawn, before settling back down against Becca. In the film, they were at the airport – Morocco seemed surprisingly rainy for a desert country – and Rick was telling Victor that Ilsa had lied when she said she loved Rick in order to get the papers they needed. 'Here's looking at you, kid.' And Ingrid Bergman had never looked as beautiful as when she said goodbye.

Lily woke up at the credits and twisted round to Becca. 'You're crying, Mum.'

'It's the film, love,' Becca said stroking her hair. 'It always makes me cry.'

Before Christmas Lily had been full of plans for going out to an all-night party on New Year's Eve, but after the day Truffle died, there were no further arguments. Instead, they were all going to stay at home and have a family supper. Becca invited Frank, but he declined, so it was just the three of them for smoked salmon and champagne. Lily's eyes were red from prolonged weeping and she only just managed to stay up until midnight before trudging off to bed.

'I wish I could take the pain from her,' Becca said to Martin as she snuggled up against him on the sofa.

'She's got to go through it – we all did.' He stroked her back. 'You coming to bed?'

'Mmm. I just want to tidy up before I go.' She got up and stretched.

'Leave it till the morning,' Martin said also getting up. 'It'll keep.'

'I suppose.' They went up to bed, each following their own routine, although without speaking, neither put their nightwear on before slipping under the duvet. They kept their eyes on each other's face as they made love, slowly, quietly, kissing each other gently, with tenderness.

Afterwards Martin gave a sigh of deep satisfaction. 'Happy New Year,' he murmured.

'And to you.' Becca stretched in bed, her body heavy. 'Any resolutions?'

'Get round the marathon. And you?' Martin wrapped his arms around her.

'The usual. Drink less, exercise more, learn to speak French.' It felt wonderfully warm and secure in Martin's arms. As she went to sleep she remembered there was one other resolution she had made, but that was one she could never share with Martin.

Becca pushed the door open to the Holburne Museum, pleased to get out of the driving rain outside. Paul was already there, and despite her best intentions and determination, her heart lifted. She hadn't seen him for two weeks. Strange how he appeared at once familiar and unfamiliar. We forget how they look over time, she thought. Perhaps if I was separated from Lily I would forget. I would carry a picture of her in my heart, but the image would get blurred.

He turned, and smiled at her. I must remember Lily, she thought as she walked towards him. I am doing this to protect Lily.

'Lovely to see you.' He kissed her cheek, as if they were friends meeting casually, but one hand on her shoulder pulled her to him so for a moment their bodies were aligned. She moved away, head down to hide her face, not wanting him to see her confusion. It was one thing to decide to give him up when he wasn't there, quite another when he was.

They walked to the ticket desk, his hand in the small of her back. Such a familiar gesture, that gentlest of pressures, protecting and guiding. One that from today she would no longer experience. She quickly glanced up at him. The light played on his cheekbones highlighting the contrast between the delicacy of the shaping round the eyes and the masculinity of the strong brows and nose that she loved. She caught herself in time. No, not loved. You couldn't love someone you didn't know. And not in the same way as a child you had given birth to.

Paul handed over a note to pay for their tickets. 'No, let me,' she said, opening her bag and searching in the depths for her wallet, not wanting to be beholden.

'Too late,' he said, smiling down at her.

Too late. The story of her life maybe, she thought as she climbed the grand stone stairs, Paul by her side. 'The first floor has all the porcelain and silver,' she said. 'We'll start at the top, where the paintings are, if you like.'

'I will follow where you lead,' he said gallantly, but paused by the window on the stairs. 'Are the gardens open?'

'Sydney Gardens? Yes, all the time, as far as I know.' Lily had spent much of the summer hanging out with her friends in Sydney Gardens doing heaven knew what. Usual teenage things, Becca assumed. Talking, listening, playing tag with childish bursts of energy before collapsing into teenagerish inertia. She didn't like to think Lily's peer group activities also included smoking and drinking.

'It's wonderful to see you,' Paul said. He was standing on the step below her so their eyes were level. 'I've missed you.'

'What, with all that skiing going on, and Christmas and every-thing?' Becca said, keeping her voice light. She wanted to stroke his face, smooth a strand of hair away, but she couldn't let herself. She could hardly bear to look him in the eyes.

'You were with me all the time. Here.' Paul pressed one of her hands to his chest. She so wanted to be able to hold him, press herself against him, the two halves coming together to make a whole. But it was impossible. She couldn't.

'We need to talk,' she said, and despite her best efforts at self-control, she felt her eyes filling with tears.

He held her chin and tilted her head as he searched her face. 'That sounds serious.' Paul dropped his hand to his side, his body language wary. 'Come on, let's go and look at these paintings. I could do with a dollop of culture after all that fondue.'

They climbed the stairs to the top floor in silence. Becca couldn't work out how to begin. How to explain to someone that you wanted to be with them, but had decided not to see them any more. It didn't make any sense. Love – not that she was in love with Paul, of course – was supposed to conquer all. People gave up everything for love, abandoned husbands, wives, children, betrayed countries, trampled on convention, swept all before them. They didn't meekly settle for something less just to avoid hurting others.

Mind you, that was what Ilsa did in *Casablanca*. She settled for fighting the good fight with her husband Victor rather than running off into the sunset with Rick. She put duty and obligation above love. Becca glanced up at Paul, thinking how good looking he was, especially with a tan from skiing.

They were the only people in the top gallery beyond the custodian. Most of the paintings were portraits. They stopped in front of a painting of a young girl dancing. 'Portrait of Henrietta Laura Pulteney,' Becca read. 'Most of the roads round here must be named after her – there's Pulteney Bridge and Pulteney Street, Laura Place and Henrietta Gardens.'

Paul peered at the portrait. 'She looks pleased with herself.'

'You wouldn't have your portrait painted if you weren't, would you? I mean, you wouldn't commission an artist when you were feeling a bit depressed, or you'd just lost a fortune. You'd only get it done when you were feeling you'd achieved something, surely.' Becca knew she was delaying the moment when she'd have to tell Paul. She had suggested the Holburne because she'd guessed correctly that it would be a quiet space at this time of year, but now she wished the gallery was full of visitors, bustling and talking, anything that filled the empty spaces of the top-floor gallery with something other than her need for him, and her determination to tell him it was over.

'Suzy had the children's portraits painted last year,' Paul said.

'Were they any good?' If only one other couple, one other person walked in right now, she wouldn't have to tell Paul, she could wait for another opportunity. She wistfully looked at the entrance, but no one else came. They were alone.

'Nothing special.' He paused, as if considering the question for the first time. 'Rather old fashioned, in fact. I suppose it's a good likeness, which is what Suzy required. That, and looking good above the mantelpiece.'

'I wish I'd had Lily done when she was younger,' Becca said. 'Perhaps not a painting, but one of those really smart photographs in a studio.'

'Why didn't you?'

'I don't know,' Becca said, moving away from him. 'No money, I suppose.' She'd always assumed there would be another child so she realised she'd subconsciously waited until he or she could join Lily in the photographer's studio, hair neatly brushed, best clothes on. Too late now. Lily didn't brush her hair at all as far as Becca could tell, let alone brush it neatly. Something deep inside her flinched from the idea of underlining Lily's solitary state with something as permanent as a photograph.

There was a bench in the middle of the room and she sat, facing away from the guard, hands clasped on her knees in front of her. Paul sat next to her. 'I can't see you again,' she blurted out.

He swung his head to look at her. 'Why not? Did something happen? What happened over Christmas?'

'Nothing, nothing,' she said, laying a hand on his arm to reassure him. 'I just can't see you again.'

'I see. Why?'

'I can't do this.' Becca leaned forwards, head in hands. 'I can't lie to everyone all the time, I can't treat Lily and Martin as if they don't matter. Whatever we have between us comes at their expense. I can't risk hurting them. And I don't want to hurt your family either. We shouldn't have let things get this far, but at least we haven't . . .' She looked up at him and thought he had never looked more desirable, more handsome, more unobtainable. 'We are not free to be with each other.'

'And if we were?' Becca turned away from him, unable to answer. Paul gave an anguished sigh. 'Do you think emotions can be turned on and off like a tap?'

She shook her head. 'I can't believe I'm saying these things to you. I want to be with you, but I can't. Every time we meet, we go a little bit further emotionally. At least, I do.' I could fall in love with you so easily, she thought.

'Don't.' He screwed his eyes up as if in pain. 'Don't do this.'

'There isn't a choice.'

'There are always choices,' he said sharply. 'I could leave Suzy. You could leave Martin.'

It was all going too far, too fast. Becca felt out of control, as if she were sliding down the mountain towards the edge and there was nothing to stop her. 'I can't . . . If you left Suzy because of me, think of all the pain you'd cause. Think of your children.'

'Children are tough. They'd get over it.'

'I don't want Lily to be tough, I don't want her to have to get over it. My parents are splitting up right now, and it's hurting me – and

I'm an adult.' She hugged her knees close to her. 'I can't do that to a child, any child, let alone my own. We have to stop seeing each other before it's too late.'

'But it already is too late.' He took her face in his hands. 'I've fallen in love with you.'

'You can't,' Becca whispered.

'I love you more and more. Every minute, every day. I've never loved anyone the way I love you now. Even when you're saying these dreadful things, I love you. I love you for being brave, and wanting to do the right thing.' His eyes were large and shining and he spoke with great conviction. He's an actor, Becca thought, trying to keep her feet on the ground. 'But darling, don't you see?' Paul continued. 'You can't just walk away. It doesn't work like that. If we know anything about life, it's that love isn't just hanging around waiting to be picked up. You have to search for it. And if you find it, you don't throw it away.'

Becca pulled her head free from his hands. 'Don't make it hard . . .'

'I want you to see what you're doing. Do you think you can live without love?'

'There'll always be the memories,' she said, echoes of Rick telling Ilsa that they'd always have Paris. But Paul wasn't being like either Rick or Ilsa. No question of self-sacrifice there. 'Please, Paul. Let me go.'

'I can't,' he said, turning away from her and putting his hand to the bridge of his nose. 'You've been the one good thing I've had these past few months. I can't let you just ruin it.'

Becca touched his shoulder, wanting to comfort him, wanting to cry herself. 'I'm sorry. If it's any consolation, I feel like death. I can hardly bear it. But I have to do this. I can't be with you, so I have to go before I get in too deep.'

'Aren't you in too deep already?' he whispered.

She stood up. 'I have to go.'

'Tell me you don't love me. Say it.'

'I don't love you.' And that was when she knew. She bent and quickly kissed him, took one last look at his face. 'I have to go.'

She turned and walked out of the gallery. She could hear Paul call her name but she carried on. If she stopped, she'd never get the strength to leave again. Becca went down the stairs faster, her feet clattering on the stone steps, her face wet with tears. Her feet were going faster, faster, her breath coming in short puffs. She put her hand to her mouth to stop the sobs coming out. And then she was in the lobby and out the front, with the rain still coming down. Where now? She guessed Paul's car was in the Holburne car park. She turned the other direction and ran through Sydney Gardens to the canal. Then down, and along, hardly looking in her need to get away from him. Rain washed her face, mingling with the tears. The towpath was covered in puddles, a few ducks contentedly quacking. She slowed to a walking pace, frightened of slipping in the mud. The rain was pelting down. Ahead, the canal went into a tunnel and she ran for it.

It was nearly as wet under the tunnel as outside. She leaned back against the mossy walls, and howled. The sound echoed round the tunnel, muffled by the rain falling in large sploshes on to the still brown water. She slid down the wall, not caring what she did to the back of her coat and crouched in a foetal position at the foot of the tunnel wall. I can't bear it, she thought. I can't bear it. I can't live without him. Oh God, help me. I didn't know I loved him. Her voice echoed round the tunnel. 'Paul, Paul, Paul.'

Chapter 20

It was a relief when the twelve days of Christmas were over and Becca could take the decorations down. 'Come and help me,' she called up to Lily. 'I'm going to do the tree,' she tried again. 'Do come down.' No reply.

Becca waited. Last year Lily had been a cheery, happy child chattering about Christmas and school and the new hamster. Now the hamster was dead, no longer rattling round on its treadmill, unloved, unnoticed until it smelled enough for Becca to yell at Lily to clean it out. I'm like that flipping hamster, Becca thought, stuck on a treadmill of work and domesticity. I gave up Paul for this. She closed her eyes. I gave up Paul for Lily's sake.

She looked at the tree. It wouldn't undecorate itself. Hey ho, she'd have to do it. Becca began to take the decorations down, wistfully aware that her hopes for Christmas had been unrealistic, designed for some 1950s happy family, with scrubbed and brushed children wearing ankle socks and ribbons in their hair, Mummy looking slim and elegant in her pinny, and Daddy neat in stay-pressed trousers and a canary yellow golfing sweater. Instead she'd got Lily, who possessed the animation of a gothic slug and Martin . . . Martin would fit quite happily into the mould, she thought. She could see him as the good father, working hard, settling into cosy slippers and pipe on his return, wielding a hammer for a spot of DIY or washing the car on a Sunday and buffing it up with a special polishing cloth. Perhaps if he'd buffed up my bumpers with as much care and attention, I wouldn't have fallen for Paul.

She took down the oldest, most precious of the decorations, the one she remembered from her own childhood, a creamy white ball decorated with a filigree of sparkling gold and swirling patterns dancing across the surface. She cupped the bauble in her hand, feeling the weight, the fragility of the glass. This had always been the one she placed last, to make sure it wasn't eclipsed by the others. It was still beautiful, even though she no longer looked at it with a child's eyes. It was older than Lily, possibly older than Becca herself. She felt a twinge of pleasure, followed quickly by a twinge of guilt, that somehow she had ended up with the family Christmas decorations. But Joanna wasn't interested in traditions, she rationalised. She probably didn't remember the glass balls, and anyway, they wouldn't have survived the trip overseas.

She put the bauble back in its tissue-paper nest in the box marked 'Fragile' and went back to the tree. But as she did so, her skirt must have caught the edge of the cardboard box and the box toppled to the floor with a muffled crash. With her heart in her mouth, she bent over the box, fingers probing the white tissue for the damage. The creamy white ball was in several pieces, the inside of the eggshell-fine glass a glossy gold. She could see her reflection in the largest piece, a golden haze of unhappiness.

'You OK, Mum?' Lily had emerged from her torpor. 'I heard a crash.'

'I broke one of the balls,' Becca said, trying for a smile.

'Oh.' Lily prodded the box with one stripy foot, the gothic look alleviated with purple stripes. Her eyes were still red from weeping over Kevin's defection. 'D'you need a brush or something?'

'No, it's OK.' Becca got up, the pieces in her hand, her body aching with the effort. 'Silly of me to be upset. It's just . . . well, we always had this decoration on the tree at Gran and Grandpa's.'

'So it's really old.' Lily didn't sound impressed. 'Didn't they want it?'

'I think Gran felt she didn't have the room to store Christmas decorations,' Becca said, letting the broken pieces slide into the waste-paper basket.

Lily drifted off upstairs so Becca put the rest of the decorations away single-handed and then took down the lights. Despite her careful efforts, they became tangled with the branches, twisting and coiling into a knobbled mass of wires. I used to love Christmas, she thought as she began to untangle them. She looked out of the window at the flat grey sky and felt there was nothing in life to look forward to, just more days of working and caring and feeling tired all the time. Term was starting tomorrow, and the relentless round was about to begin again.

Becca suddenly shoved all the tangled lights into the decorations box. What the hell. She'd sort it out next Christmas.

'Do you love me?' Becca asked. It was Monday morning, the first day of the new term, and Martin was sitting on the edge of the bed, examining the soles of his feet.

'Mmmm?' Martin picked at the ball of his left foot. There was something simian about the way he was hunched over. 'God, I've got a lot of hard skin. Did you get a new pumice?'

'I put it in the bathroom.' She pressed her lips together. Why couldn't Martin see that this wasn't a moment to worry about pumice?

'Thanks.' He got up and ambled across the room.

'I said, do you love me?'

Martin paused for a second on his amble across the room to the bathroom. 'Course.' He disappeared. A few minutes later, Becca could hear him rooting around the cupboard. 'Can't find it.'

'Look on the bottom shelf. Next to the shampoo.' I think I'm going mad, she thought. Completely mad. It wasn't supposed to be like this. She had given up Paul, and for what? Martin and his hard skin. Her own skin felt thin, like the membrane around a raw egg. It held the contents together, but only just. Easily pierced. I'm cracking up, she thought, and Martin doesn't even notice.

A cry of triumph from the bathroom. Martin stuck his head round the door. 'Found it,' he said, waving the pumice stone in his hand. His face was lit up, as if a new pumice stone was the summit of his desires. 'Thanks for getting it. Do you want me to wake Lily?'

'Do you love me?' Say yes, she willed him. Say yes, and take me in your arms. Say yes, you love me, adore me, worship me. Say yes, I am the woman of your dreams, the woman you love. She stared up into his eyes, willing him to make the right answer.

'Er, yes, of course I do,' he mumbled, looking embarrassed.

'Then why don't you say it any more?' Becca said.

Martin looked surprised. 'I do, don't I?'

'No, never.'

'That's a bit of an exaggeration,' he said.

'When was the last time?' she said.

Martin rubbed his face. 'I don't know, Becca. How am I supposed to remember?'

'You haven't for ages. I can't remember the last time. You never say it.'

'Just because I don't say it, doesn't mean I don't think it.'

'Then why don't you say it?'

Martin checked his watch. 'I can't go round saying I love you all the time. It wouldn't be . . .'

'What? What wouldn't it be?'

'I really ought to be getting on, otherwise I'll be late. We'll all be late.'

'Say it now. Tell me you love me.'

Martin shifted from one foot to the other. 'You can't make someone say these things, they've got to arise spontaneously, be part of the moment.'

'But what if the moment never comes? Do I assume you don't love me?'

'It's Monday morning,' Martin said, a hint of exasperation in his voice. 'I've got to go to work. You're my wife; of course I love you. Better?'

'Not really.' Becca picked at the duvet cover.

Martin rolled his eyes. 'I've said it – what more do you want?'

And that was the question. She didn't know. Or rather she did, chaotic dreams and emotions swirling around in a confused mass. Becca felt this was a turning point, that if Martin was to take her seriously, to put the rest of the world to one side for a minute and sit by her side and tell her that he loved her, all would be fine. I want romance, she thought. I can't live this humdrum, dreary life, day in, day out, without love. All Martin would have to do is make the teeniest, tiniest bit of effort. She looked at him with sad realisation. It wasn't going to happen. 'Can you make sure Lily's up?'

He did a thumbs-up, obviously relieved that they were on safer domestic ground. 'Will do.'

She slid into her weekday morning routine: shower, dress, breakfast. It was always hard to get back into the work routine after time off; it felt like climbing back up onto the treadmill, working so hard to gain any momentum. Martin peered out of the window, cereal bowl in hand. 'Looks like there's been a frost. I'll sort your car out if you like.'

'Thanks. Lily, if you don't eat up, we'll be late.' Becca slotted her cereal bowl into the dishwasher as Martin went outside with the car keys.

Lily poked her spoon at her cornflakes. 'I can't bear to eat cereal in the mornings, it makes me sick.'

Toast was rejected because there wasn't any peanut butter, and the raspberry jam that had been such a favourite all last year was now vile. Finally Lily volunteered that she fancied a poached egg. Becca knew that if Martin had overheard the conversation he'd be pointing out that Becca spoiled Lily. Good thing he wasn't here then. She glanced up at the clock. 'All right, I'll do you a poached egg, but you'll have to get ready as quickly as you can and then come back for it.'

Lily slouched off to finish getting her school uniform on, or so Becca hoped. She grabbed the egg poacher from the cupboard and put it on to heat. Martin came back into the kitchen, rubbing his hands and stamping his feet with cold. 'I've defrosted the car,' he said. 'And look what I found on your windscreen.' He handed something to her. A red rose, withered from the cold. Becca felt suddenly as cold as the rose. 'Someone must have mistaken your car for the girls in the flat across the road – one of them's got a black hatchback too, haven't they?'

Becca nodded. 'Was there any note with it?' Her voice sounded high pitched.

Martin shook his head. 'I must be off. See you this evening. Oh, while I remember, can you put up my sponsorship form at work? I've still got to raise at least another £250.' He kissed her forehead, and left.

Becca held the rose. It was soft and cold in her hand, tightly formed into a dense head of petals, dark red like dried blood. Her mobile phone pinged. A text message: 'I love you.'

The water for Lily's poached egg hissed and spluttered on the stove. Becca deleted the text, then tossed the rose into the rubbish bin.

Becca had never felt less like being at work as she put up Martin's marathon sponsorship form on the staffroom notice board.

'Is that for Martin?' Crystal said. 'I'll sponsor him.'

'Thanks, he'll appreciate that,' Becca said. She watched as Crystal filled in her name and address on the form.

'I've put on half a stone over Christmas. Perhaps I ought to take up running, like Martin.' Crystal paused, twisting the pen in her fingers. 'I suppose it's none of my business . . .' You're right; it isn't, Becca thought gathering her books together, as she guessed what was coming from the concerned but also interested expression on Crystal's face. How she wished she hadn't said anything to her at the Pump Room. '. . . But how are things?'

Becca toyed for a second with pretending she didn't know what 'things' Crystal meant, but that would have been a cop-out. It was her own fault for dumping her problems on Crystal. She looked around, thinking she might cry if she thought any more about Paul.

'Ah, the very ladies I wish to see!'

Becca had never been happier to see Bill. 'What can we do for you, Bill?' she said.

'I've arranged a special drama workshop for all students doing English or drama on Thursday 15 February, so can you put that in your diaries please?'

Crystal exchanged glances with Becca. 'Do we need to prepare anything? What's it about?'

Bill grinned broadly and tapped his nose. 'That's for me to know, and you to find out. You don't have to do a thing, just come along and be crowd control.' He swirled away from them.

'One more thing to worry about,' Crystal said, sighing heavily.

'You don't have to worry about me and Martin,' Becca said. 'I told . . . my friend I couldn't see him again. I gave him up.' She couldn't help it, the tears started to fall.

'Becca, you've done the right thing. I'm really proud of you.' Crystal gave her a hug.

I don't care, Becca thought. I wish I hadn't.

Strange how life carries on. The shell of Becca went about her daily business. Most of the time she thought she could manage, but sometimes she would find herself crying and have to hide in the staff loos at work. She pretended to have a heavy cold, as an excuse for perpetually clutching tissues.

'Why don't you take a day or two off work?' Martin said.

'I can't let everyone down,' she said. The demands of work were the only thing that was keeping her going.

'I'd have thought they'd be happy to give you a couple of days. You'd get better quicker, and they wouldn't get your germs. Anyone can see you're not yourself.'

No, she wasn't herself. The real Becca had died inside, distraught by leaving Paul. It had to be done, she thought. I had to do it. But then she hadn't known how hard it was going to be. She thought of Paul all the time.

Her mobile rang. His number. She held the phone in her hand, wanting to answer. Even seeing his name on the screen lightened her heart. It would be so easy to pick the phone up and speak to him, rekindle the relationship – if he would let her. And then it would start all over again, the lying, the deceit, the anxiety, the fear of being caught. Lily. Think of Lily. The phone rang on, shrill and insistent. I love you, she telepathically told Paul at the other end of the phone. But she didn't answer.

In the end Bill caught her coming out of the ladies on Monday morning, her eyes red, nose streaming and told her to take the next day off, so she did. But being at home without anything to do was worse than being at work. Becca sat in the kitchen and caught up with the Sunday newspapers. She desultorily turned the pages of the Sunday colour supplement, feeling unable to settle on any one article. There was far too much about the January sales, diets and detoxing, none of which was of interest to her. She felt she never wanted to buy anything ever again after the orgy of spending over Christmas, and let's face it, all diets came down to eat less, exercise more and the only detoxing she needed was how to flush Paul out of her heart, something no amount of carrot and wheatgrass would solve.

Becca flicked through the pages. 'Spice up your sex life! We tell you how!' screamed one of the headings. They'd chosen to illustrate the article with a long-legged model in various bits of flimsy underwear. If I looked like that, Becca thought, I wouldn't need to spice up my sex life, I'd be having it non-stop. She blew her nose. Still, perhaps she should buy something a bit less practical and more exciting to wear from time to time. 'Get your nipples pierced and drive him wild when you tell him in the supermarket!' the article suggested. Becca clutched her breasts to her just thinking about it. She didn't think pierced nipples were Martin's thing, and they definitely weren't hers.

An article on feng shui caught her eye and she read through it. It was quite clear, her happiness corner was occupied by the downstairs loo. Becca herself hardly ever used it, as it made up the last section of the utility room and was therefore subject to outside walls on two sides. Now she realised that every morning Martin took the newspaper and settled himself down to crap on her happiness.

She closed the magazine and slung it in the bin. I won't allow myself to think like this, she thought. I won't. I said goodbye to Paul, and that was the right thing to do. I can make it work with Martin. I will make it work. She clenched her fists with determination while her treacherous mind slid over to Paul. A ransom note had arrived in the post that morning: 'Help! My heart has been kidnapped. Rescue me.' She'd thrown it away, but the image of him cutting out letters from newspapers and sticking them on to the sheet lingered.

I need to move on, she thought, and make a new start. Out with the old, and in with the new. She could clear out that pile of drama school brochures for a start. Without looking inside, she tipped them into the bin. It had been a daft idea, a complete fantasy. There was no way she could afford to give up work and become an unemployed actor. But perhaps it was a sign that she needed to move on. She'd been working at Hamilton House for too long, she'd got complacent and lazy. There had to be other things she could do.

She went to the computer and turned it on. While she was waiting for it to boot she tried to think of her options. She was on a yearly contract with Bill running from September, so if she handed in her term's notice at the end of the spring term she'd be paid for the summer holidays too. That gave her a couple of months to research alternatives, with the prospect of starting something new in September. But what? She went online and found Google. For a moment she paused. She could get careers advice from Hamilton House. She typed in 'New Beginnings'. A few seconds later a long listing came up. She scanned it. There didn't seem to be much of specific interest. Try again. She thought for a second. Then typed 'Reinventing yourself'. This time there were lots of entries on the theme of being the person you always wanted to be. She rolled up her sleeves, stretched her fingers out, then started to work her way through the entries.

That night Becca woke at two in the morning and couldn't get back to sleep. Martin's rhythmic breathing infuriated her as she huddled over on her side of the bed trying to wrap the duvet around her even more tightly. She remembered the flint-knapping, and thought it was like love being tested. If the love was flawed, the flint would shatter at the first few strikes and be discarded. If it were true, the blows created a thing of beauty as well as function. The only way of knowing if the love was true was to test it. But once you found your love, your perfect flint, and had created the axehead, it was there to be used. And in using, each blow started to chip away at the perfection. It was still functional, still usable, but the sheen started to go, the edges becoming ragged and dull instead of translucent and smooth. All those small blows of selfishness, the tiny strikes of inconsideration chipping away. At any moment it might shatter, or become so chipped away that it lost its function, its meaning. Or it could remain true, a useful tool. The thing with Paul was never real, she told herself. It was never tested. Martin is real.

The night air was cold. She snuggled up to Martin, and in his sleep he turned and cuddled her. Finally she slept.

Four weeks later, Becca let herself into her parents' house, lugging a large bag full of food for Frank's fridge to get him through the weekend and the beginning of the following week, by which time June would be back home. It hadn't been exactly a struggle keeping Frank stocked with food, but it had been another thing to think about. Thank heavens June was coming back and could take over. She shied away from thinking of what was going to happen to Frank if June did leave.

'Dad? It's me,' she called, trying not to think of preparing meals for one for the next twenty years. There were voices coming from the kitchen. Slightly surprised she followed the sounds down the hall. Perhaps Frank had the radio on. 'I've brought you some supplies,' Becca said, then stopped.

Sitting at the kitchen table was her father, all spruced up and wearing a check shirt and paisley cravat, while opposite him was a grey-haired woman upholstered in a heavy, ribbed, navy cardigan and pearls from an oyster the size of the Old Man of Hoy gleaming round her neck. If she'd leaned forward just a little her bust would have formed one long continuous slope from neck to table.

'Ah Becca,' her father said, giving a start as if he'd been caught doing something naughty. 'I didn't know you were coming.'

'I've brought supplies,' Becca repeated, feeling stupid. Frank had obviously been entertaining, judging by the plates and wine glasses. So much for the visions of her father starving all alone.

The pearly woman patted her hair and gave a coy smile that didn't reach her eyes. 'Aren't you going to introduce us?'

'Ah yes. This is my daughter Rebecca, and this is Mrs Batey. From the golf club,' he added.

'We met at your parents' party this summer,' Mrs Batey said.

'Of course – how are you?' Becca replied, sticking to the safe shores of conventional politeness although she couldn't remember Mrs Batey. Had there been a Mr Batey? She glanced at Frank. He'd obviously made a huge effort – he hadn't looked this smart for years. She opened the fridge door ready to put in her food, but the fridge was nearly full. 'Why, Dad, you've hardly eaten any of the things I brought you last time. You've got to eat properly.'

'That's what I told him,' Mrs Batey chipped in. She simpered at Frank, creasing make-up that could have been used for the white cliffs of Dover. Her pale-pink lipstick had already imprinted itself on to her teacup in a pucker of a kiss. So unlike June in every way. 'At our age you can't afford to skip meals.'

Becca could feel all the hairs on her neck bristle, even though Mrs Batey was merely echoing what Becca had just said. I don't want you to agree with me, she glowered, aware that she'd slipped into sulky teenager mode. What was it about her parents that brought out her most unattractive side? Becca tried to re-establish the nicer, more adult bit of her. She started to rearrange the contents of the fridge so she could squeeze her carefully wrapped dishes in. It had become as complicated a case of manoeuvring as a Rubik's Cube. He really had hardly eaten anything at all.

Frank looked sheepish. 'Mrs Batey has been kind enough to make me a few meals.'

Becca looked at Mrs Batey again, who looked back in a slightly defiant way. Becca looked to Frank, then back to Mrs Batey. A horrible idea began to form in her mind. Surely not . . . 'That's really kind of you, looking after Dad until Mum comes back from holiday,' Becca said, smiling at Mrs Batey. 'She'll be back on Monday, as I expect you know.'

Frank took a sharp intake of breath as if to say something, but didn't.

'It sounds as if she's having a wonderful time,' Mrs Batey said, chattily. 'I've never fancied going myself, but I hear it's beautiful.

Lovely scenery. Not that you can beat Scotland for scenery in my opinion.'

'Don't know why anyone wants to go abroad. We've got every-thing we need here, in this country. Better food too,' Frank said.

'There's nothing like a good old-fashioned British roast,' Mrs Batey said and Frank nodded. The sight of them nodding in complete agreement in her mother's house made Becca feel panicky.

'That reminds me, Dad, would you like to come over to our house for lunch tomorrow?' He'd been over every Sunday since June left, apart from the last weekend when he'd been doing something else.

'Thank you, Becca dear, but I have a prior engagement.' He looked across at Mrs Batey who bridled. Becca felt sick. This wasn't happening. June had only gone away for a little while. She'd be back within seventy-two hours.

Normally when Becca came over to her parents' house she'd make herself a cup of tea or coffee, not think about asking, or being asked. Now she felt inhibited. 'I suppose I ought to be going,' Becca said, expecting Frank to offer her a coffee or tea. He didn't. He quite obviously wanted her to go. 'Is there anything I can do before I go?'

Frank shook his head. 'No thank you, I'm fine. I mustn't take up too much of your valuable time.' He moved to the door as if to encourage her to go through it.

Becca felt like a pushy salesperson who has to be escorted from the premises. 'I'll be off. Busy weekend ahead and all that. It was nice to meet you again,' she said to Mrs Batey, not quite able to look her in the eye. 'Give me a ring if you need me, Dad.' She gave him a quick peck on the cheek. 'Don't worry, I'll let myself out.'

As she closed the front door behind her she reflected that, judging from the relieved smile on Frank's face, he wasn't worried in the slightest.

* * *

'I simply couldn't believe it,' Becca said to Martin as they trundled round the supermarket. 'There she was, sitting in my mother's place.'

'Which your mother has left vacant. I need lots of low GI carbo-hydrate,' Martin said, slinging a couple of packets of rice cakes into the trolley. 'Frankly, I'm not surprised Frank's found someone else.'

'Martin!' Becca put in two multi-packs of chocolate biscuits. 'My mother's away on holiday, she's hasn't moved out.'

'You may not like it, darling, but your mother's said she wants a divorce. And while technically she's on holiday, she's as good as moved out.' Martin waggled the biscuits at Becca before putting them back on the shelf. 'We've got enough fat stored on our bodies to run twenty consecutive marathons. Can you blame Frank for looking around for someone else?'

'They're two for the price of one.' Becca put the biscuits back in the trolley, thinking it had been a mistake to go round the supermarket with Martin. 'I don't blame Dad, I blame Mum. I don't think she'll be pleased to come back and see that woman in her place. I was going to phone, but there isn't much point – she'll be back on Monday.'

'For all you know she might be delighted. Or it might change her mind. We don't know. What we do know is that it's none of our business. We've got to stop eating this rubbish,' Martin said taking the biscuits out again. 'It's nothing but empty calories. Wholegrains, that's what we should have. Wholegrains, pulses and beans – that sort of thing.'

'But they taste nice. And Lily likes them.'

Martin sighed, and put the biscuits back into the trolley. 'Anyway, what's wrong with Frank finding someone else? June might be having a holiday romance – or two!'

'That's horrible.' She stuck her lower lip out, then realised she probably looked like Lily.

'Come on, Becs, it's not really. Just because they're your parents, doesn't mean they don't want a bit of romance in their lives. You should be pleased they're fit and well and not in wheelchairs.'

'Of course I'm pleased they're fit but . . .' She knew Martin was technically right but in her heart she felt Frank and June having other relationships was just wrong. Besides, if she wasn't allowed romance, she was darned if she could see why her parents should have it. And I do want some excitement in my life beyond chocolate, she thought, following Martin as he headed round the corner in search of salads.

But Martin's hunt was deflected by Crystal coming the other way round the corner, presumably in search of chocolate biscuits too. There was a slightly awkward moment while they decided if kissing socially was something you did in the supermarket, and then Martin obviously decided it was because he gave Crystal a peck on the cheek.

'I haven't seen you for ever, Martin, since before Christmas at least,' Crystal said. She looked flustered and for a heart-stopping moment Becca wondered if she was going to let slip something about Becca's confession. 'Gosh, Christmas seems like ages away, rather than six weeks. You're looking incredible. What's your secret?'

'Willpower,' Martin said, straightening up and pulling what remained of his tummy in. Becca knew he'd lost nearly two stone and looking at him she realised he'd developed, if not a six pack, then the beginnings of a two pack. He was looking more like the man she'd originally married.

'I suppose that means you think I haven't got any. Well, you're quite right I expect, I can resist everything except temptation.' She raised her eyebrows suggestively.

'I'm off to get the rest of the list,' Martin said, waving it. 'Nice to see you, Crystal.'

'Byee,' Crystal said. She waited until Martin had gone further along into the next aisle before leaning towards Becca conspiratorially. 'I hope you've patched things up.'

'I told you we have. Forget that I said anything,' Becca said, regretting telling Crystal more than ever.

'Martin is looking so gorgeous at the moment, if you don't want him, he'll be snapped up in seconds. Heavens, it's enough to make me take up marathon running. If only it didn't involve so much exercise. Anyway, I must scoot, I've got a new bloke coming for dinner, and I've hardly got anything on my list yet,' Crystal said, despite her trolley looking full enough to keep a small cruise ship going on a transatlantic crossing. 'See you at school.'

Becca watched Crystal's retreating back. There was no doubt she was right: Martin was looking well at the moment, but as to him being snapped up ... But Frank was being snapped up, Becca thought as she walked round to find where Martin and the trolley had gone. The second June's back had turned, Mrs Batey had slipped in. Not that Martin would ever go off with someone else, but she could see him being a target for a predatory woman. He was at the far end of the aisle reading the label on a pack of humous. A youngish woman walked by him and for a second her eyes flickered over him as if in appreciation. I must try harder, Becca thought as she edged beside him. If I want things to change, I have to make the effort. Spice up our sex life, just like the magazine article said. Thinking of which ... 'I've just remembered I've forgotten the aubergine,' she said to Martin. 'You carry on, I'll go and get it.'

She nipped through the fruit and veg section to the ladies. On the way back she collected an aubergine and tracked along the aisles to find Martin. She waited until they were alone in one of the aisles before sidling up to him.

'I'm not wearing any knickers,' she whispered.

'What?' Martin said vaguely, reading the label of the low fat mayonnaise. 'I think we ought to be using the low fat version.' He put the jar in their trolley. Drat, he obviously hadn't heard her.

'I'm not wearing any knickers,' she said again, this time putting her hand on his forearm to attract his attention.

'What?' he said again, this time his attention fully engaged. 'Why not?' He dropped his voice down to a whisper. 'Have you had an accident?'

'No, of course not,' Becca said, disconcerted. She'd imagined Martin immediately wanting to whisk her away into some quiet corner, not him assuming that she was incontinent. 'It's supposed to be exciting.'

'It will be, if you trip up!' He laughed, pleased with his joke.

Becca stalked back to the ladies. So much for driving him wild in the aisles. In the cubicle she pulled her knickers from her handbag, and with them came an envelope. It was, she realised, one of Paul's letters. She usually threw them away, without even reading them, thinking it better not to look, but this one she'd grabbed for an impromptu list of Things To Do. Now, she sat on the loo seat and opened the envelope: 'I love you. Ring me, text me, email me. Anything. Life has no meaning without you. I love you. P.'

Becca leaned back against the cubicle wall. She'd assumed at the beginning that Paul would get fed up with the game and one day the letters and flowers would stop. They'd been together such a short time, although she'd felt she'd loved him at the time, the reality was that he occupied a warm, fuzzy but also distant place in her heart. She lowered her eyes, thinking that while she of course couldn't have anything to do with him, it was nice to be chased like this, to feel that you could inspire passion in a man, albeit not your husband.

She looked at the letter more closely. He'd written in ink, with a real pen, with large dramatic sweeps and flourishes. He's an actor, she thought. He's married. That was more sobering. Becca stood up, and with sudden, jagged motions, ripped up the letter and envelope and flushed them down the pan.

Chapter 21

'Welcome back,' Becca and Lily chorused as June opened her front door. Becca did a double take, stunned into silence. No such inhibitions for Lily.

'Gran! Your hair!'

'Do you like it?' June said, running a tanned hand through what remained of her bob, now cropped like a man's. 'It's so much easier to look after.'

'It's a bit dramatic,' Becca managed. 'But it suits you.' I think, she mentally added. June had never been a little old lady to Becca, but she thought of her as being as cuddly and comforting as a currant bun. Now with her hair cropped short she looked older, but striking and immensely capable, as if she was going to sail a yacht around the world or stride out across the Trans-Pennine way. All good things, just not like Becca's mum. 'You're very brown.'

'It's the wind that does it. Everyone lives a very outdoors kind of life in New Zealand, climbing up mountains, going hiking, swimming, cycling, all that sort of thing. Exhausting, but exhilarating too. I'll show you the photos in a sec – I bought a digital camera on the way out,' June said. 'A little Christmas present to myself.'

'We missed you at Christmas,' Lily chipped in, hugging her grandmother.

'Did you, lovey? I missed you too.' June kissed Lily's cheek. 'But it was nice for me to be with Joanna and your cousins – I can see you all the time, but they're on the other side of the world. Mind you, I did feel like staying out there.'

'Would you?' Becca asked.

June shook her head. 'It's too far from anywhere else, and I want to do a bit more travelling. There are so many places I want to see!'

'I'm glad you're staying here,' Lily said, leaning her head into her grandmother.

'Mmm.' June glanced towards Becca, whose senses went onto red alert. There was something going on here.

'Where's Dad?' she asked, suddenly aware of his absence.

'Off playing golf I think,' June said with a dismissive wave of her hand. 'Come into the living room. I've got something for you two.'

They crossed the hall into the living room, June and Lily arm in arm, with Becca trailing behind, feeling like the bad fairy at the christening. She wondered when – if? – she should say something to June about Mrs Batey. June had brought presents: necklaces made from shells and beads, a bright red scarf threaded with tiny green and yellow beads around the edge. Lily looked delighted as June arranged a scarf around her shoulders, while Becca wondered if she'd been wrong about there being something going on.

'Boiling mud, just plop plopping out of the ground,' June said, pointing to a photograph of a geyser. 'Stinks to high heaven.'

'Can we go to New Zealand, Mum? We could go for Christmas too.'

'We'd have to ask your father, see what he thinks,' Becca said. It occurred to her that she deflected questions on to Martin all the time. She should have said up front if she wanted to go, or not, and left it at that. She liked the idea of being there but the thought of the journey put her off. 'It's a very long way.'

'But worth it. It's made me realise how much I wanted to live beside the sea.' June took a deep breath. 'I'm thinking of moving to St Ives.'

'What? But that's Cornwall.'

'It's not the end of the world.' June squeezed Lily to her. 'You'll like it, poppet, there's lots of surfing, and the sea and—'

Becca had a vision of June surfing to the theme music of *Hawaii 5-0*. 'But why St Ives?'

'Do you remember my old friend Anna? She came to our golden wedding party. She lives in St Ives. Her husband died a bit ago, and her children have moved away, so she's alone in her house. She's invited me to come and stay for a while – well, for as long as I like, to be honest. I've spent all my life putting other people first, and now I'm going to put me first. St Ives is heaving with artists and galleries, and I've decided I'm going to become a full-time artist.'

'Good for you, Gran,' Lily said.

St Ives. Becca had a picture of it as a mass of higgledy-piggledy little fisherman's cottages running down to a harbour. She knew it had been an artists' colony in the fifties – was it Barbara Hepworth who'd lived there? 'Couldn't you be an artist here?' she said.

June shook her head making her dangly long earrings – another new acquisition – dance. 'No. I need to soak up the atmosphere. Bath is stifling me, it's too bourgeois.'

'Oh.' Becca felt completely inadequate. Hidebound. Boring. She liked Bath. 'I suppose I must be bourgeois.'

'You are, dear,' her mother said with a blithe smile. 'But never mind.'

Becca felt immensely annoyed with June. What did she mean by going off, and then coming back and telling Becca she was bourgeois, as if that was synonymous with boring. They couldn't all go off on a jolly for three months, some of them had responsibilities that they weren't prepared to run away from and expect everyone else to cope in their absense.

'While you've been away Dad's had one of the ladies from the golf club in attendance,' Becca said, faux-casually. 'She's been making him casseroles and hotpots. Mrs Beattie? Batey?' She deliberately fudged the name to make it look as though she didn't care. Which she didn't of course.

'Maureen? Never.' June shook her head. 'Now that is a surprise. I always thought she had a bit of a soft spot for your father but I never thought . . .'

Becca tried to read her mother's expression. Jealousy? Amusement? It was hard to tell. But it would only be human nature to be thrown to discover that the person you'd left behind had found someone to take your place so very quickly.

'Would it make you change your mind?' she said softly.

June shook her head and grinned. 'I'd just wish her good luck.'

On Valentine's Day Lily burst into the kitchen, school bag swinging from her shoulders. 'Anything for me?'

'Where?' Becca said, feigning nonchalance. It was mean to tease, but irresistible.

'In the post.' Lily's face was a study of intensity.

Becca was tempted to play out the drama for a little longer, but gave in. 'Three cards. They're on the side.'

Lily grabbed them. 'Tsk, you could have at least tried to disguise your handwriting, and that's from Gran,' she said, discarding two of the envelopes immediately. The other she examined minutely, trying to decipher the postcode.

'Do you recognise the writing?' Becca asked, stirring the rice and trying not to appear too avidly curious.

Lily gave a quick shake of her head and turned a little away from Becca as she ripped open the envelope. She gave a little gasp of pleasure – Becca could make out a flowery scene and plenty of throbbing red hearts. Then she opened it up and scanned the contents, a smile spreading across her face as she read.

'Who's it from?'

'Kevin,' Lily said smugly.

'Has he signed it?'

'Course not, but who else would it be?'

'You might have a secret admirer.' Lily snorted at the idea, and returned to studying her card as if the secrets of the universe were written inside. 'I thought Kevin was a mean creep and you were never going to speak with him again.'

'Mu-um.' Lily rolled her eyes at such parental stupidity. Was there something especially elastic about the membranes in a teenager's eye sockets that allowed them such extravagant rolling abilities? Sometimes it felt as if Lily was undertaking the Olympic try-outs in eye rolling.

'I take it you've made up.' Lily nodded, her smile serene, her eyes far away. 'So. Has he written something nice?'

Lily looked torn between keeping the contents private and telling. Telling won. She cleared her throat, and read.

> When winter comes and skies are dark
> And Jack Frost's fingers make their mark
> And all the world is looking black
> And all I know is what I lack,
> I think of you, your smiling face
> And everything slips into place.
> You don't know it, but you see,
> You are the sunshine and the stars to me.

'Oh Lily, that's beautiful.' Becca was amazed. There must be more to Kevin than she'd thought. It just went to show, you shouldn't judge by appearances. 'You must treasure that for ever.'

Lily sighed. 'Did you get anything?'

Becca shook her head. 'Your father never remembers.' It wasn't a lie – Martin never did remember – but not the entire truth either. Because she'd come back from work to find a small hand-tied bunch of elegant stephanotis stems on the doorstep, deliciously scented, absurdly unseasonal, and a card that read: 'To the woman I love.'

It turned out Martin had booked a restaurant for dinner on Valentine's Day. 'Oh, you didn't,' Becca said, feeling guilty because she'd said that Martin never remembered. 'You know they always whack up the prices on Valentine's day.'

Martin's face fell. 'I thought you'd be pleased,' he said, and Becca felt doubly guilty.

'It's kind of you to think of it.' She made herself smile. 'It'll be a treat.'

The restaurant was full of other couples indulging in the special menu. Red rose petals were strewn on the tables, the complimentary glass of champagne was pink, as were the candles and ribbons forming the centrepiece along with pink carnations and sprigs of shrivelled gypsophila. Becca found the trappings of romance oppressive, as if it was compulsory to hold hands and stare into each other's eyes for at least fifty per cent of the evening. People who are in love, she wanted to say, don't save it for one fancy dinner a year, they demonstrate it every day, with a million small things.

The oppressive atmosphere was felt by most of the diners as far as she could tell. Only one couple seemed to be enjoying them-selves, and they looked as if they'd rather be eating each other than the food. The rest of them sat in silence or made stilted, formal conversation. Becca wondered how many relationships broke up after the ordeal of the special Valentine's Day dinner.

She told Martin about June, and her apparent unconcern over Mrs Batey's presence. 'You'd have thought she'd have been a bit more . . . I don't know, jealous I suppose. But not a bit of it. Maybe she was jet-lagged. Perhaps I should give her a ring and talk about it some more.'

Martin sighed. 'Do we have to talk about your parents all the time?'

'I'm sorry, I didn't mean to bore you.' Becca stared crossly at the gypsophila. It would be dead by tomorrow.

'It's just – there are other things to talk about.'

'Fine. Let's talk about them.' She poked the gypsophila further into its vase so it could reach the water. The situation with her parents might be boring to Martin, but it was important to her. All Martin had to do was listen. She listened to him talking about running often enough. She dropped the gypsophila and started to fiddle with her fork, sticking the tines into the weave of the tablecloth.

I once promised myself that I'd never be one of those couples who sit in silence with their partner, Becca thought to herself. I always thought it would be terminably sad to be in that sort of relationship where nothing you said was interesting and nothing they said interested you.

She prodded her food, but even a conversation about the meal was difficult as the low lighting, presumably to make the atmosphere intimate, had the effect of making it hard to see what she was eating, and she'd forgotten what she'd ordered. It all tasted like cotton wool anyway. With Paul she never had to think about what to say, conversation flowed between them as naturally as the Avon. And he listened properly.

'What?' She realised Martin was saying something. 'Sorry.'

He looked offended. 'I was just saying how you ought to book your car in for a service; I don't like the way your engine is sounding.'

'Right. Sorry.' She brought her mind away from Paul and to her car. 'You're right, it is sounding a bit rough.'

'And last time I was in it I thought the clutch was slipping too.' Becca nodded, thinking of Paul's clutch slipping into all sorts of delicious places it shouldn't. Martin hesitated. 'Are you OK, Becca? You seem distracted.'

'Oh, no, I'm fine. Just a little tired perhaps.'

'I was wondering if there was anything worrying you?'

'No, no, nothing beyond the usual.' She shrugged and Martin stared across to the other side of the room, and they were silent like the other couples in that rosy, intimate, chilly room.

On the way home Martin broke the silence. 'I'm sorry,' he said. 'I wanted this to be a good evening for us both, and it seems to have been a failure.'

'I'm sorry too,' Becca said, disarmed by his apology.

When they got home, Martin offered to make them both a hot drink which Becca declined. 'I think I'll go straight to bed.' She went up, checked that Lily was asleep, then started to get undressed. Martin came into the bedroom.

'You were quite right – it's a dreadful night to go and have dinner with your wife.'

'I'm sorry,' Becca said again, not sure of what she could possibly say to retrieve the situation. Martin meant well, it was she who was the problem. Martin was only doing his best. It wasn't his fault she hated him for it. 'I don't think I'm myself tonight,' she said shakily, feeling close to tears. 'Everything I say or do comes out wrong. I'm sorry. You deserve better.'

'Becca.' Martin gave her a hug. 'What's the matter? There's something else, isn't there, something else that's bothering you. Is it work? You know, if you ever wanted to change jobs and say "sod off" to Bill Malcolm you could. We could manage financially until you found another job.'

'Thanks.' Becca sniffed back her tears. The very idea of leaving her job seemed to require more energy than she had. 'I'm OK, really I am. Just a bit tired maybe. I think I'm getting menopausal. I've been reading this book and it can start in your twenties.'

'But that's rare, surely.' Martin stopped undressing and patted her shoulder. 'You're perhaps feeling a bit stressed – February is always a depressing month.'

'Forty-five onwards for the first signs of menopause in most women.' She got into bed, thinking mournfully of declining fertility, not that she'd ever been a whiz in the fertility stakes in the first place.

'You're only forty-three.' Martin got into bed and cuddled up to her. 'I think you're a pretty damn sexy woman whatever.'

'Thanks.' She sniffed the last of the tears away. He put his hand on her hip. Becca froze. 'Martin, I'm sorry. Not tonight. I'm too tired.' She couldn't meet his eyes. 'And I've got a splitting headache.'

Martin rolled away, grunted a goodnight and turned his light out.

Becca stared into the darkness. Life was so painful and difficult. It seemed you only found happiness for yourself at the expense of others.

Becca pushed open the door of the church hall, feeling a strong sense of déjà vu. But this time the steps were filled with hordes of teenagers thronging around, yawning, jostling, tossing their hair. Crowd control, Bill had called it. He hadn't come in the coach with her and Crystal, but had gone earlier. He was being very mysterious about the whole project.

Crystal was already in the foyer. When she saw Becca she indicated the door to the main hall with a nod of her head. 'Bill's in there. Apparently we're not to come in until he says so.'

'What's he up to?' Becca said.

'Heaven knows. He's looking jolly pleased with himself though.'

The foyer looked as it always had, but now there were photographs from the production of *The Country Wife* up. She examined them, half wanting to point out the pictures of herself to the pupils, half praying that none of them realised that it was 'Miss' with the heaving bosom. Mind you, it was hard to see who it was under the white make-up. Her face looked like a mask.

There were some she hadn't seen before – Angela must have taken them in rehearsal. Victoria, waving her arms around. Brian, hands raised foppishly, despite his jeans and jumper. She caught her breath. One of Paul and her. He was pointing at something, perhaps giving her an indication of where she was supposed to move, and she was looking intently at him. She could feel the connection between them, the eyes focused in on each other, the intensity. It had been there all the time, but she hadn't realised. She felt for a second as if the ground moved beneath her feet. All the longing and desire for him came flooding back. They were on the same wavelength. He understood. She belonged in his world, doing interesting things, not this everyday relentless battle. She put her hand out to steady herself. No, she'd done the right thing. These feelings would pass. It was a fantasy, acting, being with Paul. Not real life. She looked up and caught Crystal's glance.

'My moment of fame,' Becca managed to say, tapping the picture of her in full costume and make-up.

'Are you going to carry on with acting?' Crystal asked.

Becca shook her head. 'It was fun, but it's not for me.' Like having an affair, she thought. Fun for some, but not for me. She gave herself a little shake. She was over all that. She'd made her decision, and suffered the pain, but that was all over.

The door opened, and Bill stuck his head out. 'I'll be ready in another couple of minutes, so take the register now.' The door shut again.

'Thanks, oh master, we were just about to,' Crystal muttered. 'Hey ho, Becca. Let's get underway.' They took the register, the students chattering with high excited voices now it looked as if something was going to happen.

Bill's head emerged again. 'They can come in now.' Crystal held the door open and the first students slowly filed through. Becca brought up the rear. She went through the door and Bill closed it behind her. The hall was dark, except for students walking around holding lighted candles. Bill must have gone mad, Becca thought for a second. What about Health and Safety?

'Remember, keep on walking around,' came Bill's voice. He handed Becca a candle. 'You're to look at everyone carefully.'

Becca looked at Crystal. In the candlelight her face was softened and the light flickered in her eyes. 'What's Bill up to?'

'Search me.' Becca held her candle close to her face so the pupils could see who she was. They appeared to be taking it seriously, moving around the dark hall in a slow and considerate manner, like taking part in an elaborate dance, although there were a couple of outbreaks of giggles.

A larger shape came towards her. Bill. She held her candle up ready to smile at him – show willing! – then practically dropped the candle. The candle lit up intense blue eyes that glittered as they stared at her, a soft smile on carved lips, and light on high cheekbones.

'Hello, Becca,' Paul murmured.

Chapter 22

She had spent so many hours trying not to think about him and there he was in the flesh. 'What are you doing here?' she whispered.

'Running a Shakespeare workshop,' he answered. 'It's what I do. Remember?'

'But . . .' Bill. Oh, but he was a crafty one. Becca stared at Paul in the darkness. 'I thought you said you weren't interested in school kids.'

'Perhaps I'm interested in school teachers.' He touched her cheek. 'I've missed you.'

Becca inhaled sharply and pulled back away from his touch. 'You shouldn't be here.'

'Where else should I be?' He glided past her to the doors, and then the lights went on. Becca blinked in the sudden brightness.

'If you could blow your candles out . . .' Paul stood by the entrance doors, his body relaxed as if talking to a couple of people and not a mass of alien school children puffing and spluttering at their candles. 'Think about what you saw when we didn't have electric light,' Paul said. 'What did you notice about the people you talked to?'

'Their faces,' someone piped up.

Paul rewarded them with a smile. 'That's right. Their faces. In

Elizabethan times, when Shakespeare was writing, they didn't have electric light. They relied on daylight, or candlelight. It made a lot of difference to the way they behaved. Suppose you were a wealthy man or woman and wanted to show off your wealth. You'd use jewellery, same as now. But where would you wear it? Think about what you could see by candlelight. Yes?'

He pointed to a girl whose hand was raised. 'Earrings?'

'Yes. Anyone else?'

'Round your neck?'

'On your head?'

'Good, you've got the idea. You can see an area roughly around the head and neck.' He drew a circle in the air around his head and shoulders. 'So the Elizabethans wore necklaces, jewelled collars, earrings, brooches on hats, anything near their faces which would show up by candlelight. What else is different when you talk to people by candlelight?'

'You whisper.'

'Very good. The candlelight creates intimate spaces. Look again.' He nodded at Bill, who turned the lights out. For a second all was darkness, then came the sound of a lighter being struck, and two candles flared up in the darkness. Paul handed one to Becca. 'Mrs Woods has agreed to be my assistant today.'

I haven't, Becca wanted to say, but she couldn't, not in front of her students.

'Now, at the moment, Mrs Woods and I are standing quite far apart. It's quite difficult to see her in the candlelight. Mrs Woods.' He beckoned her towards him. Reluctantly, Becca moved, conscious of being the centre of attention. Paul moved the candle towards her. 'Now I can see Mrs Woods properly. I'm only about – what – a few feet away. So I don't need to shout. I can talk quite softly and she'll hear.' His eyes looked up at Becca, and for a second she wondered what he was going to say next. 'And if we get even closer . . .' He pulled Becca to him. She wondered if he could hear her heart beating. 'We can have some very private conversations without anyone hearing us.' His eyes held hers then he turned away. 'Lights, please.'

The lights came back on. 'So, when we start looking at the texts, we must remember that sense of privacy and intimacy we get from candlelight. The need to be close to people, the sense of being in an enclosed world. And it's that enclosed world I'm going to be talking about today – the world of Shakespeare. I've spent my life exploring that world and I'm hoping that today, with a little bit of imagination, you're going to discover that Shakespeare's world isn't so far away from your own. OK, if you hand your candles back to Mr Malcolm by the door, and then come and join me up at the front.'

Obediently the students shuffled to Bill and deposited their candles before going to the stage end of the hall where Paul sat on the edge of the stage, the long lean line Becca remembered so well from rehearsals.

'You didn't say he was going to be here,' Crystal whispered to Becca. 'He's really good.'

'I didn't know,' Becca muttered, as she put her candle down. 'And it's one thing to pull a stunt like that, quite another to keep their interest.'

'I don't think there's any danger of that,' Crystal said. 'Look at them.'

Becca looked. Crowd control wasn't going to be much of a problem apparently, judging by the way the students were sitting quietly. Paul was waiting for them to all settle, he was completely in control. He looked across to Becca and their eyes met. Becca felt the gaze could have run scorch marks the length of the hall, like a high frequency laser, precise in its ability to cut though to the heart of matter. They could have been the only ones in the room. Run, she thought. Run away while you still can. But her feet remained where they were. He is not for me, she told herself. Don't let yourself think about him. She closed her eyes. Martin. Think of Martin. The image that arose in her head was of Martin hunched over his foot, whinging about hard skin. No. Think of Martin . . . telling a joke, laughing at Christmas. Think of Martin when we got married. Think of Martin holding Lily when she was born, how he looked then, the pride on his face. She could see him now quite clearly. Dear Martin.

'For someone who was so famous in his own lifetime, we don't know many facts about Shakespeare's life,' Paul was saying. 'Even his birthday is a guess. What we do know is that he was baptised on 26 April 1564 in Stratford-upon-Avon in Warwickshire . . .'

The day went on. Becca was caught between admiration for Paul and determination not to get carried away. She didn't want to think that Paul was the man for her, her one true love. I don't love him, she told herself. It's a fantasy, it's not real. But the truth was that he was a charismatic speaker, able to hold fifty or so adolescents' attention with the same ease he held hers. Shakespeare seemed accessible, more like a friend of Paul's, than some distant playwright.

Paul explained about cue scripts, a word Becca hadn't heard before. At the time in Elizabethan theatre, printing or copying the whole play by hand for each actor would have been too expensive and time consuming – and also would have given a chance for a rival company to steal the play. So instead, each actor was given their part on a long piece of paper – or roll, which is the origin of the word 'role', Paul said – plus their cues, three or four words from the actor who spoke just before them. They'd have to learn their words without knowing what the play was about, then listen for their cue to speak. There wasn't much time for rehearsal as often there was a different play on every night, so actors had to learn their lines properly and trust that the playwright had given them enough clues in the text to tell them what to do. 'For example, when Shakespeare uses "you" in the text, it means to stand not too far away. Thou, means, get a little closer. Thee means to get closer still. The first folio editions of Shakespeare had lines, half lines, and strange punctuation that modern scholars have tidied up – but they were actually clues that tell the actors what to do next.'

He clapped his hands together and stood up. 'That's the theory. Now, let's see it in action.' He distributed scripts from a section of an Agatha Christie play to a dozen students with instructions to obey whatever clues they thought the text gave them about where to move. Obviously, there weren't many, because the end result was them standing in a long line. Then he handed out the cue scripts for the final scene in *Romeo and Juliet*. Ten students crammed on the stage. 'Just listen, and react,' Paul said. 'Do what you hear the text telling you to do. If someone says "Look", then look where they are pointing. When the Watchman says: "here is a friar that trembles, sighs and weeps", that's the cue for the person with the Friar's cue script to tremble, sigh and weep. Listen to what everyone is saying, and you'll be fine. OK?'

Crystal raised an eyebrow at Becca; it was clear she was thinking this was going to be beyond the students. But she was wrong. Unlike the Agatha Christie, this time the students reacted and listened, and moved forward and backwards, handed over imaginary letters, looked where they were directed to. 'I'm impressed,' Crystal whispered to Becca, who nodded. Oh, he was impressive all right.

They looked at more from *Romeo and Juliet* later in the morning. Paul had picked out two of the pupils to play the parts, but he was having problems with Eddie, the boy he'd chosen to play Romeo. Becca knew Eddie was bright, but shy.

'Now what are you going to do?' Paul said. Eddie looked blank. 'Look at the text,' Paul said. '"Palm to palm is holy palmer's kiss" – what do you think they are doing?'

Eddie still looked blank, but Tamsin, playing Juliet put up her hand, palm facing out. Eddie, after coaxing, held up his hand against Tamsin's.

'Good,' Paul said, looking slightly ruffled. 'Let's carry on. "Then dear saint, let lips do what hands do." What do you think that means?'

Eddie went scarlet, then tentatively pecked Tamsin on the cheek to a background of giggles and a few cheers. 'Is that how you'd kiss the girl you've just fallen madly in love with?' Paul said, his eyes quizzical.

Eddie gave Tamsin's cheek another tentative kiss.

'More like this,' Paul said and turning to Becca, kissed her.

Becca's eyes flew open, she could hardly breathe. Her ears filled with buzzing, and over that a chorus of delighted 'Oooooh!' from the watching teenagers. How dare he! How could he? Her body felt quite limp beneath his, her whole being confused and delirious with pleasure at being kissed by him again. It was like coming home. His lips on hers, as soft, delicious, hard as she remembered. She almost closed her eyes, but then the wolf whistles started, bringing her abruptly back to her senses. This was a school day. They were not alone. People were watching. Becca pushed away from Paul, furious that he'd exposed her feelings for him through his kiss. Oh yes, he knew full well the effect he had on her, and that she was powerless to do anything in front of the others.

'It's in the text,' he said, with an apologetic smile but a mischievous glint in his eyes. It was the glint that did it. Without being aware of what her body intended doing, her hand shot out and she slapped him hard across the face.

More ooohs from the students, sparking with delight at the sight of grown-ups – teachers, what's more – kissing and slapping in public.

'Miss, miss, slap him again!'

'Kiss her again.'

'Go on, sir, do it!'

And one voice piped up, 'It's in the text!'

Becca could feel her cheeks flaring scarlet. How could she have been so stupid to slap him? She should have pretended nothing had happened, but now . . . She turned for help to Crystal and Bill, but Crystal was staring open mouthed, and Bill's expression had moved beyond thunder to something far more threatening, an electrical rainstorm perhaps. Paul's cheek showed the print of her hand as he ruefully stroked it. The challenge in his eyes had been replaced by something else, something satisfied.

'I'm terribly sorry,' he said, not sounding sorry at all.

Becca looked around. A sea of faces stared back, expectant and hopeful of further fireworks between them. Angry tears suddenly pricked her eyes. She couldn't, wouldn't cry in front of them. 'Excuse me . . .' she murmured in Bill and Crystal's direction, then marched down the aisle to the exit doors.

Out in the foyer she gulped down air. It had been going so well, and now . . . oh, how could she have been so stupid as to betray herself? What an idiotic thing to have done. She bent over clutching her stomach as if she'd been winded. The door opened and she quickly glanced towards it, expecting – hoping? – it would be Paul, but it was Crystal.

'Don't say anything,' Becca said, holding up one hand.

'Are you OK? My word, he was well out of order. That was outrageous – what are you going to do? Report him? You could probably sue Bill.'

'What for?'

'Employing someone who sexually harasses employees – I don't know. But that was something else. I mean . . . in front of everyone! What are you going to do?' Crystal's eyes bulged with expectation.

Becca ran her hands through her hair. 'I don't know.'

'You've got to do something. I'll be your witness. We could go to the papers: "Teacher sexually assaulted in front of—"'

'Stop it,' Becca said sharply.

'Oh, lovey, you're upset.' Crystal draped an arm around Becca's shoulder. 'I would be devastated. Are you going to tell Martin? He'll go up the wall, probably want to come round and beat him up.'

'Don't tell him. Please Crystal, don't say anything.'

'But, lovey . . . you've got to do something. That man just—'

'I know what he did,' Becca said. 'But I'm not going to do anything about it. I'm just going to ignore it. Pretend it didn't happen.'

Crystal took hold of Becca's hands. 'Look. I know you're upset, but really, you can't let this go.'

'I can, and I'm going to.'

Bill came out of the hall looking nervous. 'How are things, ladies?'

'You should be ashamed of yourself, employing someone like that – that's sexual harassment, you know.' Crystal looked pink in the face.

'That's a bit extreme,' Bill said, wringing his hands. Poor Bill, the idea of being sued for sexual harassment had made his jowls droop. Becca thought it would have been funny if the whole thing hadn't been so serious. She had to get out of the situation without anyone asking any more questions.

'Crystal is right. There are responsibilities that you have as my employer.' Bill visibly flinched and she could almost see his vision of the law courts floating above his head. It was tempting, just to see his bombastic balloon of self-importance punctured. But she had to think of others. 'But I don't wish to pursue that course. I think it would be best if we all forgot about it. Just assume it was all part of the theatrical experience and leave it at that.'

'I knew you would be reasonable,' Bill said, smiling with relief. 'I knew I could rely on you—'

'However,' Becca said, stopping him in his tracks. It was quite nice, this feeling of power, rather like being queen for the day. 'I would like your assurance that you will speak to Mr Fitzwilliam and tell him that the incident must never be repeated.'

'Of course, you're right, I'll speak to him at the first available opportunity.'

'In that case,' Becca said, still in regal mode, 'I think we'd better return and continue with this . . . mmm, interesting workshop.'

The rest of the workshop passed without incident, although Becca took care to avoid any contact – physical, verbal, even eye contact – with Paul. It wasn't difficult, especially with Crystal bustling round her like a flustered chicken with a fox outside the hen coop. There was the occasional ripple of interest from the students, a frisson of excitement, but it soon passed when they realised there wasn't going to be a repeat of the morning's drama. Becca had to admit it: Paul was a good teacher, charismatic and enthusiastic. But she knew that. She'd always known that about him, it was one of the reasons she'd fallen— She caught her breath. Think of Martin and Lily. Think of the people who mattered. Ridiculous to think for a second about someone else in that way, a man she hardly knew. She concentrated on what Paul was saying about Shakespeare productions, how it was common to put on six different plays over six consecutive days, how plays would drop in and out of the repertoire, completely new plays being introduced on average of one every two weeks.

'People talk about the plays having complicated language because that's how they spoke at the time. But it's not true. Listen to this . . .' He pulled out a sheet of paper. 'This comes from the diary of John Manningham, and he wrote it just as anyone today would – for himself, on 13 March 1602. "Upon a time when Burbage played Richard the Third, there was a citizen grew so far in liking with him, that before she went from the play she appointed him to come that night unto her by the name of Richard the Third. Shakespeare, overhearing their conclusion, went before, was entertained . . ."' Paul stressed the word in a suggestive manner, and got a laugh from the intently listening audience.

Crystal patted Becca's hand and mouthed 'OK?' to her. Becca smiled and nodded back. It was sweet of Crystal to be concerned for her. She turned back to listen to Paul read the rest of the diary extract.

' "... was entertained and at his game ere Burbage came. Then message being brought that Richard the Third was at the door, Shakespeare caused return to be made that William the Conquerer came before Richard the Third." '

That got an even bigger laugh. Paul surveyed the audience, as if he saw himself as a conquerer, sweeping all before him. She could see Bill guffawing, even Crystal was smiling. He held the laughing audience in the palm of his hand, Becca thought. She was the only person there without a smile on her face.

The workshop over, the students were ferried back to the college, fizzing with energy and excitement. That was a great day, Becca heard several of them say. Absolutely brilliant seemed to be the general consensus. She'd always known that Paul was good at what he did. Becca shrugged herself into her coat, gathered up her bag and folders, feeling more tired than she'd been for ages, as if all the energy had been leached out of her. She put her hand to her lips, remembering his mouth on hers.

Becca walked out of the school and down the street where she'd parked her car. Someone was leaning against it. Someone tall and lean, someone who made her heart leap and the energy she thought she was lacking surge through her.

Becca checked her stride. No. Whatever she felt, she would grow out of it. She would be in control. Ignoring Paul she unlocked the car and opened the door. She would have got in but Paul caught her arm. 'Are you avoiding me?'

She looked up at him. She wanted to reach out and touch him, bury her face in his jacket and for him to put his arm around her. 'Leave me alone,' she said, her voice as cold as she could make it.

'Darling—'

'I'm not your darling,' she spat at him. 'Go away and leave me alone.'

'But I love you.'

'Love? You humiliated me in front of my students, my colleagues, my employer. I have to teach these kids, I need their respect. I can't be kissed in public by—' She stopped, unable to finish her sentence.

'I'm sorry, it was a spur of the moment thing. You were standing there looking so kissable I couldn't help it.' He gave a charming shrug. 'You must know how I feel about you.'

'That's not my problem.' Becca thumped the side of the car with her fist in frustration. 'Just go away and leave me in peace.' She turned her head so he wouldn't see her expression, but he knew.

He gently touched the hair on the nape of her head. 'Darling Becca,' he murmured and his voice was as soft as summer sunshine. 'Don't fight.'

She put her hand over her mouth, and prayed for strength, still turned away from him.

'It doesn't have to be like this,' he said, stroking her hair.

'It does,' she said, turning to him. 'Let me go.'

'Why, Becca? Why?'

She took a deep breath. 'Because whatever I may or may not feel, you're another woman's husband, and I'm not going to break up anyone else's marriage. You have small children who need their father. And I have my husband and a daughter who I love and who needs me.'

'But I love you.'

Becca closed her eyes, then opened them again. 'I'm sorry. I can't help that.'

'You love me.' He said it as a statement.

She shook her head, not in denial, more in resignation. 'I have to go. My daughter will be at home waiting for me. I'm sorry.'

Paul hit his head in a theatrical gesture. 'I can't believe you're prepared to do this, to chuck love away. I can't believe it.'

Anger flared inside her. 'It doesn't matter what you believe, so long as this stops. You must stop sending me things, I can't accept them. I can't be with you, so let me go. No more scenes like today.'

'I want you.' His eyes burned, imprinting themselves on to her retinas.

'Forget me.' Becca held her hand against his cheek, the same place she'd slapped him, touching him one last time. It took every ounce of willpower she possessed to get into the car. Quick, quick, before she could change her mind. She turned the ignition and drove away round the corner. Her hands were shaking so much she had to pull over, and rest her head on her hands. Why did doing the right thing have to be so very hard?

'But why can't I?' Lily said, her lower lip stuck out.

'You're much too young,' Martin replied.

Becca sighed. It seemed like a rerun of so many conversations, Lily pushing boundaries, Martin manning the barricades and resisting and Becca caught somewhere in the middle. She couldn't help feel that if Martin were more flexible, Lily wouldn't push quite so much. Besides, half the time it was clear that what she was proposing was pure fantasy, it simply wasn't going to happen. So why not make cautious noises, instead of triggering screaming and slammed doors? She remembered that when she was a teenager everything seemed accompanied by slammed doors and her rushing upstairs to sob her heart out into the pillow. Not much had changed. But then, things seemed different. Becca would never have asked permission to go to an all-night rave. She would have automatically known it was out of the question and not bothered.

'It's not fair,' Lily said, scarlet faced, working herself up. Becca cleared their plates and went into the kitchen, half listening to Lily's protests and Martin's calm but dogged refusal to even consider it, which was undoubtedly incredibly annoying for Lily. She scraped the plates into the rubbish bin and put the plates in the dishwasher, then closed her eyes, remembering Paul's mouth on hers, desire flaring up, immediate and instant. No wonder love denied was such a powerful theme in literature. She went to the fridge feeling the cool air against her face and pulled out a ready-made flan. She balanced it, a knife and three bowls on a chopping board and took it through.

'Do you want some?' she said to Lily, her calm tone cutting across the heated exchange.

Lily was obviously torn between refusing the flan as part of her role as family martyr and simple greed. At least there was no danger of her becoming anorexic, Becca thought. 'Yes,' Lily said grudgingly then added, 'A very very small piece.' Becca gave her a normal-sized slice, which Lily accepted with only a hint of hesitation. 'I'm going, and that's that.' Lily spooned flan into her mouth.

The phone rang. Becca edged her chair backwards, eager to escape from another teenagerish discussion, but Martin was already on his feet. 'You stay and enjoy your pudding,' he said.

Becca waited until he'd left the room. 'You're daft,' she said to Lily. 'You ought to talk it over with me first.'

'You're always too busy,' Lily said and Becca felt a stab of guilt. 'You're always telling me to run along because you've got to work, or you've got to do the washing or you've got to do something.'

'Well, I am busy. I've got to work and keep the house nice and—'

'I know,' Lily said rolling her eyes as if Becca were saying something so blindingly obvious. 'You're always telling me how ghastly it is and how much you have to do. Don't think I don't know you'd rather not have had me.'

'Lily,' Becca said, half put out, half amused by the absurdity. 'That's just ridiculous.'

'I'm not a child,' Lily said. 'You and Dad don't know anything.'

'No, well, I thought that about my parents.'

'Not surprised,' Lily said with a snort. 'They're ancient.'

'They weren't when I was a teenager,' Becca said. She had to smile, because she could remember her own parents seeming as old as the giant redwoods of California, and about as unyielding too.

Lily pushed flan around her plate. 'You just don't trust me.'

'It's not so much not trusting you, darling. It's a question of trusting the people you're with. You're a lovely young girl, and your father and I want to protect you.' Martin came in and sat down. Becca turned to him. 'Isn't that so Martin?'

'What?' He looked at the plate in front of him as if he'd only just seen it and then picked up his spoon.

'We only want to make sure Lily is OK.'

'Yes, yes.' He started to eat.

Lily and Becca exchanged glances. 'Is everything OK? The phone call – it wasn't about work, was it?'

He shook his head. 'No, something quite different.'

'Can I get down?' Lily said not waiting for a response before pushing her chair back.

'Yes, and take your plate through to the kitchen,' Becca said automatically. Lily grabbed her plate so the spoon fell off. Becca decided to ignore the flouncing. There were times when being blind and deaf were an advantage as a parent with a teenage daughter.

'The phone call,' Martin said, pushing his plate away. 'It was from that woman I met after your play.'

'Who? Victoria?' Becca frowned. 'What did she want?'

Martin shook his head. 'The woman in the bar. The stuck-up lawyer.'

'Suzy – you mean Paul Fitzwilliam's wife? Why didn't you tell me it was her?'

'She didn't want to speak to you, she wanted to speak to me.'

'You? Why on earth you?'

'She said . . .' Martin massaged his temples as if he had a headache. 'She said you are having an affair with her husband.'

Chapter 23

They say that when you're drowning your life flashes before you. Becca wasn't drowning but suddenly every detail of her relationship with Paul flashed before her. She hadn't realised before how fast her brain worked. It buzzed with calculating exactly what Suzy knew, what she might have said, what Martin would believe.

What Suzy knew: nothing, unless Paul had said anything. And she couldn't believe that he'd suddenly spill the beans. No, Suzy was acting on her own suspicions. There was nothing concrete to go on – unless Paul had confessed to their brief relationship, and his subsequent pursuit. So, assuming he hadn't, Suzy was going on guesswork.

What Martin would believe: the thought of Martin believing what Suzy may have said made the room spin for a dizzy second. We haven't done anything wrong, she thought wildly. Whatever Suzy has said, it isn't true. We haven't made love, or, or, or . . . that steamy moment in the back of the people carrier flashed into her imagination. No, that didn't count. She needed time to think.

'You're joking,' she said in what she hoped was a calm and reasonable voice.

'No.' Martin was terse, tight lipped. She'd never seen him look at her like that.

'I'm confused,' she said truthfully. 'Did you just say Suzy

SARAH DUNCAN

Fitzwilliam has rung to say I was having an affair with her husband?'

'Yes.'

'But that's preposterous! Why would she say anything like that?' Maybe Suzy had discovered the flowers and notes Paul had been leaving her. But to call it an affair – an affair meant hotel bedrooms and candlelit dinners. Not a handful of kisses. For a second she remembered Paul kissing each finger in turn and telling her she was beautiful.

'Is it true?'

'No! No! No!' The words gushed out of her. She paused to get her breath back, horrified that for even one minute, one second, he could think that she, Becca, had . . . But you wanted to, her conscience said. I haven't done anything wrong, her heart countered. 'It's laughable.'

'I'm not laughing.'

'Nor am I.'

They stared at each other. Perhaps she should tell Martin the truth: I was feeling low and we met a couple of times before Christmas, and then I finished it. She could imagine Martin wanting to know what she meant by saying they'd met. What do you mean? Did you sit and talk? Hold hands? We kissed, she'd have to say. And then the real interrogation would start: What do you mean by kissing? How often? What sort of kissing? Did he touch you?

She couldn't tell Martin. Paul had run away with her heart, her mind, had taken over her soul. She'd believed she loved him – perhaps she loved him still. The fact that their relationship had never got further than kisses didn't make it any better. She had been emotionally unfaithful. She looked at Martin and saw the hurt on his face, the way his eyes had crumpled, and felt it was essential to repair the damage that had already been done, and protect him from any further harm.

She took Martin's hands and spoke clearly. 'I've only met Suzy Fitzwilliam a couple of times. I know she's a lawyer of some sort, and I expect she knows all about libel and slander and things like that and probably believes whatever it is she's told you, but you have to believe me, because I am telling you the truth: I am not having an affair with Paul Fitzwilliam.' The truth, but not the whole truth. Nothing about kissing, nothing about the notes. She held Martin's gaze. She could discern the struggle that was going on behind his eyes as she willed him to believe her.

'Why would she say such a thing?' His voice held the edge of defeat.

'I don't know,' she said, feeling defeated too. 'Even if I was having an affair with Paul – which I'm not – I don't see why she'd do it. It's like throwing a bomb into a shopping centre, it's as if she simply doesn't care who gets hurt.'

Martin slumped into the chair, his face drawn with misery. She stroked Martin's hand. Martin turned her hand over in his as if examining it for telltale signs of something or other. Her rings neatly stacked up on the fourth finger of the left hand: engagement, marriage, eternity. There wasn't one for infidelity.

'I can see he's exciting to be with,' Martin began, but she stopped him.

'I'm not having an affair. I'm simply not. I love you,' she said. The tears came then, she couldn't stop them, though she didn't know who she was crying for.

Martin wiped her tears, hesitated, then gave her a hug. She clung to him, burying her face in his chest. They stayed like that for a few minutes, clinging to the wreckage together.

'Perhaps I shouldn't have said anything,' Martin said eventually.

'Of course you should.' Becca sniffed loudly, and rummaged in her pocket for a tissue. 'It's better it's out in the open, it would have been awful if you'd felt you had to spy on me. What exactly did she say?'

'It seems to have become jumbled up.' Martin squeezed her hand tightly. 'She said something about, did I know what you'd been up to, and how you'd been seeing her husband. Something about a workshop last week.'

'Is that what this is about?' Becca thought hard. Perhaps this was his revenge for her rejection after the workshop. 'Yes, he did a workshop for Bill – it was very good – but it was work. Bill was there, and Crystal and all the students.'

'She said . . .' He took a deep breath as if it hurt his lungs to breathe. 'She said you were having sex with her husband.'

'She's gone mad.' Becca now felt more confused than ever. Why would Paul confess to something that he hadn't done? Images of being in the people carrier swept over her, Paul pressing against her, his hand on her. But that didn't count as having sex, surely. Maybe for someone of Lily's age, but not for an adult. Or was that the Clinton defence? She shook her head with bewilderment. 'I really don't understand this – I've never "had sex" with Paul Fitzwilliam.'

Martin was sitting at the end of the table, his hands clasped. One thumb nervously massaged the base joint of the other. She recognised a comfort gesture and realised he was wavering. She could see that this was going to be how it was from now on. Suzy had destroyed his innocence. Even if he accepted Becca's word, there would be a tiny piece that would question her actions and wonder: was there any truth in them. Why had Suzy done it?

She realised she was shaking slightly, her heart racing. She felt sick and elated at the same time. I want to tell him the truth. I don't want to lie. How sordid it all was. I want to tell Martin about how I feel, how Paul keeps saying he loves me, and how it's so hard to keep fending him off.

'I need a drink.' Becca grabbed a bottle of rioja from the rack and began opening it, her fingers clumsy. To love Paul meant hurting Martin. She couldn't hide from that. It meant lying and cheating and being deceitful and all those things she so despised in others.

She poured out a glass and took a swig, her heart pounding as she tried to look calm. What would an innocent person do? Carry on as normal. Becca couldn't think what normal might be. Load the dishwasher, wipe the kitchen surfaces. If only they'd got a dog, she could take it round the block.

'Are you all right?' Martin said. He was looking at her in a puzzled way.

'Yes, yes. Fine,' she said, smiling brightly. No, that must look too much like covering up. 'Actually, no. This Suzy business has upset me. I can't think why she'd do such a thing.' And then it hit her. 'Of course!' she said, grinning. 'Why didn't I think of it before? She's got the wrong person!' Becca got up, unable to sit still. 'Don't you see – he must be having an affair with someone else and . . .' Becca stopped, suddenly thinking about the implications of what she'd said. Paul was having an affair with someone else. All the time he'd been saying he loved her, he was seeing someone else. Having sex with someone else.

Martin stood up too. 'Come to think of it, I don't think she asked for me by name, she just launched straight into what she was saying. I'm sure that's right, I don't think she said my name, just hers, and then I said yes, and she said the stuff about my wife. She didn't say your name either.' He started to laugh. 'I can't believe it. She must have made a mistake. Or even phoned the wrong number, yours might have been next to his mistress's in his phone directory or on his mobile or whatever. I've done that before, think I'm phoning one number, and I'm actually phoning the person below them. What a stupid thing to do. And to think I—' He stopped suddenly.

'Believed her?' Becca lightly finished his sentence.

Martin came across and held her. 'I'm sorry, darling. Just for one second I did. I'm so so sorry. I should have known. I should have trusted you. I should have known there would be some simple explanation. I'm sorry.' He kissed her hair. 'Forgive me.'

And what could she say but whisper, 'Yes'?

* * *

'"O beware my lord of jealousy; it is the green-ey'd monster which doth mock the meat it feeds on."' Becca looked up at her class. 'What's Iago doing in act three scene three?'

'Telling us that jealousy looks like Shrek,' Eddie said.

'Very funny,' Becca said drily. 'Anyone else?' Tamsin had her hand up, so Becca nodded to her.

'He's telling Othello to watch out for jealousy, but he's also feeding it.'

Becca smiled at Tamsin. 'And how's he doing that?'

'By telling him that if Desdemona could deceive her father, to marry Othello, it also means that she could deceive Othello.'

'Good. So we could say that in this scene, Iago feeds the monster while ironically warning him about it. Do you think there are any other examples of jealousy in the play?'

They were more experienced now, more forthcoming. They knew what was expected of them. They talked about Rodrigo's jealousy of Desdemona choosing Othello over him, and Iago's jealousy that Othello had chosen Cassio to be his lieutenant. They discussed the meaning of the word, and although she hid it well, directing the discussion back and forth, all the time Becca's own green-ey'd monster grumbled and stirred. Had Paul really been seeing someone else? Surely not. He couldn't have. That would imply he was some sort of horrible lothario, taking advantage of women. Not Paul, the sensitive man who'd been so sweet and understanding. On the other hand, there was his urgency in the back of the car. Perhaps he was after only one thing, like men were always supposed to be, according to old-fashioned comedians. Who could it have been? Angela? Unlikely. Then who? The questions whizzed round inside her head like angry bees swarming, but getting nowhere.

'It's Becca.'

There was a pause. 'Becca,' Paul said, turning her name into a caress. He sounded delighted to hear her.

'You know why I'm ringing.' She leaned back against the door of the stationery cupboard, just to make sure no one would come in.

'If you're pregnant it's not my fault,' he said jauntily. 'Though not for want of trying.'

'Suzy rang up Martin and accused us of having an affair,' Becca said cutting across him. She stared at the multi-coloured files stacked up on the shelves next to the boxes of paperclips. Bill liked to recycle as much as possible, she could see the corners of the top file were inked in by some bored student.

There was silence at the end of the phone. Then a long drawn out sigh. 'Shit. Why?'

'You tell me.' Becca pressed her lips together. 'Didn't you know?'

'No.' He sounded stunned. 'When was this?'

'Yesterday evening. Why would she do that?' Becca helped herself to a bulldog clip from the box next to the paperclips and snapped it together.

'I don't know . . . look, we need to talk face to face. I can't do this over the phone. Are you at school now?'

What if Martin found out? It would look suspicious. Becca attached the bulldog clip to the green file. 'I don't know about meeting. I don't think it's a good idea.'

'Meet me in the park after school, and we'll talk then.'

'Becca.' He kissed her cheek in greeting, that faintly elusive lemony scent filling her nostrils. She thought his face looked leaner, taut with strain perhaps.

'I haven't got long,' she said, digging her hands into her coat pockets. 'What the hell is going on?'

'I've no idea. Honestly.' He twisted a dog lead in his hand. 'Tell me what happened.'

'Suzy rang Martin and said you were having an affair with me. Or rather, we were having sex. Hasn't she said something to you?'

He shook his head. 'I was away over the weekend, didn't get back until late last night, then she went to work early this morning. I expect I'll hear all about it this evening.' He sighed, then put his arm around Becca. 'But what about you? Are you OK? How did Martin take it?'

'He wasn't best pleased, as you can imagine,' Becca said, moving forwards away from Paul's arm. She was only too conscious of his physical presence as it was. 'But we talked it over, and sorted it out.'

'That must have been rough.'

'It was.' Becca pulled her coat around her. 'She didn't actually use my name. I thought it might have been a mistake, I thought she might have meant to call someone else.'

'Someone else? Who?'

Becca shrugged. 'How do I know who you see?'

'Oh, Becca.' He laughed. 'Do I detect a touch of the green-eyed monster?'

'Certainly not.'

He turned to her. 'Darling Becca, you are the only woman I want.'

'Apart from your wife.' Becca walked on, her feet tapping out her annoyance. Annoyance at him, annoyance at herself for giving him the idea she was jealous.

'So you told Martin it must have been a mistake of some sort, and he believed you.' Paul whistled, and the dog ran over, before darting off again.

Becca nodded. It was disturbing that Martin hadn't believed her at first. But of course, she hadn't been entirely faithful. Life was becoming a series of grey gradations, not black and white. How faithful was faithful? She supposed each couple worked out for themselves what was tolerable. Trust was a fragile thing, easily broken. She looked up at Paul, and for the first time wondered if she could trust him. 'I don't know what's going on, but I don't want to be part of it. I want you to stay out of my life.'

'Becca—'

'I mean it, Paul.' Her hands were trembling. 'Stay away from me.'

He put his arms gently around her, and she allowed herself the luxury of relaxing against his chest. 'We'll sort something out,' he murmured.

It took everything she had to extract herself. 'No. No sorting out. I can't pretend I don't have . . . some feelings for you, but I don't want this. I want to go back to where I was, before I met you.'

'Sad? Lonely? Anxious? No one to talk to?' Paul's eyes were clear. 'You were like some neglected treasure tucked away and forgotten about when I met you. Don't you remember?'

'It wasn't like that.' Becca tried to remember. She'd thought she was getting her life together, was being positive, getting on with things. Coping. Obviously not coping as well as she'd thought. 'And even if it was, it was better than this.'

'Better than being loved?' He tilted her head. 'Because I do love you.'

'Don't say that to me.' She turned her head away to look at the dog, tail wagging happily as it investigated some smell at the foot of a chestnut tree.

'I know you better than you know yourself. You want to come with me but you're afraid. Don't be. We could be so happy.'

'At other people's expense?' She shook her head. 'You don't know me at all. I'm going back home now. I don't want me or my family disturbed by you – or your wife – again.'

'Suzy's a law unto herself.'

'That's as maybe. I'm serious, Paul. No more cards, no more letters, no more flowers. Go back and make things up with your wife – you loved her once.'

'He doesn't love you,' Paul said suddenly. 'He doesn't appreciate you, not the way I do or—'

'Don't talk about Martin like that,' Becca said. 'I won't listen to you.'

'I love you. I'd do anything for you.'

'Then leave me alone.'

They had walked right through the park, and had reached the children's playground and skatepark. A group of skateboarders were swooping up and down the half tubes watched by a gaggle of boys and girls in school uniform. One had a familiar shock of black hair.

'Lily!'

Lily turned, registered her mother, then sheepishly detached herself from the crowd. 'Hi, Mum.'

'What are you doing here? You should be at home by now.'

'I came to see the guys practising.' The dog bounded up to her, and Lily knelt and stroked it, undeterred by dog breath. 'Is this your dog?' she said to Paul. 'He's gorgeous.' The dog rolled over on to its back, presenting a soft black furry stomach. Lily gave it a vigorous scratch. 'What's he called?'

'Oberon.' Paul glanced at Becca, whose lips twitched despite her shredded nerves.

'Come on, Lily, I'll give you a lift home. Where's your school bag?'

'Over there.' Lily left the dog with obvious reluctance and went over to her friends to collect her bag.

Becca quickly turned to Paul. 'Goodbye.'

He held her hand. 'Don't say it.'

She took her hand from him. 'Goodbye, Paul.'

Chapter 24

The dining-room table at June and Frank's house looked more like a jumble sale than anything else. Becca recognised things from her childhood, prints of famous paintings, pots, a World War I medical kit that her grandmother had used. Becca lifted the lid. It hadn't been used very much, judging by the number of bandages left.

'I don't think Clarice was that keen on nursing,' June said, peering in too.

Becca slammed the lid down. 'You can't get rid of all this.'

'I don't want it any more,' June said simply.

Becca prodded a wooden rhinoceros with her finger. Its horn had been broken, but she could remember it taking pride of place on her parents' mantelpiece when she was a child. It was supposed to stay with them. 'What are you going to do with it all?'

'Well, obviously you have first choice, but anything that's left over I was going to give to the Friends of the Holburne for their summer fair. I don't suppose any of this is worth much.'

Not much in money, Becca felt like saying, but worth a million memories. She picked up one of the jugs. It had been hand made and the honey-brown glaze dripped like caramel over a custard-yellow base. In the spring June had always filled it with an abundance of daffodils and put it in the hall where it created a pool of welcoming golden light. 'I'd like this,' she said.

June took it from her. 'It's a nice jug,' she said turning it round in her hands, a slight smile on her face, as if she too was remembering.

'Perhaps you should keep it,' Becca said.

June smiled, and put the jug down. 'I'm aiming to take as little as possible with me when I move,' she said. 'Hopefully I'll find some little fisherman's cottage and paint it all white, and have nothing but empty space and blank walls.'

'That sounds a bit bleak,' Becca said.

'I expect I'll soon fill it up with things,' June said absent-mindedly. 'Do you think Lily would like this doll?' Frank had brought it back from some trip abroad for either Becca or Joanna.

'I think Lily's a bit too old for dolls,' Becca said. She felt like saying, that's my doll, but she couldn't be sure if it had been hers or Joanna's. She felt cross with June for dismantling her life. It was as if all the foundations of Becca's childhood were being sold off for a few pennies.

'Perhaps Lily could come up and choose some things she might like at the weekend.'

Becca nodded. 'I'll ask her, although Lily's arrangements are always a bit vague. It depends on what everyone else is doing. They all seem to hang out in a big mass and flock this way and that with no particular direction.' Except that Lily's direction was firmly towards Kevin after the Valentine's card. 'I could bring her up on Saturday – oh no!' She ran her hands through her hair. 'It's the twenty-third this weekend, isn't it? I've got this stupid conference to go to in Oxford. I keep on forgetting about it.'

'Probably means you don't want to go.'

'No, I don't. I got bounced into it by Bill ages ago.'

'What's it about?'

'It's an educational conference on using drama in education, whether for teaching English, or social skills or stuff like that. It should be interesting but I want to stay at home this weekend.'

Relations with Martin had been edgy since the weekend and Suzy's phone call. She'd thought they could have a lovely family weekend together, do things like go for a walk in the countryside or along the canal. She was intending to lure Lily with the promise of Sunday lunch out at a pub. 'Drat. I wonder if Martin's remembered. Probably not.'

She looked over at June who was holding the honey-glazed pot again. 'Are you OK?' To her surprise, June looked round with tears in her eyes. It was the first time Becca had seen her mother look vulnerable for ages. Her heart leaped. Perhaps she was regretting her decision to leave Frank. 'If you changed your mind about going,' Becca said gently, 'I'd think it was really brave. Sometimes the right thing is to stay.' June nodded. Encouraged, Becca continued. 'It's brave to admit you've made a mistake, and I'm sure no one would blame you for having a blip. Fifty years is a long time for anyone to stay married.'

'I did stay,' June said, turning the jug over in her hand. 'The man who made this was someone who . . . was special to me. He wanted me to leave Frank and go with him. But I couldn't do it.'

'What are you saying?'

'It's all very ancient history now, but a long time ago, when you and Jo were small, I met this man – he taught pottery at the evening class. Nothing happened,' she added quickly. 'Times were different. It might have been the sixties, but people didn't hop into bed with each other willy-nilly, at least, not ordinary people like us.' June gave a small laugh. 'I haven't thought about him for years. But I used to. I used to think about what would have happened if I'd gone with him. My life would have been very different, that's for sure.'

'Why didn't you go?' Becca whispered.

June sighed. 'I used to tell myself I had you and Joanna to think about. But to be honest, I think I wasn't brave enough to face all the uproar it would have caused. And I was brought up to be loyal – we all were at that time. You stuck with your marriage through thick and thin. You didn't expect as much as you young people do nowadays. I don't know. Perhaps I should have gone. Perhaps because I didn't go then, I'm going now.'

Becca stared at her. 'You're not going to him are you?'

'Heavens no. I've no idea where he is. He's probably a stuffy old man like your father by now.' June tapped the jug and it made a faint pinging sound. 'No, this time I'm going for myself. I'm going to have an adventure. Do you want the jug?' Becca shook her head, stunned by her mother's revelation. 'No, I didn't think you would. Never mind. It can go to the jumble sale.' June looked around the room, at all the things she had acquired in a lifetime of accumulating. 'You know, I thought I'd be really upset, clearing all this stuff away and getting rid of my things. But now it's come, I can see that they're only things. I've had them, enjoyed them, and now it's someone else's turn.'

Becca shook her head, trying to take it all in. She was tempted to tell June about Paul, but then realised she hadn't heard from Paul since their meeting in the park. So he'd taken her at her word, and was leaving her alone. There was no point in discussing it with June; it was over, and the fewer people who knew, the better.

'I know you've found this all very hard, but be pleased for me, darling,' June said gently, not realising what Becca was thinking about. 'This is what's right for me.'

Becca let herself in through the back door, her mind still on June's extraordinary revelation. All she could think about was that June had nearly had an affair. Her mother. Her ultra respectable, ultra conventional mother.

'Is that you, Mum?' Lily was in the dining room. That meant she was on the computer instead of doing her homework.

'Sorry I'm a bit late, sweetheart. I was up at your gran's. Is your father around?'

'Dad left you a note.'

It was lying on the kitchen side. 'Gone to training session with Ian. Back later. Martin.'

What did 'back later' mean? Back in two hours, back for supper, back at midnight? Typical, bloody typical. What does he think this is? Some hotel? Something in her mind clicked and she whizzed back in time to a memory of June banging around in the kitchen at home muttering about Frank: what does he think this is? Some hotel? Back later indeed. Serve him right to come back later and find we'd all vanished.

Becca's heart missed a beat. Had her mother thought about vanishing at that point? She tried to re-create the scene in her mind. She could conjure up the kitchen with its hospital-green painted units, the wallpaper scattered with little bundles of vegetables, purple turnips and orange carrots and round scarlet splodges for tomatoes. There was lino on the floor – was it chequered? Becca couldn't remember. What was her mother wearing? An apron? A shift dress? She couldn't picture her. Joanna was there, her eyes round as she watched their mother, but Becca couldn't conjure up an image of June beyond a fuzz of anger and resentment.

Becca went to the fridge and took out the salmon fillets she'd intended for their supper, but her mind was on June. She'd always assumed June had been happy in her role as homemaker, but this memory didn't fit. She tried to reach back for other memories from her early childhood but they eluded her. She'd always said that she must have had a blissfully happy childhood because she couldn't remember anything about it, but now she wondered. Perhaps she had been suppressing all the bad stuff.

There was a sudden wail from the dining room that pierced her heart. Lily rushed through the kitchen and upstairs, slamming her bedroom door. Becca ran upstairs after her. 'What is it? What's the matter?'

Lily was lying face down on the bed among bits of torn paper, head cradled in her arms. Becca sat on the bed next to her, and stroked her hair. 'Lily, sweetheart, what's the matter?'

Lily suddenly twisted round and clung to her, sobbing into Becca's lap. Becca could only murmur, 'There there, it's all right,' and other soothing nonsense as Lily wept her heart out. When it sounded as if the sobbing was dying down she pushed the hair back off Lily's face. 'What's the matter?'

'It wasn't Kevin,' wailed Lily.

'What wasn't?' Becca said.

'The Valentine's card. It wasn't him. All the time I've been thinking he wrote that poem, and everyone has known it wasn't him. They've all been laughing at me.'

Becca felt Lily's pain, her loss of face. She stroked her head, trying to think of a way to help. 'Never mind, it was a lovely card to get. And think, you've got an unknown admirer. That's far more romantic.'

'He's not unknown. It's Sam,' wailed Lily as if that was the worst thing that could possibly happen to a teenager.

'Sam can't be all bad.'

'He's a nerd.'

'Better than a creep then,' Becca said, feeling desperate. 'And you'll always have that card to treasure.'

'I've ripped it up.'

'No – it was a lovely poem. No one's ever sent me anything like that.'

'But it wasn't Kevin.'

Becca held her while Lily cried and cried. If she could have taken Lily's pain into herself she would have. Poor Lily, the path of her first love certainly wasn't running smooth. Perhaps it was because she'd been thinking of June earlier, but now she had another brief flashback to a woman crying in a darkened bedroom and Becca putting her arms around her and saying she'd make it better. The Becca in her memory had been young, a small child, and the crying woman had been June. Becca sat very still while Lily sobbed into her lap and the darkness gathered in the corners of the room.

Eventually Lily ran out of sobs. She curled up like a baby on the bed and allowed Becca to gently wash her tear-streaked face with a flannel dipped in cool water. A bang downstairs alerted her to Martin's return. She heard him thump up the stairs, two at a time, and came out of Lily's room to meet him on the landing.

'Hi, there – did you get my note?' Becca could feel a layer of sweat lying on his skin as he kissed her and it took all her willpower not to wipe her face.

'Supper'll be ready shortly,' she said, then lowered her voice. 'Lily's had a bit of an upset. Boy problems.'

Martin raised his eyebrows, then went and showered, while Becca went downstairs to finish making supper. Poor Lily with her boy problems, Becca thought. Poor Becca with hers. Still, she'd made it clear to Paul that he wasn't to get in touch. She had done what June had, turned away another man for the sake of her family. No, that was unfair. She loved Martin. She loved him for his good humour and kindness, his generosity. She loved him for his little quirky ways, the way he tried to do well. But now she recognised another niggling question: had she made the wrong choice all those years ago? Martin was loveable, but there was no question that Paul was more exciting and charismatic. In some ways he reminded her of the lecturer, with his energy. She tried to remember him but he had been overlaid by Paul's image.

But Paul had gone from her life. A part of her felt a loss. His letters and cards, while she hadn't wanted to receive them, had been the major excitement of her day. She had felt she was starring in a Technicolor version of her everyday life, one filled with glamorous lovers and romantic gestures. Now it was back to the kitchen and domestic life, she thought as she put the pasta on to boil.

Over the meal they talked about their days, or rather Martin talked about his day, the running programme, the sponsorship –

'which isn't going too well, you couldn't nudge a few more people at work could you?'

Becca agreed to nudge anyone and everyone. Lily sat heavy-eyed and only managed to eat two forkfuls of food before slipping away upstairs.

'Did you think my parents were happy together?' she said suddenly, interrupting Martin in full flood.

'Er – well, obviously they weren't as they're getting divorced.'

'But before that. When we first met. What did you think of their marriage?'

'I don't think I thought anything. Just, they were your parents.' He shrugged. 'I can't really remember.'

She opened her mouth to start telling him about June's almost affair, then stopped. It suddenly seemed too close to her own almost affair with Paul. Instead she said, 'I'd forgotten it's that stupid conference thing this weekend. Had you remembered?'

'Is it this weekend? I know I put it in my diary.'

Becca started to clear the plates. 'I don't want to go.'

'Don't, then.'

'I'll have to, unless I can persuade Crystal or someone to go instead of me. It's a shame. I wanted us to do something as a family, maybe go out for Sunday lunch and have a walk.'

'Another time. I've got to do my first long run this weekend anyway, so maybe it's for the best we're not going yomping across the countryside.'

Becca touched his shoulder. 'Martin, you do believe that I haven't had an affair, don't you?'

He reached up to her. 'Of course,' he said, just a few seconds too late.

'I'll give you a lift to the station,' Martin said on Friday afternoon. He'd made the effort to get home early so he could be with Lily while Becca went to the conference.

'I was going to take the bus,' Becca said. 'You don't want to get caught up in all the traffic.'

'No problem. You're always giving me lifts to the station, so fair's fair.'

'It's greener by bus. Besides, haven't you got running?'

'Yes, but we're running later this evening. Una wanted to get something done beforehand, and I can't let her run on her own in the dark – it might be dangerous.' His voice sounded indulgent. Becca flicked a look towards him.

'I wouldn't want to risk you getting stuck in the traffic and being late for Una.' Her voice sounded sharper than she'd meant. It was natural that Martin was concerned for his running partner, he was that sort of man.

'No, it's quite all right. If we go pretty soonish, I can run you up and be back in plenty of time.'

So that was decided. It meant that she didn't have to go quite as early as she'd thought, had ten minutes in hand. But it only made her feel nervous, as if there was something vital she should have been doing in that ten minutes. It would have been better to go early and wait at the station, rather than have this no-man's-land of time.

Finally the clock ticked past and it was time to go. She hugged and kissed Lily. 'I'll be back on Sunday, with luck by lunchtime, and maybe we can go and do something.'

'Cool,' Lily said. Becca thought she wouldn't mention the idea of the walk. She hugged her again as if it were the last time she'd ever see her.

Becca sat in the passenger seat of Martin's car, staring out of the window. She couldn't shake off the feeling that something was going to go wrong. She'd heard of people getting premonitions about train crashes, or other disasters. Perhaps this was one of them. It felt as if she'd left something behind but she couldn't think what. I should go away more often, she told herself. I'm becoming housebound and neurotic about leaving my family. 'Be nice to Lily,' she said. 'She's having a bit of a rough ride.'

'We'll be fine,' he said, glancing at her before turning back to his driving. 'I thought we could go to the cinema tomorrow – see that film about Jane Austen and have a pizza afterwards.'

'Wow, that is being a good father,' Becca murmured. Martin hated period dramas. She only hoped that Lily would appreciate it. 'I thought you said Jane Austen should be a brand of tampons.'

'Yeah, with the tag line – don't make a drama out of your period.' Another glance to see how she'd taken it.

Becca laughed. 'Well, I hope you enjoy it, and if not, at least Lily will.' Poor Lily. She looked so pale and unhappy. Damn that Kevin boy for breaking her child's heart.

'Here we are,' Martin said, driving on to the station forecourt. 'You should be in plenty of time for your train.'

Becca clutched the handles of her bag. 'I've changed my mind. I'm not going to go.'

'Darling, why on earth not?'

'I – I – I'm worried about Lily. She's been awfully upset over this boy . . .'

'Don't be silly, we'll manage. Besides, Bill will be pissed off if you don't go, won't he?' Martin said. He got out of the car and took her overnight bag from the car boot, then opened the passenger door. 'Come on, hurry up, or you'll miss your train.'

She got out of the car, feeling as if fate was conspiring against her. They walked into the foyer and Martin checked the display board. 'Five minutes to go. Perfect timing.'

'You don't have to wait.'

'I'll take your bag up, at least.'

They walked in silence up the stairs to the platform. The station guards checked Becca's ticket, and let Martin through to say goodbye.

'Do you want a tea? A newspaper?'

Becca shook her head. 'Why are you being so nice to me?'

'Aren't I always?' His eyes dropped down. 'I'm sorry. I know you're having a bit of a rough time, what with your mum and everything. Me always out running. That bloody woman phoning.' He sighed. 'You deserve a break. So, off you go, have a nice time talking about Shakespeare or whatever you're going to do and don't think of us. Just enjoy yourself.'

'Martin—'

'Ah – here's the train coming now.' The train pulled in, and they walked to the far end of the platform. Martin opened the train door and put her bag inside. 'Can you manage?'

'It's not heavy,' she said.

He slammed the door shut. The guard whistled, and the train pulled out of the station. Becca watched as Martin standing on the platform became smaller and smaller, and then, as the train eased round a curve, vanished.

The conference was taking place in a large hotel. Becca dropped her bags in her room and quickly rang home to say she'd arrived safely. Lily had sounded a bit droopy, she thought as she freshened up then went downstairs to register. She hoped Lily would be OK.

Downstairs she was directed to a large reception hall. She collected her name badge and a conference pack, and looked at what lay ahead of her that evening: registration drinks, a talk, then the opening dinner. She pinned her badge on to her jacket, took a glass of red wine from a waiter and sat down at a small table to look at the schedule for Saturday. There was a complicated timetable, with most of the hourly slots having an option between four or five speakers so delegates could choose their path throughout the day. She sipped her wine. OK – what would she choose for the nine until ten slot?

Sometimes the choice was easy, sometimes hard. But she carried on ticking the relevant boxes until she came to the last time slot: four to five. A New Approach to Teaching Shakespeare: Speaker, Paul Fitzwilliam.

Chapter 25

W as Paul there? Becca swiftly looked round the room, but couldn't see him among the crowd. Inwardly she cursed herself for not having thought of this before. It was obvious that Paul was a potential speaker. She knew he talked at conferences, and while this was slightly out of his area – hence his slot in the late afternoon when some delegates would have given up and gone home – she'd known that he was interested in getting his work with Shakespeare known to a wider audience than just theatre professionals.

Becca was tempted to leave right there and then, but Bill expected her to report back and would be angry if she didn't. The brownie points she'd gained from not making a fuss about Paul kissing her at the workshop would be lost. She looked around her. There were hundreds of people attending the conference, there was no need for their paths to cross. As he was speaking late on Saturday, he would probably skip the rest and just turn up for his talk. Maybe he might stay for a drink afterwards, but he'd be bound to want to get back home. So long as she kept a low profile, there was no need to panic. And to be honest, should they bump into each other, she was surely capable of being friendly, polite, and distant as befitted a professional conference.

In fact, she didn't see him that evening, although she kept

checking the faces at the tables around the large hall. He wasn't there. Becca went up to her room feeling perversely cheated. She rang home, but there was no answer, so instead she opened a mini bottle of wine from the minibar – hang the mega cost, it was on Hamilton House – and settled down to watch Friday night television.

The room was furnished in hard stiff fabrics, with a turquoise colour scheme: turquoise curtains, turquoise bed covers, turquoise carpet. The walls were striped off-pink, cream and turquoise. It wasn't seedy, but there was nothing glamorous about it either. A businessman's hotel room, anonymous and impersonal. She guessed that she could be in any country in the world, and not know the difference. If I were home, she thought, I'd be doing the same but I'd have my feet across Martin's lap and we'd be eating chocolate as a Friday night treat.

Saturday proceeded without incident. The talks she'd chosen were interesting, and Becca enjoyed most of them. It was fascinating talking to other teachers and she took part in a lively discussion about the pros and cons of drama coursework over lunch. She'd almost forgotten Paul.

Almost, but not quite. After lunch she took care to check the lecture room she was in, to keep her eyes out for a tall figure. She had the advantage over him because she knew he was there, while he was ignorant of her presence. She changed her schedule and chose the afternoon talks on the basis that the rooms they were being held in were furthest from the one Paul was speaking in.

At four that afternoon Becca was sitting in a small room listening to a talk and thinking of Paul who was giving his talk on a completely different floor. She wondered if he'd attracted a large audience, if they were attentive. Perhaps he was fielding lots of difficult questions. He'd probably enjoy that, she thought, smiling. It would appeal to the fighter in him. She had no doubt that anyone who attended would be won over by his enthusiasm. With a start she realised that people around her were clapping. The talk was over, and she'd hardly listened to a word.

Next on the schedule were drinks at 6.30, followed by the plenary speech, and then dinner. Becca trailed down the corridor, wondering how to occupy herself for the next ninety minutes. Go to her room, have a cup of tea, put her feet up for an hour, then get ready for the evening she supposed. The thought of a cup of tea made with proper milk rather than those little cartons of UHT treated milk appealed, and having it outside her turquoise room appealed even more. She went to reception and ordered tea for one.

A black notice board with gold stick-on lettering announced their conference, an AGM and a wedding reception, and there were plenty of people about, the mix more varied than Liquorice Allsorts, some walking purposefully, others loitering and checking watches as if waiting for an important announcement. Grannies took tea with grandsons, men with laptops on their knees talked business, tourists examined maps and complained of sore feet. People busied themselves with a variety of activities here in the hotel reception, and not a single one of them was Paul.

A waitress brought the tea. Becca sat on the edge of her seat and sipped it, wondering how best to pass the next couple of hours. At home, if Lily was around, they would sometimes watch television at this time – there was usually one of those programmes of video clips of people making fools of themselves, brides slipping at their wedding and showing their knickers, dads falling off ladders and ending with the can of paint on their heads. Becca and Lily liked the animal ones best, cats sticking their heads in unlikely places, dogs eagerly jumping up as if on mini trampolines. A tall dark man came through the revolving doors and her heart leaped. Paul! The man turned. It wasn't Paul.

She fidgeted with the sugar cubes now knowing why she was drinking tea in the lobby. UHT milk or not, she should be in her room and instead she was hoping that she might accidentally bump into Paul. She picked up one of the cubes and examined it. How did the crystals stick together in such perfect little white cubes? Perhaps when you dissolved one you were also adding a dollop of secret glue to your tea.

She put the cube on the table. I love him. Then another cube on top. I love him not. Another cube. I love him. I love him not. She was creating a substantial tower. I love him. I love him not. The tower trembled, then collapsed. There it was, foretold in a stack of sugar cubes. She didn't love Paul. I do, her heart countered. Of course I do, or why else would I be here in the lobby?

She poured another cup of tea and stared at the sugar bowl, unable to answer her own question. Was it really love she was feeling? Not the same love she felt for Martin and Lily. That was like breathing. Was he really the person she fell in love with? Was he worth loving? Wasn't he simply a charming surface that she'd projected feelings on to? Becca had to put her teacup down, her hands were shaking so much.

A hand touched her shoulder. 'Becca?'

And she turned, as she'd known she would, and smiled at him. 'Hello, Paul.'

He sat next to her. 'What are you doing here? Of course, how stupid of me. You're at the conference too. But you didn't come to my talk.' Becca shook her head. 'Never mind. You know the gist of it from the workshop, but there's quite a lot of other material I'd have liked to show you – photographs of productions, copies of some of the platts, entries from Henslowe's diaries, I've even got a copy of an original cue script—' He stopped and looked away. 'I'm sorry, I'm boring you. I get carried away.'

'No, it was interesting. What are . . . platts? Was that the word?'

He nodded, eyes lighting up. 'They were like the plot outline and would hang in the wings so the actors knew what happened in each scene, which characters were in it, and who played which parts. They're fascinating documents, for example, you can tell which of the actors were company shareholders because they're called Mr Fitzwilliam, or whatever, the hired actors were just Fitzwilliam, and the apprentices were known by their first names or nicknames. But enough about Shakespeare. Tell me about you. Have you enjoyed the conference so far? Has it been worth it?'

'I've enjoyed it. Some of it's been very interesting. I went to one talk . . .' and they began to talk about the conference in a relaxed and friendly way. Paul was such a good listener, Becca thought. He looked so intently interested in her thoughts and opinions. She felt herself speak more confidently, more fluently as if they were old friends. And Paul's attitude to her was that of an old friend. There was no hint of their previous relationship, it was back to how it had been before they'd kissed, but better because there was a warmth and appreciation there hadn't been before. It was good that he'd stopped sending her messages and saying he loved her, it really was. Now they had the chance to be friends.

When Paul stood up, Becca was thrown by how reluctant she was to finish their conversation. 'It's been great speaking to you,' he said. 'But I'm dying for a drink and I've got to take my stuff back to my room, so I'm going to head on up.'

Becca stood up too. 'You're staying over?'

Paul nodded. 'Suzy's taken the kids off to visit her sister, so I thought I might as well, rather than rush back home.'

'Are things all right at home?' Becca said.

Paul made a face. 'Not really. But you mustn't blame yourself for that, it really wasn't your fault. The fault was entirely mine. As Suzy tells me so very often.'

'I'm sorry.'

'All part of life. I have tried taking your advice to make up with Suzy, but Suzy doesn't appear very keen to be made up to.' He struck a theatrical pose. 'I am summoned by a large gin and tonic and I must go.'

'It was good seeing you again.'

'And you. So it's goodbye then.' He touched Becca's cheek, smiled, then kissed her. For one second his arms were around her, his skin next to hers and she trembled as she murmured goodbye.

He picked up his briefcase and turned to go, then turned back with a cheeky grin. 'Unless you fancy joining me. I could show you my platts.' His eyes were alight with mischief and Becca found herself grinning back at him.

'It's big,' Becca said with surprise as Paul unfolded a large sheet of printed paper.

'About two foot by three foot. Look, you can see the hole where they would have hung it up on a peg backstage.' He pointed at a square hole in the middle of the paper. 'This is a copy of the original at Dulwich College, where all Philip Henslowe's papers ended up. Philip Henslowe was the manager of the Rose Theatre at the time when Shakespeare was acting at the Globe next door.'

Becca read a bit out: ' "Enter King Gorboduk with 2 Counsailers. R Burbadge Mr Brian. Th Goodale. The Queene with Ferrex and Porrex and som attendants follow. Saunder. W Sly. Harry. J Duke. Kitt. Ro Pallant. J Holland." Was that Richard Burbage who was Shakespeare's friend?'

'One assumes so. Did you see the cue scripts I prepared for the workshop? This is a copy of an original.' He shuffled among his papers and pulled out a long piece. 'What modern actors call parts, they used to call lengths – you can see why.'

Becca bent her head over the text. 'This is fascinating.'

'The evidence is there and all the actors who've worked with cue scripts are excited by it. It makes so much more sense of the texts but it's an uphill struggle getting the academics to accept it.

The guy who first developed cue scripts discovered no one had thought about how they rehearsed plays in Shakespeare's day, they simply assumed it was in the same way that we do today – if they thought about it at all. The academics don't like the idea of being told they're wrong by lowly theatre folk. But the plays were written to be performed, not studied.'

He rummaged among the papers. 'I'll show you some photographs of cue script productions. That's *Measure for Measure* in Japan, that's *Macbeth* and *Romeo and Juliet*, I did those for . . .' He flicked over one of the photographs. 'That was for a festival in Germany. And these ones are all from the States – they like me there, they're more open minded.'

'Don't they like you here?' Becca said looking at the photographs.

'Not much. I've ruffled too many feathers. Oh, that's an old one, not sure how that got in here. That's me at the RSC. God, I look young. Look at that hair.'

Becca touched a photograph of a young Paul, his hair flopping over his forehead, the stare at the camera intense and dark. Her finger was only a few centimetres from his. Millimetres. He had lovely hands, with long fingers. She thought of them on her body, touching her. So close.

'Were you with Suzy then?' Her finger traced the photograph.

His finger joined hers. 'No. I must have met her a couple of years later.'

The room felt incredibly small, filled to the brim with aching desire. She looked up at him, and suddenly thought, what if I kiss him? Every scrap of normal brain had vanished, pushed to the further reaches of her skull cavity by the big, throbbing statement of: I want to kiss him. His head was near hers as he bent across to examine the photograph, turning slightly sideways so she saw the line of his neck disappearing down into his cornflower-blue shirt. This is ridiculous, she told herself. Stop it now. This was a mistake. Go.

She straightened up and as she did, Paul did too. The papers caught, flipped up, and cascaded to the floor, spewing photographs and photocopies.

'God, I'm sorry,' Becca said, kneeling to pick them up.

'No, it was my fault,' Paul said, kneeling too. Their heads bumped. Becca sprang away as if Paul were on fire. Which was ironic, given that she could feel her own cheeks burning, her insides consumed with the heat of wanting him to kiss her. But it's such a cliché, some mad bit of her brain thought. The papers on the floor leading to a clinch. She stood up, her arms full of photographs.

'Sorry, they're out of order.' And so am I, she thought. She realised they were staring at each other. Paul's face was serious. The air was still between them. Her heart was pounding. She swallowed. 'I must go.' She turned for the door, breaking the eye contact. 'Thanks for showing me the platts and things.'

'Becca . . .' Paul caught her shoulder and her heart missed about six beats. She felt she had shot from turbo-charged acceleration and smashed straight into a brick wall. 'Don't go.'

'I think it's better. You're married.'

'And I can't tell you how much I wish I wasn't.'

'Every marriage goes through rough patches,' she said, still with her back to him.

'My rough patch seems to be lasting a lifetime.'

With a blinding flash of clarity, Becca knew that this was the moment she should leave. She should say something anodyne like, never mind, hang on in there, I remember how difficult it was when Lily was the same age as your children – except it hadn't been. Or, have you tried talking it over with a marriage guidance counsellor?

'I don't know what to say,' Becca said truthfully. 'Everything seems banal or trite because I don't know you well enough to say something meaningful.'

'Don't you know me? I feel I know you. I felt it when we first met. A sense of connection. That you were the person I was meant to meet.'

Becca put her hand to her chest. Her heart was beating so fast it threatened to escape from her ribcage. There was no room to breathe. Becca stared at the carpet as if the swirling pattern held the answer to the meaning of life. 'You mustn't say these things to me. Please don't.'

He touched her shoulder. 'Turn around and look at me.'

She shook her head, but allowed him to turn her around then pull her gently towards him, one hand cupping her head. I could still go back, Becca thought for one blinding moment. I could still pull away and leave. She turned her face up to his and rested one hand on his shoulder.

His mouth was soft on hers, soft and sweet as she'd remembered. Past and future were gone. All that was left was an intense awareness of the present, the here and now. Exploring, delighting, all her conscious thought fully engaged in what she was doing at this moment, kissing Paul. His hands were everywhere, burning against her skin. She felt breathless and dishevelled, holding his body to hers. Paul's hands were untucking her shirt, then were inside it, skin on skin. And then they were falling on to his bed, mouths clamped together, hot and sweaty, she could hear Paul kicking his shoes off, he was kissing her neck, his breathing heavy, his hand pushing up her skirt.

'Too fast, too fast,' she breathed, pushing his hand away.

'I want you,' he muttered, and she buried her head in his chest so she didn't have to answer, thoughts whirring round her head faster than her racing heartbeat. Did she want him?

'I need time . . .' she panted.

He pressed against her as if he hadn't heard, his weight pinning her to the bed, his tongue pushing hard inside her mouth and she realised that she might not be able to stop him. I don't know this man, I don't know him, she thought in panic. I am grappling on a hotel bed with a stranger. 'Paul, no. You're hurting me.'

To her relief he pulled back. 'Sorry,' he mumbled. 'Getting carried away a bit. Shit, is that the time? I've got to shower and change before dinner – I'm one of the after-dinner speakers.' Paul rolled away from her completely and stood.

'I ought to change too,' Becca said, sitting up, thrown by his change of mood from loving to businesslike.

'Come and join me.' Paul indicated the en-suite shower room with suggestively raised eyesbrows.

Becca shook her head. 'My stuff's in my own room, I'll change there.'

'OK. Meet you back here? We can go into dinner together.'

'OK.'

He kissed her, a long lingering kiss. 'See you back in fifteen minutes. Hey, you could help me run over the notes for my speech.'

She nodded, and he shut the door.

Becca waited a couple of seconds and then she heard the gush of the shower going on. As if it were the starter's pistol, she was off. She grabbed her bag and coat then ran from the room. Down the corridor to the lift, up another two floors, then down more corridor to her room. She swiped her keycard and entered, slamming the door shut behind her. She slumped against it. Now what?

Seventeen minutes later Becca knocked on Paul's door. He opened it. 'Come in, come in. You look lovely. I'm just putting a couple of last-minute touches to my speech.' He turned back into the room and Becca followed him. 'Do you want a drink?'

'No thanks.' Becca waited.

Paul scrabbled around on the top of the desk. 'Now, where was I? Ah yes.' He picked up a piece of paper. 'This was it. Tell me what you think of this.' He held it out to her then stopped. 'You've got a suitcase.'

Becca nodded. 'I'm going back now.'

'Not staying . . . ?' Becca shook her head, and he sat on the edge of the bed with a thump. 'I don't understand. What about the dinner? The conference? What about us?'

Becca sighed. 'There is no "us". I'm sorry. I thought of going straight away, but felt I owed you an explanation. The thing is . . .

the thing is, that if I stay, I'm basically staying the night and that's crossing a line I don't want to cross. We don't really know each other very well. I hardly know myself. What I've realised is that I'm not the sort of person who can lightly go into an affair, play around, and then come out the other end without touching the sides. And even if I was that sort of person, I suppose it all comes down to choices.' She smiled at him. 'I find you hugely attractive. Life is exciting when you're around. Your company is stimulating, and fun, and things happen. I like being with you. A huge part of me wants nothing more than to sleep with you.'

Paul scratched his head. 'Why do I think there's a "but" coming . . . ?'

'It's been really hard, because I do have feelings for you. You're very loveable but . . .'

'There it is.'

'But.' Becca took a deep breath. 'I made a choice to be with Martin a long time ago. I've never regretted that choice, until you came along. You were right – I was feeling low and unappreciated. You made me feel like the star in my own life again, that I was someone who things happened to. And I so needed that.'

'Then why aren't you staying?'

'Because that's not what it's about. It's fun and exciting because it's just the surface. It's all the thrills, but you can't live like that. It's not real life. Tell me my favourite food, my favourite record. Do you know which side of the bed I like to sleep on? Do you know what I'm most scared of, or what makes me happiest?'

'Yes to the last one – me!'

Becca laughed. 'Sometimes. And the saddest too. But all those things are part of me, who I am, and I don't know them about you, and you don't know them about me.'

'But getting to know is part of the fun.'

'And then what? You can't keep that level of excitement up for ever. Real life sets in.' Real life with Paul must be frustrating, she thought, however charming he is, like having another extremely demanding child. Poor Suzy. 'Why did Suzy ring Martin? Did you tell her about us?' Paul looked at her, his eyes wide and innocent. Too innocent. 'Why on earth did you do it?'

Paul looked annoyed at being caught out. 'I wanted you to see how much I loved you.'

'That's so . . .' Becca stared at Paul, unable to articulate what she felt. How could he have been so irresponsible? There were other people – their children – to consider. 'How could you be so selfish?'

'I told Suzy we'd been having an affair. That wasn't a lie. I wanted to shake things up, stop you playing the martyr and putting duty and obligations before love. You wanted me, I know you did. You still do.'

'Not now,' Becca said her eyes wide at how she could have been so mistaken. 'Didn't you think about your children? No wonder Suzy doesn't want to make up with you – I wouldn't.' She picked up her suitcase.

'He doesn't deserve you,' Paul said. 'I love you.'

'I don't deserve him,' Becca said sharply. 'I haven't been a very good wife to him these last six months. I don't think I've been a good wife these last years. We've lost sight of each other, got too wrapped up in our own little worlds.' She walked to the door. 'It's time for me to go home.'

Back in Bath, safe at home, Becca paid off the taxi driver, giving him an enormous tip for bringing her back to Martin. There were lights on in the house – it wasn't that late, only 9.30. She let herself in through the back gate as she usually did. As she stopped by the back door to hunt for her keys she glanced at the kitchen window. There was Martin, but not on his own. Una was with him, and Martin's arm was around her shoulder and he was kissing her.

Chapter 26

'What the hell is going on?'

'Becca!' Una and Martin sprang apart as Becca burst in. Martin jumped up, guilt mixed with surprise on his face. 'What are you doing back?'

'What's she doing here? What's going on?' Becca was stunned. Martin, kissing Una, in her kitchen. She couldn't breathe.

'I asked Una back for a glass of wine,' Martin said, still looking surprised. 'She needed help with her report.'

'Martin's been very kind, and helpful,' Una said, getting up.

'I bet.' Very kind, and very very helpful, by the looks of things. So this was how it felt. This was how Martin must have felt when Suzy called him. Oh, but she had been so stupid not to realise. Her chest twisted internally into a painful knot. 'How long has this been going on?'

'There's nothing going on,' Martin said.

'Look, I'd better be on my way,' Una said, picking up her fleece. 'Really, Becca, it's not what you think.'

'And how do you know what I think?'

Una glanced at Martin. 'I don't want to cause any problems.'

'Good. That's good,' said Becca, as her brain seethed with devastating put-downs. 'I'm sure there won't be any problems – I mean, it's usual for a wife to come back unexpectedly and find her husband kissing another woman. And where's Lily?'

'She's having a sleepover at Grace's. Becca, it was a peck on the cheek,' Martin said, coming towards her. 'Don't be silly—' He put out his hand to touch her shoulder, but she pushed him off.

'I don't think I'm being silly here.' Becca put her hands to her head. A peck on the cheek? Was it? Did they think she was stupid – his arm was around Una, he was kissing her. 'I can't believe I've come home to this.'

'I'm on my way,' Una murmured. 'See you, Martin.'

'I'll show you out.' Martin glanced at Becca. She couldn't believe it. Martin. Martin! She'd left Paul, and come back to – her breath was coming in sharp jagged jerks. She could hear Martin's voice in the hall, saying goodbye to Una, telling her not to worry, he'd explain. Explain what? Becca thought.

'Explain what?' Becca said as Martin came back into the kitchen. She could have punched Una for simply existing. 'What the hell is going on?'

'I'm sorry, I'm sorry, I'm sorry. You came in at just the wrong moment. There's nothing going on between me and Una, she was feeling a bit depressed about work, that's all. I gave her a hug and a kiss, as a friend. That's all.'

'No.' Becca shook her head. 'No. No, no, no. You don't hug and kiss friends, not when you're married and she's an attractive young woman. Oh God.' She pressed her face in her hands. This wasn't happening. Oh, she knew about that spur of the moment thing, the way a man comforted a crying woman. Paul had comforted her when she'd been upset over Martin. The circles go round, inter-connecting. One thing leads to another. And she knew how it could lead elsewhere, to unsought directions. 'You were kissing her. How can it mean nothing?'

Martin took her hands and peered earnestly into her eyes. 'Because you know me. Because you know I wouldn't do anything that might harm our relationship. You have to believe me. Una was feeling really low, and it seemed the right response at the time, a peck on the cheek, and that's all. She's listened to me banging on about my problems, it was fair enough I listened to her.'

'What sort of problems?' Becca said, looking at him with horror and removing her hands from his. 'You haven't talked about us have you?'

Martin couldn't have looked more shifty than if he'd been selling used cars. 'A bit.'

'What have you said? "My wife doesn't understand me"?' She felt sick with jealousy. What if Martin left her? Una was young, attractive, available. Oh God.

'Nothing like that.'

'What then?' Everything seemed wrong. She had come home with such good intentions, such a need to make up, such a need to compensate for her deficiencies. And then this! But who was she to complain about what Martin had been doing, when she had been kissing Paul with passion just a few hours earlier. She poured herself a glass of wine with shaking hands.

'I know how it must seem, and I'm really sorry but there's nothing going on.' Martin sat down next to Becca. 'I'm not stupid. I know you think my running's pointless. I also know that you never seem to have time for me any more, if it's not the acting, it's something else. And when I try to talk, or do something nice like go out for Valentine's Day, you're not interested. I expect I'm a bit boring compared to your theatre group.' He rubbed his eyes, as if they were sore. 'I know I shouldn't have kissed Una. She's an attractive girl, and I like her. You could say I have a bit of a soft spot for her.' He paused, then spoke very deliberately, very seriously, looking straight at Becca. 'But I would not for one second risk our marriage for some fling. It would never be worth it. You have to believe me.'

Becca put her hand to her mouth, fighting back the tears. Martin didn't know what she'd done, what she'd been about to do, that she on the other hand *had* been ready to risk their marriage for a fling. He thought he had to convince her to believe that there was nothing between him and Una, as she had had to convince him to believe there was nothing between her and Paul after Suzy's phone call. The difference was, she did believe him, and she was the lying one, the weak one who'd put their marriage at risk. 'I believe you, Martin, I really do. And I'm sorry if I've been neglecting you. I didn't mean to. Everything's gone wrong. Ever since Mum said she was leaving Dad, it's all been wrong. Me, you, everything.'

'Ah, honey, I'm so sorry. I will try harder.'

Becca sniffed. 'So will I. And I'm sorry too. I should have . . .' But there were rather a lot of things she should have, or rather shouldn't have, done. In the end she resorted to just shrugging.

Martin got up, taking the wine bottle to the kitchen worktop where he found a cork. Becca still had some wine in her glass, which she drank down.

'How come you're back today? Was there some problem?' Martin said, pushing the cork deep into the bottle.

Becca spluttered on the wine. Ages spent rehearsing various scenarios on the train became wasted as her brain went blank. 'There was only the dinner and some speeches left this evening, and not much going on tomorrow so I decided to skip it. I'd got a headache,' she said, brushing splatters of wine off her cardigan.

'Are you feeling better now?'

'Not really,' Becca said. A wave of emotional tiredness came over her and she could feel her eyes well up. 'In fact, I think I'll go up now.'

'I'll join you in a sec.' Martin held her shoulders. 'I'm sorry for kissing Una. It really was a spur of the moment thing, and meant nothing. Will you forgive me?'

Becca nodded. 'Of course.' She went to the stairs and paused, foot on the tread. If I go up now, she thought, I miss the opportunity for ever. I'll have to spend the rest of my life lying to him about what went on with Paul. I'll have to take care with every word I say. Whenever the phone rings I'll always be worried in case it's Paul, whenever we're out with Crystal I'll worry because she might let something slip. I'll never be able to discuss it, and it will filter through and destroy our life together, even if Martin never finds out the truth. I will always know I have lied again and again to him. And if he does find out, I can say goodbye to any chance of happiness together after all the lying and deceitfulness. Is that what I want? She turned and went back to the kitchen.

Martin looked up from loading the dishwasher and smiled at her, a big innocent, warm smile.

Becca pleated her cardigan in the fingers of her right hand. 'I've got something I want to tell you.'

Becca lay alone in the vast and chilly expanse of her bed contemplating the crack on the ceiling and the motto that honesty was always the best policy. That must have been dreamed up by someone who had never tried being honest. She curled up into a foetal ball, hoping that sleep would come to her despite having eluded her all night. If she hadn't felt ill before, she did now. It was a strange sort of pain, one that consumed her whole body, making every corpuscle ache, every molecule moan. She hadn't felt this bad since she was a teenager. Teenage love, teenage pain. Perhaps it was just the pain of relationships that you forgot once you'd settled into a pattern with one person. No pain, no gain. But she'd got all the pain, and for what?

Martin was in the spare room.

He had been dignified after the initial shock, quietly taking himself up to bed. 'I need to think,' was all he said. So she had to wait. She'd hoped he would come across to her in the night, but he never came and she lay there, getting colder and colder, despite the duvet and an extra blanket. She played out scenarios in her head where she crept over to him, but the fear of rejection was too great.

Instead she lay, unable to sleep despite her eyes feeling swollen. She longed to close them. But they seemed as unable to rest, staring out into the darkness, all the time her mind running over and over that same moment: on the stairs, with her foot on the tread, about to go upstairs and never say anything to Martin ever.

Why did I say anything?

Because it seemed a good idea at the time.

She had to stop acting on impulse. She would be sensible and mature and make considered decisions from now on. Think before you speak, and all that. Why couldn't she have done that before now? She'd been told often enough. There was no reason to suppose that her keeping the secret of Paul would have meant the end of their marriage – plenty of women kept secrets. But not her. No, she was the one who had to blurt out the truth at all costs. The room had gradually lightened and she realised it was dawn and another day was starting.

She heard a noise and sat up in bed. Then a knock at the door. 'Come in,' she said, feeling cold as ice with fear at his formality. Martin pushed the door open. He looked more serious than she could remember seeing him, all humour gone from his face. 'You look like I feel,' she said, desperate to say something to lighten the situation. He stared at her, but Becca felt he wasn't seeing her. 'We need to talk. I'll be downstairs.'

In the kitchen the wine and glasses were still left out, giving the room a sordid, unfinished feel. Becca could feel the chasm between them. She clicked the kettle on, then quickly cleared the glasses into the dishwasher. 'Tea? Coffee?'

'Tea. Thanks.' He stared out at the garden. He was already dressed in his tracksuit and trainers ready to go running. Becca tightened her dressing-gown tie around her middle.

He turned away from the window. 'I'm going to move out today.'

Becca stared at him, open mouthed. 'No, you can't. If anyone should go, it should be me.'

He flickered a glance over her, the first sign that there was life behind his zombie demeanour, as if he wanted to say – Too right it should be you. But what he said was, 'Lily would never forgive me. She needs you.'

'You mustn't go. Not like this. Please, Martin. Can't we try?' Becca pressed her lips together. She wanted to go down on her knees and beg him to stay with her, to give it one more go, not to give up on their marriage. But Martin was looking like a man made of stone, another man, not her warm and loving Martin. The thought occurred to her that he would never be her warm and loving Martin again and she thought she would be sick. She clutched her stomach and swallowed the bile down.

'I obviously can't give you what you want. You want another man.'

'No, no, I want you,' she cried.

He shook his head. 'Obviously you don't.'

'I do, I do. You're all I've ever wanted.' Don't cry, she told herself. Stay calm.

'The thought of you and—' He turned back to the window as if the view of the clothes line in the garden outside could solve all their problems.

'I've told you nothing happened.'

He turned round. 'Nothing?'

Becca hung her head. 'Kissing yes, but more than that, no. We never, ever had sex. And I finished it – it was over before it started, just a moment of madness.'

He dug his hands deep in his pockets. 'The thing is, I thought our marriage was perfect. I thought whatever happened, we'd get through it. It never occurred to me that you didn't feel the same way.'

'I felt you didn't love me any more,' Becca said in a small voice.

'Of course I did.'

'Then why didn't you show it?'

• • •   300   • • •

Martin shrugged. 'You can't go round all the time acting like a teenager.'

'There's some middle ground, you know.'

'I can't fake it. It's not worth anything if it isn't real.'

'I'm not asking you to fake it.' Becca tried to think of ways to explain. 'You gave me saucepans for Christmas.'

'You said you liked them.'

'As saucepans, yes, but not for my Christmas present.' Becca felt like crying. 'It's not about the bloody saucepans, it's about what they symbolise. They make me feel like a domestic drudge, not an attractive woman.'

Martin stared at his feet. 'I can't do anything right.'

'Martin, no, I didn't mean that. I love you. I want you to stay. Please, don't go.' He shook his head. 'Please, please. Give it some time. Don't go in anger. Wait a little. Please, Martin. For Lily's sake at least.'

'For Lily's sake.' He paused, as if considering, then nodded. 'OK, I'll stay for the time being. We'll see how things go. Right now, I'm going for a run.'

'With Una?'

He gave her a sharp look. 'Yes. Any problems with that?'

'What else did you expect?' Crystal said, hands on the side of the pool, her face pink from the heat of the water. 'Martin's an attractive guy – and even more so now he's lost that bit of surplus. Decent men are hard to find, they get snapped up as soon as there's a whiff they might be coming on to the market. Did you really think he was going to hang around while you snogged some other man?'

'He didn't know I was snogging someone, as you put it.' It had been Crystal's idea that they should go to the spa in half term. Becca felt she needed gallons of boiling water to cleanse her of her sins, but so far all that had happened was the skin on her fingers looked like albino prunes. 'Oh, Crystal, I can't bear to think about Martin going off with her. He's shutting me out. He won't talk to me, he cuts me dead, he won't discuss anything. At least he's stopped saying he's going to move out, but that's about it. And he hasn't stopped going running with her.'

Crystal shook her head, making her curls bob. 'Men need constant attention, if you leave them too long, they wander off.'

'What about him paying me attention? He made me feel less important than his running shoes.' Becca waved her hand in front of her face to try and get some cooler air on it.

'Men don't work like that. Men can't see the point of all the stuff we like.'

'They ought to.' The water in the pool started to bubble.

'Yes, they ought to, but they don't.'

Becca looked sideways at Crystal. 'If you're so switched on, how come you're single?'

'Cos it's easy to see with other people, you can't do it yourself. That and years of self-help books.' Suddenly Crystal looked coy. 'Besides, I am with someone at the moment.'

'Really? Who?' Becca shifted to get the bubbles against the small of her back.

'Just a bloke.' Crystal gave a token shrug of indifference, then leaped in, not even waiting for any encouragement. 'His name's Jim, and he's a chemistry lecturer up at the college, and he's utterly gorgeous.'

'I hope it works out.'

'I think he might be The One.'

'I never thought Martin was The One,' Becca said slowly. 'We just grew together. I always thought I was lucky because I married my best friend.'

'Doesn't everyone think that?' Crystal said. 'Otherwise, why would you want to marry them? Shag them, yes, but marry them, no. Anyway, what went wrong?'

'I don't know. Yes, I do. I felt my life was being measured out in washing cycles. Relentless, non-stop domestic stuff. Stupid things like getting up early on Saturday morning to put the first load of washing on before rushing to the supermarket. Get back home, unload the shopping, then swap the washing loads round. Hang stuff out to dry while the next load washes. And so on through the day until you end up with a massive pile of laundry to iron at midnight.'

'Didn't Martin help?'

'Yes, he helped, but it's not about how much help they give you, it's about the fact that you have to ask every time. It's always your responsibility, you're the one who's saying can you do this, can you do that. And if you don't, nothing happens and you end up living in a slum.'

'That's part of being married.'

'Why? It's not for better, for worse and the ironing stack. Recently I looked into Martin's eyes and thought I didn't know him at all. He was someone quite different.' Crystal snorted as if she thought Becca was being ridiculous.

'Or perhaps it was me who had become someone different,' Becca said. She remembered back to the beginning when she'd first kissed Paul, the heady feeling that she had been born again, the escape from the dreary reality of everyday life, the excitement, the delicious sense of her body waking up like Sleeping Beauty being kissed awake by the handsome prince. The trouble with being best friends with your husband was that best friends didn't usually want to have wild passionate sex.

Crystal pursed her lips. 'Well, Becca Woods, you have to decide if you want that husband of yours or not.'

'But he doesn't want me,' Becca wailed, tears mingling with sweat.

'He's still at home, though, whatever he says.' Crystal ducked her head under the water. 'Don't worry, Martin isn't going to leave. He'd have gone by now if he was really going to go. Why on earth did you tell him about your fling?'

'I was fed up with there being lies between us,' Becca said, hoping Crystal was right. 'I thought, my parents' marriage is breaking up because they haven't been talking to each other and telling the truth about how they feel. So I thought I'd better come clean, otherwise I'd end up like my mum.'

Crystal pushed her wet hair from her eyes. 'If you ask me, truth in a marriage is severely overrated.'

Becca went over to her parents' house. Frank let her in. 'Becca, you're just the person I wanted to see. Can you give me a few minutes?'

Becca nodded. 'But is it OK if I talk to Mum first?'

'She's upstairs in her studio. I'll make us some coffee,' and he bustled off. Becca went upstairs, wondering if this was the first time she'd heard her father offer to do something domestic. She opened the door to the studio, but to her surprise the canvases had vanished. June was halfway up a ladder by the window.

'Wonderful, your timing's perfect. Give me a hand with these curtains, will you?'

Becca stood below her, and helped support the weight as June hung them. 'They don't seem quite your taste,' she said, running the chintzy material through her fingers.

'Maureen's lent them to me. The estate agent said the house will sell better if each room is clearly defined as to its function. So this is going back to being a bedroom.'

'You've had an estate agent round? You didn't tell me.'

'Didn't I?' June waved an arm as she came down the stepladder. 'We're moving to separate houses, so of course we're going to sell up. You'll never guess how much the agent valued it at. Of course, house prices have gone up everywhere. Did you know that St Ives is the same sort of price as here?' Becca shook her head. 'I hoped there'd be a bit more of a difference but never mind. I only need a small place, just enough for me and my painting and the occasional guest.' She gave Becca a hug. 'I can't wait to get there.'

'You know what you told me the last time? About the potter,' Becca said. 'I wanted to ask you – did you regret not going with him?'

'Oh darling, it's all water under the bridge. I honestly haven't thought about him for at least twenty years, if not more.' She patted Becca's shoulder. 'There are more important things in life to be getting on with, rather than fretting over some man.'

'But did you regret it?'

'Maybe for a time. I suppose it's the idea of the life you might have lived. But look at me now! I have two lovely daughters, and lovely grandchildren, and I'm off on an adventure. I'm going to live by the sea. I can't think of what might have been, I can only enjoy what is.'

'Coffee,' Frank called from downstairs.

'Would you bring one up for me, there's a love. I want to get the bed made up.' Becca offered to help but June shooed her away. 'I can manage. You go and talk to Frank.'

Frank was looking about ten years younger every time she saw him, Becca thought as he poured the coffee. He'd arranged everything nicely on a tray, including a plate of biscuits. 'Now, Becca, I trust your judgement. Have a look at these.'

He fanned out a batch of estate agents' details. Becca took them from him and flicked through. 'But these are all flats.'

'Bachelor pads.' Frank looked smug. 'There's even a penthouse suite. I quite fancy that.'

Becca found this new playboy version of her father hard to adjust to. 'But what about your garden? You love gardening. What about your roses?'

'It'll be a shame to lose the garden, but it's a bit of a tie, to be honest. All that watering in the summer. And it's only going to get worse with global warming, you know.' He nodded at her as if he was passing on some insider knowledge. 'It's going to be either watering from May to October, or going in for Mediterranean plants, and I don't fancy them much. I never really took to lavenders and santolinas. They're not as satisfying as roses and dahlias. You can't have a relationship with a santolina in the same way you can with a hybrid tea.'

Becca was speechless. All her life Frank had tended his garden with love and care – more care and attention, June had sometimes said, than he paid to her. And now he was giving it all up. It would be a red sports car next. 'What'll you do instead?' she whispered.

'Maureen – Mrs Batey – and I are going on a tour,' Frank said with relish. 'We're aiming to do all the golf courses in Scotland. Maureen reckons we can do at least four a week. She wants to do a bit of other stuff too – shopping and all that. But mostly it'll be golf.' He loosened his tie around his collar with an air of satisfaction. 'She's quite a nifty player, is Maureen.'

Saturday night, and Becca had prepared a nice meal for them both as Lily was out, staying over with Grace for the night. As she lit the candles she wondered if she was overdoing it, but Martin didn't comment. On the other hand, he might not have commented because he hadn't taken much notice. Becca thought of when she and Martin had first started seeing each other, how they had told each other everything. Their hopes, their fears, their dreams. They'd talked about their parents, their childhood, the sad times and the bad times. There were things she'd told Martin that no one else in the world knew. She could remember lying in bed staring into Martin's eyes as if there were no barrier between them, the polished shell of adulthood peeled away to reveal the vulnerable naked child underneath. And now there were nothing but barriers.

'I thought we could watch a DVD afterwards.' She'd got the new James Bond out, which she knew Martin had wanted to see.

Martin shrugged. 'Whatever you want.'

He settled down on the sofa next to her, the paper folded over to the Sudoku on his lap, as if to make it quite clear he wasn't watching the DVD with her, just happened to be on the sofa at the right time. The familiar music came up. Martin had wanted to see it in the cinema, but Becca hadn't been as keen, even though she'd heard good things of the new Bond's attractiveness. Lily didn't want to go either. It was the sort of film men went to with their sons, for a bit of male bonding over explosions and fast cars. Martin would have liked a son to do DIY with, and go to James Bond films with, who'd be able to discuss the finer points of a decent pint. Boys together. Becca looked across at Martin, who was clearly now enjoying the film. She stared at the television screen seeing instead of a card table, an image of a little boy, tousle haired like Martin, running and laughing with delight as he was scooped up into his father's arms. Her eyelids began to droop. Vaguely in the background she heard the Bond music.

Becca was woken by the doorbell ringing. For a minute she couldn't place the sound. Heavens, she must have dropped off. She looked across at Martin who was fast asleep, his mouth open slightly. The doorbell rang again, and Martin blinked awake, his eyes sleepy like a lion's.

Becca checked her watch. 'It's after midnight.'

Martin rubbed his face. 'Probably kids larking around.'

The doorbell rang again, and this time there was no let up. They looked at each other, then went to the door. Martin opened it, and Lily collapsed on the doorstep as if dead.

Chapter 27

Becca tried to pull Lily up, but she was a dead weight, her legs as immobile as sandbags. She held Lily's face in her hands, but the eyes were unfocused. A line of dried spit traced its way across her face.

'What happened?'

'She had a bit too much . . .' A boy hovered on the front path, dark hair obscuring half his face. Not Kevin, who was stocky. This boy was painfully thin, even with a thick knit jumper smothering his top half, and jeans flapping around his legs.

'Who are you? What's been going on?' Martin crouched by Lily.

'The others went, but she needed to come home.'

'Where have you been? Lily said she was at Grace's,' Becca said.

'I just wanted to make sure she was OK.' The boy shifted on his feet. 'Is she all right?'

Lily moaned, her arm flailing around as if she was trying to make contact with something. 'Lily, darling, are you OK? Can you hear me?' Becca turned to the boy. 'Is it just alcohol – has she taken anything else?' She didn't know what to do – should she go to hospital? The thought of her poor Lily having her stomach pumped made her feel cold all over.

The boy shook his head. 'Don't think so. She had a bottle of peach schnapps.'

'You bastard, how could you?' Becca said, imagining her poor child being force-fed peach schnapps. 'How could you do it to her?'

'I didn't,' the boy said indignantly, backing away. 'I said it'd make her sick but she wouldn't listen.'

Martin put a hand on Becca's shoulder. 'Are you sure that's all?' he said calmly to the boy. 'I promise I won't be angry, but it's really important we know what she's taken.'

The boy shook his head. 'Nothing else. Just the schnapps.'

Martin nodded, then turned to Becca. 'Best get her up to bed.'

'Don't you think we should call an ambulance or something?' Becca tried desperately to think of anything useful she could remember about alcohol poisoning. 'Has she been sick?'

The boy shook his head. 'She'll be OK, won't she?'

'Oh God, I hope so.' Becca clasped Lily to her, feeling this was her fault. If she'd paid as much attention to Lily as she had to Paul, Lily wouldn't be like this now. 'Wake up, darling, wake up.'

Lily mumbled, 'I'm sorry, I'm sorry, I'm sorry. Oh, Mum,' she said, as if she'd only just realised Becca was there. 'I'm so sorry.' Relief flooded over Becca. At least she was conscious and talking.

'Lily, can you hear me?' Martin said, holding her head so it didn't loll everywhere.

'Dad – I'm sorry,' Lily wailed. 'I feel awful. Oh Dad, help me.'

'I will, love. I think she'll be OK,' Martin said turning to Becca. 'Just one hell of a hangover in the morning. Best thing is to get her to bed.'

'You don't think she needs to go to hospital?' Becca said, looking up at him.

Martin shook his head. 'I don't think she's that bad, so long as we watch over her.'

'I'd best be getting home myself,' the boy said, starting to edge backwards along the front path. He took one last look at Lily, sprawled on the doorstep, then turned and ran down the street.

'Thanks for bringing her back,' Becca called after him.

Martin stood up. 'Come on, let's get her upstairs.'

Becca had seen cartoons where characters' legs had turned to rubber; but she'd never seen it in action before. Lily's legs appeared to become boneless. They alternatively sank and supported in a random manner. It would have been funny if it hadn't been her little girl. Martin tried to hold her, but she slithered out of his arms like jelly, so Becca tried to help lift her from the other side. Her weight was extraordinary, and her legs wayward. Becca and Martin staggered up the stairs, Lily wedged between them.

'I'm sorry, I'm sorry,' Lily kept muttering, flinging her arms around. Somehow they got her to bed, where she collapsed like a beached starfish.

'Help me get her into the recovery position,' Becca said, pushing at Lily's inert body. Between them they managed to get Lily over on to her side, and Becca tucked the duvet around her.

Lily started whimpering. 'Make the room stop moving, Mum. Make it stop.'

Becca stroked her forehead. 'I can't, darling.' She turned to Martin. 'Can you get some water?' Martin nodded, and left.

'It hurts, it hurts.' Lily closed her eyes, then opened them again. 'Make it stop.'

Martin came back, and held a glass of water to Lily's lips. Lily sat up, half supported by Becca, and managed a few gulps. Then her eyes closed and she subsided down onto the bed.

Martin stood holding the water glass. 'She ought to have some more.'

Becca nodded. 'If we can get it down her. Come on, darling. Try and drink some more water.'

Lily roused herself to sitting, then her face went white. 'I'm going to be sick.'

Martin had the presence of mind to grab the waste-paper basket just in time. Shame it was a wicker one. Sick oozed out of the sides.

'Dump it in the bathroom, I'll sort it out later,' Becca said to

Martin, as Lily started to cry. She turned back to her. 'You'll feel better now you've been sick.'

'What happened? Who was that boy?' Martin said.

'What does it matter? She's home, and safe.' Becca turned back to Lily. 'There there, darling.'

'My head hurts.' But Lily seemed more at ease, as if in less pain. Her eyes slowly shut.

Becca stroked her forehead, thinking that maybe she'd sleep now. 'What if she's sick in her sleep?' she whispered to Martin. 'Isn't that how Jimmy Hendrix died?'

'I'll stay up with her,' Martin said, pulling up a chair. He stroked Lily's tangled hair. 'Oh, Lily, my sweetheart. Why peach schnapps?'

Lily moaned, and was sick all over the sheets.

It took some time to change the sheets and clean Lily up and get her back to bed, but they managed together. Becca lay down on the bed, her arms around Lily. After a while Lily's breathing settled into a regular rhythm. Becca looked up to see Martin watching them, his face drawn and tired.

'I'm sorry for what I did,' she whispered, holding out her hand to him. 'Won't you forgive me?'

But he shook his head, the pain etched on his face, and wouldn't speak to her.

In the morning Becca felt exhausted, and Martin looked as if he hadn't slept for a thousand years. Lily was bright-eyed and hungry, cheerfully munching through toast and peanut butter.

'The advantages of being a teenager,' Martin growled. 'Now, young lady, you've got a lot of explaining to do.'

The story came out gradually with many digressions and random statements. Kevin had asked Lily to go to the rave; they'd said no. She'd gone anyway. It had been fun at first. They'd met up with other teenagers in Sydney Gardens, then gone to buy alcohol from the off-licence.

Becca assumed a neutrality she didn't feel. 'Why peach schnapps?'

'It was on special offer. Three for two,' Lily said.

Martin looked at Becca. 'Her mother's shopping habits already,' he murmured.

'We bought cider as well,' Lily added, as if that was a mitigating factor. They'd gone back to Sydney Gardens. Then friends of Kevin's turned up with cars, ready to go on to the rave, but Lily felt ill. Kevin's friends refused to take Lily in their car. The others piled in, leaving Lily behind. 'Kevin left me,' she said, her mouth puckering up and eyes filling with tears. Becca hugged her. She felt Lily's hot forehead press against her chest, and she was filled with murderous intent towards Kevin, who had left her precious child behind when it suited him. The thought of Lily, alone and drunk in Sydney Gardens, was too horrific to contemplate.

'Who was the boy who brought you home?' Martin asked gently.

Lily shook her head. 'I can't remember,' she wailed. 'I can't remember anything.'

'He was tall and thin,' Martin started, but Lily was crying properly now and his questions were drowned out.

Becca hugged Lily. The intensity of her love and relief that Lily was safe and with her, resonated through her body. My precious child. She kissed Lily's black hair. In the end they settled Lily on the sofa, wrapped up in a blanket as if she were ninety-four, watching children's television. She looked very young as Becca tucked her up, far too young to be going to raves and pubs.

'I'm sorry, Mum,' Lily said, looking up with sooty eyes.

Becca kissed her. 'You're back safe and that's the main thing.'

Back in the kitchen Martin had made coffee. 'Thank God she's safe.' He stopped, and she knew he was trying to control his emotions. 'When I think what might have happened—'

'Don't,' Becca said with a shudder. 'Thank heavens that boy looked after her. God knows how he got her home, she was so out of it.'

'You called him a bastard at one point.'

'Did I? I was so worried about her, I was desperate. You were wonderful – I don't know how you kept so calm.'

'I didn't feel calm.'

'All I could think about was my darling girl was ill, and I couldn't do anything to stop it. I feel it's all my fault,' she added in a low voice.

'I don't see why,' Martin said.

'I've been so wrapped up in what I've been doing, I've hardly noticed what Lily's been up to.'

Martin sighed. 'If it's anyone's fault, it's as much as mine as it is yours. I've been busy too, thinking about work, and the running. I haven't been a good father to Lily. Not the way you've been a good mother. But I will try harder.' He looked at Becca directly. 'Do you want me to pull out of the marathon?'

Becca was stunned. 'But you've trained so hard for it.'

'It's taken up a lot of my time and head space. I should have been here more.' He shook his head. 'Maybe none of this would have happened if I'd been around more.'

'Every parent has problems with teenagers, it comes with the territory.' Becca looked at her hands. 'I'd hate you to give up the marathon. I know I haven't been as supportive as I could have done but . . . I'm also proud you've got this far. I couldn't have done nearly as much.'

'Hey, I haven't run it yet. I might crash out with cramp or something.'

'Don't you dare.' She sipped her coffee. 'Do you think it would have been any easier if we'd had more children?'

'I don't know. I expect there'd have been other problems.'

Becca turned the cup round in her hand. 'Would you have liked more?'

'We've got Lily, that's enough. Quite enough right now.'

'You could always have more.' Becca thought of Una, so young and fit. There was an uneasy silence between them.

'You're assuming the fault was yours. It might have been mine,' Martin said, frowning. 'I know we've always gone along with the idea that it was your problem, but there isn't any reason for it. It's just as likely to have been me. I should have agreed to go for tests – I knew you wanted me to. The thing is . . . I didn't like the idea of it being me who had problems. Low sperm count sounds pretty pathetic really. When we had Lily, I told myself it was proof we didn't have problem. Give it time, and we'd have more . . .'

Martin stood up and went to the window while Becca waited. 'It's hard, being a man sometimes. Women say they want a bloke who's caring, and sensitive and considerate, and then they go off with some bastard who treats them badly. I know I'm not an alpha male. I can't offer you excitement and yachts and fast cars. I don't make shed-loads of money, or have an exciting career. I just bumble through life as best I can trying to look after my family. But I haven't done well with Lily, and I know I'm not enough for you. I've always known you felt you'd settled for me.'

'That's not true,' Becca said.

'Isn't it? Isn't this bloke just like the lecturer you went out with? The one who broke your heart.'

'Maybe he was,' Becca said. 'But I didn't choose him. I could have slept with Paul at the conference. It would have been easy enough, and no one would have known about it. But I didn't. I chose you.'

'I don't think it's that simple.' Martin put his coffee down. 'I'm going to go for a run.'

'Isn't this supposed to be your rest day? Martin, please, stay and talk to me.' She reached for his arm, but he sidestepped her.

'It's not just about your choices, is it? It's about what I want to choose as well. I may not have been the best husband in the world but I've been a loyal one. I've never even thought of looking elsewhere. But now all that's changed. When I think of you with him . . .' He shook his head.

'I can't bear to think of you with Una.' Becca tried to smile at him. 'It hurts me to even say her name.'

'Yeah, but nothing happened with her, whereas you . . .' Martin opened the door. 'I need to work this out on my own. I'm going running.'

Lily appeared to have no ill effects from her excursion, but over the next three weeks Becca noticed she stayed close to home. Grace came round several times, and they disappeared into Lily's room. Kevin wasn't mentioned. Once, when Becca was trying to find a letter she'd written on the computer she came across a file that Lily had written. 'Mean People' was the title. Tempting fate, Becca opened it, hoping she wouldn't find her own name. She needn't have worried. The list was divided into Mean People; Mean People I don't speak to; Mean People I HATE. The last group contained one name in capitals: KEVIN.

Becca wondered if Martin had a secret list of Mean People. She guessed so. At least, he was avoiding her as if her name headed his list. Of course it could have been that in these last few weeks in the run-up to the marathon there were more training sessions, longer runs. They were careful with each other. It was intolerable, but had to be tolerated.

The day before the marathon, Becca took Lily to the Costume Museum as inspiration for Lily's coursework. Becca hadn't been for ages, even though as Bath residents they had free entry. Lily pressed her nose against the glass cases and made notes, drew sketches.

'Imagine wearing that every day,' Becca said. 'Look at the embroidery, it's all hand done.'

Lily looked at the dress. 'Are you and Dad getting a divorce?'

Becca shook her head, startled. 'I hope not.'

Lily digested this. 'Then why is Dad sleeping in the spare room?'

'It's just temporary,' Becca said, hoping she wasn't lying. 'Dad needs his sleep what with the marathon.'

'Oh. That one's like the dress you wore in the play.' Lily pointed.

'So it is.' She squeezed Lily's shoulders. 'Perhaps Angela copied it.'

They wandered around the exhibits. At one point there was a selection of corsets to try on. Lily squeezed herself into the tiniest one she could find. 'I can't breathe,' she gasped.

'That's nothing,' Becca said, tugging on the strings. 'Shall I go tighter?'

'No. Yes. Ow!' Lily squeaked, sticking her tongue out. 'You've cut me in half.' Becca wrapped her arms around Lily and they stood like that in front of the mirror. Lily rested her head back against Becca's shoulder. Mother and daughter, caught in a moment in time.

'I love you,' Becca whispered.

Lily twisted round to kiss Becca's cheek. 'I love you too.'

Once they'd got Lily out of her corset, they moved on to the exhibition of costumes from various Jane Austen films. It was interesting to read the designers' notes, how some of the styles were exaggerated to emphasis a person's character, so Willoughby got an extravagantly swirling cape to go with his romantic hero appearance. Becca stared at the cape. It was the romantic dream; the tall, dark, handsome man on his white horse, his cape swirling around him. Paul would have played the role to perfection.

Becca moved on to the next case. For Jane Austen, the romance was confined to the period between a girl becoming aware of men, and the marriage. Marriage stopped romance. She looked at a costume from *Pride and Prejudice*. Lizzie Bennet had her choices to make, and chose bravely and wisely. Becca stared at the mannequin. But a woman in Jane Austen's day had limited choices. These days there were hundreds of choices waiting to be made through life. Look at June, off to discover a new world in Cornwall in her seventies, Frank and his penthouse flat, and the golf courses of Scotland. Life wasn't a full stop at marriage, if it ever had been. Doors were always opening, it was just the romantic ones that were closed.

Becca wondered which doors she would open during the rest of her life. She'd been searching online for possible options and found a degree course in theatre arts she could study by distance learning. As she read through the list of modules options her mouth watered like being confronted with a box of delicious chocolates. She wanted to do them all. Where it would lead, she didn't know, but secretly she liked the idea of perhaps getting involved in arts administration, perhaps something to do with theatre in education.

Becca turned to look for Lily. There she was, sketching at the far end. She started to go to her, then realised it wasn't Lily after all, it was another person with a sketch pad. And a purple feather bolero.

'Angela? Hi, how are you?'

Angela looked up from her pad. 'Becca! It's good to see you.'

'I love your drawing. Is it for the next production?'

Angela shook her head. 'No, we can't afford to do more than one costume drama a year. This is just for me. We're doing *The Killing of Sister George*. This summer, after the Ayckbourn. You ought to audition.'

'Oh no, I don't think I could,' or should, she thought inwardly. Lily joined them and Becca put her arm around her. 'This is my daughter, Lily. She's also interested in costume. Angela did all the costumes for the play I was in. And the stage management too.'

'Too many jobs,' Angela groaned. 'I need an assistant. Why don't you come along with your mum and help with the costumes?'

If Becca had suggested it, she knew that Lily would have put on that mutinous look and made that strange intonation of the word 'mum' which managed to convey equal amounts of disgust and despair that a parent could be, like, so uncool. But Angela, with her purple feathers, was obviously as cool as an American fridge. 'I suppose I could,' Lily said. 'What'd I have to do?'

Angela explained about getting the costumes together and all the props, while Becca watched Lily nodding. Strange how teenagers could be so ghastly at home, and yet so polite and charming in public. 'Tell you what,' Angela said. 'The auditions are going to be in three weeks' time. Why don't you come along with your mum then and I'll show you round. You can help me with the auditions if you like.'

'Would I have to act?' Lily said, pulling a face.

'No, just be nice to people, and tick them off the list. *Sister George* is going to be Brian's baby. Though quite why he wants to direct a play about an unhealthy lesbian relationship is beyond me.' Angela fluffed her feathers. 'Have you heard the news? Paul and his wife are off to New York, so he wouldn't be around even if we could afford him.'

'New York?'

'Yes, his wife was offered a job there. God, it must be incredible to live in that sort of world, getting head hunted, flying to New York, changing where you live just like that. I sort of fancy it, but to be honest, I couldn't be doing with it myself. Not in real life.'

'No,' Becca said. 'Not in real life.'

Chapter 28

They got back from the costume museum later that afternoon. Lily dashed into the house, but Becca stayed to give the car a quick tidy up. Lily had been eating sweets in the back by the look of it, and there were many other stray bits of paper. She remembered for a second the back of Paul's car, the detritus with the spat-out sweet. She shuddered. So sordid.

Becca went into the house with a bag full of rubbish. As she stepped over the threshold she realised someone wearing a hoodie was hovering by the garden gate.

'Hello,' she said, turning round and thinking 'mugger'. The person moved from behind the overgrown leylandii and stood where she could see him. He was tall and thin, and Becca recognised him as the boy who'd brought Lily home that night.

'Hello,' she said again, more warmly this time. 'Have you come to see Lily?' He nodded. 'I'll call her down. What's your name?'

'Sam.' The word was squeezed out.

'You're the poet,' Becca said, remembering the Valentine's Day card. Sam showed he was by going scarlet, as far as she could tell from under the mop of black Rasta dreads. 'Lily!' she called up the stairs. 'Come on down – Sam's here for you.'

Lily came clattering down the stairs, then stopped as she saw Sam. 'Hi,' she said in a teeny-weeny, un-Lilylike voice.

Sam stared at the floor. 'Hi.'

Becca shoved the bag in the rubbish bin. 'I can't say thank you enough for what you did on Saturday. We're so grateful you looked after Lily.'

Lily rolled her eyes. 'Mu-um,' she hissed.

Sam shrugged bony shoulders. 'S' OK.'

'Would you like a cup of tea? Orange juice?' Becca tried to keep the conversation going.

Sam shook his head. 'No thanks.'

'My dad's running the marathon tomorrow,' Lily said suddenly. 'You could come with me, if you liked.'

Sam cleared his throat. 'OK. See you then. Bye.' He loped back towards the front gate.

'I've got the latest Cradle of Filth CD,' Lily called after him. 'Would you like to listen to it?'

Sam nodded, and they trailed upstairs, feet heavy on the treads as if wearing hobnail boots. A few seconds later the familiar thud thud thud emanated from Lily's room. But this time Becca just smiled.

The original plan was for the men's running team to go as the Magnificent Seven. Martin had quite fancied wearing a ten-gallon hat and a tin star to run in, but at the last minute it dawned on marketing that it was possibly unwise to suggest the team from IT were a bunch of cowboys. Instead they were provided with Lycra running kit, emblazoned with the company logo, in the colours of snooker balls: pink, yellow, red, green, brown, blue and black. They'd drawn lots: Martin had ended up with pink.

'It could be worse,' he said to Becca as she stood with Lily at the entrance to the recreation ground under rows and rows of red and white bunting flapping in the breeze, all carrying the logo of the main marathon sponsor. 'Ian ended up with brown, and he looks like a turd. Still, I suppose you could say I'm in touch with my feminine side.' He played with the tag of the windcheater zip. 'I ought to go and warm up.'

'You'll be fine,' Becca said, touching his arm. 'You know you can do it.'

'Mum, stand next to Dad. I want a picture of you together.' Lily was dancing around them. They stood awkwardly side by side, not sure of what to do.

'Put your arm around Mum,' Lily instructed. Martin hesitated then put his arm round Becca and squeezed her shoulder. An everyday gesture that once she would have accepted as entirely normal, but now it felt strange and slightly disturbing. 'Smile!'

They smiled.

'Now kiss Mum,' Lily commanded. Martin pecked at Becca's cheek. 'Daad, do it properly.' There was an edge to Lily's voice.

Martin kissed the side of Becca's mouth. It hurt that he couldn't bear to kiss her properly.

'I've got to go now,' he said briskly. 'There's a group warm-up.'

'We'll go and wait at the start,' Becca said, taking refuge in arrangements. 'I said I'd meet Crystal there – she's bringing her new man.'

'Hey, Martin! Get over here!' They turned and saw the rest of his team. Becca noted glumly how lithe they all looked, especially Una. It was one of those uncomfortable equations: those who run marathons do not have issues about their weight whereas those who don't, have to watch how much chocolate they eat.

'I must go and join them,' Martin said, half turning away from her. 'Lily, come here and give your old dad a hug.'

Lily put down the camera and hugged and kissed her father. 'You'll be brilliant,' she said. Then Martin jogged off. Halfway he turned and gave them a thumbs-up. They gave thumbs-up in return.

'Good luck,' Becca called out to him as his group of runners moved off.

'Come on,' Lily said, tugging at her arm. 'Let's go and watch the start.'

They walked along the river towards the weir. There were hundreds, if not thousands of people milling around, chattering excitedly. More were coming up from the railway station, the runners in tracksuits, family and friends carrying banners.

'We should have done a banner for Dad,' Lily said.

'Never mind, we'll just cheer very loudly.' They walked up the steps by the weir to Laura Place. Strange to be there when it was closed to traffic. Already there were spectators lining Pulteney Street, even though there was an hour before the start. Becca examined the race programme. 'Why don't we watch the beginning, then we can go across to Queen Square and cheer him on from there, and then come back here for the finish,' she suggested.

She wondered how many of Martin's teammates knew about their marital problems apart from them. It was quite possible none of them knew. She wondered, if they were told that either Becca or Martin would have had an affair, how many of them would guess it was her rather than Martin. Martin looked about ten years younger and was about twenty years fitter since taking up running. Had she felt threatened by that? Had there been deep down some worry that he would leave her for some ambitious young woman from marketing? Except that an ambitious young woman wouldn't have gone for Martin if she was aiming to sleep her way to the top. Martin had reached about as high as he was going with the company, marathon or no marathon. These should be the years they consolidated their positions, and saved for the future. They still could be – if they made up.

Her mobile rang, and it was Crystal. They arranged to meet on the steps outside one of the grand houses on Pulteney Street in ten minutes. 'Is Sam coming?' Becca asked Lily.

'He said he'd meet me by the start.' Lily checked her phone for the time, a contented smile on her face. 'But that's not for ages.'

Becca looked at her. It looked as if Sam was going to be a fixture, judging by her expression. 'Do you think you'd like to do the costumes with Angela? Even if I decided I didn't want to audition for a part in the play . . .' The idea of Brian directing *The Killing of Sister George* took some getting around 'I'd take you along and introduce you to everyone. I expect Victoria will be there.'

'I'd like that,' Lily said. 'Angela seemed well cool.'

They walked on, dodging around the milling people. 'Can you see Crystal anywhere?' Becca craned her neck, trying to spot her. 'Sorry,' she said automatically as a woman bumped into her.

'Sorry, my fault,' the woman said equally automatically before stopping.

It was Suzy. 'How nice to see you,' Becca said on social autopilot.

'It's . . . ?' Suzy looked vague.

'Becca,' Becca said. For an instant she wondered if Suzy would acknowledge her. 'We met at the after-show drinks before Christmas.'

'Becca . . .' Suzy echoed. The skin round her eyes tightened and she gave a sharp intake of breath as she obviously realised who Becca was.

'This is my daughter Lily,' Becca said.

'Hi.' Lily vaguely waved a hand, then her face brightened and she dropped down to her knees. 'Hello, gorgeous!' The dog rushed forward on its lead and enthusiastically licked her ear while Lily giggled and hugged it and told it it was a good dog again and again.

'She likes dogs,' Suzy said. Becca wondered what she really wanted to say to her. You bitch, probably.

'Adores them,' Becca replied, thinking about what she'd like to say to Suzy. I'm sorry for what happened, and I hope things work out between you and Paul. 'Do you know someone who's running?'

'My company fielded a team,' she replied, her lips tighter than a gallon of Botox.

'My husband's running for his company,' Becca said. If the

conversation got more stilted it would have the perfect view of the race, Becca thought. And yet neither of them seemed able to leave the other. Too much unsaid, too much unsayable. 'Did you bring your children to watch?'

Suzy shook her head. 'They're with Paul.' She swallowed after mentioning his name as if it had been an effort to talk naturally of him. Down at their feet, Lily was burbling endearments to the dog and getting a thorough clean.

'He's a good father,' Suzy said, looking directly at her. Forced close together by the people pushing around them, Becca realised that her eyes were an extraordinary mix of colours, greens and browns and flecks of blue. 'Though not a perfect husband.'

'No one can be perfect,' Becca said carefully. Around them the crowd milled and pushed and talked in excited voices, and the radio station covering the event played loud music, but the air round Suzy and Becca felt still and charged with meaning. 'But we love people for their imperfections, don't we?'

'Do we?' Suzy lifted her chin, and her sharp eyes blurred as if they had lost focus. She tried a smile, but it didn't quite work and Becca realised she was close to tears. 'I suppose we have to.'

'Especially when they haven't done anything wrong,' Becca said gently, startled by this vulnerable version of Suzy, the scary dragon lady who so obviously loved Paul desperately.

'Haven't they?' Suzy said, her eyes hopeful.

Becca wanted to give her the reassurance, uncertain exactly where on the scale of marital wrongdoing came a man declaring extravagant love for another woman. But Suzy was a lawyer, and lawyers dealt in facts, and the facts were that adultery had not been committed however much it may have been intended. 'Not to my knowledge,' she said firmly.

'He gets carried away and says things he doesn't mean. I suppose it's part of being an actor,' Suzy said, her expression soft as if talking about a favourite child and Becca realised that part of Paul's attraction for the perfectionist, driven Suzy was his unpredictability, his mercurial enthusiasm. Not so much a question of opposites attracting, but complementing, each giving the other what they lacked.

Lily stood up. 'I love your dog,' she said, rather unnecessarily as she'd been proclaiming undying passion for the last five minutes. Becca crossed her fingers that Lily wouldn't say anything about having met the dog before.

Suzy looked down and gave the lead a wiggle. 'He's a bit of a problem at the moment. We're moving to New York,' she flashed a look at Becca, 'and can't take him with us. So he's going to have to go to the RSPCA up by the university.'

'And then what?' Lily said, her face appalled.

'The worst case is, he'll be put down. I sure they'll find a lovely new home for him,' Suzy carried on quickly over Lily's gasp of horror. 'I'd look for one myself, but I don't have time.'

Lily tugged at Becca's arm. 'Mum, please.'

'No,' Becca said. 'Out of the question.'

'But, Mum, pleeeeeese, he'll be put down otherwise, and he's gorgeous, I'll look after him, I'll take him for walks – he can go running with Dad – and pleeeese, Mum, he's so lovely. I'll do everything for him, you won't even know he's in the house.' Lily was jumping with excitement and her face shone with enthusiasm in a way Becca hadn't seen since the summer. Becca caught the look of amusement on Suzy's face and she knew that both of them were thinking of dog hair and dog smells and the overall responsibility that went with dog ownership.

'Lily, I can't,' she said weakly. 'Not a dog.'

'Here's my number,' Suzy said, handing Lily a business card, with a sly slightly malicious glance over to Becca. 'You can have a think over the weekend and then call me. I have to go, I'm meeting friends.' She hesitated, then held out her hand. 'It was nice meeting you again.'

'And you.' Becca nodded, suddenly thinking that it had been nice, and that despite the frightening exterior, Suzy might have become a friend. 'Good luck in New York.'

'Thanks.' Suzy smiled, and moved into the crowd before calling out, 'Ring me about the dog.'

'I will,' Lily called back. She nestled up to her mother. 'Mu-um . . .'

'I'm not even going to talk about it,' Becca said, detatching Lily from her arm. 'And we must go too and find Crystal. She'll think we'll have vanished. I hope she's found a good place, there seem to be loads more people about now.'

The crowds were now three or four deep against the barriers, and making their way up Pulteney Street was difficult, what with all the other people with the same idea. Luckily Crystal had found a good place on the raised pavement outside one of the big houses.

'And this is Jim,' Crystal said, clinging to the arm of a pleasant-looking man with such unmemorable features he should have taken to a life of crime instead of chemistry, safe in the knowledge that no one would ever pick him out of an identity parade. But the chemistry was definitely there between him and Crystal, they couldn't stop touching each other, and having little in-jokes. Becca felt excluded.

Lily suddenly shrieked, 'Over here!' She waved both arms in the air and jumped up and down. Becca turned, and saw Sam loping towards them through the crowd. He was already taller than most of the people there, despite his tall boy's stoop.

'Hi,' he said with a vague wave to Becca. 'Hey, Lily.'

'Hey.' Lily was about a foot shorter than him, not helped by her tendency to stare at the pavement. Then she looked up at him through her fringe. Becca watched Sam's reaction. No doubt about it, he was smitten.

'When do they start?' Crystal said, twisting her head. The crowd had grown until it was filling the pavements on both sides of the wide street, and looking back down Pulteney Street towards the bridge, Becca could see the runners gathering around the start, their heads bobbing as they jogged on the spot. The tannoy system crackled constantly with comments from the local radio station, but the noise from the expectant crowd came close to drowning the speaker out.

Becca checked her watch. 'About five minutes,' she said. 'The serious runners go first, then the fun runners start ten minutes later. Martin's number's 2617. He's dressed in pink Lycra, top to toe.'

'You're kidding.'

Becca shook her head. 'Sadly, no. Still, look on the bright side, at least we can't fail to see him.'

'Oh,' Lily squealed. 'They're starting.' They all craned their heads to try to see. Spectators got their banners ready, some were charity posters, others simply cheering their family runner on. Even Becca, who rarely felt inclined to shift above walking pace, regretted not having joined Martin in slipping on the trainers back in the autumn. Perhaps if we'd trained together, I wouldn't have been attracted to Paul, she thought. The family that jogs together, stays together. She glanced at Crystal, happily chatting to Tim, and Lily, up on Sam's thin shoulders so she could see better. And she was alone, while Martin ran with Una.

She felt something push against her knee and looked down. A small boy, hardly more than a toddler, was nuzzling her leg. 'Hello,' she said bending down.

He looked up, and his face puckered with the realisation that Becca wasn't his mother. She looked around and saw a young woman with a buggy standing on the far side of the steps. 'There she is,' Becca said, pointing.

He abruptly let go of Becca's leg and toddled off to the woman, grasping her legs tightly. The woman absent-mindedly leaned down and stroked his hair, apparently oblivious that he'd wandered off. Safely with his mother's skirt tight in one fist, the little boy turned and stared at Becca, sucking the ears of the stuffed rabbit he held.

She smiled at him, but he stared back, unsmiling, dark eyes wide, too young to appreciate the excitement of the marathon.

A cheer from the spectators brought Becca away from the child and back to the race. She realised that she'd managed to miss the start, and that a bobbing mass of runners was heading through the gateway and up Pulteney Street, long legs stretching. After the leading runners came the fun runners, to more cheers and shouts, and cries of encouragement. The noise of the crowd rose, and now Becca had people pressing at her back, in much the same way she was pressing into the people in front of her.

'They say it's going to be a fast time today, as the weather's not too hot,' a man in front of her remarked to his companion. Martin will be pleased at that, Becca thought.

'There he is,' Lily shouted from Sam's shoulders. 'Dad, Dad!' She waved frantically with one arm, the other pressed the camera to her face as Becca could distinguish flashes of pink, yellow, green and blue as the team passed and then were gone. Lily scrambled down and grabbed Sam's hand. 'Come on – if we cut across Pulteney Bridge, we'll see him go through Queen Square. See you, Mum,' and she was off in the opposite direction to the runners, dragging Sam along with her.

'Do you want to go?' Crystal said.

'I don't think we'll get through the crowds in time,' Becca said, shaking her head and watching that final flash of pink go round the corner past the Holburne. 'I hadn't realised there'd be so many people. I'm going to stay here and get a good place to see Martin when he comes round the second time, when the runners are more spread out. You go if you want to.'

Heads turned as there was a sudden surge of noise from the crowd further up, an explosion of sound bouncing between the Georgian houses, screams and shouts. All the heads of the spectators turned up towards the Holburne, and the tannoy stopped broadcasting the names of notable runners.

'Something's happened,' the man in front of Becca said to his companion. 'A collision, I expect.'

The tannoy lurched into life. 'Will runners please keep to the far right going round the corner. Will runners please keep to the far right going round the corner.'

'Sounds like an accident,' the man in front said. 'Or someone's had a heart attack or something. Too soon for cramp.'

Martin. Something buzzed in Becca's ears. She knew, just knew it was Martin. 'Martin went round the corner just before,' Becca said, looking at Crystal. She could feel the tension in her voice. 'I'm going to find out what's happened.'

She began to push through the crowd not caring if she was rude. She vaguely heard Crystal calling to her that it would be fine, Martin was fine, but she didn't stop, her mouth set in a determined line. She had to get to him. So many people, so many people in her way. Why wouldn't they move? Why wouldn't they let her through? She wanted to yell at them to clear the way, but they were too busy cheering and clapping and beeping horns and waving football rattles to take any notice of her. And in the distance came the sound of an ambulance.

Becca got to the top of the street, by the Holburne. Runners were still making their way past, directed by the stewards, but she could make out a knot of people on the left side of the street, about fifty feet from where the road turned the corner. Screens were being put up, people in yellow fluorescent jackets were busy directing spectators away from the site, lifting barriers to funnel the runners past. And then there it was. A bright pink cap, lying limply on the road.

Chapter 29

'Martin,' she screamed, but her voice was swallowed in the clamour of the crowd, the noise of thousands of feet running, running, running, and the ambulance siren getting louder and louder. She pushed forwards heading from the screens.

A man's voice. 'There's nothing to see here, please move on.'

She vaguely registered the darkness of his uniform. 'Please, please, it's my husband. Please.' She stared up into his face, not seeing it, willing him to let her through. Everything hung on his decision. 'Please, it's my husband,' she said again.

He swung the catch that held the barriers together and pulled one towards him to make a gap. She slid through it and he caught her arm. 'I'll take you through.'

They got nearer the screens. People with walkie-talkies were busy directing everyone around the screens, the runners separating like fish around a rock, seething, bobbing, but there seemed to be this still centre, like a spotlight that followed Becca round. 'Poor bugger,' she heard one steward say as they passed.

It was part of some film where everything goes into slow motion. She looked up and could see the policeman talking to one of the men in a fluorescent jacket, see their mouths moving, see their heads turn to her, the embarrassed, harassed, sympathetic looks, the man with the fluorescent jacket and the walkie-talkie had missed a bit when shaving that morning she noticed, she could see the tiny patch of darker stubble on the underside of his left jaw. Someone trod on Martin's peaked cap, scuffed it over to the kerb.

'Martin,' she screamed again, and pushed past the men, for a second registering their surprised faces, their mouths making the shape of 'no', and she was behind the screens and there was a man lying on the ground in the recovery position, covered with grey-brown blankets, surrounded by other people kneeling beside, including one dressed top to toe in pink Lycra.

'Martin.' And the film suddenly speeded up and there she was, sobbing into his shoulder. 'I thought it was you,' she cried. 'I thought it was you.' And she held on to him as though she would never ever let him go. And Martin held on to her, his shoulders shuddering, her Martin, alive and in her arms.

The ambulance siren suddenly stopped and seconds later the crew rushed to the man on the ground. 'Can we get a bit of room here,' one shouted, but even as they spoke the people kneeling moved back to let them work, feeling for vital signs, then clamping an oxygen mask to the man's white face. Becca recognised the brown top.

'But I thought Ian was fit, the fittest of you all,' Becca said, clinging to Martin's arm. She recognised other members of the team standing in the background, Una in tears with her hand over her mouth being comforted by the MD in green. Becca held her breath. 'Is he . . . ?'

'I don't think so.' Martin shook his head, his face nearly as white as Ian's. 'Christ, Becca, I couldn't believe it, we were all running together, and then suddenly he just went. I thought he'd stumbled, went to help him up, then realised he was unconscious. I can't believe it.'

'I've just thought, has anyone got Val's mobile number?' the MD said, his face nearly as green as his outfit. 'We should call her, she's bound to be watching somewhere.'

'I've already called her,' Martin said, and Becca was proud that, although as stunned as any of them, Martin had thought to call Ian's wife. He was good in a crisis, she thought, remembering how he had dealt with Lily when she was drunk. He was a good man. She held his arm tightly, flashing back to the moment when she thought it was Martin who'd had the heart attack, and Martin put his arm around her. 'It's OK,' he murmured.

A white-faced woman Becca recognised as Ian's wife was ushered past them. 'Ian!' she gasped, falling to her knees beside him and bursting into tears. The ambulance crew exchanged glances and opened their mouths to get her out of the way, but Martin was there first.

'Val, love, he'll be fine, but the crew need space to look after him,' he said as he gently helped her stand up. She nodded, hand over her mouth, her eyes wide and full of tears.

Becca gave Val a hug. 'Ian's in the best hands,' she murmured, trying to match Martin's calmness despite her own emotional turmoil. The ambulance crew were manoevering Ian, flipping him up and on to a trolley. Ian moaned as they moved him, and waved an arm as if trying to pull off the mask. At least he's alive, Becca thought as the ambulance crew tucked him firmly on to the trolley. Thank God.

'Will he be OK?' the MD blurted out.

'He's coming round, that's a good sign,' one of the crew said, with a calmness that astonished Becca. 'But we need to get him in as soon as possible.' With practised speed they clicked down the wheels, and pushed the trolley into the ambulance. Val climbed in the back with Ian and one of the crew. The other slammed the doors shut, then climbed into the cab. Siren on, they zoomed away leaving Becca, Martin and the rest of the team standing in the street.

'Can you move along please,' cried the stewards, taking down the screens and pushing the barriers back to their original positions. Becca realised that there were still runners going past, as the screens went back.

'What should we do?' Una said. 'Do we go to the hospital, or what?'

'I don't know,' the MD said, looking around. 'Martin, you trained with him. What do you reckon? Should we run?'

'I don't know,' Martin said, his arm around Becca's shoulder. 'It seems wrong somehow, to carry on running.'

'But Ian loves running,' Una said. 'He'd want us to carry on. Besides, there's all that money we've raised for charity. We'd have to give it back if we don't run.'

'Ok. Executive decision: we're running,' the MD said. 'I mean, it's not as if he's died.' Becca exchanged a look with Martin. 'OK, team, let's get out there.'

'You don't have to if you think it's wrong,' Becca said in a low voice to Martin.

'I know. But Una's right, Ian would want us to run.' He squeezed her shoulder. 'Besides, I don't think Lily would forgive me if I didn't run.'

'She's waiting to see you at Queen Square,' Becca said, suddenly realising, and fishing her mobile out of her bag. 'She'll be worried you haven't come round yet. I'll ring and let her know you're OK.'

'Thanks.' He bent his head and kissed her quickly. She stared up into his eyes. Then he kissed her again, longer this time, before setting off with the remaining team. 'See you at the finish.'

Becca stood and watched them join the mass of runners, her hand to her mouth, remembering his lips on hers.

Becca waited for Martin outside the cardiac ward. People came and went– visitors? Doctors? Nurses? It was hard to tell unless they came with flowers or stethoscopes round their neck. Everyone seemed to walk purposefully as if they knew where they were going. Becca and Martin had had to follow the signs to the ward. Sunday afternoon. Prime time for hospital visiting.

The last time she'd been in hospital was when Lily was born.

Then the nurses had bustled and babies cried and she too had wept from exhaustion, but the atmosphere was positive. They would be going home with their babies. Here the atmosphere was different. This was the ward where you lived, or died. She noticed that every visitor used the antiseptic hand wash before entering the ward.

The swing doors to the ward pushed open, and Martin emerged. 'How is he?' Becca said, standing up immediately.

'They think he'll be all right,' Martin said. 'Val says he came round in the ambulance on the way in, and he's now stable, not needing oxygen any more or anything. Mind you, he's wired up to so many machines it must be draining the national grid. But he's going to be all right.'

'Thank God for that,' Becca murmured.

'Let's get back home. I'm dying for a cup of tea,' Martin said.

Becca thought the expression ironic, given the circumstances. 'I should have made you one while you changed, but I didn't think.' On their way back from the race she'd insisted on driving home so Martin could shower and eat something before visiting Ian. 'You won't help him by passing out in hospital,' she'd said, putting scrambled eggs in front of Martin, the quickest meal she could think of. But she'd forgotten tea. They began to walk back to the main reception.

'Was it a heart attack?'

'Yup, complete heart block, whatever that is. He's going to have a pace maker fitted and then apparently he'll be as right as rain. He was saying he was going to run the marathon next year in under two hours.'

'Val must have looked pleased at that,' Becca said. Martin looked round blankly at the corridor. Becca smiled, knowing a sense of direction wasn't one of his talents. She pushed open the double doors to the stairs and Martin followed her.

'She didn't look exactly thrilled. Makes you think, doesn't it? He's nearly ten years younger than me.'

Becca nodded. 'I couldn't bear it if it had been you.'

'It'd take more than that to get rid of me.' Martin put his arm around her shoulders and squeezed as they walked down the stairs and into the main reception area. 'Though under two hours might do it. Bad enough doing it in two hours seventeen.'

Becca felt her eyes fill with tears. 'I parked on the far side,' she said, as they left the central hospital door. They walked towards the car. Becca's hand brushed against his, and somehow they were walking hand in hand. 'Two hours seventeen sounds pretty impressive to me. How are you feeling?' Becca asked.

'Not too bad. I expect I'll be in agony tomorrow, but right now . . .' he paused, taking a deep breath and stretching, 'Right now, it's good to be alive. When you're young you treat each day as if there are plenty more to come,' Martin said. 'Makes you realise that there is actually only a finite amount of time left. If you knew this was going to be your last day, would you behave differently?' His hand was warm in hers, his grip firm and reassuring.

'Of course.'

They reached the car. 'What would be different?'

She looked directly at him. 'I'd tell everyone who mattered to me that I loved them.'

'Ah.' He smiled, then opened the car door. 'Let's go home.'

They drove in silence. Becca leaned her head against the car window feeling the coolness against her forehead. I don't want to be alone, she thought. I don't want to rip my life to shreds and hope I can make something better from the wreckage. I want to build on what I have. They turned down the familiar street. Becca could have done this journey with her eyes shut, and yet today she looked, really looked, at all the houses they passed. She saw the new curtains at number six, that number nine had trimmed their hedge. Someone was painting the upstairs bay window of number fifteen, the scarlet cloth dangling from his jeans pocket a bright splash of colour against the honey stone.

Martin pulled up outside the house. Wordlessly they got out of the car and went in. Becca slipped her coat off, and after a moment's hesitation, Martin took her hand and led her upstairs.

Skin on skin. Known, yet new. She felt shy with him as he undressed her, his hands soft, his touch light, as if this was the first time. Each hair stood erect as his fingertips traced the line of her arms. Hands clasped, they slid into bed. Bare legs entwined, his foot fitted exactly under her instep. She stroked his face, as if learning him with her fingers, his eyes large and gentle, skin taut across his cheekbones, her fingertip running along his lower lip. He bit it lightly, playfully, and she laughed as his teeth nibbled her skin sending sensations rippling over her body. Her hand grazed the surface of his skin, warm and smooth, running the length of his body, feeling the curve of his skin at his hip, and down, his hands on her, she felt pliant at his touch, soft and supple, skin quivering.

The room was quiet except for their regular breathing, the light dim as the spring afternoon light filtered in through closed curtains, their skin gleaming where the light caught it, dissolving into soft smokiness under the covers. She felt she could dissolve into the warm air as he touched her, rolling over to luxuriate in the sensations travelling throughout her body, his mouth on hers, tender and affectionate, everything was calm and unhurried and she was flowing, her body liquid like molten gold pouring over the edge and falling away as he took her. Their breathing quickened, the rhythm accelerated, she clutched his arms, his shoulders, fingers digging in, no longer fluid but taut with longing, overstrung like a bow waiting for release, she pressed against him, determined, eyes shut tight, oblivious to everything except the hunger he had ignited within her, and, steady, steady, her breath juddering as she arched her back up to him, and now, now, now.

She subsided in his arms, face pressed into his shoulder, breathing his warmth in with every inhalation, every muscle relaxed and unstrung. He stroked her hair, his hands gentle and loving, and she nuzzled into him like a cat curling up in a sunbeam.

'Lily will be home soon,' he whispered in between giving her tiny kisses that dappled over her face like summer rain. She stretched out, toes and fingers flexed. Her body felt burnished inside and out, skin satiny to the touch. She gave him a wide, sleepy smile.

'I suppose we ought to get up,' she said, not moving. She wasn't sure she could ever move again, all her bones had dissolved away into nothingness. She trailed her fingers languorously over his chest. He sighed deeply and closed his eyes, but after a few seconds opened them again and rolled away from her.

'Cup of tea?' he asked, sitting on the edge of the bed.

'Mmm,' she replied, rolling on to her front and stroking his back. 'That is, if you don't fancy seconds.'

'Later,' he said, smiling.

'Is there going to be a later?' Becca said seriously.

He nodded, equally serious. 'If you want.'

'I do,' Becca said. 'I do.'

Chapter 30

'Come on, Becca,' Martin called up the stairs. 'If we don't go soon we won't get back in time for rehearsal.'

'Just changing.' Becca undid her work trousers and the zip shot down, released from the strain of being done up. Running made Martin so slim, but it was making her put on weight which was the most unfair thing she'd ever heard of. Bad enough panting round and round the park, but to then discover you were getting fatter was just unfair. She supposed it was all the extra eating she felt she could get away with now they ran together three times a week. Trousers off and in her bra and pants, she popped into the bathroom and on to the scales to assess the damage.

Becca peered down at her toes, trying to avoid noticing her tummy – a difficult feat since it stuck out so much. Strange. According to the scales she'd lost weight. She stepped off them, and then back on. Still the same result. She patted her tummy. Obviously she was becoming an apple having been a pear shape all her life. It was what happened to middle-aged women unless they were careful.

'Come on, Mum. We're all waiting,' Lily yelled and Ronnie barked in sympathy. Ronnie – the dog formerly known as Oberon – was transforming Lily from a tubby goth into a sleek princess, although she kept the jet-black hair (a teenager had to rebel somehow). Becca had fudged Ronnie's origins to Martin, just saying the previous owners were friends of a colleague. Lily was true to her word; these last two months since Ronnie had joined them she had been most attentive to his every whim. She washed him, fed him, petted him, brushed him, walked him, ran with him and in return Ronnie had given Lily eternal love and shed vast quantities of black hair that collected in corners of the room and needed sweeping by Becca on a daily basis. Other than that, she had to admit that she liked having his hairy black face around the house.

'I'll be down in a minute. Martin, can you put the casserole into the oven – it'll have heated up by the time we get back.'

Sucking her tummy in, Becca went back into her bedroom and pulled on her tracksuit bottoms and a running crop top. Even though it was the end of May she toyed with grabbing a sweater. The weather hadn't been that good. On the other hand, she'd be teased mercilessly by Martin and Lily if she took one and didn't wear it. Becca decided against it, then checked her watch. Martin and Lily were just fussing, there was plenty of time. It wasn't that bad, they could always cut back the running by five minutes and that would give plenty of time to shower, eat the casserole and then get to the arts centre in time for rehearsal. Lily was taking her role as assistant stage manager very seriously, getting her homework done the minute she got in from school, and ticking Becca off whenever she was late.

Becca stretched her arms up, easing the tension from her back. Never mind, this was the last play she was going to act in for the foreseeable future, assuming she started the theatre studies degree course. And if she finished the course . . . goodbye Bill, goodbye Hamilton House and teaching, hello new career as a creative arts adminstrator. Strange to think that in the future she might not go to drama school, but she could end up running one. She'd already made tentative approaches for work experience to the drama school in Bristol as well as the theatre-in-education department at the Theatre Royal in Bath.

There was the possibility that one day, if she followed that route, her path might cross with Paul's. But that was over and done with, she thought, as she looked for a band to tie her hair back with. The woman Becca had been then wasn't the woman she was now. She smiled at her reflection in the mirror, admiring the new sleeker haircut that had taken off some of the length without losing the weight. A grown-up haircut. She tied her hair back, twisting the caramel strands up and back into a ponytail. Her face looked a little rounder than usual, she thought as she smoothed back some loose strands.

'I've put the casserole in,' Martin called. 'Get a move on.'

'All right, all right,' Becca muttered. Martin was coming to rehearsal too, having been co-opted by Lily to be set designer and builder. Lily had also roped in Frank, who trudged around back-stage like a Wagnerian dwarf but at least he'd been deflected from DIY coffin-making. Although Becca had to admit, that was mainly Maureen's doing. Maureen took the phrase 'mustn't grumble' literally, and had filled Frank's life with golf, bridge and three square meals a day. Frank looked happier and fatter than Becca could remember. Sam was designing the posters. Becca had seen the prototypes which always featured beautiful young girls with shiny jet-black hair who bore no similarity to the cast.

The only family member Lily hadn't drawn in was June, who had decamped to St Ives the second the house in Bath had gone under offer. They were all going down to see her at half term next week, Martin as well. He was taking a week off before he started his new job within the company. There had been some redundancies but it had meant promotion for Martin. Becca sat on the edge of the bed to put her running socks on. As she leaned forwards her breasts ached, and she wondered if she ought to try a different running bra. She'd never thought of herself as being particularly big up top, but since starting running they'd frequently ached and felt heavy and full, much as they were before a period.

Perhaps that's it, she thought. My period must be due soon. The last time was . . . ages ago. She couldn't remember having one over the Easter holidays. The last one she could remember was way back – was it February sometime? March? Two or three months ago at least – she gasped, hand to mouth, head buzzing with the implication. No. It couldn't . . . she couldn't . . . She crossed the landing to the main bathroom.

'Come on, Mum.' Lily's voice floated up the stairs.

'Hang on, I'll be down in five minutes. I've just got to do something . . .' She sounded quite normal yet when she saw her reflection in the bathroom mirror she looked wild-eyed. It had to be here somewhere . . . She scrabbled around in the bathroom cabinet, heart pounding. There it was, tucked away at the back, the spare test Lily hadn't used.

Her hands shook as she tipped the second pregnancy-testing kit out of the packet, quickly reading through the instructions. Three minutes, don't touch the tip, keep it upright. She felt sick and had to lean forwards to let the blood rush back to her head. Calm down. This isn't happening. At my age you expect to start missing periods. She stood up, keeping her breathing controlled. I'll do it, just to prove there's nothing to worry about, she thought.

She sat down to pee, trying to get the pointed tip of the test mid-stream. Mission accomplished she sat back and waited. Three minutes wasn't a very long time. One hundred and eighty seconds, and then she could get on with her life.

The second hand ticked round. Three minutes, and a lifetime. Two minutes fifty-nine, fifty-eight, fifty-seven . . . As Becca sat staring at the tip of the tester she put her hand on her stomach, feeling its roundness taut, not flabby, as if full of promise and secrets. I'm imagining things, she told herself, it's no different from usual. I can't be. It's impossible. I'm too old. I'm not pregnant. Being pregnant would be ridiculous. Being pregnant would be inconvenient. Being pregnant would be . . . wonderful? She spread her fingers wide over her stomach. Was there life there? Was there a baby?

Don't think about it. Of course she wasn't pregnant, she was doing the test just to confirm that. If she were pregnant though . . . Martin had been sleeping in the spare room right up until the marathon at the end of March. Two months ago. They'd come back from the hospital and then . . . and then . . . Making love then had been like an affirmation of life; perhaps it had also created a life. She checked her watch. Two minutes thirty-five, thirty-four, thirty-three . . . The first window was now saturated, the blue line clear. The moisture was creeping up the second window, but there was no sign of any line appearing. It's a false alarm, Becca thought, face in her hands, overwhelmed with – relief? Regret?

The second window was now saturated, and no line showed. One minute forty-eight, forty-seven, forty-six . . .

No, it wasn't going to happen now. Becca put her hand on her stomach, her eyes filling with tears. One minute twenty-one, twenty, nineteen.

The first line was bleeding slightly, its blueness almost insolent in contrast to the emptiness of the second window. She wiped her face. You silly woman, she thought. Getting upset over nothing. Two minutes were gone. It was over. Look on the bright side, a baby would have been impossible at her age. No, not impossible. They could have worked something out. In some ways it would have been perfect timing, she'd have had the summer holidays and then could have gone on maternity leave from Hamilton House. She could have carried on with her course even with a small baby in tow. A Christmas baby.

Becca shook her head and blew her nose on a bit of loo paper. It was all hypothetical, she told herself, ignoring her aching heart. She was just being silly. She had Lily, her own darling child, and that was enough for her. A baby at her age? Ridiculous. Still, she couldn't help taking one last look at the tester stick.

No. She was imagining it. She wanted to see the line, and her imagination was supplying it. Becca stared at the tester. The line was faint, but there. Both windows. She wasn't imagining it. Becca put her hands to her face and stared at herself in the mirror. The grin stretched across her face and her eyes shone. She couldn't cope. She would cope. It was ridiculous. Fantastical. She laughed, and then stopped.

'Becca? Are you running or not?' Martin downstairs sounded quite cross.

'I don't think I'd better,' she called to him, quickly wiping the tears from her face.

She heard him run up the stairs. 'What's the matter?'

'Nothing's the matter,' Becca said, opening the bathroom door.

'Then why aren't you running? You're not giving up already?'

Becca shook her head and held up the pregnancy-testing kit. 'I think I'm . . .'

She watched as it took him a few seconds to realise what she was talking about. His eyes flew up to hers, his mouth open in astonishment. 'You're . . . ?'

Becca nodded. 'I think so.'

A grin spread over Martin's face and with a whoop he picked her up and swung her round, and Becca wrapped her arms around his neck and buried her face in his warm shoulder, never ever wanting to let go.

Lily stomped upstairs. 'What's going on? Isn't anyone going running? We'll be late for rehearsal at this rate.'

'We've got some news,' Martin said, setting Becca down but keeping tight hold of her hand. 'Some wonderful news.'

Becca held out her hand to Lily. 'I'm going to have a baby.'

'That's disgusting,' Lily said in the same horrified tones she'd greeted steak when she was a vegetarian. 'That means you've been . . . you've been . . . doing it!'

Martin and Becca looked at each other, feeling like naughty children being told off. ''Fraid so,' Martin said.

'It's appalling, it's so . . . so . . . irresponsible. I mean, like, you're old. You ought to know better.' Lily put her hands to her face rather like Munch's *The Scream*. 'Omigod, that's so embarrassing. No one must know.'

'I think they'll have to,' Becca said, holding out her hand. 'Darling Lily, you don't really mind, do you?'

Lily took her hand. 'I s'pose not,' she said, sniffing. 'Mind you, it had better be a boy. If it's a girl, it's got to go back. And now – can we go running? Pur-leese?'

'In a minute,' Martin said. Lily rolled her eyes and stomped down the stairs. Martin stroked Becca's cheek. 'I'd better go – will you be all right?'

Becca pressed her cheek against his hand. 'Of course.'

Martin's eyes were warm on hers. 'I love you,' he said.

'I love you,' she whispered back, smiling as her eyes filled with tears.

Downstairs they could hear Lily call to the dog, and its nails scratch on the wooden floors as it scampered to join her. 'Guess what, Ron? We're having a baby!'

'Don't cry,' Martin said, gently wiping Becca's face. 'We're having a baby.'